THE CANADIANS

INTRIGUE AND INDIANS, POLITICIANS AND PRIESTS!

STEPHEN NOWELL—a handsome young man who would carry the scar of being kidnapped as a boy far into the future—shapes Canada's history as he recreates his own.

SARAH NOWELL—the strong-willed beauty who lost her husband and son Stephen to the Indians vows to recover them at all costs—or die trying.

SOCONO—the fierce Indian who guards Stephen's life from afar. He killed *his* father but would give his own life to save Stephen.

LALONDE—the conniving, tortured Jesuit who seeks bloody revenge against Stephen.

MOLLY BRANT—the proud Indian princess who saves Stephen's life and becomes his first love.

CANADA—a land of challenge so vast that all who come there must fight—or perish!

THE FORGING OF A CONTINENT INTO TWO POWERFUL NATIONS!
THE CANADIANS!

THE CANADIANS

by
Robert E. Wall

I

Blackrobe

SEAL BOOKS
McClelland and Stewart-Bantam Limited
Toronto

BLACKROBE
A Seal Book / February 1981

ISBN 0-7704-1670-5

Seal Books are published by McClelland and Stewart-Bantam
Limited. Its trademark, consisting of the words "Seal Books"
and the portrayal of a seal, is the property of McClelland and
Stewart-Bantam Limited, 25 Hollinger Road, Toronto, Ontario
M4B 3G2. This trademark has been duly registered in the Trade-
marks Office of Canada. The trademark, consisting of the word
"Bantam" and the portrayal of a bantam, is the property of and
is used with the consent of Bantam Books, Inc. 666 Fifth Ave-
nue, New York, New York 10103. This trademark has been duly
registered in the Trademarks Office of Canada and elsewhere.

PRINTED IN THE UNITED STATES OF AMERICA

0 9 8 7 6 5 4 3 2 1

For my wife, Regina

A GENEALOGY

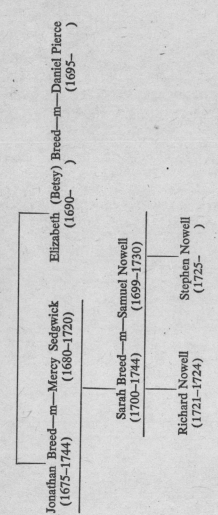

Jonathan Breed—m—Mercy Sedgwick
(1675–1744)   (1680–1720)

Elizabeth (Betsy) Breed—m—Daniel Pierce
(1690–   )   (1695–   )

Sarah Breed—m—Samuel Nowell
(1700–1744)   (1699–1730)

Richard Nowell
(1721–1724)

Stephen Nowell
(1725–   )

Part One

For the Greater Glory

I

1730-1731

The Reverend Samuel Nowell strode up the sloping path that led to the home of his father-in-law. Behind him lay the village of Charlestown. At the top of the hill, Nowell paused and looked back. The village could only vaguely be seen, lost in the glare of the afternoon sun as it struck the waters of Back Bay. Across the strait that connected the bay and the harbor, the triple hills and the church steeples of the town of Boston could be seen more clearly.

Both Boston and Charlestown were exactly one hundred years old that year. But the Boston of the third decade of the eighteenth century had become a town of fine houses, horse-drawn carriages, and ladies and gentlemen dressed in clothes of the latest cut and wearing wigs of the latest style. It was a far cry from the Puritan community founded by refugees from Anglican persecution. Charlestown, on the other hand, had remained closer to its roots. Its streets were still hard-packed dirt that was dusty in summer and muddy in winter. One could still find pigs foraging loose in Charlestown's lanes. No swine snorted its way through the better streets of Boston. Had one tried, constables would have shooed it off. In the poor sections of Boston—the north end along the harbor front—a loose pig would have been basted over hot coals, with little concern for the rights of the owner.

Nowell knew that he might never see Charlestown again. He had just completed his last Sunday afternoon lecture as assistant to Pastor Byles. Tomorrow he would leave Charlestown and take his family west to his own church. Tomorrow he would leave the place where he had spent his entire life except for the six years at Harvard, leave the place where he was born, where he had married Sarah Breed, and where their children were born. Thinking of Richard, his first-born, brought a pained expression to Nowell's face. He had bought

3

a gold locket for Sarah to celebrate the child's birth. There was a large gothic *N* engraved on it, and she had worn it continually from that day on. She had cut a lock of Richard's blond hair and placed it in the locket's square casing. But now Nowell could barely remember what the boy had looked like. The only memories that remained were the image of a child with fair hair like his own and the feeling of strength in the boy's grip as he played with Samuel's finger. But he could remember well the agony of the all-night vigil, watching life ebb from his son's body with the fever and with every cough. Many children died that summer from throat distemper, but none was more mourned than Richard Nowell. The birth of a second son, Stephen, the next year had not altered the sense of loss he felt.

Now he was leaving this place of his birth and his sorrow. He was going into the wilderness to be a true pastor—not just an assistant to a healthy, middle-aged pastor here in Charlestown. He had driven a hard bargain, even rejecting two offers from more established towns, which had not offered enough, before he accepted the offer from Northfield's selectmen. Northfield, too, had tried to offer only £45 and a house with no mention of firewood. Nowell had demanded £50, a house and a whole winter's wood cut and stacked each year. The selectmen agreed rather ungraciously. They needed a minister, and Nowell, it was clear, was a good one. And so after almost ten years in the Breed House, Samuel Nowell, his wife and five-year-old son were leaving.

Nowell turned and continued up the path to the heavy, nail-studded oak door of his father-in-law's house. He opened it and stepped inside. The ground floor had originally consisted of two rooms built on either side of a center chimney. To Samuel's right was the room that had once been kitchen and dining room combined. After the lean-to had been added to the back, the kitchen, pantry and servants' quarters had been moved there, and Breed had converted this room into an elegant dining room, as befitted a wealthy farmer, a town selectman and a member of the General Court. The room was dark in the late afternoon. No one had come yet to light the candles, and since the day had been warm, there had been no need of a fire. The heavy oaken table was set with the family's best pewterware. Nowell noted eight place settings. Pierce will be eating with us again, he thought to himself.

On the left side of the entryway was the sitting room, which glowed with the refraction of the late afternoon sun through lead-paned windows. Miss Betsy Breed, his father-in-law's 40-year-old sister, and her suitor of many years, Mr. Daniel Pierce, were seated together in the window seat, holding hands. Samuel wanted to get upstairs and tried to avoid the couple, but Pierce caught sight of him in the doorway. He dropped Miss Betsy's hand and coughed.

"Reverend Nowell, sir," he said nervously. "It is good to see you."

"How are you today, Mr. Pierce? How is business?" Samuel regretted asking the last question almost immediately. Pierce, a fur merchant, dealt with trappers who roamed as far as Nova Scotia to the north and the Great Lakes to the west. But Pierce was not very successful. Montreal and Albany were the great fur centers. Boston was too out of the way. Pierce seemed to have staked all his hopes on a marriage to Miss Breed and the dowry that such a marriage would bring to him from her brother, Jonathan. Jonathan Breed, however, was utterly contemptuous of Pierce and had repeatedly rejected Pierce's requests for permission to marry his sister. Only Betsy's obvious love for the man had stayed Jonathan's desire to ban him from the house.

"Business," said Pierce after some pause, "has picked up a bit. Tell me, did you meet my man, Wiggins, yesterday?"

"Yes," said Nowell. "He has agreed to take us west with him to the Connecticut and then lead us up to Northfield. He seems a rather unsavory fellow though, Pierce. Can he be trusted?"

"Unsavory is a mild word for Wiggins," laughed Pierce. "But he knows the woods. You can rely on him."

Samuel took advantage of a slight pause in the conversation to make his excuses and continue upstairs. He frowned to himself as he turned from the room. The middle-aged lovers seemed slightly ridiculous and frivolous. He climbed the twisting stairway to the bedroom he shared with his wife and child. The door to their room was half opened and he stood staring at his wife as she dressed their son for dinner.

Sarah Breed Nowell was thirty years old. Although many Charlestown women looked old at that age, there was still much girlish beauty about her. Her hair was black, her skin well tanned. Many of Boston's best folk regarded that as a detraction from feminine beauty; even Samuel wished his wife would behave more like other women of gentle birth and keep out of the sun. But Sarah was her father's child and, although acquiescent to her husband in almost every other way, she would not give up her love of the outdoors. Joseph Moulton, a ship's carpenter, who worked in the Hammond

5

shipyard in Charlestown, had taught her to sail as a girl, and her ever-indulgent father had purchased a small skiff for her. Up until her confinement with Richard, she had continued to sail about the Mystic River, Back Bay and the islands in Boston Harbor. Motherhood had curtailed some of her activities, but it had also added a ferocity to her character.

When Richard died, Sarah did not cry. For two days she sat in the bedroom next to his cradle. After the funeral, she returned to her home and never mentioned Richard's name again. She still wore Samuel's gift about her neck, but he knew without looking that the blond lock of hair had been replaced with a lock of black hair belonging to their second child. Samuel frequently visited the little grave in the churchyard, but he was always alone. When Sarah became pregnant for the second time, Samuel feared that her experience with their first child would affect her attitude toward the second. And he had feared rightly. From the day that Stephen was born, Sarah had been fiercely protective of him.

Samuel shifted his gaze from his wife to his son. Stephen, naked to the waist, stood before his mother as she brushed back his hair, then reached for his shirt from the bed. Stephen's hair was black like his mother's, but straight and unruly, while hers showed some tendency to curl. In complexion, however, he was totally unlike his mother; the boy's skin was very fair. His ribs pressed almost painfully against the pale skin of his chest and his collarbones rose sharply from his shoulders. His most striking feature, however, was his eyes; there was a penetrating blueness to them that was accentuated all the more by the thinness of his face. He was a very beautiful child.

"I missed you both at the service this afternoon," Samuel finally said after standing in the doorway unnoticed for some moments.

"Samuel, you startled me," answered Sarah. "Father asked me to stay at home to supervise Hannah's cooking. He wants everything just right this evening and he wants to eat early—just as soon as he comes back."

"Where is he?"

"He's gone over to Bunker's Hill with George to fetch the herd. They strayed over there again."

"Well," muttered Samuel, "at least he is consistent. On our last day in Charlestown he embarrasses me by profaning the Sabbath with manual labor and then he keeps my wife and

6

son from hearing the word of God. I will be glad when we leave this house at last."

"Hush, Samuel," Sarah admonished. "Father will be home any minute now and I do wish our last night together to be pleasant."

Samuel was the first to enter the dining room. Jonathan Breed insisted on the old practice of having the servants eat their meals with the family, even though none of the best families allowed this any longer. Nowell felt that such practices might have been appropriate fifty or even thirty years earlier, when the houses consisted of one or two rooms and when servants might well be the children of respectable families who were placed out in order to gain a God-fearing upbringing. But Hannah and George were not that type of servant. They were honest but base-born people. Samuel was sure that even they were disquieted by Breed's vaguely democratic self-indulgence.

Hannah entered the room carrying a lighted taper. Before long all the candles in the dining room, on the polished oaken table and on the lowboy against the wall opposite the fireplace, were flickering and casting shadows. The room glowed with rich warmth.

Sarah and Stephen came into the room together. Stephen's excited eyes took in the room at a glance. Normally the boy would have eaten earlier in the kitchen by himself, but this was his last evening with his grandpa.

Just as Sarah managed to settle Stephen at the table, a burst of loud laughter in the kitchen, followed by a shriek of glee from the cook, Hannah, gave ample warning that the master of the house had returned. Moments later Jonathan Breed, followed by George and Hannah, burst into the room. Breed was fifty-five years old but still in the prime of health. His hair had turned gray but, as George had been heard to say on many occasions, his muscles were like oak. He was barrel-chested, and a pot-belly rose to meet his chest. He had just washed his face and hands in the kitchen, and the lye soap and cold water that had been applied with some vigor had added to the color of his face—a color that hard work in the sun had begun.

"Father, your boots are still muddy." Sarah knew that it would do little good to complain. As usual, Breed merely smiled. He chucked Hannah under her ample chins.

"Hannah will take care of them for me later. Won't you?"

7

Then he tousled Stephen's hair, for which he received an exasperated look from his daughter, who had spent the last ten minutes before coming to the table trying to train the boy's unruly cowlick. Stephen looked at his grandfather with pure adulation. Their eyes met. For all the differences in their age and size, they were alike in the penetrating blueness of their eyes. Neighbors seeing the two together in the village had commented to Breed that he would never be able to deny his grandson.

Betsy Breed and Daniel Pierce entered together from the sitting room.

"Who asked him to stay?" asked Jonathan.

"I did," flashed Betsy. "It's my house too and Daniel is my special friend."

"It's whose house?" shouted Breed.

"Father," Sarah said in warning.

Normally Jonathan would have continued the fight, but his mind was on a more pressing problem—the loss of his daughter and grandson. He followed Sarah's warning and dropped into his chair at the head of the table, which Hannah took as a signal to go to the kitchen and begin serving the meal. She reentered the dining room carrying a steaming earthenware pot, which she set before Breed. Then she hurried out again, returning just as quickly with a platter of hot cornmeal bread and two pitchers, one filled with cool milk and the other with cider. As soon as Hannah had taken her place at table, Breed picked up a large serving spoon and prepared to attack the contents of the pot in front of him; however, Samuel lowered his head and folded his hands and was joined in this position by all the others.

"Oh, Lord, we thank Thee for the food that has been set before us and we ask Thy blessing on all of us seated at this table."

"Amen," said Breed loudly. But Samuel was not finished.

"For those of us who are about to travel far into the wilderness, we beg that our journey will be fruitful and that Thy work will be done. For those who remain behind, we beg Thy grace so that they will continue in Thy ways and keep holy Thy laws. Amen."

No sooner was the last word spoken than Breed pierced the crust on the hot pigeon pie with such force that some of the brown gravy leapt from the pot and landed with a splat on the table. Immediately the delicious aroma of the pie mixed with the scent of warm cornbread. Plates were passed to the head of the table, where Jonathan placed pie and bread on each. Then the pitchers were passed around; there was cider for all but Stephen, who received milk.

After his third helping of pie and his fourth mug of cider, Breed launched into the topic that was on all of their minds but that they hoped he would not raise.

"Well, Reverend son-in-law, you still have a mind to take my only daughter and my only grandson into your Godforsaken wilderness?"

"I think what Reverend Nowell is doing is highly commendable," said Daniel Pierce.

Breed turned on him angrily. "When I want your bloody opinion, I'll ask for it."

Pierce, realizing he had misjudged Breed's temper in his attempt to ingratiate himself with Nowell, started to apologize. But Breed would not let it drop.

"Why don't you leave?" said the older man.

Pierce, taken aback, started to protest. But Breed would not listen. "Go on. Get out," he shouted.

Pierce pushed his chair backward and stormed out of the room. Betsy Breed, nearly hysterical, rose and ran after him.

"If I'd have known he was that easy to get rid of, I'd have ordered him out a lot sooner," said Breed. "You haven't answered my question, Samuel," he continued.

Reverend Nowell put down his mug of cider. "Yes, Father Breed, I intend to go and my family will accompany me."

"Why, man, why?"

"Because," said Samuel, "the country is just as you described it—Godforsaken."

Sarah leaned forward and touched her father's calloused hand. "Father, we have been over this many times before. Can't we spend a pleasant evening—our last evening together for God knows how long?"

"No, by Christ," he said. "This is too important and time has run out." He turned to his son-in-law. "Samuel Nowell, you are taking this woman and this boy whom you claim to love from a comfortable home, from medical care." He looked over quickly toward his daughter. "Is there a doctor in Northfield, Sarah?" She winced but his argument missed the mark. Everyone at the table knew that he was contemptuous of all physicians.

"It is God's work," responded Nowell.

"Well, there is God's work to be done in Malden too, and it's a hell of a lot closer. Why did you reject their offer? Was it God's work or was it the bloody wood?"

Samuel stiffened in his chair as if slapped in the face. Sarah stifled a cry, rose from her chair and, taking Stephen by the hand, left the room. Nowell rose from the table to follow his wife and son. "I will overlook your remark to me, sir. I shall assume that it was the cider speaking, not my esteemed father-in-law."

Breed, his face flushed even more than usual, shouted at Nowell. "If you take that woman and that boy away from me tomorrow, you are no son-in-law to me."

"We intend to go."

"Then go, sir, and you can all go to hell while you're about it."

Samuel turned, walked out the door of the dining room, and closed it behind him. Hannah rose and began to clear the table. When she left, Breed was left alone with George. Breed left the table and went to the lowboy, opened the cabinet and removed from it a large leather-bound family Bible. He opened it to the blank pages in the back, which served as a family genealogy. He stared at it. Almost all the names had death dates next to them—most recently the names of his beloved wife, Mercy, dead almost ten years, and his grandson, Richard. Tears came to his eyes.

"They are really leaving, George," he said after some moments of silence. "I don't think I will ever see them again."

"Surely there will be visits," said George rather lamely.

"I need something stronger to drink," said Breed, pushing the Bible aside. He reached into the lowboy again and pulled out a bottle of rum. "Northfield is a dangerous place," he said, pouring some rum into his mug. "The Indians burned it out in the last century and it will be a prime target for the French when we war again."

When Breed finished his bottle, he fetched another from the kitchen. By that time George had fallen asleep, slumped over the oak table. But Breed sat up far into the night. The fire burned out and the drippings from the candles ran down the sides of the holders and began to accumulate on the surface of the oak table. Still Jonathan Breed sat, with only the rum for company.

The river front of the town of Springfield was busier than it had been in some time. Three boatloads of trade goods for the western tribes had arrived from Hartford, while an equal number of boats carrying local produce was about to head

10

downriver. The wharf bustled with sweating men loading and unloading. At the foot of the wharf the local public house did a booming business. The day was hot and the work was hard. Several Indian traders sat on benches in front of the tavern drinking rum from pewter mugs, while several Stockbridge Indians, Christian Indians from the Berkshires who had temporarily fallen from God's grace, were sleeping off the drink and dancing of the night before in the empty lot next to the tavern.

Sarah watched as her husband spoke to Isaac Wiggins, the trader who had agreed to lead the Nowell family to Northfield overland by wagon. Samuel had been attempting to make arrangements to send the Nowells' goods from Springfield to Northfield by boat, since the trail to that remote town would not take a wagon. Stephen and he would travel by horse and by foot on the overland trail, while Sarah would accompany their belongings.

Sarah had disliked Wiggins from the moment she set eyes on him. He had worn the same set of stained buckskins day and night all the way from Charlestown. She knew from the smell of him that he had not washed at all during that same period and for God knows how long before. The front of his shirt was badly stained with tobacco, which he chewed and spat out regularly. His aim was none too effective, since his four front teeth had been knocked out in a brawl. The missing teeth, more than most things about him, disturbed Sarah. The gap gave his face, already blotchy with years of hard drinking, a hideous leer when he opened his mouth. Then there was the way he stared at her; he frightened her with that stare. She could not bring herself even to speak with him, much less to trust him. But Samuel seemed to think him acceptable. Samuel settled his business with Wiggins and returned to the river bank where his wife and son were awaiting him.

"Wiggins suggests that he and I leave overland for Northfield before dawn tomorrow. We will send a boat back, and you will still come north by the river with our belongings. Let's go back to the inn, have supper and retire early." They started to walk in the direction of the tavern.

"I'm really upset that no one from Northfield is here to greet us," said Samuel. "Wiggins says that he sent my letter on ahead with one of his colleagues several days ago. Certainly it should have arrived there in plenty of time for the selectmen to send a delegation."

"Papa, are we going to ride a horse?" asked Stephen. "Am I to go with you?"

"Don't interrupt me, boy," his father said with some irritation.

Sarah responded by slipping her arm through Samuel's as they continued walking. "Don't fret, Samuel; perhaps you will meet the selectmen on the trail tomorrow."

The common room of the inn was large and drafty. There were about fifteen tables scattered about it, most in front of a huge stone hearth, in which a fire was burning to take the early evening chill out of the room. The innkeeper, a small, balding, fidgety man, gave the Nowells a table in the corner away from the fire. Samuel did not complain because the afternoon had been hot; those who sat before the fire would soon be very uncomfortable.

The innkeeper set a plate of sliced venison and cheeses, a pot of brown beans and a pitcher of beer before the Nowell family. The crackling of the wood in the fireplace and the warmth given off by the flames created a welcome homeliness. The trek from Charlestown had been difficult; Wiggins had little patience with the incompetence of a preacher when it came to driving a horse. He liked preachers almost as little as he liked the Indians from whom he made his living. His belittling remarks had infuriated Sarah and only Samuel's glances in her direction had quieted her. Her greatest fears, however, had been for Stephen. There had been no room in the wagon for sleeping, and every night Sarah had insisted that the great feather quilt be unpacked and spread on the ground for Stephen. Wrapped in softness, Stephen fell asleep looking at the stars, cradled in a downy womb.

As their meal progressed Wiggins and his friends entered the common room, accompanied by one of the Indians. All of them had started drinking well before the sun had set. Wiggins called loudly for more rum, and the innkeeper, anxious to avoid trouble, quickly brought him a large tankard.

"Not just rum, you idiot. When Isaac Wiggins asks for rum, he wants hot rum with butter."

Almost instantly a poker was thrust into the fire and a crock of butter appeared on the table in front of Wiggins. He stuck a dirty finger into the crock and brought it to his mouth, where it disappeared into the gaping hole. He noticed the Nowells sitting in the far corner of the room and made a mock bow.

12

"Jesus, if it ain't the holy family," he said. "Good evening, preacher. Get to bed early and remember to wake me up in the morning. Without me you couldn't find your way to hell, much less to the flea-bitten town that hired you."

When Nowell ignored the insult and continued his meal, Wiggins lost interest. He turned his attention to the Indian, who had fallen under the table.

"Damn, Hackett, why did you let that bug-eating son of a bitch come into a white man's house?"

"I dunno, Isaac, he just followed me. Besides, there's something weird about him. He isn't like the others."

"He's drunk, isn't he?" responded Wiggins. "He's like all the rest of them murderin' bastards. We ought to take him out and shoot him."

"I don't think this one is with the Stockbridgers," said Hackett, a gruff man with black chin whiskers. "And I seen signs upriver. I don't like it."

"You mean you were too drunk to know where you were goin'. You set out to deliver the Reverend's letter to Northfield and you ended up back here drinkin' without ever gettin' there. You're worse than this Indian here." With that he kicked the Indian out from under the table and onto his back.

"Let's get him out of here," said Wiggins.

"I don't think any of us are in any condition to carry him."

"Carry him? I'd rather carry garbage than carry an Indian," quipped Wiggins. "Here, I'll wake him up." Wiggins reached for the lacings at the front of his buckskin pants. Standing over the unconscious Indian, he urinated on his chest and face. Wiggins' companions broke into uproarious laughter. But the Indian stirred not an inch.

The innkeeper gathered up every bit of courage he possessed and demanded an end to any indecency. "My God, Wiggins, there is a lady and a man of God in the room."

"To hell with them both," he retorted.

"Issac, let's go," said the slightly more sober Hackett.

"Not till we wake the Indian." He reached into the fire and extracted the heated poker. Before any of his friends could stop him, he thrust the poker into the unconscious Indian's face, causing a sickening hiss, like hot metal dropping into cold water. The Indian screamed, grabbing his face. He vomited and, staggering to his feet, stumbled out of the inn.

13

Nowell grabbed Sarah, who by this time was shaking as if overwhelmed with chill. Stephen was crying with fright. He led both of them quickly to their room.

That night, as she lay comforted in her husband's arms, just before falling asleep, Sarah pleaded for the first time with her husband to return to her father's house.

"We have no choice but to go on, Sarah. It is God's will," he responded.

She lay quietly, her face against his chest. All she could think of was Wiggins—his cruel face, his leering smile. She shuddered. Her last thought before sleep came was the comforting one that Wiggins was leaving tomorrow with Samuel and that she would never have to see him again.

Samuel was dressed and standing before the recently re-kindled fire in the deserted common room before the gray light of false dawn. But Wiggins was not yet up. As the pink light of true dawn began to lighten the sky to the east, Hackett, clearly the worse for wear, stumbled into the inn from the yard. From the bits of weed that clung to his clothing, it was clear that he had spent the night where he had fallen after the revelry in the inn.

"Wiggins told me to take his place. He ain't leadin' ya today."

"But I paid him in full yesterday," objected Nowell.

"Well, it's like this," said Hackett "Ya gets me or ya don't go—least not today."

"Do you know the trail to Northfield?" asked the preacher.

"I been there before," Hackett replied belligerently.

Sarah came down the stairs from the bedroom holding Stephen by the hand. The innkeeper spread a light breakfast of toasted bread and milk on the table for the mother and son while Samuel, who had eaten earlier, helped Hackett with their horses. When Samuel returned from the stable, he sat down beside his wife and told her of the change in plans.

Stephen was too excited to eat. He had never ridden a horse before and he immediately joined into the argument.

"Please Papa, let's leave now," he shouted gleefully.

Samuel paid no attention to the boy. He was concerned about his wife. "I'm not sure I should leave you here alone, Sarah."

"I'm sure I'll be safe here. I would not enjoy the long overland journey with Wiggins—and his helper is hardly

14

better. This way I can go in greater comfort by boat with our possessions."

After breakfast, with firm promises from the innkeeper to see that Sarah was well taken care of, Samuel and Stephen mounted the back of one horse, while Hackett climbed unsteadily onto the back of the second. Sarah kissed Samuel on the cheek, knowing full well that she would receive a look of annoyance for her efforts. Samuel believed that public affection between a minister and his wife was inappropriate. Stephen, leaning over the side of the horse while holding on to his father's coattails for support, threw his free arm about his mother's neck and kissed her. Samuel dug his heels into the horse's side as soon as Stephen released his grip on his mother. The horse moved quickly to join Hackett, who was already moving down the road. Sarah stood alone, watching them until they followed the road to the right and the woods swallowed them up.

The trail from Springfield ran along the river bank through the towns of Hadley and Northampton. The father and son enjoyed the cool morning air and the pleasant breeze coming off the river. After they left the horses at Deerfield and set off afoot, however, the journey became more difficult. Hackett paid little attention to his charges, and on frequent occasions, as they walked single file, he allowed a branch he had pushed aside to snap back and strike Samuel, who followed him.

The sun was high in the sky and hot by midafternoon. Hackett had called numerous halts to the march. During these rest periods he would brace his back against a tree, pull out his flask of rum, tilt his head back and swig another large gulp.

As the afternoon wore on, Samuel became more and more nervous. "Mr. Hackett, I realize now why we could not continue on horseback. This trail has become very difficult to follow. In fact, I'm not sure that we are still following a trail. I think we should be traveling northeast. We are clearly not doing that."

"Hold your peace, Reverend," responded the guide. "I know where I'm going. If I were you, I would do more fretting about the kid, see that he don't wander off and get himself lost." Nowell looked up to see Stephen a good hundred paces off, picking the blossoms that grew on the bushes encircling the clearing where they rested. Samuel strode off to fetch his son.

Hackett decided to stretch out the break. As he watched

the minister start across the clearing, he muttered unflattering comments about the clergy to himself. He let his head fall back against the rough bark of the tree trunk and took another gulp of rum. He closed his eyes and listened to the buzz of the honeybees as they diligently worked their way among the blossoms. He really didn't know where he was. He had lost the trail at least forty-five minutes earlier. But if he found a stream he would be all right.

He heard the chirping of the squirrel sitting on the branch overhead. Another squirrel answered. The first stopped his chatter. Hackett opened his eyes and froze. The squirrel above his head had also frozen and was staring at something behind Hackett's head. Hackett turned to catch sight of a swollen, pus-oozing face which not even the zigzag stripe of purple war paint could hide. It was Hackett's last sight. The tomahawk crashed into his skull.

So loud was the noise of Hackett's death that Nowell, startled, turned around to observe the cause of the disturbance. What he saw forced him into action. At first he started to run to help the guide. Then he stopped, realizing that would bring instant death to himself and his son. One of the Indians was already busily removing what was left of Hackett's scalp from his head. The two others had noticed Samuel, and they began to race across the meadow toward him and Stephen. Samuel ran to Stephen, scooped up the frail body of his son into his arms, and made for the underbrush.

The thorns of the briars ripped at his coat and tore gashes in his arms and hands as he pushed them aside to make a path for himself. The boy began to cry but Samuel had no time to hush him. To stop was to die. He pushed his way through the densest underbrush and entered a grove of young evergreens. Here, too, the lower branches slapped at him but in his desperation he did not feel them. He broke through the grove into another meadow. He dared not stop to listen for his pursuers. They were behind him. Even if they could not see him they could hear his frantic efforts to escape. He raced toward a rise at the end of the meadow. Several large rocks stood at the top of it and beyond the rocks he could hear the roar of water falling.

Stephen, catching his father's fear, was now quiet, his eyes wide. He seemed to grow heavier and heavier. Samuel knew that he was nearing the end of his endurance.

He made for the sound of the water, perhaps only instinctively aware that the waterfall's noise would drown the sounds of his escape. But it was too late and he was too tired.

As he reached the top of the rise, an Indian broke into the clearing. He halted, raised his musket, aimed and fired. The ball struck Samuel in the shoulder. He staggered but he did not fall. His only thought was to protect his son, and to do that his instincts told him to remain standing. The second pursuer had continued to race after him while the other had halted to shoot. Now he was upon Samuel, and he could almost feel the oily, sweetish smell of him. The Indian raised his tomahawk to strike. Samuel's arm rose to ward off the blow. The handle of the axe struck his arm with a thud and the flat side of the blade struck Stephen, gashing him across the eyebrow and causing blood to splatter over his face. Terror engulfed Samuel and he remembered no more.

He awoke several hours later and wondered why he was still alive. Night had fallen and he was lying against a log next to a pale and unconscious Stephen. The boy's bleeding had stopped, but the wound was ugly. About twenty yards away he could hear the ripple of the river and he realized that he had been carried some distance. His shoulder throbbed and his eyes were not focusing clearly. One of his captors, seeing that he was awake, thrust a slice of dried meat at him. It looked unappetizing but in his hunger he gulped it down. Stephen began to stir and then opened his eyes. Samuel covered his mouth softly with his hand and whispered in his ear.

"Hush, my son, please don't cry out. Your father is here. You will be all right. I promise you, you will be all right."

The days that followed were one long tortuous haze for Samuel. For some reason, his Indian captors had not killed him or his son. But he knew that each morning was a new test, and he prayed for the strength to meet it. If he could make it to his feet despite the pain and the weakness, then he would live for another day. If he failed, they were both dead. That first morning after his capture, he knew that it had been Wiggins who had caused their pain. He had not seen much of the Indian whom Wiggins had maimed at the inn, but one look at the face of the warrior who seemed to lead the band was enough to tell him that it was the same man.

The first two days of capture were much the same. They lay hidden during the daylight hours. Samuel tried to clean the wound on Stephen's forehead and the one in his own shoulder. He made bandages from portions of his shirt. Stephen would be scarred but he would live. As for himself, he knew the ball was not lodged in a vital area, but it was there and that was enough. Unless he received medical

17

attention, infection would set in and he would surely die. He thought of Sarah and feared for her, but his immediate concern was for Stephen. He had to live for the boy's sake. That was all that mattered for the moment. The boy must live.

With the coming of darkness the four warriors uncovered two small birch canoes. They loaded their captives in one with two paddlers and set out on the river. The first night they passed Northfield. Samuel, sick with the pain in his shoulder and weary from his cramped position in the tiny craft, could still make out the outlines of the houses of the town. The canoes were paddled near the far bank to avoid detection, but so bright was the moon's reflection, turning the river waves to silver, that a careful observer could have seen the dark, silent forms as they glided past the last of Samuel's world. No one was watching.

After leaving the settlements behind, they traveled continually, day and night, stopping only for a few hours' sleep. The Indians seemed in a great hurry. As they entered the valley of the upper Connecticut, the river narrowed and the current grew swifter, forcing the paddlers to work harder. The rich meadows on both banks were deserted except for the occasional deer or raccoon surprised on the bank by the sudden appearance of the silent canoes.

Now the Indians seemed not to object when Samuel spoke to Stephen. The boy was conscious most of the time now but weak from loss of blood. His wound was healing well. Samuel tried to assuage Stephen's fright by telling him that the Indians were not going to kill them and that they were taking them somewhere—possibly to their village, where they would be held for ransom.

"Never forget, Stephen, that you are English; your name is Stephen Nowell; you are my son and a servant of God. Most of all, never forget that your mother and grandfather are alive. They will ransom you and bring you back to safety."

"Grandpa will bring us both home, Papa," the boy responded.

Samuel nodded.

Samuel removed the bandage from his shoulder and stared at his wound. For the past two days he had not been able to ignore the sick smell of infected flesh. It was as he had feared. The wound was swollen and oozing pus, but it was the stench of gangrene that told him he would die. They had left the Connecticut and were traveling overland, carrying their canoes. He did not know how much farther they would have to go, but he was determined to keep going for the boy's sake. The Indian with the scarred face gave the word to begin moving again, and Samuel got to his feet slowly. Stephen could walk now, and he took him by his small hand and began the painful trek forward.

The trail they followed was a clear one. Samuel could not have known it, but it was the trail that the Abenacki of St. François had followed for years when they descended upon the New England towns. At midafternoon they rested. The Indians offered the boy and his father more of their food and water. The leader gave the word to begin the march anew, but Samuel realized that he could not get up. He had failed. He knew what Indians did to captives who could no longer walk. He began to pray.

Scarface, whose wound was healing but still hideous, bent over Samuel to see why he had not responded to the gestures to begin again. But instead of the flash of the tomahawk, there were orders given to one of his braves to get Samuel to his feet and to support him as they walked. The brave refused. Scarface, with a shrug of his shoulders, ignored the affront to his leadership and, with a sweep of his arm, roughly raised Samuel off the ground and stood him on his feet. He started to fall again, but the Indian caught him under the arms and supported his weight.

Samuel lost track of time—day or night did not seem to matter. In his few lucid moments he was all the more aware that he had been and would again be delirious. They were traveling by canoe again. As he lay on the bottom of the craft, his head propped against the stern, he could see only a great expanse of water on all sides. They were moving across the choppy surface of a great lake. Dark forms loomed high above him, cutting off the sun—evil giants, their heads touching the low-hanging clouds and their feet planted firmly in the water. They lined both shores like a guard of honor.

They left the lake and he was carried again. His moments of lucidity grew further and further apart. Again they traveled in canoes, this time rapidly downstream with the current. He heard the sound of rapids and perhaps he was carried again. It didn't matter any more. He opened his eyes. He was in the canoe and the sun was low in the sky. But on the right bank of the river, he could see a town, a European-style town with houses and streets. They must finally have reached Northfield. The selectmen would be waiting for him. He must be ready to meet them. But why couldn't he rise? He must be

19

about the Lord's work. These people needed him. He closed his eyes again. He must sleep. He was too tired to rise. He had suffered much. He was sure they would understand, even if he had driven too hard a bargain about the cords of winter wood.

Isaac Wiggins awoke with a start. He sat bolt upright and looked about the room. He had been drinking for seven straight days, but the last night had been the worst of the binge. He looked down at the naked woman who lay beside him and could not remember who she was or why her face was bruised. He chuckled to himself. It was not the first time he had awakened in bed with a strange woman, nor was it the first time he had amused himself at a woman's expense. And certainly he hoped it would not be the last time. He thought perhaps he might try for a bit more amusement, but the ringing in his head and the queasiness of his stomach convinced him otherwise.

The woman stirred and opened her eyes. She smiled at him, revealing some blackened and broken teeth. Wiggins pulled his knee up toward his chin and then thrust his foot into the woman's naked belly, shoving her over the edge of the bed. She yelled as she hit the floor. "Son of a bitch," she screamed at him. "What did you do that for?"

"Don't ask me questions at this hour of the morning," he responded. "Especially while I'm still trying to figure out why I ever wanted a slut like you in the first place."

She picked herself up off the floor and walked to the dresser, on which her clothes lay in a heap. She pulled her shift over her head and down over her shoulders. Opening the door of the room, she turned and looked at him. "Don't worry about the pox or something like that. You didn't run any risk. You said you were too drunk to get it up. But then I guess you have to say that all the time." She spat at him and ducked out the door.

He cursed and reached for the water pitcher beside the bed to throw it at her, but she was gone before he could grasp the handle. He pulled his buckskin shirt on and found his moccasins under the bed. His head still hurt and his eyes ached as he entered the taproom and was confronted by the nervous innkeeper, who kept rubbing his hand over his balding head.

"Mr. Wiggins, I must protest the noise that came from your room last night. It was extremely disturbing to the other guests. I'm afraid that I have taken as much as I can from you. I am going to have to ask you to settle your account and leave this inn."

Wiggins was sorely tempted to punch the little man in the face but he decided against it. Springfield was an important layover spot for his business, and this little rodent in front of him ran the only inn in the whole region. He would have settled up and left as he had planned to do except for one small problem. He had no money left after the orgy of drunkenness he had indulged in.

His reluctant host seemed greatly relieved that Wiggins had taken the eviction so well, and he tried in his very nervous fashion to play the gracious innkeeper once again. "Before you leave, Mr. Wiggins, I would appreciate it if you would speak to the young woman whose party you led here— Mistress Nowell. She has been waiting here in Springfield for word from her husband, the minister, whom your man led to Northfield. Certainly enough time has lapsed for them to reach their destination and send back boats for the Nowells' belongings. The young woman has been extremely upset and wants to speak with you."

Wiggins followed the innkeeper into the side alcove, where Sarah sat nervously toying with her cup of breakfast tea. She stood up as he approached her. "Mr. Wiggins, I've had no word from my husband. He has been gone for over five days. Three days were all it should have taken for them to arrive at Northfield."

"Well now, lady, Hackett really ain't the best man I've got. He gets confused and he probably got them lost a bit. So the delay really ain't all that unusual."

"I can't wait any longer, Mr. Wiggins. I must contact Northfield. I will pay to be guided there immediately."

"I ain't going to Northfield, lady. I'm heading over into Iroquois country and that's over in New York—west of here."

"But you can't just leave me here," Sarah begged. This man revolted her as no man ever had before, but she had no one else to turn to until she got to Northfield.

"I suppose if you was to pay up my tab here," said Wiggins, "I could take off the next day or so to follow your husband and that poor excuse for a guide, Hackett."

Sarah arranged with the innkeeper to keep her family's possessions until she could have them shipped to Northfield. The innkeeper did his best to put her fears to rest, but she was

21

still terrified. In the past few days she had gone from vague concern to abject fear. There was no comforting explanation for the delay in hearing from Samuel. At first she had remained in her room except for meals; then she had taken to sitting in the taproom despite her embarrassment when drinkers would stare at her. When this grew unendurable, she had begun walking along the river front, straining her eyes, looking upriver for the boat from Northfield. But none came. In desperation, she had asked the innkeeper to approach Wiggins.

The guide arranged for horses to carry the two of them, and they set off the next morning. They rode along the river bank single file, with Wiggins in front. Sarah was grateful for the lack of conversation. She was frightened, and proximity to Wiggins only increased her uneasiness. Once she jumped when a fish broke water in the river next to her. Wiggins turned around on his horse and leered at her in amusement, but he said nothing and continued to ride.

When they arrived in Deerfield, Wiggins made inquiries about Samuel's party. The livery stable owner told them that, like themselves, the Hackett party had arrived from Springfield and had started out for Northfield on foot. He had not heard from them since.

Again Wiggins and Sarah set out single file along the trail, this time on foot. Isaac Wiggins knew these woods and had no trouble following the trail. He easily saw where Hackett had gone wrong and led his party astray. Wiggins also saw what Hackett had never seen. There were signs all over the woods of an Indian party that had been following the two men and the boy. He said nothing to Sarah about the Indians. There were no fresh signs; had there been, he was perfectly prepared to abandon her to her fate.

The trek through the woods was beginning to have a calming effect on Sarah's nerves. She was oblivious to the very things that Wiggins paid most attention to. Instead, she heard the singing of the birds as they flitted from branch to branch and the hum of the bees. One zoomed just by her head and she had to duck. The breeze was a good one, and the branches of the trees above her head swayed with the force of it. Her senses seemed especially alert. She could smell the sweet scent of the blossoms, which grew abundantly in the clearings, where the sun could break through the forest and reach them. But then there was another smell—a sweet smell, sickeningly sweet. Sarah could not recognize it, but Wiggins knew what it was immediately. He waved Sarah on ahead of him and allowed her to enter the meadow first. As she pushed aside the branch in front of her, she gasped and her free hand went to her mouth and nose. She started to moan, a low animal-like sound. Hackett's remains were spread about the base of the tree that had been his last resting spot. Wild animals had been at him and the stench of death was everywhere.

Sarah thought she was going to be sick but she gained control of herself. She did not think that the corpse in front of her was Samuel because of the buckskin clothing, but she had to be sure. She forced herself to look at what remained of the face. She turned to Wiggins, who stood watching her. "This is not the body of my husband, Mr. Wiggins. We must keep searching. My husband may have escaped."

"There ain't no escaping what got Hackett, Mrs. Preacher," he said cruelly. "Your man is lying around here somewhere. Indians don't take men captive unless they plan to burn them. But these bastards are not locals. Locals wouldn't have the nerve to do this. These were priest Indians from Canada. They have a long trek back home—they didn't have time to burn your man. They just knocked him on the head and took his hair. If you're lucky, they didn't do the same to the kid. Maybe they took him with them."

There was a truth to his words. Sarah could not weigh the evidence before her with any accuracy, but she had heard enough stories as a child and young woman about frontier massacres to believe that Wiggins knew what he was talking about. She knew in her heart that she would never see Samuel again. It was Stephen, then, whom she must save.

"We must search for my husband's body and then we must follow the savages and retrieve my son." She was fighting for control of herself and it was a fight she was determined to win.

"You are a gutsy one," said Wiggins. "I haven't got time to go scrounging through these woods looking for dead bodies, and besides, there has got to be more of them red devils hanging around here, just waiting for fools like us to come and do the Christian burial thing."

"You just told me they would be in a hurry to get back to Canada, and I believe you were right with your first evaluation."

"Don't argue with me, woman," Wiggins shouted at her. "We're going back to Springfield."

"Quite to the contrary, Wiggins, you are going to take me to Northfield as you agreed. At least there I will find humane

23

people who will help me discover the fate of my family."

Wiggins turned and headed back out of the clearing. Sarah called after him to wait. He ignored her cries, and she had no alternative but to follow him or be abandoned in the woods. She ran to catch up with him.

"Isaac Wiggins, do you hear me? I want to go to Northfield." She picked up the end of a birch branch that was lying across the path and, using it as a cudgel, she hit him across the back.

Wiggins turned to face her. He smiled menacingly at her and then he lunged for her wrist.

"No bitch can hit me and get away with it," he shouted. He held her wrist and prevented her from using the stick a second time. His grip had the force of steel and, shaking her wrist, he forced her to drop her weapon. She swung at his face with her other hand. He ducked the blow and twisted her arm back. Then with his free hand he clutched at her bodice, ripping the cloth of both her dress and her undergarment. He tore them away, leaving her naked to the waist. Her hands went to the dress to pull it up and cover herself. She was defenseless, then, when Wiggins' fist smashed into her jaw. Dazed, she collapsed into a heap on the ground; her assailant fell on top of her. He tried to kiss her but she jerked her mouth out of the way.

"So much for the nice stuff, then, bitch," he gasped.

She felt his hand reach up under her dress. She arched her body off the ground to avoid his touch, to no avail. His hand weighed on her naked chest, holding her down. He leaned all of his weight on her with one hand, while he loosened the string in the front of his buckskin pants. Then he thrust her skirts up about her waist and attempted to enter her. She twisted away. Once again his fist struck her jaw and she remembered nothing more.

Sarah awakened in the late afternoon. She had been left to lie where she had fallen. She rubbed her jaw. Although it was swollen, she was sure there was no serious damage. She had been scratched and bitten and when she moved her legs, she groaned. She had been used brutally and she ached. She touched herself with her hand and pulled it away again with revulsion when she felt the stickiness. She rolled over onto her stomach and began to weep, her whole body racked with sobs. Her tears of pain turned to tears of frustration and anger. Slowly and gradually the sobbing subsided and a creeping apathy began to take control.

She fell asleep. She did not know how long she dozed, but when she awoke the sun had not yet set. She was alone in the woods. Surely Wiggins had left her here to die after what he had done to her. She could count herself lucky that he had not seen the need to murder her.

She pulled herself off the ground and tied the front of her dress to the sleeves on either side. She straightened her petticoats and skirt. The late afternoon sun pointed out to her the direction she knew she must travel to reach the river. And reaching the river now had become a necessity. Northfield lay on the river, even if the trail to it ran inland. If she could reach the Connecticut and head upriver she would be safe. She faced the setting sun and began to move painfully toward the west.

She walked for about an hour, forcing branches of trees back out of her way. She knew that she was not on any trail, and had little hope of finding one. The sun was gone; darkness fell swiftly on the woods. She was lost. The night grew chilly. Sarah huddled down next to a large tree trunk. Her hand went to her throat and closed around the locket Samuel had given her. Was he really dead? She knew Wiggins was probably right and she had lost her husband as she had lost her first-born. But what of Stephen, her beloved Stephen? Who would be taking care of him now? She began to weep again and then fell asleep, her shoulders shuddering and her breath catching even as she dreamed.

Susannah Gage bent over the huge iron cauldron, stirring it with a canoe paddle. She yelled at Eben, her ten-year-old, to fetch more wood for the fire. The fumes that rose from the pot stung her eyes and offended her nose. Even after twenty years of life on the frontier and just as many years of soap making, she found the task no easier. As usual, she had hauled her pot, animal fats and ash away from the cabin and taken them down to the river. At least the smell would not invade her home unless the wind changed. The fire was burning strongly and she was sweating. She wiped her forehead on her long sleeve.

A boy partly tumbled and partly jumped down the river embankment to the mud flat with his arms loaded with split logs. "Get some more," she ordered.

"Ah, gee, Maw," said the boy, but the rest of his complaint never left his lips. Instead, his eyes widened and he stared beyond his mother and down along the river's edge.

Susannah turned around quickly, reaching for the musket

she always kept at her side. But she saw that she would not need the weapon. A few yards downstream, half in and half out of the water, a woman stumbled along. Her clothes were torn to shreds and her naked breasts hung from the top of what had been a fine dress.

Susannah dropped her musket and yelled at Eben to help her as she ran toward the woman in the water. She caught her just as the woman began to fall once again. "There, there, dear," she comforted. "I've got you."

"I'm Sarah Nowell, the wife of the new minister," mumbled Sarah as she collapsed into the ample bosom of Susannah Gage of Northfield.

Jean LaGarde of the Society of Jesus was saying his morning mass in the mission chapel of St. François Xavier. Behind him his congregation of gaily clothed warriors and squaws sat, listening attentively. The children, wearing loincloths, were a bit noisier and very fidgity. It had taken tremendous efforts on his part to get the parents to place even this little clothing on their babies, but God's house required this decency. He knew for certain that as soon as mass was over and the children were set loose on the village, they would be naked once again and would remain so until next Sunday brought them back into the Lord's house.

The chapel was the most awe-inspiring building in all of St. François. The sawmill at Trois Rivieres had sent cut boards so that it might be built in the European fashion. Carpenters in Quebec had hand-carved the wooden pews. The Abenacki worshippers had painted them in bright colors, depicting scenes in the life of Christ as related to them by the priests. Purists in Rome might complain about Christ being dressed as a warrior of their culture and the Virgin as an Abenacki princess. But this bothered LaGarde not at all. Jesuits were trained to adjust and mold the faith to the needs of the congregation.

He had been chaplain now for three years, unhappy years for him. As a boy he had thrilled to the stories of the Jesuit mission in Canada. He had heard with awe of the horrible sufferings and death of Brebeuf and his companions at the hands of the Iroquois, and he had made up his mind to join their holy company. His family, nobles resident at the Court of Versailles, had objected. As the youngest of four sons, he could properly choose a career in the church, but surely, his family thought, he should aspire to a bishop's chair and a rich living rather than to the vows of a religious order. In the long run, with the assistance of the King's own confessor, who was a Jesuit, he had won his argument and received the blessing of his father, the Marquis.

As a novice of the Society, he had begged Father Provincial to send him from France to Canada—to the missions. He had been told to be patient. The vow of obedience kept his enthusiasm in check. Finally, after fifteen years of training, he had been allowed to come to the missions. He was to be a martyr, not to fire and the knife in the hands of the heathen, but rather to frustration and failure.

In addition to classical languages, and of course French, LaGarde had mastered Spanish and Portuguese and he could carry on a conversation in heavily accented English. But the Indian languages seemed to be beyond his grasp. For three years he had labored over the Abenacki tongue in despair. He rejoiced in guiding the souls of his flock on their paths to heaven, but he suffered that he could not speak to them with the intimacy that true knowledge of their language would give. His sermons in Abenacki were listened to gravely by the adults, but the children laughed until corrected by their parents. He realized that in correcting their children, these very indulgent parents were paying him a great honor; it forced him to try even harder.

The sermon this morning, however, had gone well. He had struggled with it late into last night and he was pleased with the results. He turned to give his blessing to the congregation.

"Ite missa est."

In the back of the chapel a glum-faced Brother Hubert caught his eye. As he turned to read the last gospel, the opening lines of the Gospel of St. John, the priest was hard-pressed to keep his mind on what he was reading.

Brother Hubert was in the tiny sacristy waiting for the priest at the end of the mass. While LaGarde unvested, the lay brother told him of Socono's return. "You must come to the river, Father. He has returned with two captives. White captives."

The priest was startled. "Whites? *Anglais?* Is Socono mad? There's no war with the English." Without waiting to return the precious vestments to their closet, LaGarde left the chapel and followed Hubert to the stream that flowed by the town.

As LaGarde approached the large crowd by the shoreline, his first shock was seeing Socono.

"My God, man, what has happened to your face?" he said in Abenacki.

Hubert, to LaGarde's chagrin, translated the priest's shock into a more understandable Abenacki and then retranslated the warrior's story into French for LaGarde.

The priest knelt down and placed his ear to the chest of the man who lay in the bottom of the canoe; then he touched the boy's forehead. "The man is dead, but the boy lives. Carry him to my house. Socono, you and your braves take the body and bury it. Then come to my house and I will try to help you with your face." Hubert again relayed his instructions and then rushed off to help Socono with the burial. Seeing that there was no one left to carry the boy, LaGarde lifted the frail body of Stephen Nowell into his arms and carried him away from the canoe toward the rectory.

Late at night in his study LaGarde pondered what he should do. The boy lay sleeping in his bed, wrapped in one of the priest's own nightshirts. He had washed the boy's body carefully and then cleaned and bandaged his wound. The boy had not regained consciousness. LaGarde's heart went out to him. He stood and walked to the window. Fires were burning in the stoves of all the houses in the village. The smell of smoke hung heavy over the town. He was proud of all that had been accomplished here and now he feared for it.

St. François was one of the oldest Jesuit missions. For years the priests had gone deep into the wilderness of Maine, to work in the Abenacki villages. But they had seen all their work thwarted by agents from Boston. The heretics corrupted their converts with lies and whiskey and finally even made war on the priests themselves. The solution, as with the Mohawk mission, was to bring their converts out of the wilderness to the St. Lawrence valley, where the mission, its priests and its Christians could be placed under the protection of the troops of His Most Christian Majesty of France.

Thus St. François Xavier had grown along the banks of the river bearing the same name, some miles upriver from where it flowed into the mighty St. Lawrence. As well as the church, there was a fort with several cannon. The Indians had abandoned their crude huts and had adopted wooden European-style houses. They were a Christian, God-fearing community. They were not afraid to protect themselves, and they would without hesitation make war upon the enemies of the great King in France and the good fathers who cared for them. But now LaGarde feared for them.

The Society of Jesus, despite all its accomplishments, its

28

glorious victories for Christ in Europe and in the missions, despite the blood of its martyrs, aroused jealousies on all sides. In France the order was powerful but its enemies, both Protestant and radical Catholic, attacked it, using its special devotion to the Pope in Rome as an excuse to accuse it of disloyalty to the crown. The present governor of New France was no friend to the Society or its missions. A raid on the English, unauthorized in Quebec, would be used against the work of God. It fell to him to cover the tracks—all for the sake of God's sacred work.

He turned away from the window and returned to his desk. He pulled pen and ink from his drawer and placed a sheet of paper in front of him. Before writing the letter, from long habit, he wrote the letters *A.M.D.G.* at the top of the page. They were the first letters of the Latin motto of the order to which he belonged—*Ad Majorem Dei Gloriam*—"For the Greater Glory of God." He wrote the report in Latin, feeling that language would offer him greater security.

Very Reverend Father Provincial, the Peace of Christ,

I hasten to inform you that one of our Christian converts of this mission, who was sent into the English settlements on the lower Connecticut by myself at your request, has returned with very little useful information but he has, nevertheless, placed us in a very difficult position. In the course of scouting in the English towns he was very brutally treated by some of the inhabitants and frightfully maimed. He determined to seek revenge. Some miles outside the main settlements on the river, he ambushed a party of settlers containing one of his tormentors. The others in the party were innocent and the scout wished to spare them. His companions failed to discriminate and wounded the other members of the party. The scout managed to save a man and child and brought them back to the mission. The man died just before arriving at St. François. The boy lives. It would, however, have been better for the Society and this mission if the child had died as well.

A raid deep into English country will surely be reported and complaints will be made to His Excellency in Quebec. Inquiries will be made about the mission Indians. As you know, we have strict instructions from the governor to maintain the peace. If it becomes known that it was our Indians, the wrath of His Excellency will surely fall upon us.

I need not remind you, Reverend Father, that the unwarranted enmity against our holy company is shared by many close to His Excellency. News of this indiscretion must be kept from those who hate us. The body of the man has been disposed of. I can rely completely on the silence of my charges here at the mission. The soldiers in the fort were drunk as usual and have no idea of what has happened.

There remains the problem of the boy. He is young but no doubt will remember much of what has happened to him. I suggest that we keep him here at the mission and inform no one of his survival. All inquiries about him will be evaded. I remain yours in Christ.

Jean LaGarde, S.J.

The message was on its way to Montreal by the first light of dawn.

The boy's eyes were covered with bandages. The priest had meant to cover only the wounded eye, but his bandage had been tied clumsily. He was a poor nurse. He would have to get Brother Hubert to tie it properly. LaGarde sat by the boy's bed reading the Latin prayers of his breviary. The boy tossed in his fever and then his body went rigid. The priest realized that he had awakened, but awakened in total darkness. LaGarde moved the bandage away from the boy's good eye and patted his shoulder softly. "Rest, my son," he said in his strange English.

"Where am I?" whimpered the child. "Where am I?" he called even more loudly as panic began to take hold of him.

The priest stroked his hand. "You are safe now, child. You were injured. But now you will be all right. Lie back. You will be safe now." He placed his hand on the boy's forehead to test for fever. He was very warm.

"How are you called?" LaGarde asked.

The boy began to cry again.

"Hush, now," the priest comforted him. "You must be a man. You must not cry. You must tell me your name."

In his darkness Stephen tried to think of his name. He heard a voice from out of that same darkness that surrounded him. "You are Stephen Nowell," said the voice.

"Your name, boy?" asked the priest once again.

"Stephen Nowell."

30

"Ah, good. Now tell me what happened to you."

The child began to cry once again. He clutched the priest's hand in his.

"I don't remember," he said.

LaGarde sat back in his chair. "Go to sleep, my son," he said over and over again. "It will all come back to you in due time." In his soul he hoped that it never would.

Three months before, René Demarais, provincial of the Society of Jesus in New France, had agreed to Jean La-Garde's suggestion about the English brat. Now he was beginning to regret his decision. Certainly, he had hoped never to have this confrontation. He had agreed to LaGarde's suggestion about the Nowell boy last summer only because he could think of nothing else to do. The Jesuits were under constant attack from Jansenist elements still present in the government of New France and in the Ministry of Marine. The Gallican movement in the French Church was older even than the Society, and it was the Society's sworn enemy. Other foes saw their special approach to matters of conscience as immoral.

Demarais could remember the shock of the simple curé of his home parish in Normandy. He had returned home for a family visit and had offered to help the pastor of the church with confessions. He had given the sacrament to Monsieur LaPorte, a merchant whom the whole town despised for his price gouging. The curé would have demanded complete contrition, while he, Demarais, the Jesuit, had advised the merchant that he had not sinned if he had one sufficient reason for his actions. Demarais smiled when he thought of the hostile looks he had received from the rabble of the parish. "We Jesuits are more suited to the consciences of kings and statesmen than to those of common folk," he mused aloud.

The provincial had little use or patience for the arguments used against the order, but he had to respect the power of some who used them. What did the governor of New France, resident in Quebec, hope to gain by sending the boy's family upriver to Montreal to visit him? Did His Excellency suspect something, or was he simply trying to foist a difficult problem onto someone else? Whatever the governor's motives, Demarais knew he had no more choice now than he had last summer. An innocent scouting expedition in preparation for future troubles had gone astray. And why should not the Society mount such expeditions? The peace with England could not last very much longer. And then, with war, His Excellency would come knocking on the door, begging for the information that the Jesuit Indian converts had brought back to the missions and to him. But this one expedition had gone wrong and innocent people had been vicitimized. Nothing, of course, had happened to them that would not have been perfectly acceptable in time of war, but there was no war. The tragedy was not his responsibility, but it had fallen to him to straighten it out and to protect the Society of Jesus. LaGarde had been right to take the steps he had taken to hide the existence of the boy. Who would have guessed that the family would have been able to come this close to the truth?

There was a knock on the door and Brother Francis, his secretary, led a red-faced, well-dressed older gentleman and a younger dark-haired woman into his office. Demarais rose from behind his desk. "Monsieur Breed and Madame Nowell," he greeted them in heavily accented English. "His Excellency has notified me of his promise of assistance to you. Would you please be seated." He pointed to two straight-backed wooden chairs that stood before his desk.

Demarais noted how carefully the woman helped the older man into his chair. He noted how physically frail he was. He had the frame of a giant, but it was clear that he had been ill. Where once muscle had bulged, now flesh sagged. The woman, he knew, had been through great torment and his heart went out to her. But he also noted about her an aura of great strength of character and an extraordinary determination. "How may I assist you?" he asked finally.

Sarah spoke up immediately. "Reverend Father, my father and I are on a mission of mercy and seek your help. Some months ago my husband and son disappeared in the woods in the western part of our home, the province of Massachusetts."

"How terrible for you," said the priest.

"I've hired guides to scour the woods," interjected Breed, "and I have attempted to apprehend the scoundrel who was paid to guide my daughter and her dear ones—all to no avail. We have discovered no bodies save that of one of the guides. We have found not a trace of my son-in-law or grandson."

"It is a terrifying story, sir. But why have you come to me, or to Canada, for that matter? I would have thought that the authorities in Massachusetts or in New York would be of more assistance. The Mohawk of New York are a fearsome people. Would it not be more fruitful to search among them? They have terrorized the very city in which we sit for years and have murdered our priests without compassion."

"I'm glad you agree that it is toward Indians we should look. We found signs of them red devils all over the woods and there was an unfortunate incident involving an Indian the night before the disappearace. The savages who attacked Mr. Nowell's party were from this neck of the woods, Reverend, of that there can be no doubt."

"Why are you so certain of that, Mr. Breed?"

"Because your sons of bitches have been coming down on us in New England like the four horsemen from the good book for as long as I can remember," said the older man.

"I'm sorry that you think it necessary to cast aspersions on our wards."

"It's no slur to speak the truth, sir. The devils who attacked my family were either Mohawks from your pesthole in Caugnawaga across the river or they were that worse bunch of Abenacki at St. François. The innkeeper in Springfield told me that no Iroquois were present in Springfield. So I'm betting on St. François."

"My understanding, monsieur, is that you have already visited Caugnawaga and that you found no trace of your loved ones."

"So you know more than you let on. Don't you?" said Sarah.

The Jesuit merely smiled.

Sarah continued. "Every sign leads now to St. François. They must have been taken there. Since your people run the place, you must know something about it. Please, Father, you must help us."

"I'm so sorry, my dear," said the priest. "I can't help you. I know nothing." He did pity her and his natural inclination was to tell her what she wished to know, but the greater claim on his heart was held by holy obedience and the protection of the Society.

Sarah sank perceptibly in her chair and tears came to her eyes. But she would not be beaten. "I don't believe you, "she said quietly.

Demarais tried to control his reaction. He was accustomed to deference from women; he did not like the arrogance of this one. "I don't understand, madame. My English is not the best."

"I think you are lying," Sarah repeated.

Demarais turned to look at the old man. "Monsieur Breed, I believe your daughter is too distraught to continue this interview."

"Oh, I'm just fine," said Sarah with vehemence. "Listen to

33

me, priest," she continued. "I have nothing more to lose. I've lost my husband and son and I've nearly lost my sanity, but I will hold on just as long as there is a chance of finding my family. If Samuel and Stephen are dead, so be it. If they live, then you know something about them. Of that I'm sure. And you won't help me. But so help me God, someday I'll find them, with or without the help of the likes of you."

Demarais was angry now. "Monsieur, I'm afraid I must ask you to leave and take your daughter with you. I'm sure you, as a gentleman, will agree with me that she has succumbed to her grief and does not know what she is saying."

"I'll take her now," said Breed. "But she hasn't succumbed to anything." He stood and smiled down at his daughter with pride. "Whatever she says goes for me too."

They left the door open, and the Jesuit had to get up from behind his desk to close it. He stood watching them walk down the corridor away from the porter's office, out toward Rue St. Paul. They would follow it to Rue St. Gabriel, where they were lodged.

He turned and slowly walked back toward his desk. "I must write immediately to LaGarde at St. François," he mumbled aloud.

Daniel Pierce paced the floor of the sitting room of the Auberge St. Gabriel. He had walked the streets of this town all day. Montreal was a superior fur town. Great trading canoes continually traveled the St. Lawrence from Frontenac, Niagara, Detroit and the lakes beyond. Here they met ships from France, which crowded the river front under the guns of the small fort on Isle Ste. Helene. Pierce was determined somehow or other to become a part of this scene, which offered so much more than the pittance that came to Boston through the indulgence of the Albany fur barons.

But his immediate concern was with Breed and his daughter. He had wanted to accompany Sarah and the old man when they interviewed the priest, but Sarah would not hear of it. The search for the boy and his father was going on too long. Pierce had drawn on all of his resources to help Breed, and things had changed as a result. No longer were there any gratuitous insults from Breed. No longer was he the unwanted guest; Breed had become more and more dependent on him. And he had helped. His connections in the fur trade had made it possible for Breed to hire woodsmen to scour the forests north of Springfield. He had hoped that they would find the bodies of Samuel and Stephen; he was not sure what he would have done if they had found any evidence that the two were alive. But none of his men had found anything. He was happy to report this total failure to the old man.

The one conversation he had not reported, however, was the secret meeting with Wiggins in Albany. What filth that man was, but useful filth. Wiggins had agreed to work exclusively for Pierce for a healthy sum of money—all of it supplied unknowingly by Breed. The old man's purse was bottomless when it came to funds to find the little brat. Wiggins was to spend all of his time searching for signs of the Nowells. If he found anything, he was to report it instantly—but to him, Daniel Pierce, alone.

Wiggins was to stay away from Breed and his daughter. The wretch seemed especially pleased about this last part of the bargain. For some reason Pierce did not understand, Wiggins, who seemed to fear nothing, was wary of Breed and especially wary of Sarah. He made it very clear that he did not wish to have anything to do with Sarah, and he questioned Pierce especially closely about what she had said and done when she had been rescued at Northfield. Something strange had happened between those two.

But now Pierce was determined to use Breed's tragedy to his own advantage. There was no question in his mind that if he asked Breed for permission to marry Betsy, it would be granted. The old man was in his debt. But why should he marry the older woman for a dowry when the young heiress was available? His ambitions were loftier now.

The door to the sitting room opened and Sarah and her father entered.

"Did the priest have any news?" asked Pierce.

"Nothing," said the discouraged Breed.

"I'm so sorry, sir."

"He lied, Father. I know he lied," said Sarah.

"You have no proof, daughter."

"Call it intuition. Maybe it was the look on his face. He knows things that he refuses to tell us. The way he tried to pass the blame onto New York Indians—all of it was loaded with guilt. I just know he lied. We must try at St. François immediately."

"I will see to it right away," said Pierce. He was intrigued by the woman's conviction. Perhaps these priests did know something. If they did, he would make sure that Wiggins was assigned to watch them carefully in the future. "Mistress Sarah," said Pierce, "I will have my agents watch these priests continually."

Sarah looked at Pierce quizzically. She wished she knew what his game was. Surely he must know that he had already done enough to earn him Betsy's hand. She doubted now that her father could continue to oppose the marriage, not after all he had done to help the family.

Jonathan walked wearily toward his bedroom door. "Right now I am very tired," he said. "I think I will nap. Thank you, Daniel, for this last favor and for all that you have done since this sorry business began. I am afraid that I have misjudged you and abused you in the past. I hope you will allow me to make up for it."

"It is the least that I can do, sir," said Pierce.

"No," said Breed. "It goes beyond friendship. I simply don't know what we would have done without you." The old man entered his room and closed the door behind him.

Pierce turned to Sarah. "Can I be of further assistance to you, Sarah?"

"No, I think I will retire also."

"Then I will leave you and get on with the St. François investigation. But do not forget, Sarah, I will always be here if and when you should need my services."

Sarah lay down on her bed. She felt uneasy about this exchange with Pierce. She could not put her finger on just what it was that disturbed her until just before she fell asleep. He had called her Sarah. Never before had he been so familiar.

Pierce went to his own rooms but only to pick up his coat. Leaving the hotel by the back door, he walked down the alley until he reached Rue St. Paul. He continued down this street to a warehouse with a full view of the Jesuit residence. He stood in the shadows and waited. Before long the back door that led to the kitchen of the house opened and Brother Francis stuck his head out and looked in both directions; then he stepped out and walked toward the river front. Pierce followed him as closely as possible. The lay brother accosted an Indian who had been asleep on the dock. The Indian had been drinking and the brother was forced to shout at him. Pierce knew very little French, but it was sufficient for him to discover the secret. He made out the words "garçon, St. François, LaGarde." His men would be on the trail of the Indian as soon as he could get word to them. The boy at least was alive, and he was at St. François. The Jesuits would soon have him out of there, but he would know where they took him. It was a piece of information that would never find its way to Jonathan Breed or Sarah Nowell.

Rough jacket of Pierre sufficiently. She wished his knee
and himself was quite uncommon know that he was alread
then and so to this tiny town, for it was evident now th

II

1740

Stephen stepped quietly out of the kitchen door of the
house. Leaning against the door post, he slipped his shoes on
his feet. He could barely see across the road to the wharf and
the harbor walls. Dawn had not yet come, and the predawn
darkness always seemed to him to be the darkest part of
night. He walked briskly toward where he knew the walls
were located, turning to his right at the foot of the stairs that
led to the ramparts above. The night air was chilling and
Stephen wished to hurry his tasks along. The market building
loomed out of the black in front of him. The only light
showing was from the shop of Savard, the baker. Stephen
opened the shop door and was greeted instantly by the aroma
of freshly baked bread and rolls.

"Good morning, Savard. I have come for the fathers'
bread. Is the bundle ready?"

From the back of the shop where the ovens were, the
sweaty and flour-covered baker stood up from the table where
he was forming his dough into crescent-shaped rolls. "Good
morning, young master," he said as he bowed to the boy.
"The breads are in the basket by the door."

Stephen reached for the basket and began to squeeze and
test the bread and rolls. Savard contributed about fifteen
loaves of bread daily for the maintenance of the Jesuit
fathers. Since this was more than they needed, they gave half
of the contribution to the convent of Ste. Ann, and the sisters
in turn gave much of their portion to the patients in the
hospital they maintained. Savard enjoyed high standing in the
community for his charity. But in the five years that Stephen
had been charged with collecting the daily bread from the
baker, Savard had tried many times to slip in yesterday's
leftovers. Brother Richard, the cook, had whipped Stephen
soundly the first time he had returned with stale bread, and

the boy had vowed never to make the same mistake again.

"All seems in order, Savard," he said. "Thank you in the Lord's name."

"Good day to you, Master Etienne."

Stephen closed the door behind him and stepped off again into the chilling night air. He walked down a darkened rue Dauphine to the convent of the sisters. The porter's lodge for the convent stood at the corner of rue Dauphine and rue d'Orleans. When he arrived before it, he placed the basket down on the cobblestones and pulled the bell rope. Sister Marie Louis is growing more deaf each day, he thought as he gave the rope a second and more forceful pull.

Every morning he brought bread to the sister porter. Since he was a male, he could of course never enter the convent proper, only the lodge of the porter, and he knew none of the nuns who lived in the convent.

The heavy top half of the wooden lodge door swung open and the lamp from the table behind outlined the wizened face of a nun. "Who is there?" she inquired, peering unseeingly into the black night outside. It was not only her hearing that was failing her.

"It's me, the bread man," joked Stephen. Every morning they went through the same ritual. "Who else could it be, Sister?"

"Why, it might be the Archbishop of Paris come on a visitation and I would have to give him a proper welcome," she responded.

"Well, it is only me, poor Etienne, the bread boy."

"Ah, poor Etienne, come and sit down. I have a bit of fresh butter. Perhaps we might share one of the rolls before you go."

"Sister, I am shocked. You know that today is a fast day."

"Bah on fast days. You are too young to be fasting and I am too old. Wait till I get the butter and we will each have a roll." The old nun went to the rear of the lodge and shuffled back, carrying a small dish of butter and a pitcher. "I found a bit of fresh milk—good for a growing boy like you." She sat down heavily in her chair. "How many years have you been coming to my lodge, Etienne?"

"Five," he responded.

"That long? I remember when they first brought you here. That was longer—must be nine years ago now. You were such a sick little tyke. They brought you to our hospital. I

38

was a nurse then, before they exiled me to this useless task. I nursed you, boy, and there never was a better nurse than me. Look at you now." Her old hand touched his face, tracing the blue scar that cut through his eyebrow. "You are not what I call strong—too skinny and too pale. That cook of yours should have spent less time warming your bottom and more time filling your belly."

"Brother Richard is a good man, Sister. You know that."

"I haven't seen the man since I left the hospital to become official greeter to archbishops and bread boys," she responded. "What you really need to make you strong is some sunshine. Sunshine like we had in Avignon when I was a girl. I am an old lady and I am going to get older and it is all because of the sun I soaked up as a child. But you, where do you grow up? On this wretched island where the fog blots out the sun nine days out of ten. You will be lucky to see twenty, Etienne."

She went on this way every morning. Soon, thought Stephen, she will begin to remember more than just the warm sun of the south of France, and she will begin to cry. He was determined to escape. "Sister, I will be late for mass. I must return home," he lied.

"But you haven't eaten your buttered roll."

"You eat it for me, Sister. It should not go to waste. That would be wrong."

"Ha, I can tell you live with the Jesuits. You reason just as they do. Trying to tempt an old woman, and on a fast day. But I suppose you are right." She tested the roll with her finger and sighed. "Even the fresh ones are too tough for my old teeth. They hurt when I bite into anything."

"Well, Sister, then I suggest that you dunk the rolls into the fresh milk and eat them as mush. Then nothing will be wasted."

"Etienne, I think you will make a fine Jesuit. And when you are a priest, I will have no one else for my confessor. With your help I will cheat the devil for sure."

"You need not worry about the devil, Sister. You are one of God's special ones."

"Be off with you, boy. You're just trying to flatter me. Next time you will be expecting pastry instead of just butter and milk." She opened both halves of the door and playfully shoved him outside. Then she turned back to the table on which rested the nuns' share of the bread. Removing a roll, she broke it in half, spread the fresh butter thickly on one of the halves, poured out a tumbler of milk and dunked her roll. "I wonder if I could get some pastries away from Mother," she mused.

Stephen retraced his steps back toward the market and home. The sun's rays broke over the tops of the hills behind the lighthouse, lightening the blackness of the sky to a dull gray. That may be the last of the sun we see today, thought Stephen as he reapproached the ramparts. He climbed up the steps toward the guard post. Karl would just be starting his guard duty. Stephen watched as the sergeant and the replaced sentry marched out along the parapet toward the next guard position. Once they were out of sight, Stephen called softly to his friend.

"Over here," answered the soldier. Playfully he lowered his musket and challenged the intruder. "Halt, Bastonois, or I will shoot."

"First an archbishop and then a heretic. Sic transit," said Stephen. Stephen approached his friend, and as he did the contrast between them grew more pronounced. Karl was as bullish as Stephen was slight. He was ruddy complexioned and even in his uniform the muscles of his chest and arms bulged. His legs were like logs shoved into breeches and stockings. He was over six feet tall, with blond hair and blue eyes. His home was Zurich and he had come to serve as a mercenary under King Louis. Most of the garrison's common soldiers were Swiss like Karl, although, unlike him, most were French-speaking Calvinists. Karl was a German-speaking Catholic, who spoke French with a heavy accent.

Stephen approached the wall, where in wartime cannon would be placed, and stood in the empty embrasure. One could see almost all of Louisbourg harbor from this spot on the circular battery. Far across the kidney-shaped harbor he could see smoke rising from the Grand Battery. He could see the muzzles of its great guns pointing, it seemed, toward the Circular Battery and the town walls, but in reality they were pointing off to the right toward the harbor entrance.

"It is almost breakfast time," said Stephen. "They are cooking over at the Battery."

"Over at the Island, too," said Karl. "You can't see the fort from here but you can see the smoke." He pointed out toward the burying ground, beyond which stood a heavily armed fort on an island in the channel entrance to the harbor. "But I will have to wait at least two more hours for my breakfast."

"Here," said Stephen, "have a roll." He shoved one of Savard's specialties into Karl's hand.

"I thought you'd never offer," joked Karl. "It is going to be another Isle Royale day," he said, munching the roll.

Stephen knew exactly what he meant. Out beyond the great bastions and the enormous walls on the landward side of the town and beyond the swamps and woods to the south of the walls—between Black Cape and White Point—they could make out the sea, or rather they could see an enormous wall of fog where the sea should have been. The fog was approaching the town and would soon blot out most of the traces of day.

"Have you heard yet from the rector, Stephen?" asked Karl.

"No, he hasn't answered my application yet."

"Are you sure you want to become one of the fathers?" asked Karl. "I know that I could never do that. Imagine not having another woman for the rest of my life. My God, I'm only seventeen. If I live to eighty, that is sixty-three more years. On the average of one wench per week, that is . . ."

Karl's mental arithmatic broke down at this point. Stephen disliked it when Karl displayed his soldier's attitude toward sex. Perhaps it was because he was only fifteen and had no experience. Perhaps it was because he might not ever have any experiences. He tried to get back to the original subject.

"I am likely to hear at any moment from Father LaGarde. If he is willing to consider my application to join the Society, I will begin the Spiritual Exercises immediately and I won't be seeing you for at least thirty days. And perhaps, if I am admitted as a novice after the retreat, you will not be seeing me for a very long time after that."

"No more outings with Socono, eh Stefan?" Karl offered. "When he took us on those treks through the woods, that was great fun, wasn't it? By God, you are good at that Indian stuff, Stefan. That ugly red bastard is the best shot with a bow I have ever seen. But I can shoot a musket better than him. Nevertheless, the two of you could live in the woods for weeks with ease. I would die before a week was out."

"They are good times, Karl, aren't they? But they will have to stop once I am novice. I doubt that I will even be allowed to leave the house."

"Have you told Socono?" asked Karl.

"He knows. I think he has always known that I would become one of the fathers. I think he spent the time he did with me—teaching me to hunt, canoe and speak Abenacki— so that Father LaGarde would send me home to St. François with him."

41

"You speak that heathen tongue almost as well as Socono does. I think LaGarde is jealous of you."

"Why should he be jealous of me? He is a great man. He is the youngest son of a nobleman. Now his brother has inherited the title and serves the King in the ministry of foreign affairs. He has been a missionary and now he is superior of a major house of the Society. I owe him everything. He has cared for me for almost as long as I can remember. He tried to find out about my parents and if I had any relatives. He has been like a father to me. I am not worthy to be his brother in Christ, but I will try."

Karl was silent for a few moments after Stephen finished speaking. "Can I have another roll?" he asked finally.

"No, you can't," said Stephen. "I have given away too many already. I have to get back to the house with what I have."

"See you tomorrow, Stefan, and remember my poor stomach."

"Maybe," said Stephen, laughing as he descended the steps to the street below.

The fog had completely enveloped the town by the time Stephen returned to the house of the Jesuits. He entered from the back, through the kitchen. Brother Richard had almost finished making breakfast for the five priests and five lay brothers who comprised the community. The priests would just now be completing their morning masses. The brothers had attended an earlier mass said by Father LaGarde. Stephen, as usual, had attended mass with the brothers.

In many ways his status in the house was unique. He labored at menial tasks with the brothers. He helped Brother Richard in the kitchen and Brother Michel in the laundry room. But, unlike the lay brothers, Stephen attended school. The priests of the house had each undertaken to oversee some aspect of his education. In this manner and with liberal application of the switch, Stephen had learned to conjugate Latin and Greek verbs. He had translated Cicero and Horace. He knew of the many travels and tribulations of Odysseus. Father Mercier had introduced him to the mysteries of geometry and trigonometry. Fr. Gregoire had taught him to identify the constellations, and together they had studied the heavens through the astronomer-priest's telescope. Secretly, Stephen enjoyed Socono's study of the stars far more. Socono taught him to use the stars to find his way home at night through the woods. Fr. Gregoire was not interested in finding his way home at night through the woods; he had no intention of being in the woods in the first place—day or night—if he could help it. Most recently Fr. Lalonde had begun to introduce Stephen to the logic of Aristotle.

As Stephen stepped into the kitchen, Brother Richard looked at him sternly. As usual, he had dawdled with his friends and had delayed the placing of the bread on the table. Since Great Silence, observed in all religious houses from evening until after mass the next morning, was still in effect, Brother Richard said nothing. Instead he flashed him the sign of a V, using his first two fingers. Stephen instantly understood *Ille vult videre te*—"He wishes to see you." The *he* always referred to Fr. Rector—Fr. LaGarde.

Stephen knocked softly on the superior's door and opened it. Fr. LaGarde was sitting at his desk and looked up to observe the boy as he entered. Ten years had passed since he had lifted Stephen's almost lifeless body from the canoe. The boy had grown tall, and although he had not yet filled out, he seemed to grow healthier as he grew older.

LaGarde smiled at Stephen. "Well, Etienne, I have your application before me. I am pleased that you have decided to apply. But before I make any decision there are several questions I must ask."

"Yes, Father," the boy responded meekly.

"I have been your confessor for the past five years. It was I who baptized you in the true faith; it was I who heard your first confession and gave you your first communion. I know the state of your soul and I am convinced that you have been a good boy, walking in the way of the Lord. But there are several disturbing matters to discuss. It has not gone unobserved that you are happiest when you go off hunting with Socono. Perhaps in a mission such as ours we should not be disturbed by such a tendency. But the life of a Jesuit is not just the hard life of the missionary. Before he can do such work for God, he must have prepared himself as a scholar. Training in philosophy and theology will take years of your time. You may go to the missions and live among the savages, but always you must be prepared to return to our houses for renewal and more study. I have no doubts about your ability to learn, but do you feel that you can pull yourself away from those you love and from a life that you find more pleasing in order to obey the commands of Jesus as spoken by your superior?"

Stephen considered the question for a moment. Then he smiled. "I have always obeyed you, Father. Haven't I?"

43

"It will not always be me telling you what to do, Etienne. But to go on, have you completely rejected the ways of your ancestors? Have you rejected the English heresies?"

"You know I have, Father. It was you who first taught me the truth. I was very young when I was found. I knew very little of my parents' heresy."

"Then why have you persisted in calling yourself Stephen Nowell?"

"I suppose because it is my name."

"It is your English name," LaGarde responded.

"I accepted it when everyone called me Etienne Noel. Especially when you decided that my birthday would be celebrated on Christmas day."

The priest shrugged. "It is all the same. As you know, Etienne, members of the Society retain their names when they take vows. We do not take on a religious name to indicate a transition to a new life. But that does not mean we do not have a transition. Your stubborn clinging to your name, not adopting a totally new French name at your baptism, has worried me. Perhaps it is a sign of hanging on to old ways, old ideas—an older life."

"Do you insist that I change my name, Father?" asked Stephen.

"I wish to be assured that there are no vestiges of heresy in you, my son, before I admit you as a novice in this house," answered LaGarde.

Stephen bowed his head and in a low voice spoke to the priest. "What is to be my name then, Father?"

"In due course," the priest responded. "In due course. But your submission is sufficient evidence of your good intentions. Return to my room this evening and we will begin the exercises."

Stephen spent the rest of the day nervously toying with his chores and absentmindedly attending to his schoolwork. Time seemed to drag on endlessly. The evening meal, eaten in silence while the scriptures were read in Latin, was almost unendurable. Evening prayers in the chapel were worse. Finally the hour of his appointment arrived, and he had to stop himself from racing down the corridor from his room to Father LaGarde's.

Stephen knelt before LaGarde's chair. "We will begin the Spiritual Exercises of St. Ignatius this evening. When you return to your room, I want you to turn your attention—your whole heart and mind—to the points of meditation I will give

44

you this evening. In particular I want you to contemplate on the worst of all sins. Can you tell me what you consider to be the worst possible sin?"

Stephen pondered the question for a moment and then answered. "Since our Lord commanded us to love one another, I suspect that hate would be the greatest sin."

"That is well said. Hatred of one's fellow man is a grave sin. But hatred of God is an even greater sin."

"How is it possible to hate God?" the boy asked.

"One hates God by allowing love of oneself to replace one's love of God. It is pride that is the greatest sin, my son. Pride was the sin of the angels. Etienne, think of the beauty of Lucifer—the lightbearer, God's most perfect creation. But his pride grew to such proportions that he challenged the power of the Lord and said he would not serve. In a blink of an eye the glorious Lucifer is cast into the pits of hell and becomes the hideous Satan. Love yourself more than your God, Etienne, and you will find yourself in hell with Lucifer. Tonight before you sleep and tomorrow morning when you first wake up, I want you to imagine yourself in hell. I want you to feel the fire as it consumes and blackens your flesh.

"When I lived with the Abenacki, I saw them burn captives. They dressed them in skirts made of bark and led them to the stake. They did not burn them in one big fire, but slowly, first one limb and then another. And the next day the stench of burned flesh would hang over the village. You could not escape it. But hell is worse than the Abenacki fires. The captives eventually ended their sufferings—they eventually died. Not so the sufferers in hell; the fires of hell burn forever. Tonight, Etienne, place yourself there. Feel the fire, the pain. For if you continue to live a worldly life, you will surely end in such suffering."

The boy kenlt in the chapel, trying to concentrate. The red vigil lamp flickered in front of the altar. In the darkness he tried to place himself in hell's fire as the priest had requested, but it all seemed so forced to him and false. He could make no headway. Sighing, he rose from the kneeler, genuflected and blessed himself. He was tired. He would try again in the morning before mass.

He returned to his room, blew out the candle immediately and took off his clothing in the dark. His white nightshirt, so carefully laundered by Brother Michel, lay draped across the kneeler at the foot of his bed. He found it without difficulty

45

with the help of the moonlight that came streaming through his window. Pulling the shirt over his head, he climbed into his cot. He fell asleep almost immediately.

Stephen opened the door into the dark room. The heat of the room was overwhelming. His body broke into a sweat. He wiped his brow. As he pulled his arm from his forehead, he had to stifle a scream. His sweat was red. It was blood. The walls of the room began to close in around him, changing the room into a corridor. He turned to go back but the wall, where the door had stood but moments before, had opened into a cave. But was it a cave? The pulsating edges of the cave were alive. It was really a gaping, toothless mouth. Where the tongue should have been, there were flames leaping out. They crept along the floor toward him. He backed away but the floor began to move him toward the mouth. He screamed as the flames engulfed his body. The hole ahead grew closer and closer.

He awoke with a start, drenched with sweat. He lay back on his bed, taking deep breaths to release the tension; then he realized for the first time that his penis was erect. He turned on his side and tried to think of something else, but again and again his attention returned to the bulge in his nightshirt. He fought the temptation but his hand, almost against his will, reached under the shirt and he made contact with himself. Slowly he moved his hand. He sighed and let his body relax. Slowly he allowed himself to drift into a euphoric peace as the tension left him.

"I don't know what came over me. I tried to resist the temptation, Father, but I couldn't. I am overcome with grief."

"I believe you, Etienne. Your confession is a sincere one."

"But to sin so seriously the same night I began my retreat. What is it a sign of, Father?"

The priest thought a moment. "Etienne, I believe that your sin was related to the meditation I gave you. Your sin is essentially one of pride. You place love of your body above your love of God. It is a sign to you from God that your soul is in great danger. You must change your life. Your confession, however, is to me a clear indication of your willingness to change."

Stephen had been overwhelmed by the enormity of his sin almost immediately after the act. He had risen from his bed, thrown on his shirt and breeches and rushed down the

46

corridor to the rector's room. LaGarde was still awake and answered the boy's knock.

"Will you reject me, Father?" Stephen asked.

"Not for this sin, Etienne. Your sin is forgiven. But you must do penance and the penance will be severe."

The boy bowed his head. The priest continued. "You will accept in the spirit of love twenty-five strokes with the cord, which I will administer to you here immediately."

"Yes, Father." Stephen realized that this would be hard to bear. But he had been whipped before, although never before with the cord.

But LaGarde continued. "Tomorrow morning, at breakfast, you will confess your sin to the entire community."

Stephen gasped. He opened his mouth to protest but LaGarde silenced him. "If the sin is one of pride," he said, "then the penance must be one of humiliation." Stephen said nothing.

The boy removed his shirt and knelt on the floor before the crucifix on the priest's wall. He bowed and kissed the floor, straightened up and awaited his punishment. LaGarde removed the whip from his desk drawer. It was made of woven white cord and was about two feet in length. The first foot was the handle; the second consisted of three separate strands of cord joined to a common base.

"I will not be gentle with you, my son," he said. "If I am gentle with you now, Satan will surely be hard on you later."

He struck Stephen a blow across his back that nearly knocked him forward onto his face. He gasped but did not cry out. Immediately three ugly red welts rose in sharp contrast to the pale skin of his back. The second blow struck his right shoulder with the same sinister effect. The third crisscrossed the marks of the first. With the tenth stroke, Stephen's back was a mass of welts. The eleventh broke the skin and blood trickled down his back, accumulating at the waistband of his breeches and staining the cloth. Still the boy refused to cry out, although he no longer knelt upright but hunched forward in anticipation of the next blow. At the twentieth stroke he fell forward and his chest hit the floor, causing him to grunt. He wiped the tears that streamed down his face with his forearm and pushed himself to an upright position with his other arm. LaGarde, breathing heavily with exertion, renewed the punishment. The twenty-third blow brought a low moan from Stephen's lips and as the last stroke hit him, he fell forward again.

LaGarde gently wiped the blood from Stephen's back as he lay stretched on the rector's cot. The boy felt the fiery sting of vinegar applied to his wounds to stop the flow of blood and begin the healing process. The cure was almost as painful as the whipping. Stephen broke down completely and began to sob, chest-wrenching sobs. The priest took his hand and attempted to calm him.

"I know how you suffer, my son. But you had to learn the lesson. Your sin brought you fleeting pleasure and your punishment has brought you harsh but also fleeting pain. How much worse would it have been had God not allowed you forgiveness and caused you to die in sin. The pains of hell are no longer just an abstraction to you. You now know pain, but only a fraction of what you could have felt."

Stephen squeezed the rector's hand. "Thank you for being my teacher, Father," he gasped.

"You try to sleep now, Etienne. Spend the night on my cot and I will pray for your soul." He turned from the bed and walked to the spot of Stephen's recent suffering before the crucifix. He fell to his knees and stretched out his arms in the form of a cross. Stephen watched him kneel motionless in prayer. His breathing quieted and he drifted off into a fitful sleep.

When he awoke in the morning, LaGarde was gone. Stephen lifted the upper part of his body from the cot with his arms. He gasped as little streaks of lightning seemed to spread down his back from his shoulders. He sat up gingerly and placed his feet on the floor. His shirt lay across the room on the rector's desk, where it had been neatly folded. There was a pitcher of fresh water on the desk, with a clean towel lying beside it. Stephen splashed some of the water onto his face and more under his arms and on his chest. After drying himself, he very carefully draped the towel over his shoulder, grasping the hanging end with his other hand. He ran the cloth softly over his back. The towel came away unstained. None of his wounds had reopened. He put on his shirt and tucked it into his breeches, ran his hand through his black hair and washed out his mouth.

He left the rector's room and walked down the corridor toward the chapel. Mass had just begun and Stephen slipped into the last pew, unnoticed by the other members of the community. LaGarde looked haggard as he turned to bless the tiny congregation of lay brothers. His eye caught Stephen's and he smiled.

Stephen approached the altar for communion. This was

48

always the great moment—the moment when his body would unite with the body and blood of Jesus. LaGarde placed the host on his tongue and Stephen was filled with a joy he found hard to control. He returned to his place at the back of the chapel. He felt at peace and he knew that he could face the humiliation required of him.

He was the last to leave the chapel after mass. He prayed for about an hour. When he entered the refectory, the whole community had assembled. The other priests had finished saying their masses and had joined LaGarde and the brothers at table for breakfast. Instead of having Stephen's customary place set at the last table near the kitchen door, the rector had commanded that the boy be seated at the rector's own table, in full view of all of the fathers and brothers.

Stephen bowed to LaGarde and requested his permission to make a confession to the community. LaGarde nodded approval. Stephen knelt and, bowing low, kissed the cold stones of the floor. Stretching his arms out in the form of a cross, as he had seen others do during his nine years in this house, he spoke in a loud voice so that all could hear.

"Reverend fathers and brothers in Christ, I confess to Almighty God and to you that I have sinned by foully debasing my body by a sin of self-abuse. I beg the forgiveness of my Lord Jesus and I beg your prayers to help me never again to sin in this manner." Finishing his confession, he again kissed the floor and stood up. LaGarde signaled him to sit down across the table from Father Lalonde. The reading of the scriptural text for the day began. Lalonde was laughing softly; then, in a voice that LaGarde could not have heard even had he not been so intent on the reading, Lalonde said, "My God, boy, you really do love to make a spectacle of yourself, don't you?" Stephen did not reply but continued to eat, his face aflame with shame.

For the next week LaGarde guided Stephen through the life of the Savior, from his birth on the first Christmas to just before his suffering and death. They sat together in LaGarde's study at the last moments of the long day in a religious house, just before evening prayers and bed.

"Tomorrow morning, Etienne, I want you to rise two hours before mass and I want you to meditate on the points I have raised this week. I want you to think of the Lord's humiliation, the omnipotent Godhead taking on corrupt human flesh and becoming man. I want you to continue by contemplating the goodness of his life, his sinlessness, his goodness to his brothers, you and I. And I want you finally to concentrate on this evening's story, the raising of Lazarus from the dead. The goodness of Christ is seen in this ultimate kindness to His friend, the granting of the gift of a renewed life."

"The story of Lazarus reminds me of my own life, Father," said Stephen.

"How is that, Etienne?"

"Because I too was raised from the dead and given a new life. I was found in the wilderness and brought to you. But I wonder if Lazarus remembered his earlier life. I remember so little."

"Your analogy with Lazarus is true only in the spiritual sense," said the priest, obviously annoyed at Stephen's intrusion of a personal note into his points for meditation.

But the boy continued. "I came from among the Bastonois. My parents, then, whoever they were, were heretics and I too seemed destined to a life without a knowledge of the truth. I wonder who my parents were. Has no one ever inquired of me, Father? If they are dead, are they in hell? I hope not. I hope that somehow or other Jesus found a way to save them."

"Etienne, I see that you are in no mood to continue our points for meditation this evening," said LaGarde. "The time has come for a break in the exercises. Tomorrow is Saturday. Try to meditate as best you can tomorrow morning. I will get word to Socono to come after mass tomorrow and take you hunting. It will do you some good, and perhaps next week you will be able to concentrate less on yourself and more on the Lord."

"I did not mean to be inattentive, Father."

The priest patted his shoulder. "It is not altogether unusual to order a break in the exercises after a week. Do not fret about it. Enjoy yourself tomorrow. It may be a long time before you have another chance to feel free in the woods that you love so much."

Stephen meditated poorly the next morning; even La-Garde's mass seemed boring. After mass he went to the kitchen. Brother Richard had packed some food for his lunch—slices of bread, cold meat and a small flask of wine. Stephen nodded his thanks to the brother, not wishing to distress him by breaking silence, and slipped out the kitchen door into the foggy streets of the town. He walked directly toward the Hotel Dieu and toward the convent.

The fog was particularly thick, but on mornings such as this one it had a tendency to burn off quickly. Stephen could have walked through the town of Louisbourg blindfolded. There were mornings in winter when it was impossible to see more than two feet in front of yourself, but residents like Stephen navigated the streets effortlessly. He came to the porter's lodge and gave the bell his customary two yanks.

"Who now?" the voice of Sister Marie Louis came from behind the door. "The bread has been delivered already. Who can be at my door at this hour?"

Stephen placed his mouth to the mid-door crack so that she might hear him better. "If it is not the bread boy, then it must be the archbishop," he said.

The door swung open and the old lady stood in the doorway smiling. "Your Excellency, please enter my lodge. You do me and my sisters such a great honor by visiting our humble convent."

Stephen made a mock bow and extended his hand for her to kiss his nonexistent ring. Instead she slapped his hand aside and hugged him.

"Oh, Etienne, I have missed you. Richard is not much of a bread boy."

Stephen smiled at the thought of pompous old Brother Richard being called a bread boy.

"He refused to talk. The first time he came I spoke to him. He reminded me of the Great Silence and hasn't spoken a word since. Never has he offered me a roll. I have eaten them anyway. But with you I never felt guilty. Now I suffer great pangs, not just in my teeth but in my soul. Great Silence—nonsense. I haven't paid attention to that for the last twenty years. When I was a nurse on night duty I suppose I was not to speak with my patients, not to comfort them in their suffering. You can tell that Richard has never been anything but a cook. Great Silence, indeed. But enough of Richard. How are you handling things, boy."

"I am well, Sister."

The old woman put her hand to his face. "The retreat has been hard for you," she said. "I can tell. I can see suffering in your eyes. I know what you go through. My order's rule is based on the Jesuit rule. I made my thirty-day retreat more than sixty years ago. But I will never forget it. I know, boy, I know." She patted his cheek.

"It is not so much the meditation and the silence, Sister. But the retreat is one of election. I am supposed to determine what I want to do with my life. And it is causing me to ask questions about myself. I don't know anything about myself. Who am I? Where am I from? How can I determine my

51

future when I don't know how to fill in my past? Every time I mention my past, Father Rector grows impatient with me."

"How can I help you, Etienne?" she said sympathetically.

"You were in Louisbourg when they brought me here. Was there anything that could give a clue to where I was from?"

"Don't you remember anything, Etienne? You were not so young that you should have no memories."

The boy dropped into a chair near the door. "I have only impressions. I remember a house. I suppose it was my parents' house. And I can almost recall my mother's face; at least I suppose she was my mother. But how I came to be lost in the woods and how I came to be here—of those things I remember nothing. The last impressions I have are of a journey, of traveling through the woods and of lying out of doors at night, very warm, and looking at the stars."

"I don't think I can help you, Etienne. I have told you everything I know. You were brought to the hospital by two Indians. I don't know if I had ever seen them before or if I have seen them since. I can't tell one Indian from another. Father LaGarde told Mother Superior that you had been found in the woods south of here, in Acadia. You had no papers, nothing. You were in a fever from the wound. Father LaGarde had doctored it but it had become infected. You were raving, out of your head, and would answer no questions. You spoke no French and the words you did speak I couldn't understand. Mother said you spoke English. When your fever broke and you regained consciousness, you could only remember your name. That is all I know. We have always assumed that you came from the Bastonois. They had taken over the towns and fort in Acadia. Maybe your parents were going there when you were separated from them—like the boy Jesus in the gospel."

Stephen brooded for a moment. "I suppose I should put it all from my mind," he said. "I certainly will have to if it interferes with my retreat. Father Rector will not put up with these distractions. He has given me today as a holiday to go hunting with Socono. But I would like Karl Stiegler to come with us too."

"Ah, he is a dear boy," said the old nun.

"Not according to Father LaGarde and Brother Richard. Richard called him a foul-mouthed bastard."

"Richard, that one," she muttered. "He would say that of anyone who used the spoken word."

"I would like to see if Karl can obtain a day's leave. I have enough food for myself and Socono will bring pemmican. Can you spare a bit of food for Karl?"

"I have some good cheese that the Intendant sent over for Mother Superior. I suppose I could let you have that. She has been putting on a few pounds anyway; she can do without it. A growing boy like Karl needs it more than she does," she rationalized as she walked to the back of the lodge where she kept her stores. "A bit of this morning's bread would not be missed either. That should do it."

Stephen thanked her by kissing her forehead when she returned with the bundle of food.

"Off with you now and enjoy your day, boy," she commanded.

"Goodbye, Sister," he yelled as he left and began to trot off into the morning fog.

She wiped her eyes and closed the lodge door softly.

The afternoon sun had burned off the fog and the day had grown hot. Stephen lay on his stomach absolutely motionless as the sweat trickled down his face and blurred his vision. Inside his shirt it coursed from his armpits, chest and back, staining the gray-brown cloth a darker shade. He was concealed by underbrush on all sides and his arm, holding a bow already equipped with an arrow, lay stretched out in front of him, resting on a rotting log. He stared over the log toward the clearing, which began only a few feet past where he lay.

He had selected this spot with Socono earlier in the day, after noting deer signs in the clearing and finding the path that they used to get to the stream, which flowed about twenty feet behind Stephen. Here he would wait, downwind from the deer, and be ready for them when they came to drink and feed.

He had been lying there relaxed for almost three hours when a smallish buck strode boldly into the clearing. Stephen was taken by surprise. It was too early for deer to be feeding. Normally they would rest during the heat of the day and come to feed when the sun grew cooler. At first he wondered if Socono, lying hidden on the other side of the clearing, had been surprised too. He knew better, of course. Socono was never taken by surprise.

For the next twenty minutes Stephen remained frozen, awaiting Socono's signal—the chirp of a squirrel. He could not see him, but he knew that the Indian would be working himself slowly forward, in order to get a clear shot. Then he heard the signal. He counted to three and leaped to his feet. Socono's arrow struck the deer in the neck. The buck turned to flee and charged almost directly at Stephen. He could see the animal's eyes, red with fright. Stephen drew back the bowstring, aimed and fired. His arrow bit deeply into the deer's chest. The buck changed direction and charged into the bushes.

From across the meadow Socono raced after the deer. Stephen stopped to pick up the quivver of arrows that lay at his feet. He notched an arrow in the string and ran toward the path that the deer had taken. About seventy-five yards into the underbrush he found Socono, standing before the deer, which lay quivering where it had finally fallen. It was still alive.

"Stand clear," Socono warned Stephen in Abenacki. No warning was needed; Stephen knew that the feet of the deer were as sharp as razors and, although this buck was near death, one kick could tear open its tormentors' flesh.

Socono walked behind the buck. He grabbed its head under the chin and, with one deft sweep of his knife, he slit its throat. Socono waited a few minutes to be sure that the animal was dead and then he stepped over it. He drew his knife again and, with another rapid stroke, he opened the buck's belly, allowing its intestines to spew onto the ground. He reached into the bloody cavity with his free hand and drew out the deer's liver. The Indian would have preferred to eat the raw liver right then and there, but he knew that Stephen would object. The boy would eat raw liver if he had to—Socono had seen to that—but like all whites, he preferred to cook his food, turning the tender liver into brown leather. He knew also that the boy would wish to save some of the liver for his friend, the soldier, who waited for them by the pool some three miles downstream. Socono's arms and chest were covered with the deer's blood and intestines, and he knew he would enjoy a swim once they joined Karl.

Stephen drew pieces of leather cord from the pouch at his side and began to tie the buck's feet together. Socono whacked away with his tomahawk at the trunk of a birch tree about four inches in diameter. Once he had felled it and cleaned it of branches, he placed the pole through the bound feet of the animal. Stephen took one end and Socono the other; together they walked into the stream and followed its course southward.

"Hail, the great hunters return," joked Karl as Stephen and the Indian, carrying the deer, found him. The pool was a natural one, formed as the waters of Freshwater Brook fell some three feet over a ledge into a hollow below. It formed a crystal clear pool of chilling water some ten feet deep. The water flowed out of the pool again on the south end and began its journey to the sea, another mile to the south.

Karl sat naked on a rock on the far side of the pool, soaking up the afternoon sun. Stephen crossed the stream above the ledge and joined Karl on his rock, while Socono fastened the hind legs of the buck to a tree branch and hauled the deer off of the ground, its antlers hanging about a foot off the forest floor. He then prepared a small fire and began to roast the fresh liver. Stephen opened his pouch and produced his meat, bread, cheese and wine, spreading them on the flat rock before his friend. When Socono had roasted the liver to his own satisfaction, but not really to the satisfaction of Karl and Stephen, he too joined them on the rock.

When they had finished eating, Karl announced his plans for another swim. "How about you, Stefan?" he asked. "Are you brave enough to freeze your ass off in that water?"

Socono had already stripped off his buckskin pants, which were all that he was wearing.

"No," said Stephen. "I'm not much for swimming today."

It was hot, and he would have enjoyed a swim, but the marks of the beating he had received were still visible on his back; he was ashamed to let his friends see them.

Socono dove gracefully into the pool and swam underwater to the other side. Karl followed, jumping into the water with a great splash.

"Jesus," he yelled, "the water is even colder than it was before." He pulled himself back up onto the rock, satisfied to have cooled himself off but not wishing to stay any longer in the cold water. "You are a quiet one today, Stefan," said Karl. "What is bothering you?"

"I don't know," responded Stephen. "I suppose the retreat is more than I bargained for. I can't seem to get it out of my mind that I don't know anything about myself. I don't know who I am."

"You really think that is important, Stefan?" Karl started to laugh. "I know who I am and it hasn't done much for me. I know I am a bastard and that I come from a long line of bastards. My father was a bastard and his father before him.

Or so my mother says. Although how my mother knew who my father was is a great mystery to me. She never told me his name."

Socono swam back from the far side and rejoined them, holding on to the rock with his elbows and allowing the water of the pool to flow over his body.

"Tell Socono that his cock will shrivel off if he doesn't come out of the water," said Karl. Socono understood French well enough, and Stephen did not feel the need to relay the message in Abenacki. Socono, perhaps fearful that the Swiss boy's prediction might come true, pulled himself out of the water.

Karl continued to recount his family history. "My mother, now there was a woman. The greatest whore in Zurich."

"Karl," interrupted Stephen, "if Father LaGarde could hear you talk, his ears would . . ." He was about to say *shrivel*, but remembering Karl's recent remark to Socono, he failed to finish the sentence.

"No, Stefan, it is true. My mother was the best whore in the city and I pimped for her from the time I was ten until I was fourteen. Then I joined the French army. Yeah, old Mama, she was really something. I sure do miss her." He laughed and then fell silent.

Socono asked Stephen in Abenacki why the soldier had so insulted his mother. "I don't think he was insulting her, Socono," Stephen responded. "Or at least he doesn't intend to insult her." He remained quiet for some moments and then added, "At least he knows who she is."

The Indian looked at him searchingly. "You would prefer to know that your mother was a woman of no morals who sold herself rather than know nothing about her? This I do not understand, little brother. A woman such as the soldier's mother would have her nose cut off among my people."

"Karl knows where and to whom he was born. Sometimes I feel that I just happened. The Micmacs found me in the woods and that's when Stephen Nowell began."

"The Micmacs did not find you," said Socono softly.

Stephen looked him directly in the face, only to see a mask of stoic disinterest take control. "What did you mean by that?" he asked.

"I know nothing, little brother. Perhaps the blackrobes can answer your questions."

The sun was setting behind the low hills at their back when the three men crossed the marshes that stretched uninterruptedly from the stream to the town. Before the sun had disappeared, they had arrived before the great walls of the city, loaded down with the carcass of the buck. They had decided to take it to the military barracks and to let the army butchers skin it and hang it for seasoning. The fathers would receive a hindquarter once it was ready.

They reentered the city by the west gate. The massive walls loomed above them as they passed through. Stephen could not help but stare upward. "It is really an overwhelming sight, isn't it, Karl?"

"What?" asked the sweating soldier.

"The strength of the fortress," responded Stephen.

"The hell it is," said Karl. He handed one end of the pole he carried to Stephen and walked over to the side wall of the gate while Stephen and the Indian looked on. Karl lifted his foot and struck out at the stone jutting out to form a corner. The blow set the stone free of the grip of the mortar and moved it a good two inches out of line.

"If I can do that with my foot," he said, "you can imagine what a forty-two-pounder can do. This fortress has been built on this godforsaken island to protect the entrance to the St. Lawrence River—the gateway to New France. No one is supposed to be able to attack Quebec or Montreal as long as this place stands. The defense of New France depends on this fortress, and although they haven't even finished building it, it is already falling down."

Stephen was shocked. "How did this happen?" he asked.

"They've used sea sand in the mortar. It's too fine. It won't hold."

"But the engineers know better than that, Karl. Why don't they stop it?"

"You are an innocent, Stefan. Don't you know what is going on in this town? This west gate is bad and it is the same over at the Grand Battery and the Island Battery. It is better over at the King's bastion and the Queen's bastion. Inspectors are more likely to look there. What's happening here is a crime. Instead of having a great fortress, we are likely to end up with a great pile of sand. Do you know why the troops have not been paid in three months? Oh, they tell us that it is because the pay ships have been delayed in France. Do they take us for fools? The sailors from the *Vengeance* told us that she carried our pay. She has docked, loaded, refitted and sailed and still no pay. But the officers always seem to have money. The Intendant is well heeled and the Governor dines on the best. While we troops—we are only Swiss after

57

all—we eat garbage. The building of this fort has made many a greedy man wealthy, all at the expense of good King Louis."

But it was not in Karl to remain angry for too long. He smiled at his friends and took the end of the pole from Stephen. "You go home now, little priest. It has been a good day. I hope Father LaGarde does not find you too corrupted after a day with me."

Stephen smiled back and said goodbye to Karl and Socono. "It has been a good day," he repeated.

Stephen entered the Jesuit house by the front door. Father Lalonde was sitting in the porter's lodge, filling in for Brother Jean.

"Good evening, Etienne. I hardly recognized you in your hunting clothes," he said. "It is always difficult for me at the best of times to see how you fit into this house, but if you dress like a common ruffian and spend your time racing through the woods like a savage, you must forgive me if I fail to recognize you as one of ours."

"Forgive me, Father," said Stephen. "I forgot myself. I should have returned by the kitchen door."

"That would have been more appropriate, boy." The priest rose unsteadily from his chair behind the desk. The boy caught the unmistakable smell of brandy from the priest. He started to go back out the door again.

"Hold, boy, where do you think you are going?"

Stephen stopped. "I was going to go through the kitchen, as you suggested, Father."

"Come over here and help me," ordered the priest. "I am not feeling well. One would think that a boy in the midst of the Spiritual Exercises of our founder would be looking for opportunities to perform good works."

Stephen approached the priest and offered him his hand to help steady him as he walked to the door of the lodge. The priest staggered slightly and fell against Stephen, throwing his arm about the boy's neck.

"Help me down the hall to my room," the priest ordered. Stephen led him carefully as the man leaned on him for support. "Do I offend you, Etienne? I'm drunk, you know. Do you plan to run off and tell LaGarde?"

"I would hope, Father Lalonde, that you would tell Father Rector."

"Ah, noble Etienne. You will never really be one of us. You have the instincts of an Englishman. Never snitch on anyone

—fair play and all that. All these years living in a Jesuit house and you still don't know that the essence of the Society of Jesus is snitching on one another and on everyone else in the world. How else could LaGarde control us all?"

They had reached the door to Lalonde's room unobserved. Stephen turned the knob and entered. By now he was actually carrying the priest. He dropped him onto his cot and Lalonde did not move. Stephen thought the priest had passed out, and he had turned to leave when Lalonde stirred.

"Why don't you stay a while with me, boy?" he said sleepily.

"I have to change my clothes, report to the refectory to help Brother Richard and then get points for meditation from Father Rector. I will not have time to stay and talk with you, Father."

The priest smiled and turned his face to the wall of the room. "You never do understand anything, do you, Etienne?"

For the next six days Stephen followed LaGarde through the suffering and death of Jesus.

"My son, I want you to contemplate the cause of the Lord's passion and death," said LaGarde on the evening of the sixth day. "Why His agony of doubt in the Garden of Gethsemane? Why the scourging and the crowning with thorns? Why the nails through His hands and feet? Why the piercing of His side with a spear? Why His death?"

"It was as you have always taught me, Father," said Stephen. "It was so that man could be saved. Jesus reopened the gates of Heaven for all by His suffering and death."

"But, Etienne, why were the gates of Heaven closed in the first place? It was due to sin—to Adam's sin, to your sins, to my sins. We forced Jesus to suffer and die. You pounded the crown of thorns into His skull. When you abused your body that first night, you drove a spear into the side of our Savior. Your sins have killed Jesus."

"But I love Jesus, Father."

"If you really did, you would not sin, ever again. You would spend the rest of your life in atonement for the sins you have committed already, which brought the Lord's agony upon Him. You should never again think of any act as indifferent. It is good and therefore relieves the sufferings of the Beloved One, or it is evil and constitutes a stroke of the hammer to drive in a nail. If you truly loved Jesus, you would make a commitment to Him—to strive to discover His will and to do it always."

"But how can I know God's will?" asked Stephen.

"That is one of the great consolations of the religious life," answered LaGarde. "We always know God's will. All we must do is be obedient to the voice of our superior. He speaks with the voice of God to us."

"But what if our superior tells us to do what is wrong?"

"Holy obedience is a binding vow, Etienne. You are safe if you obey and lay the burden of subtle morality on the one whom you obey."

"But should I not follow my conscience?" asked Stephen.

"Of course," said LaGarde, "as properly formed by obedience."

"What of those who live outside the vows, Father?"

"For them it is more difficult. They must follow the teachings of our mother, the church."

"But I have done that, Father, and I have still sinned."

"Then you must work even harder. You must strive for perfection."

"But how can I do that? How can I be perfect when I can't even control my own sins of the flesh?"

"That is a question that you must strive to answer, Etienne. I will help you. Jesus gave us the answer to your question, and before the Exercises are over, I hope that you will have come upon it yourself. If not, I will aid you."

Stephen walked along the base of the outer walls of the King's bastion—the citadel. Ahead of him he could see the angle of the Queen's bastion and he walked toward it. Shortly after passing the last of the walls of the town, he broke through the trees and marshland and walked onto the rocky beach. He had spent most of the afternoon at the pool, but he had not been able to concentrate there. It was too full of memories of Socono and Karl and good but worldly times. He had trekked through the marshes and been bitten by innumerable mosquitoes. It had been frightfully hot in the woods, and the sea breeze and the sound of the surf striking the rocky shoreline provided a welcome respite.

He sat on a rock with his back to the setting sun, looking out at the gray sea, now touched with gold. It has come to this, he thought. I must make up my mind. What do I do with my life? Do I spend it in what might be a fruitless search for the past or do I devote myself to the God who loves me?

He had thought that the decision would come to him only after a great emotional struggle or even that the heavens would proclaim it with thunder and lightning. Instead it came to him quietly. He knew what he would do. He stood up from the rock and walked back toward the town.

He knocked on LaGarde's door, but there was no answer. He returned to his room. He would inform the priest later of his decision.

LaGarde had heard the knock but he had not responded. He sat with his back toward the door, looking out the window at the last faint light of dusk. On his desk was a letter from Demarais, his superior. The orders were explicit. He was to discontinue the Exercises. He was to inform Stephen that in the view of the Provincial he needed further education before he could be admitted into the Society—education that could only be obtained in France. The Provincial had ordered him to take the boy to Europe as soon as possible. LaGarde could guess the real reason. The boy's family was once again on his trail.

"After all these years," the priest said to himself, "they still seek to know the truth." LaGarde would see if he could book passage on the next ship leaving Louisbourg for Brest.

Stephen tossed in his sleep. The excitement of the day and of his decision had kept sleep from him for a long time. When it came it was not the deep sleep of a mind at ease. He tossed again, and he pictured a white, frightened face leaning over him. He heard a voice.

"You are Stephen Nowell," the voice said again and again, louder and louder.

III

1740

The offices of Breed, Nowell and Pierce, Merchants, were located in Charlestown for reasons of both sentiment and convenience. Sarah Nowell sat at her desk, looking out the window across the broad river toward the hills of Boston. Her fingers played absentmindedly with the gold locket she wore about her neck. Pierce had objected when she first rented the warehouse and offices, arguing instead for space on Boston's wharves, but Sarah, as representative of the senior partner, her father, had insisted on Charlestown. Her father would never have visited the offices if they had been in Boston, but there was a chance, a very small one, that Breed would pay a call on her in the Charlestown office. Sarah sometimes insisted on the need for her father's signature and in that manner lured him away from his room at the old farmhouse, which he now rarely left.

Sarah's desk was piled high with paper—bills of lading, invoices, accounts to pay, money drafts, all matters that were inappropriate to her station and sex (as Daniel Pierce always said on those occasions when he had the audacity to criticize her and to challenge her ordinarily unassailable control over the shipping end of the business). Today she had worked steadily at the pile, dictating letters to poor Edgar Rudge, her hard-pressed secretary and accountant. Gradually the finished pile had grown, had equalled and then surpassed the unfinished pile. But as the afternoon wore on, she grew weary and dismissed Rudge to his outer office, where he would labor away with much scratching of quill on paper until she sent him home. Then she would leave the office for her room at the Breed farmhouse.

Her mind was not at ease. Yesterday's visit from Elisha Parker, the customs man, had unnerved her, and his insinuations of possible irregularities in the firm had been downright insulting—especially coming from Parker, the most corrupt customs official in the King's service. And that was an opinion shared by most of the merchants of Massachusetts. Sarah herself had been paying him regularly for almost seven years to look the other way when the shipments of molasses came from her agents in Jamaica, Barbados or, more importantly, from French Santo Domingo. He had clearly hoped to pry more money from her by suggesting that ships of her firm had transported rum distilled from her molasses to Isle Royale and had returned to New England with cargoes of Canadian furs. This was not illegal under English law, but the implication was that Pierce would have to be involved with the Canadians to get away with such dealings.

Sarah had been enraged. Trading with the Canadians of New France was to her reprehensible. She was a merchant and as interested in profit as any merchant, but the Canadians had trained Indians to murder her husband and steal her son. They sickened her.

Sarah grinned as she recalled Parker's face when she had risen from her chair, bent over her desk and, looking him straight in the eye, had called him a "bloody liar." She was sure that Parker had never before heard a gentlewoman use such language. Normally she didn't use it either, although a lifetime in the house of Jonathan Breed had taught her much worse words. Parker could count himself lucky that she had not punched him in the eye. Before he had the opportunity to recover from his shock, she had summoned Rudge and informed him to show Parker to the door of their establishment.

Still, she puzzled over what, other than greed, could have motivated him. He never would have tried blackmail unless he had something substantial to work on. Yet every aspect of the overseas trade was under her control. Not a ship left Boston harbor under their company's registry without her knowing by heart its cargo, its destination and its master. Pierce ran only the fur trade part of their business. Was it possible that he had somehow become involved in shipping as well? She did not understand how he could have, and that in itself disturbed her all the more. She was determined to learn everything about his affairs, and if he had become involved, she would stop him.

Her relationship with Daniel Pierce over the past ten years had been tempestuous. Before the loss of Samuel and Stephen, she had paid him no attention at all. Afterward, she had realized that she had been mistaken to underestimate the man. It was he who had arranged the search of the wilderness between Springfield and Northfield as she lay unconscious in the widow Gage's bed, and her father, that bull of a man, sat paralyzed with fear that he would lose her too.

It was Pierce who had arranged their visit to Montreal and the Indian villages of Caugnawaga and St. François. At first she had expected her father to take the lead, but he had deferred to Pierce. That made sense when it came to making arrangements; after all, it was Pierce who had the contacts with the woodsmen. But even in their inquiries with the Jesuit priests and with the French Governor, Jonathan Breed let Pierce dominate until Sarah intervened and took control.

It became even worse after their visit to the squalid little Indian village of St. François. She could still remember visiting dirty cabin after dirty cabin in the company of an overly solicitous Jesuit brother. She would never forget the looks of hostility and fear on the faces of the inhabitants, and she had dreamed ever since of the scalps hanging on poles in front of the cabins. They were mostly the scalps of whites, and to this day she could not shake the thought that the scalps of her husband and son might have been among them. It was obvious to her that her father was haunted by the same thought, but as she grew stronger with each passing year, he grew weaker.

Jonathan Breed had spoken very little on the return trip from Montreal. As they sailed Lake Champlain on the clumsy-looking lake boats, Sarah had seen him look off toward the shore, peering into the dense forests, almost expectantly. And then he began to cry softly to himself. He was a broken man.

Sarah's reaction had been entirely different. Samuel and Stephen were lost, probably dead. She would never give up looking for them as long as there was any chance that they lived, but she was determined not to halt her own life or to devote it to mourning.

She had never told about what Wiggins had done to her; she never would. But she had vowed to herself that never again would she be in a position, either in mind or body, to be abused by anyone—especially a man.

No sooner had she made this resolve than Daniel Pierce had proposed marriage to her. It happened on the return trip from Montreal. Her first instinct had been to laugh, but she had checked herself. He sat facing her across a small fire that one of his trappers had built for them when they made camp on Wood Creek, the small stream that connected the southern tip of Lake Champlain and the Hudson River. His eyes reflected the embers of the fire as he looked at her, and the effect was to turn what was normally a bland, inoffensive face into something rather sinister. He frightened her. He was not the simpleton she had always thought him to be. There was something extremely offensive in his blatant move away from her aunt to her for the sake of improved prospects. That audacity had not been apparent in the past. She felt even more exposed and more determined to protect herself. The moment also offered her the opportunity to exploit a plan she had been formulating ever since she had visited St. François.

"I'm flattered, Daniel," she had forced herself to reply. "But Betsy Breed is my aunt and for all practical purposes the only mother I have ever had. I love her and I thought you did too."

"I'm not a romantic, Miss Sarah," he responded. "I love neither you nor your aunt. I am offering you the protection of a man at a time when I believe that you need that protection more than my dear Betsy. I never asked Miss Breed to fall in love with me and I do not expect you to love me either. I ask only that you comfort me, and in turn I will see to the fostering of your interests."

"You seem to forget yourself, Mr. Pierce," Sarah said with all the haughtiness she could muster. "I already have a husband."

"I don't mean to be cruel, but I don't really believe that you ever expect to see your husband or your son again."

Sarah winced but she knew he spoke the truth. The moment had come to reveal her plan to him. "You may be right, Pierce," she said. "But I do not intend to marry again or to comfort anyone unless I have a mind to. I will do what may even be better from your point of view. I will invest in your business with whatever small sum Samuel has left to me, and I will convince my father to turn over Stephen's portion of his estate to me immediately. I will also invest that in your business on two conditions."

Pierce had been absentmindedly picking at the twigs and weeds that had attached themselves to his coat and staring into the fire as Sarah spoke. But as she began to outline her plan, he looked directly at her once again. Even by marrying Sarah he had not hoped to get his hands on the Breed money immediately. His renewed interest was obvious to Sarah. "What are the conditions?" he asked softly.

"First, you must marry my aunt. Nothing less than that will make her happy, and I am determined that one member of this family shall be happy."

"Until very recently marriage to your aunt was my main goal in life," said Pierce truthfully. "It has always been your father who stood in our way."

"I'm sure that has all changed now," said Sarah.

"And the second condition?"

"The second condition is that I become your business partner."

Pierce smiled. "Obviously, Sarah, if you invest your money in my firm, you become my partner."

"I don't think you understand, Daniel. I do not intend to be just a stockholder in the business. I intend to play an active role."

"But you know nothing about the fur trade."

"We will branch out. I will leave to you what you know best. It will be my responsibility to expand the firm with our new capital into other areas of trade. Boston merchants are making money in the West Indian trade, particularly in rum. After all, rum and furs go together."

And thus the firm of Breed, Nowell and Pierce had been formed at a campfire in the middle of the New York wilderness. Sarah had insisted that her father's name be included and, even more, that it come first. She smiled again, remembering the look on Pierce's face when the nameplate was first screwed on the door of the firm's Charlestown offices. She was not sure which was harder for him to swallow, the nameplate or the marriage to Betsy, but he swallowed both.

The new firm had been successful, and its operations had become a full-time task for Sarah. She and Pierce had divided responsibilities from the very beginning. Jonathan Breed played no role whatever. He had agreed to his sister's marriage out of gratitude to Pierce for the role he had played in the search for his grandson. He had surrendered Stephen's intended portion of his wealth without a murmur, asking Sarah only to invest it wisely for Stephen, so that when he returned the portion would have multiplied enough to care for his grandson's needs.

Sarah took the entire sum and purchased rights to a shipment of molasses due to arrive from the French West Indies. She reserved only a small portion, to be paid to the Boston customs collector for turning a blind eye to the transaction. French molasses was cheap because the French

66

government discouraged the production of rum, which might prove a potent competitor for cheap brandy in the fur trade. Rum production could undermine an important home industry. French planters, having refined their sugar, could only dump the waste molasses or sell it illegally to Boston merchants at incredibly low prices. The import duty in Boston on this foreign commodity, if collected, would make its importation unprofitable. But by bribery Sarah and other merchants like her avoided the duty. Her profits from this first venture alone were greater than Pierce's profits in the fur trade had been for the past three seasons.

But still Sarah was not satisfied. She was determined to increase profits on Pierce's side of the firm as well. He traded rum, not molasses, for furs. It was her idea to use her profits to open their own distillery. Pierce had resisted the idea; he could not believe that she would take one successful risk and then risk even more with her new scheme. Sarah prevailed. She did not ask him to use the meager profits of the fur trade; the capital came exclusively from her side.

Sarah's distillery began turning molasses into rum two months later. She charged the market price to other purchasers of rum, but Pierce received his rum at cost. His expenditures were far less than any of his competitors, and he was able to trade for more furs at a lower cost to himself. The fur trade profits surged ahead.

But still Sarah was not satisfied. Once she had the distillery operating with a profit of its own, she invested in the purchase of her own schooner. The advertisement in the *Gazette* had described it as a well-broken-in vessel of medium age but sound condition. However, it was the price that intrigued Sarah. For six months she had searched the paper and the announcements posted on the doors of shipping companies, looking for just such a bargain. As soon as she read this notice, however, she knew she had to see the ship. She knew something about smaller vessels from her girlhood sails about Boston harbor, but there was only one man in Boston whom she would trust when it came to sailing ships. Before the hour was up she had enticed her old teacher, Joseph Moulton, senior shipwright at the Hammond yards in Charlestown, to leave his job. Still covered with sawdust and wood chips, he crossed over to Boston with her.

Not far from the ferry slip in the North End, they found the ship mired in mud. "Well broken in, you say," chuckled the old man. "More like well broken in two." But he pulled a small ledger book from his vest and began to take notes busily. Gingerly, they walked the planks laid over the mud flats until they were close enough to touch the hull, which towered above their heads. Still the old man took notes.

"Can anything be done with it, Joseph?" Sarah asked finally, the pleading note in her voice partly affected to work on the old man's fondness for her.

"Might be able to turn some of the timbers into middlin' fair firewood," he teased. But his seasoned eye had searched the entire hull for signs of rot and he had seen none. After they obtained permission to board and Moulton had sounded the cargo holds, he pronounced her ready for retirement but still able to sail (although he himself vowed he would never risk being a passenger in her).

Sarah bought the schooner that very day. She named her the *Betsy* and convinced Moulton to work on refitting her in his off hours. Lawrence Hammond, owner of the yards, who was the richest man in Charlestown, and Anglican, and long her father's bitterest political foe, complained of the arrangement. Therefore, Sarah convinced Moulton to work full time for Breed, Nowell and Pierce. When Daniel Pierce objected that a firm involved in fur trading, distilling and trading with the West Indies had little use for a shipwright well past has prime as a worker, Sarah agreed but stoutly refused to let him go. In fact Pierce, with his objection, had planted the idea for further ventures in her mind.

But for now, all her attention was devoted to the *Betsy*. She made the trek daily from Charlestown to the wharf in Boston, where the schooner had been floated with some difficulty. Moulton had supervised the hauling of the ship into drydock and then managed the crew of workmen as they replaced broken planks, recaulked and ordered new masts and spars. When Sarah paid the sailmaker for the new set of top-quality sails, she did it with the last of the money she had set aside for Stephen's trust fund. The distillery was making money, but everything else was under Pierce's control, and she knew she could not count on him to help her. Once again she had risked everything on a gamble.

It took six months to restore the *Betsy* completely. Sarah and Joseph stood on the wharf together and watched with pride as the workmen knocked loose the stays and allowed the hull to slide down the greased runway into the river. The ship bobbed and bounced in the water, but Moulton and his crew knew their work. Soon the ship righted herself and floated proudly. Once it was afloat, the workmen placed the masts into position and fitted the sails.

A ship with no master, though, was not worth very much to an enterprising woman. Sarah had to find a captain and a crew, and she had to find ones who would work for nothing other than anticipated earnings. Again it was Moulton who came up with the solution, the day he barged into her office in Charlestown and pronounced one name: "William Vaughan."

"What?" asked a startled Sarah.

"William Vaughan. He's your man."

She continued to look at him blankly.

"Your ship's master. Vaughan. New Hampshire man. The best seaman in New England."

"Then he has a ship," she said.

"Nope. No one will hire him."

Now she looked interested. "Why?"

"Because he drinks like an Irish priest. Lost his last ship off Cape Ann because he was drunk."

"Well then, he's just the man to turn our ship over to—especially since we've invested every last penny we have in her. Old man, have you finally lost the last of your good sense?"

"Old man indeed. Look, little girl, we need a competent seaman who will work for nothing. That's no small order. William Vaughan is a competent seaman who can't get work. I think he's made to order."

"What about the drinking?"

"Send someone along to control him," said Moulton.

Sarah thought for a moment and then she jumped from behind her desk, rushed to Moulton and kissed the little man on top of his head. He had solved two problems with which she had been struggling. "Where can I find Captain Vaughan?" she asked.

"Well, let's see," said Moulton. "It's about noon. Right now that sot will be sitting in the taproom of the Cromwell's Head in Boston."

Sarah's eyes turned toward her cloak, which hung on a peg behind the door. Moulton followed her eyes. "No need to rush, Sarah. That stubborn old cousin of mine who operates the ferry will not sail during his noon hour. It will be 1:30 before you reach the inn."

"But I may miss him."

"Not Willy Vaughan," said Moulton. "He'll be there when you get there. He has no place else to go."

Not only did Captain Vaughan have no place to go, but he was in no condition to go anyplace when Sarah finally arrived at the Boston side of the ferry. She found him just where Joseph had said he would be, and he was drunk, very drunk. Sarah rented a room in the inn; the innkeeper and his black slave carried the captain up and dropped him rudely onto the bed.

The innkeeper stepped aside to allow Sarah to leave before him, but she ignored his gesture. "I want a tub of water brought in here," she said. "Cold water. And I want this man shaved and bathed. Innkeeper, I want your cook to send up a pot of hot coffee—black and strong."

"I'll have both sent up immediately, Mistress Nowell. I'm sure, however, that in the interests of your unblemished reputation and the reputation of my inn, that you will proceed downstairs while Josiah, my servant, takes care of the captain."

"Not on your life," said Sarah. "I'm not letting this man out of my sight until he's sober, and then I doubt if he will get rid of me for sometime thereafter."

The innkeeper looked at her in dismay.

"Be off, man," she said. "You've been paid. Now bring the water and the coffee."

After he left, she helped Josiah get the captain out of his filthy clothing. He stank of perspiration and stale beer. She ordered the servant to round up some new clothing for him. He was a large man and his recent years of dissipation had not completely destroyed what had been a handsome and sturdy body. His face was blotchy with drink but Sarah noted that he was probably younger than she was. At first sight she had thought him to be over forty-five, but it was now clear that he was under thirty-five.

The innkeeper arrived with an empty wooden tub and was scandalized to see Sarah staring at the naked man on the bed. Josiah, who from bitter experience knew that his master blamed him for all that went wrong in the inn, pulled the bed covering back and draped it gently over the unconscious form of the sea captain. He then departed and began to haul heavy buckets of water into the room, filling the tub. The innkeeper remained behind to guard the reputation of his establishment from the likes of this supposed gentlewoman.

When the tub was half filled, Sarah halted Josiah and ordered him to lift the captain off the bed. He carried the huge hulk and propped his rear on the edge of the tub. Sarah gave the signal and Josiah allowed Vaughan to slide over backward into the ice-cold water. Vaughan emerged like a surfacing whale, spewing water. The shock had returned him to consciousness; he splashed his arms and legs about and blew water from his mouth and nose. Most of the water landed on the floor.

"What in the name of Christ is going on here?" he yelled. Again on signal, the black man pushed Vaughan's body back down into the ice water.

"Scrub him," was all Sarah said.

Vaughan was still too drunk to resist the bath. When Josiah had finished, he hauled the captain up out of the water. Sarah reached over the bed, pulled a blanket off it and handed it to Josiah, who wrapped it around Vaughan's bluish body.

By this time Vaughan's eyes had begun to focus, and he saw Sarah standing in front of him. The blanket had fallen away. Most men, realizing that they were naked and being stared at by a strange woman, would have covered themselves instinctively. Not Vaughan. He looked her in the eye and smiled. "And who are you?" he asked, his speech still slurred with drink.

"I'm your new boss," she said.

He looked down at himself. "And what's my new profession?" he asked with an amused smile. He tried to step out of the tub, missed his footing and sent the tub and its entire contents splashing all over the room, while his massive body struck the floor with an enormous *splat*, spraying water in every direction. He struggled to his knees and, with Sarah's help, he made it to the bed and sat down. He grew cold again, and Sarah helped him wrap another cover about his body.

The innkeeper was in a rage, insisting that his floors would be ruined by all the water. He yelled at Josiah to get a mop and clean up.

"Shut up, you," yelled Vaughan.

"How dare you yell at me, sir? You, a man who has not paid his bill to me in two months."

"Consider yourself paid," said Sarah.

Vaughan looked at her, trying to focus his eyes. "You are either a very kind woman, or whatever I do, I must be superb at it." He started to laugh, but now his head had begun to hurt and laughing proved too painful. He grabbed his forehead with both hands.

Josiah arrived with his mop, together with the innkeeper's wife, a large pot of coffee and a stone mug. Sarah spent the next hour pouring coffee down Vaughan's throat while Josiah shaved a week's growth of beard off his face. What emerged

71

from their efforts was a man whom Sarah found attractive. His features were large. His nose was straight and slightly veined on each side. His eyebrows were thick and dark, framing dark blue eyes, which were his most attractive feature. They danced with amusement, and when the joy in them combined with his smile, she found him ruggedly handsome. The muscles of his chest and shoulders were strong; only his stomach muscles sagged. He had once developed a considerable girth about his middle, but drinking and infrequent eating had left him sagging.

Sarah liked what she saw. She hoped he was redeemable, and she was determined to try to redeem him. She would pay the innkeeper by borrowing the money from her father. She would keep a careful accounting and charge it against Vaughan's share of any profits. She paid for his room for the night, to allow him to sleep it off, but she was back at the inn first thing in the morning, standing by the foot of his bed as he awoke.

He groaned when he opened his eyes. "I need a drink," was the first thing he said. Then he raised his head very tentatively and stared at her. "I remember you," he said. "You're my new boss."

"Indeed I am," said Sarah. "And the first rule for those who work for me is that drunks don't drink."

He looked angrily at her. "Who are you calling a drunk?"

"You are a drunk, Captain Vaughan. I know all about you. You lost your sloop, the *Sprite*, almost a year ago, and with her you lost your crew and cargo. You haven't worked since, and you never will get another ship—certainly not in a New England port. In addition, if you don't stop drinking you will soon be dead."

"Get the hell out of my room," he said in anger.

"On the contrary," said Sarah, "it's my room. I paid for it."

"Then I'll get the hell out," he said. He rose from the bed, realized he was naked, but got out of the bed anyway. "Where are my clothes?" he asked.

"I've taken them and thrown them away."

"The hell you have," he responded in amazement. "What do you want from me, woman?" he asked more softly.

"I want a ship's master and I've been told that you're one of the best."

"I used to be the best. But given what you know about me, why do you want me? I've developed a new talent. Some seamen have an instinct for home port. They can find their

72

way through any storm and bring their ships home safely. Me, I've found a new instinct. I can find a reef where there's not supposed to be one. I'll find a rock for you." The bitterness and self-pity poured out of him.

"I know all about your instincts, Captain, and the only new instinct you've developed is for the bottle."

"Well, you have a point there too," he said. "So why do you want me? Have you a ship you want to collect insurance on?"

"I want you to sail my schooner, the *Betsy,* to the islands, pick up molasses, bring her back to Boston and make both of us rich. In short, I can't pay you. You'll have to take a share of profits."

"What makes you think I have it in me to sail to the West Indies?"

"You're a good seaman. You'll find your way there. The only thing that could stop you is drink, and you won't be doing any. I'll see to that. You'll be taking me on as a passenger."

He looked at her and his eyes smiled. "You think you can rehabilitate me, don't you?" he asked finally.

"You are the only derelict, beached sea captain I've got." She smiled back at him.

"But could you step outside now and find me some clothes? If someone should walk in here, they might get the wrong idea."

"You shouldn't worry about that, Captain. My husband was a minister, a very proper man. My father is a member of the General Court. But me—for the past few years I've been standing the merchant community on its head. I'm a woman who runs her own business. I smuggle rum; I run a distillery and sell rum to the heathen Indians, making them more heathen—all things a man could do without anyone raising an eyebrow. But a woman? If some of my husband's old associates entered this room, they would be surprised only by the fact that *I'm* dressed."

Sarah spent the next two weeks sobering up Captain William Vaughan. It was not an easy task. A whole year of drinking had taken a heavy toll on his will power. But whenever he weakened and tried to slip away or enter a tavern, someone was always following and stopped him. Sarah enjoyed his company, and he quickly realized that she had all the strength of character that he lacked. Before long he began to look forward to going aboard the *Betsy* and taking a hand in the preparations for her first voyage.

A knock on the door and the appearance of Rudge interrupted Sarah's thoughts. "Yes, Rudge. What is it?"

"You asked me to let you know when Mr. Pierce returned, Mistress Nowell."

"Good. Ask him to drop by my office before he leaves for home, would you?"

"Yes, madam," he said and closed the door softly as he left.

Sarah looked back toward the window. The sun would be gone shortly. It would be a beautiful sunset. But the sunset on land could not compare with the beauty of the sunset on the calm seas of the Caribbean.

She had realized that she loved William Vaughan when they were about five days out of Boston. They had had supper together in the captain's cabin, which had been commandeered by the owner, while the captain had displaced his mate. Then he had walked with her on the small quarterdeck. They said very little, merely watching the sun drop into the sea. When all light had left the sky, he turned to the helmsman and set the course for the next watch. Then he escorted her below. On board deck she had responded to his touch and to the very closeness of him, but now as he walked with her to her cabin, she became frightened. He could sense her panic and it surprised him.

"Is the lady who set all the busy tongues of Boston to wagging nervous?" he asked. They were standing at the door of the cabin. "I'll not come in if you don't want me to," he said softly to her.

She almost asked him not to, but then she looked into his eyes and saw the love there. She took his hand and led him into the cabin.

Once inside, he took her into his arms and kissed her. He led her to the captain's bed beneath the great windows in the stern of the ship. He undressed her gently and then removed his own clothes and lay beside her, stroking her face and breasts. She shivered under his hands.

"Why are you frightened?" he asked.

"I'm not very experienced," she said. "My husband was not really much of a lover; he saw it as his duty to me and therefore to God. I think he really resented the pleasure he took from me. It reminded him too much of his humanity."

"What about you?" he asked.

"I never received any pleasure from him. I loved him, but I can't say it was a physical love."

"And what you feel for me, is that physical?"

"Yes, and it frightens me."

"I won't hurt you, Sarah," he whispered in her ear.

"But there was another time—another man." Tears started to fall down her cheeks. "He did hurt me. He took me against my will and, oh God, how he hurt me," she cried.

Vaughan tried to hush her and kiss away the tears. He held her gently in his arms and rocked her, kissing the soft black curls of her hair. She stopped crying and lay quietly with her head upon his bare chest. He held her that way until she fell asleep.

He rose during the night without awakening her and went above to check on the night watch and to alter course. When he returned to the cabin, she was sitting up in the dark, waiting for him. He crossed the cabin toward the bed and she opened her arms to him. He kissed her and, removing his shirt and deck pants, he crawled under the covers with her. He moved his mouth to her breasts and began to kiss them. She lay back on the pillow and sighed with contentment. He pushed his body down lower until he found her navel with his tongue and then he traced a line with his tongue downward. As he moved he could feel her muscles grow tense, but he stroked her stomach with his hand and continued to seek her with his tongue. When he found her, she gasped and then was flooded with pleasure. She ran her hands through his black hair and let fear flee from her.

William Vaughan took on an important role in Sarah's life from then on. They never discussed marriage and they never really lived together, but they slept with each other whenever they could. When he was in port they would meet at his rooms in Boston or he would come after hours to her offices in Charlestown. All of Boston knew about them and they made no effort to hide their relationship. The community was scandalized by their love, almost as much as it was scandalized by the success of their business.

Sarah's voyage to the West Indian islands had proved to be another turning point. She met the merchants and planters of Kingston, Jamaica, and those of St. Kitts and, even more important, she met those of Cape François and Martinique. The *Betsy* returned to Boston with molasses purchased so cheaply and sold so dearly that all of Boston could talk of little else. The daughter of Jonathan Breed—for years a member of the General Court of Massachusetts—was a smuggler. She was not just a merchant who purchased smuggled consignments of molasses or even arranged for the smuggling; she was herself a common smuggler, bringing the forbidden goods in on a ship on which she herself sailed, unchaperoned, in the company of a man of easy morals. Her profits had been enormous.

When Sarah returned to Charlestown, Breed, Nowell and Pierce had a new, if minor, partner—William Vaughan—and Sarah had someone she trusted. She refused to be dependent on him, but at least he was someone to whom she could tell her thoughts and express her fears.

Pierce continued to press his demands that Joseph Moulton be retired or, better yet, fired. He was astounded to learn that the firm had instead begun a new venture—their own ship-yard to rival Hammond's—and that Moulton was to be the manager. Sarah wanted more ships, fast vessels that could make the round trip to the islands more quickly than the dumpy tubs used by other merchants, ships that could, if necessary, outsail any revenue cutter disposed to interfere with an honest woman's business. Moulton would build those ships in their own yard.

And build he did. Within five years of its founding, the firm of Breed, Nowell and Pierce was a major force in the Great Lakes fur trade, competing successfully with the French; it was a major importer and smuggler of West Indian molasses; it was the second largest distiller of rum in Massa-chusetts. The firm owned and operated a fleet of vessels, as well as building and repairing its own ships and those of others in the firm's Charlestown shipyard.

Sarah was a very wealthy woman now, or at least Stephen was very wealthy. Those profits that she did not reinvest she set aside in a trust fund for her son, and those profits were considerable, even after Pierce took his large share and Moulton and Vaughan took their very small ones.

Sarah had not changed her lifestyle at all. Aunt Betsy had refused to leave the Breed house after her marriage—one of the few acts of self-will in all of her fifty years—and so Pierce moved in. Reluctantly Sarah surrendered her room, the room she had shared with Samuel. She moved into Betsy's smaller room. Every evening, when the sun finally dipped behind the hills of the mainland to the west of Charlestown peninsula, Sarah would leave her office and climb the hill to her father's house, and every evening she would take her meal with the family and servants.

The sun had slipped behind the hill now and still she looked out the window, playing with her locket. Again a knock upon the door interrupted her reverie. "What do you want now, Rudge?" she said gruffly.

"It's Mr. Pierce, Madam, as you requested."

Daniel pushed by the smaller man with impatience. "What is it you want, Sarah?" he said as he entered.

"Close the door, Rudge," she said and then waited until he complied. "I asked you to drop by, Daniel, because I had a visit from our old friend, Parker."

"Why? Did you forget to pay our monthly, eh—what do you call it?"

"Try bribe. That stupid I'm not. But I have some doubts about you."

Pierce managed to look vaguely insulted. "Well, it is your activities that require the bribing of Crown officials, not mine."

"You profit from it, Daniel, as I do and as does every merchant in Boston. No, I didn't forget to bribe him. He came to blackmail me. He suggested that our firm has moved into direct trade with Montreal."

Pierce looked away from Sarah and gazed out the window. In a rather offhand manner, he shrugged his shoulders. "He must be losing his control. Where could he have gotten such a notion?"

"So help me God, Pierce, I hope it is not you who has given him this lever against us. Are you involved in the trade?"

"Why should I do that?"

"Because you're greedy and you always have been. All these years you have demanded to be paid your complete share of company profits, even though I have never asked to receive any from your side."

"But there are so few profits on my side, Sarah. And the overhead grows and grows."

"Never mind that. It isn't the profits or lack of profits in the fur trade that I want to talk to you about. I want an answer to my question."

"I'm not involved. But if I were, what of it? Some of the top merchants in this community are slavers. Is trade with New France so much worse than that? You have not had any qualms about selling rum to the Indians for their furs."

Sarah looked uncomfortable. "There is a difference. The Indians buy the rum because they want it. And I'm not selling it to the heathens who bring havoc to our frontier. I'm not selling to Canadian Indians."

"The distinction is a fine one," said Pierce.

"No, it's not," she shouted. "I tell you now, if you're involved I want you to get out and get out immediately."

After Pierce left Sarah's office he walked deliberately toward his own. "Bitch," he said softly as he closed the door. But it was not soft enough not to startle Rudge, who sat on his stool facing Sarah's door. Pierce walked to his desk and collapsed into his leather chair.

How could Parker have learned? Somebody in his network had slipped or had been bought. Pierce bitterly resented Sarah's dominance of the firm and he always would. He had worked hard for ten years to conceal those feelings. The business had once been entirely his; he resented her intrusion, even if she had made him a wealthy man. And he had wealth she knew nothing about. Eight years ago he had taken steps that would guide the rest of his life. He had returned to the Jesuit residence and met with Father Provincial; he had told the Jesuit all that he knew: the boy had been taken to Louisbourg. He had promised not to reveal the Jesuit secret for a price—entry into the Montreal fur market. It had been the opportunity of a lifetime, an opportunity to bypass the Albany monopoly of the Western trade. He was the only Englishman involved in the French trade, under a false name, of course. But even the Jesuit superior had not been strong enough on his own to arrange this. Demarais had given him access to the authorities in Quebec; it was they who had arranged the creation of the dummy firm in Montreal. In turn, he had promised to become the eyes and ears of France in New England. His men, under the supervision of Isaac Wiggins, went everywhere and returned not only with furs but with information. That information found its way to Quebec.

Pierce's fur interests in New France had prospered beyond his dreams. To achieve this wealth he had betrayed his country and risked the hangman. But he had no intention of being caught. It was clear to him now, however, that he had made a mistake. Sarah was on to him, and she would never cease her snooping until she got to the bottom of the situation. In the process she surely would uncover more dangerous information—that he had kept knowledge of the boy's whereabouts to himself. He had time. He had covered his tracks extremely carefully, but he would have to be even more careful in the future. Parker could be silenced with enough money, and his trade could be stopped for a while.

But now that the seed of doubt had been planted in Sarah's mind it would linger, and one day, he knew, he had always known, he would have to eliminate her. If she left well enough alone, he would wait until the old man died. Then he would take Sarah out of the way and he would inherit all through Betsy.

He had plotted the whole thing out that night before the campfire after Sarah had rejected him and gone to sleep. How could she have rejected him, his honorable offer, and then taken that drunken sot, Vaughan, into her bed?

For now she served his purposes. She was good at what she did. She had the knack of making money. But one day it would all be his. He would cover his tracks and leave her be, unless her snooping showed signs of success. Then he would push up the day for eliminating Sarah. The bait would be the boy. He would have to get word to Wiggins to watch the Jesuits at Isle Royale even more carefully.

IV

1741

Stephen was led down the dark, silent corridor of the College Louis le Grand's dormitory wing by the ancient Brother Denis, porter of the college. The corridor floors were dark brown marble, and the plaster walls had been painted a slightly lighter shade of brown. There was no illumination except that from the roofed cloister, which ran parallel to the corridor on the right. The day was dark and very little light penetrated through to the hallway. The darkened walls were covered with paintings and woodcuts depicting Jesuit saints such as Ignatius Loyola, Francis Xavier and Francis Borgia, but most of them showed Jesuit martyrs in various stages of torture. There were young men hanging on crosses with lances driven through their sides and shoulders. Their bemused executioners were clearly oriental, probably Japanese. Other priests in different scenes stood half-naked and in prayer as Indians, covered with gore, poured boiling water over their heads or cut open their vitals with hideous knives.

Stephen followed the brother without much enthusiasm. He was still reeling over the speed with which his life had changed. One day, on Isle Royale, he had expected to enter the Society and had made his decision to do so. The next day he was told to prepare to sail aboard the *Vengeance* on her return to the naval port of Brest. He was told only that the provincial in his goodness had arranged for him to receive a proper education before admission to the order.

He had hated the voyage across the Atlantic. LaGarde's standing as both a nobleman and a priest had obtained for them the finest accommodations possible on the crowded vessel, but LaGarde had insisted that Stephen remain in his cabin, and he was terribly seasick. He knew that had he been able to remain on deck, he would have withstood the nausea more easily. But the seas were rough and LaGarde feared for his safety.

They arrived in Brittany exhausted, but the worst was yet to come. LaGarde had booked the overland coach to Paris; the roads were terrible and Stephen felt more buffeted on land than he had on the seas. They arrived in Paris in the middle of the night and Stephen was not able to catch even a glimpse of the city. He arrived with the priest at the porter's lodge in the early hours before dawn. LaGarde filled out the required papers and signed the college's records.

College Louis le Grand was the most renowned of all the Jesuit colleges in France. Only the sons of the nobility were enrolled, and therefore Stephen's admission had been arranged carefully. He was officially admitted as Etienne LaGarde. His sponsor was the Reverend Jean LaGarde, but the implication was that he was the illegitimate son of LaGarde's older brother, the Marquis de St. Contest, servant of the King and future Minister of Foreign Affairs.

When the house was awake Stephen had been told to follow the porter to his lodgings. He carried his own trunk and stared at the wall scenes of Jesuit disasters and triumphs.

"Number seventeen. This is your room, sir," said Brother Denis as he opened the door.

Stephen entered a scene of chaos. Two of the three beds in the room were unmade. Dirty laundry was strewn over the backs of chairs or lay in heaps on the floor. There were two young men sitting among the chaos. As the door opened, each had made frantic motions to pick up whatever was closest at hand, but when they saw that it was only Brother Denis, they relaxed.

"Gentlemen," said the old man, looking about him with dismay, "this is your new roommate, Monsieur LaGarde, ward of Reverend Father, the brother of the Marquis de St. Contest." Both young men approached Stephen and made formal and graceful bows. "The elder of these two scoundrels is Louis, eldest son of the Duc DeLuynes. He is destined for the navy after this term. The other is Charles Gozin, nephew of the Marquis de Montcalm de St. Veran. He is destined for the gallows but for the efforts of the Society of Jesus."

"We are both delighted to meet you, Monsieur," said Charles. "Especially since we were momentarily concerned that you might be Father DesGouttes."

"Where is the other young gentleman?" asked Brother Denis.

"The prince is in the chapel," answered Charles. "The Poles are fanatics about everything they indulge in. Prince Michal Wroblevski drinks harder, fights harder, screws harder and prays harder than anyone else at the college."

"He also keeps his bed made and his part of the room neat. He studies his Latin, Greek and philosophy and, as far as I know, has never been flogged at assembly by Father Des-Gouttes—unlike some other young gentlemen of noble birth who are currently within the sound of my voice," said the old brother.

"The prefect of discipline plays favorites and he is confessor to the Queen. He can't go around beating the bare bottom of her favorite cousin, can he?" said Louis.

"It seems to me he doesn't worry about beating the bottom of the son of the Queen's closest friend," added Charles.

"I will leave you to your new friends now, Master Etienne," said the brother. "God help you."

After the brother had gone, the two boys returned to their former postures. Charles groaned as he picked up his Latin text and began to read. Louis threw himself on his unmade bed and was almost instantly asleep. Stephen remained standing sheepishly at the doorway with his trunk still hoisted atop his shoulder. He had started to speak when suddenly the door flew open again and, standing there, almost filling the doorframe, was a tall and handsome blond youth. "Let me help you with that," he said to Stephen and with a deft move of one large arm, he swept Stephen's trunk into his own grasp.

Louis DeLuynes tossed in his bed, awakened by the return of his roommate. "You don't have to be polite to him," he said, looking up from his pillow. "He's a new boy and he's a nobody. I think he's St. Contest's bastard."

"You are perpetually charming, Louis," said the newcomer in strangely accented French. "My name is Michal Wroblevski." He pronounced his first name as if it were Me-How. "What's your name?"

"Etienne, Etienne LaGarde."

"Well, Etienne, welcome to the pigsty these two noble Frenchmen call home. We will have to make some room for you. I assume you were not expected or they would have added a bed. Louis graduates into the navy at the end of the term and so Father Prefect must have put you in here because we will be having the first vacancy. We will drop off your trunk here," he said as he dropped Stephen's belongings onto his own bed. "And then we will find you something to sleep on. Louis, you and Charles, go find Etienne a bed."

"The hell I will."

"No bed, Louis, no Polish Latin wizard to help with your translation for class tomorrow."

"But we will have to steal it from an underclassman."

"Since when did you worry about taking something from an underclassman?" asked Michal.

DeLuynes rose from his bed with a curse and pulled his companion out of his chair. The two of them left the room grumbling.

"You're not from France, Etienne, are you?" said the Pole.

"No, I'm from the colonies, from Isle Royale to be exact."

"From Canada, I knew it. Your accent is good, like mine. I was raised in Lorraine and I've been at Court but everyone knows I'm not French the minute I open my mouth. It will be the same for you. They will never identify Canada in your speech, but they will know it's not Paris—not Versailles. By the way, if you're from Canada, you will have nowhere to go for the Christmas holidays. What will you do?"

"I assume I'll spend them here."

"Nonsense. You must come home with me."

"To Lorraine?"

"Of course not. Not any more."

"To Poland?"

Prince Michal laughed. "Most assuredly not. No member of my family has been welcome in Poland since the fall of King Stanislaus. While the Saxon sits on the Polish throne the Wroblevskis and the Leczinskis stay in France. No, Etienne, my sister and I stay with our cousin, the Queen. I'm inviting you to visit the most fabulous palace in the world at the most fabulous time of the year to be there. I'm spending Christmas at Versailles."

Stephen's eyes lit up at the thought, but he was guarded in his response. "I'm not sure Father LaGarde would be happy about it."

"Nonsense. Didn't Louis say he was St. Contest's brother? Well, the marquis is in the Ministry. Certainly your guardian would allow you to spend some time with his brother—especially if he's your father."

Stephen had been instructed to say nothing on this point and so he merely smiled.

"Louis will be at Court as well," continued Michal. "His father is a great favorite of my cousin. Her Majesty. Oh, well, I guess there is no accounting for taste, even among queens."

Louis and Charles returned carrying a bed, which they shoved through the door with great difficulty. Michal and Stephen grabbed a corner and helped them steer it toward the one small section of the jammed room that was empty.

"He'll need a blanket," said Michal.

"No need," said Louis. "I've found one for him." He tossed a not-too-clean gray cover onto the bed. Michal looked at DeLuynes strangely but then helped Stephen spread the blanket.

While the other three boys attended various classes and tutorials that day, Stephen spent his time visiting his new instructors and obtaining assignments for the Saturday morning classes. Each of the instructors was pleased with the state of his knowledge. Their confreres at Louisbourg had done their job well. Stephen was placed in the most advanced Latin rhetoric class; his Greek was regarded as satisfactory; he was well ahead of his class in mathematics and astronomy. He had a start on logic, and it was agreed that he should be allowed to try to master some of the complexities of Aristotle and St. Thomas, matters usually left to university studies. He was also to receive fencing and dancing lessons.

The next morning Stephen was introduced to the dreaded Father DesGouttes, prefect of discipline and Latin rhetoric teacher. The students of the class, who included all three of Stephen's roommates, sat talking among themselves until the priest entered the room. He was a square man. He had tied the sash of his Jesuit habit in such a way as to disguise any waist he might have possessed. His face was also square, made so by his jaw. His upper body, especially his shoulders, was enormous. His complexion was ruddy but his temperament was clearly sour.

When he entered the classroom, the boys stood and grew silent. They remained in that position until he gave the word for them to sit. He opened the first of a pile of books on his desk and began to read to himself. Finally, he spoke aloud. "Today, gentlemen, I intend for us to cover one of the great court defenses delivered by Marcus Tullius Cicero, Pro Archia. Wroblevski, perhaps you will recite for us the opening lines."

Michal rose and began. *"Si quid est in me ingeni,*

84

judices . . ." The prince recited flawlessly the first ten paragraphs of the oration.

DesGouttes glared at Michal and interrupted. "As usual, your recitation is excellent. But now let us get back to normal. DeLuynes, suppose you tell us, in your deathless French prose, just what is the meaning of those lovely Latin phrases of the great orator."

Louis rose, to the twitters of his classmates. He bowed to the left and to the right. "Well, Father," he said, "Cicero with characteristic humility is telling us that he is a genius and that he is going to help his good friend Archius."

"Stick more closely to the text, Louis," said the priest.

For the next three minutes, the young man managed barely to get by, explaining constructions and meanings. Finally, DesGouttes told him to sit down.

"LaGarde, you, the new boy. Take up where he left off." Stephen rose. He began to translate the Latin into a flowing French. The priest rose from his desk and went to the window, turning his back on Stephen. At one point he broke into a laugh at Stephen's choice of words. Stephen stopped translating and looked up from the text. The priest turned to face him again.

"LaGarde, this is a class in rhetoric. You will have to learn to overcome minor distractions if you are ever to excel in public oratory."

Stephen was angry; he had worked hard last evening on the translation, and it was a good one. He started again. He had not gone beyond the next sentence, however, when he was suddenly overcome by the desire to scratch his belly. The itch was incredible. He misread the next line. DesGouttes was now convinced that he had memorized it.

"We've already had the memory work from Wroblevski. Sit down, LaGarde, and don't try to bluff me again."

Stephen was about to object, but the look on the priest's face convinced him to keep quiet. He sat down. Louis started to laugh.

"There is nothing for you to laugh about, DeLuynes," said the priest. "Your performance was a disgrace. Next Thursday holiday, young man, you will spend in your room learning to translate this text with greater fluency."

Louis' smile disappeared completely and now the whole class began to laugh aloud. "Silence," yelled the Jesuit. "Any more noise and you will all join DeLuynes." There was instant silence.

Stephen could keep his mouth shut, but he was having a terrible time sitting still. His armpit and his groin itched. He squirmed in his chair, his gyrations did not escape the attention of his roommates. Charles and Louis sat grinning. Finally Louis raised his hand.

"What is it, Louis?" asked the priest.

"It's LaGarde, Father. He keeps moving. He is distracting me from my work."

DesGouttes glared down at Stephen. "You, new boy, sit still."

Stephen froze in place. He started to sweat, controlling an overwhelming urge to sink his nails into his flesh. As soon as the class was over, he ran to his own bedroom, pulled off all of his clothes and began to scratch. Michal followed him into the room and found Stephen examining his skin, on which small welts had appeared. "You had better not come in here. I don't know what sort of pox I have but it may be contagious," Stephen said.

"No fear," said the Pole. "I suspected it at first and now Louis has just confirmed my suspicions, with a little persuasion. He took your blanket from the porter's lodge. It belongs to Brother Denis' dog. You are merely flea-bitten, my friend." He started to laugh. He left and returned shortly with two buckets of water and a bar of lye soap. Stephen washed himself thoroughly, then he pulled the gray blanket off his bed. He looked at Michal and both of them nodded simultaneously. They lifted Louis' bedding off his bed and placed the porter's gray blanket on the bottom. Then they remade the bed.

Later that evening, after they had been studying for at least an hour, DeLuynes hopped off his bed and yelled, "You bastard," diving at Stephen.

Michal blocked his way. "Was it only funny when the Canadian itched, Louis? I think you ought to calm down and go back to studying."

"It's a joke, Louis," said Charles. "Back off."

Seeing that he could expect no support, DeLuynes cooled down and returned to his bed. He stripped all the bedding from his bed, cursing all the while.

The days that followed blended into one another. There was constant studying; classes; verbal abuse from the prefect. Finally the promised holiday arrived; it began like every other day at the college. First they attended mass, followed by a breakfast eaten in silence. But after breakfast and a quick cleaning of their room, accomplished with the fatalistic acceptance that it would have to be redone since Louis was remaining behind by himself, Michal, Charles and Stephen left the college grounds for a trip to the heart of the city of Paris.

It was Stephen's first daylight view of the town, and the noise, the crowds and the smells almost overwhelmed him. He followed the lead of his two friends as they pushed their way down the street. Stephen was inclined to step aside as people came pushing by him. Michal and Charles, however, with frequent use of elbows, pushed aside men, women and children. Stephen soon realized that if he did not behave in the same manner, he would fall behind.

There was little sunlight in the streets. The houses rose high above the boys as they shoved their way though the throngs. Some of the buildings rose as high as seven storeys and stooped dangerously, overhanging the narrow streets. It had rained the night before and the downspouts of the great houses had poured the rain into the streets below. All the water had collected in the gutters in the center of the streets, creating streams where only stagnant pools had existed before. Stephen got his feet wet immediately when he tried to cross the road and misjudged the depth of the water.

They reached the river at a spot where the buildings seemed to pull away, revealing the spires of the great cathedral of Notre Dame sitting on its island in the river. But it was not to the great church that they headed; Michal and Charles took a side street into the Latin quarter. Stephen had no idea where his two friends were heading until they ducked into a small tavern. He followed them.

A roar of greeting rose from the throats of the drinkers in the tavern as Michal and Charles entered. Everyone in the place knew them by name, but very few of the tavern inhabitants were students from the college. Most were university students who normally would have either disdained or ignored the young schoolboys. But they were the type who were not easily ignored; it was clear that they were very popular.

The tavern owner threw his arm about Michal's shoulder and stuck a mug of cheap red wine into his hand. "If it's not my good friend, the Polish prince, "he said rather drunkenly.

"André," said Michal, "you must meet my new friend from Canada, Etienne LaGarde. Etienne, this is André. He runs the dirtiest and the lewdest tavern in all of the Latin quarter. Do nothing he tells you, and in particular, if he offers you one of his girls, do not accept. They are all diseased."

"A great pleasure to meet you, sir," said André to Stephen. "Everything the young prince says is a lie, but who am I—only a peasant just out of the fields—to contradict a prince, even if he is a prince of a race of barbarians who blow their noses with the same hands with which they eat. But a prince is a prince."

Michal said something that Stephen couldn't catch because of the laughter and cheering that greeted a group of musicians, who came into the room from behind a pile of wine kegs at the far end. The three young men found a table for themselves and André brought wine for Charles and Stephen.

Stephen was bewildered by the noise and the good cheer, none of which he had ever experienced at Louisbourg. He desperately wished to belong, not to be different any more. He was determined to follow the lead of his new friends. Charles clapped him on the back. "Cheer up, Etienne, and drink your wine. We have to be back at school before dark, when Brother Denis will lock the gate. That gives us only about five hours to get drunk, get laid and get back."

Stephen downed his wine, and a second mug was placed in his hand. He offered to pay but Michal insisted that it was Charles' turn. Charles protested that it was always his turn—or Louis' turn.

Michal looked offended. "You know that I'm a prince in exile. I am impoverished but I am a man of honor. When my family succeeds in chasing the Saxon pig from the throne of Poland, you know I'll reward you."

"The Elector of Saxony and King of Poland, whom you refer to as a pig, has the recognition of the King of France, despite the fact that yours is the pro-French party and includes the Queen of France."

"Minor setbacks for the cause," laughed Michal. "Soon there will be a Pole, or at worst a Frenchman, on the throne of my troubled land. Perhaps I shall be king."

"God protect the women of Poland if that is the case. There won't be a virgin in the land—except the Virgin Mary."

They continued to drink. Each was now on his third mug of wine. Stephen, who was less used to drinking, was beginning to feel rather peculiar. Suddenly Michal stopped smiling and began to stare at the far wall of the tavern. Charles, who knew what was coming, stood on the table and shouted for all to be quiet. The Pole was preparing to sing. Suddenly the whole tavern was hushed. Michal sang softly in a beautiful tenor voice. Stephen could not understand the words; in fact, no one in the room understood, but the song was an emotional one. Tears came into the young man's eyes and then flowed freely down his cheeks. Stephen sat entranced by the beauty of the melody and the obvious pain of the singer. When Michal had finished there was a long moment of silence, then broken applause and finally a roar of approval. Michal wiped the tears from his cheeks with his sleeve and, smiling, he made a sweeping bow to all in the tavern.

"That was beautiful," Stephen said to Michal as he sat down. "What was it about?"

"Probably about some sow of a peasant girl stolen from him by the Saxon. What a bore," joked Charles.

Michal gave him a withering look. "There are some things you do not joke about, Frenchman," he said. Then, turning to Stephen, he continued, "It is a song about my country, which is my mother—the only mother I have ever known."

Charles ordered more wine, and before André could serve it, Louis DeLuynes entered the tavern. He stood at the entrance, searching the faces of the crowd for his friends. Charles noticed him and stood on the table once again and waved toward his friend. "Louis, over here." DeLuynes saw them and crossed the room. "How did you escape, Louis?" asked Charles.

"I simply walked out of the college."

"But won't they check up on you?" asked Stephen.

"I don't give a damn," said Louis. "That useless old man is not going to ruin my holiday, especially on a saint's day when all Paris is celebrating."

"You're going to have a sore rear tomorrow after Des-Gouttes gets finished with you, my friend," said Michal.

"He wouldn't dare, not with my graduation set for Christmas. No last-year man has been flogged during our whole stay at Louis le Grand. Besides, he knows that my father has the Queen's ear and he could lose his post at Court if he is not careful."

"Well, it's your ass," said Charles. "André, another wine for my friend here. *Carpe diem.*"

After two more rounds and an extra two for Louis so that he might catch up with his roommates, none of the young men was very sober, including Stephen. His head was spinning. He needed some air and he badly needed to empty his bladder. Michal decided to join him in the back alley.

After the other two boys had left the table, Louis threw his arm about Charles' shoulder. "Charles, my friend, isn't your uncle, the Marquis, always spouting off to the King about the proper defense of the colonies in America?"

"My uncle is a great soldier. Someday he will have the chance to prove his point."

"I have no doubt of that. But in the meanwhile I think you ought to do something for Canada in honor of your uncle. Now the only Canadian we have at hand is our new friend, Etienne. I think you and I ought to put up enough cash with André to obtain for him the services of Mlle. Sophie. A gift from the nephew of the Marquis de Montcalm to Canada. Sophie," he yelled. "We have a client for you."

"Sophie usually gives the clap," said Charles.

"So, another gift to Canada from France."

Just as Stephen and Michal returned to the table, a broad-hipped and coarse-looking woman of about thirty sauntered across the room, to a chorus of whistles. When she arrived at the boys' table, Louis and Charles rose and pointed at Stephen. "He's the one," they both agreed.

Sophie reached across the table and took Stephen by the hand. He was just sober enough to realize that he didn't want to go with this woman, but he was afraid that if he said no, the others would mock him. She led him, redfaced, across the sawdust-covered floor to the room behind the wine kegs. Applause and catcalls accompanied them.

Michal looked a bit distressed, but since Stephen had not objected, he saw no reason to interfere. The other two boys followed Stephen and Sophie to the room behind the kegs to observe the occasion but were disappointed when Sophie slammed the door in their faces and bolted it.

"I don't much care for an audience when I work," she said. She reached for the buttons to Stephen's breeches and was shocked when he pulled away from her. "You have something different in mind, dear?" she asked.

"I'd just like to stay here and . . . maybe talk," he stammered.

"I understand," she smiled. "Those other boys arranged this without your knowing, didn't they? You've never done this before, have you?"

Stephen shook his head.

90

"Well, it's pretty good and I can make it very nice for you if you want to try it."

"I think I had better not. No offense meant, but I think I'd rather not try anything."

"Well, they can't have the money back. Let's go back out then. I've no time to waste on shirkers."

"Could you wait for a few moments? Just long enough to let them think . . . that maybe . . ."

She laughed. "I'll do better than that. Those ruffians need a good lesson anyway." She started to speak very loudly, well aware that three sets of ears were at the door. "That's it, boy," she yelled. "Just stick it in there. My God, it's a big one. Oh, you're killing me." She started to moan and finally to yell and scream.

Stephen laughed when he realized what she was doing. His reputation as a great lover was being established before his eyes. Had he been more sober, he would perhaps have thought that such a reputation was not suitable for a future priest, but he was not very sober.

After her yelling stopped, Sophie again approached Stephen and began to undo his buttons. Again he pulled away, but she ignored him. "Now button up on the way out," she said.

Stephen did as he was told and as he left the room, he bumped into his three wide-eyed friends. Michal was the first to break the trance; he yelled for more wine to celebrate the arrival of a great lover to College Louis le Grand. The whole tavern broke into cheers.

The four of them returned to school just before Brother Denis locked the gates. They were very drunk but they knew that Denis would look the other way. Poor Louis, however, had misjudged the power of his father and the insecurity of Father DesGouttes. The Friday assembly began with the public flogging of a very hung-over Louis DeLuynes.

The rest of the term flew by for Stephen. He enjoyed his classes and even Father DesGouttes no longer terrified him. Since he was almost always prepared for his classes, he had little to fear from the priest. The deliberate insults were an attempt to force him to get control of himself and to continue with the task despite distractions. Those who became angry usually ruined the translation and received poor grades. DesGouttes particularly admired the unflappable. Stephen did equally well in his other studies. Even his fencing reached the point where the master did not totally despair of his survival in the violent world of eighteenth-century France. But dancing seemed beyond his capabilities. He had no desire to learn the complicated steps, and even after he learned them, he seemed physically incapable of performing them with any grace.

But most of all Stephen enjoyed the companionship of his classmates. He and Michal were fast friends and he was close to Charles as well. Louis was another matter. They were not openly antagonistic but the little pranks like the flea-infested blanket continued. Stephen soon realized that DeLuynes was no friend; he was really no one's friend. Stephen was so starved for friendship that Louis' aloofness saddened him; with the exception of Karl Stiegler, he had never associated with anyone of his own generation before. But Louis De-Luynes was a loner with a meanness about him. When Charles or Michal played a prank, it was for the sheer fun of it, but Stephen felt that Louis did what he did because he liked to see other people uncomfortable.

Stephen continued to see Father LaGarde even though the priest spent most of his time traveling to different convents, giving retreats to nuns. He never told the priest about the escapade on that first holiday. He continued to go with his friends on their visits to Paris, but he never again allowed himself to drink quite so much or to be maneuvered into embarrassing circumstances. The priest never directly questioned Stephen about his plans for the future, and since Stephen had no intention of changing his plans, he never raised the topic himself. As far as he was concerned, his future lay with the Society of Jesus. He would join just as soon as they would admit him.

The Christmas holiday season was upon them, however, before Stephen mentioned to LaGarde Michal's invitation to spend his vacation at Court. To his surprise, LaGarde seemed pleased by the prospect. LaGarde was also planning to be at Versailles. He would be visiting his brother, the Marquis de St. Contest, who had apartments in one of the Ministry buildings. When Stephen relayed this news to Michal, he was shocked to learn that the prince had no place to stay at court but was relying on his sister, a lady-in-waiting to the Queen, to find rooms for Stephen and himself. Rather sheepishly, Stephen returned to the priest and asked if he could find space in the ministry apartments for the two young men. LaGarde arranged it for them.

All the avenues that led into Versailles were broad. Well before they arrived at the great gates of the palace, Stephen was able to glimpse the rooftops from the window of the coach. Both Father LaGarde and Prince Michal had visited the Chateau many times, and they did not share Stephen's excitement or his surprise, when he realized that the palace was really several buildings; not just one.

As the final turn down the avenue brought them to an open view of the great iron gates and the courtyard in front, Stephen poked Michal with his elbow and asked excitedly about the buildings they were passing, which were far larger than the King's bastion, the largest building in Louisbourg. Nonchalantly but with a slight smile, Michal informed him that they were the horse stables.

The coach drove up to the gate. A guardsman stopped them and sought identification. LaGarde had a pass from his brother, which was more than adequate to admit them into the Place d'Arm. The coach continued across the courtyard to a second gate, the gateway to the Chateau itself. Only those with close connections to the King were able to proceed any further.

The priest and the two young men disembarked from the coach at this point. The ministry buildings were off to the right of the Chateau proper. Stephen started to pick up his trunk, but a withering glance from LaGarde halted him. The coachman and his helper climbed down from their seats and picked up the travelers' luggage. As they crossed the courtyard on foot, LaGarde whispered to Stephen, "Etienne, remember how I have instructed you. Everything at Court is etiquette. You do not carry anything that someone else of a lower rank than yourself can carry. You do not open doors for yourself. You wait for ushers to do that for you. You do not knock on any door. You scratch politely."

Stephen rolled his eyes skyward and glanced at Michal.

"He's right, Etienne. Watch me and do everything that I do or they will write you off as a country bumpkin."

The Marquis de St. Contest was closeted with the Minister for Foreign Affairs and could not receive them. His servants showed them to their rooms. An elegant suite was provided for the Jesuit, but Stephen and Michal were shown into a drab little room with two beds and a washstand. It was, of course, a much nicer room than the one they shared at the college, but Stephen had thought that Michal's closeness to the Queen would have produced more elaborate arrangements. Michal had no complaints. "Her Majesty," he said, "doesn't even know I'm coming. It is also a surprise to my sister Manya. We must head over to the Queen's apartments. We might be invited to supper, and I'm starving."

The two boys crossed the royal courtyard and entered the marble courtyard. Stephen could not keep himself from gaping at the enormity and the beauty of the honey-colored sandstone exterior of the Chateau, as well as the magnificance of the formal gardens and fountains surrounding it.

Michal carried with him a pass from the captain of the Queen's guard, which gave him permission to pass through the marble courtyard and up the Queen's staircase to her apartments. The stairway itself was of ivory-colored marble, while the ballustrade that bordered it was made of a variety of different marbles—pink, light green and dark green. The stairway rose to a landing, turned to the left for four short stairs and then to the left again. As they approached the top of the second landing, Stephen halted his ascent and looked about him. He had never seen such splendor in his life. Everything was marble and gold. To the right of the landing were giant doors of wood painted white and gold, through which one entered the Queen's apartments. To the left, in a niche in the wall, was a trophy depicting doves and cherubs holding the royal monogram. Dominating the whole of the landing, however, was a huge chandelier hanging from the white and gold ceiling, its droplets of crystal reflecting the light of the candles in blue, pink and gold.

They were admitted through the door on the right into the Room of the Queen's Guard. It, too, was magnificent, filled with red and white marble with a giant hearth of the same material. The walls and the ceilings were covered with heroic paintings. Yet the room was cluttered. Everywhere there were racks of arms, muskets, lances and swords. Screens had been set up to hide camp cots placed there for the soldiers of the Queen's guard. Several guardsmen were crowded in front of the great hearth, where a fire burned beneath a giant mural showing a sacrifice to a pagan god.

Michal showed the captain of the guard his pass and asked for an audience with the Princes Marijeanna Wroblevska. The captain disappeared through another door, returning after about five minutes and waving them through into the room he had just left. This room, too, was filled with people, mostly ladies in flowing gowns with great powdered wigs on their heads. Stephen wondered how they managed to keep their necks from bending and how they could walk.

A young woman moved across the carpeted floors toward them. She was dressed in a light yellow gown of fine silk, with a strand of magnificently matched pearls about her neck. On her head she wore a wig of modest height, into which pearls had also been interwoven. Stephen had never seen anyone so beautiful in his life. He knew instantly that she was Michal's sister; the resemblance was striking. But where as Michal was large and blunt, she was delicate and slight. Her cheekbones were prominent and colored, not with rouge like those of the other women in the room, but with a natural blush of youth. Her chin was pointed and her complexion flawless. She smiled at Michal as she approached.

"Sister, I wish you to meet my good friend and classmate at the college, M. Etienne LaGarde. M. LaGarde, my sister, the Princess Wroblevska." The girl curtseyed toward Stephen. He bowed as deeply as he could, wishing desperately that he had paid more attention to the lessons offered by the dancing master at the college. He felt suddenly very shabby, even though he was dressed in his best outfit.

The girl spoke rapidly to her brother in Polish and then excused herself, promising to return soon. "Manya will try to arrange for us to have supper in the Queen's private apartments. Only a few friends are usually invited. The Queen has already been excused from the King's formal table this evening, but most of these people who are waiting around will dine there. No doubt the King's new mistress, Pompadour, will reign supreme again tonight. Manya said she was in residence. She can't afford to stay away from Louis for too long; he has a roving eye, does your Most Christian Monarch."

The girl returned and once again curtseyed to them and they again bowed in return. "Her Majesty, Maria Leczinska, commands the presence of both of you at her supper this evening in the Cabinet Doré. Would you follow me, please."

Manya led them out of the salon by the rear door, which led to the Queen's private apartments. The room they entered was exquisite. Its paneled white walls were decorated in gold with tiny mythological figures. There were six chairs upholstered in cream-colored Chinese silk surrounding a highly polished teak table of light brown veneer. In the corner of the room stood a harp of gold, whose frame was entwined with gilt laurel leaves. Liveried servants were lighting the candelabra on the table, while others carried in the covered trays filled with dishes for the light supper that was to follow. Two bewigged gentlemen stood before the mirrored hearth, holding out their hands for warmth, although this small room was quite comfortable in contrast to the great salon they had just left.

Manya presented Stephen and her brother to the two other men. One was M. Oudry, painting instructor and confident to the Queen. The other gentleman turned out to be the Duc DeLuynes, Louis' father.

"So, you are Louis' roommates," said the duke as they were introduced. "He has written me concerning you in particular, LaGarde. You seem to have some excellent connections."

Stephen smiled politely but said nothing.

"It seems that my son will be delayed in coming to court. Something about some Latin translations for Father Des-Gouttes. I've given him a free hand with that boy. He wants to be a sailor, but no matter what he wants to be, I say give the Jesuits a free hand with a boy and they will make a man of him."

Oudry looked offended at the remark but said nothing. It was clear that he did not agree.

"Louis will be here for the Christmas celebrations and then he will be off to the naval base at Toulon for his training," said the duke.

Manya had slipped out of the room while the men were speaking, but she returned, coughed politely to obtain their attention and then bowed deeply toward the door through which she had just entered. All the men followed her example. A round-faced, middle-aged, almost dumpy woman entered and acknowledged their obeisance. She was wearing a bright red dress trimmed with black fur. She had removed her wig, and her own graying hair was covered by a cap of black fur and lace.

"Gentleman and Manya, please rise and come to table with me," said the Queen of France.

After a brief grace was said by the Queen, the servants began to serve the cold meats and slightly chilled red wine that were to be their meal.

The Queen ate in silence until she finally noticed her cousin. "Michal," she said, "I was so pleased when Manya told me you were at Court. You must present your young friend to me."

"This is M. LaGarde, Your Majesty, ward of the Reverend Father Jean LaGarde, youngest brother of the Marquis de St. Contest. He is my roommate at the college. Even more interesting, he is from New France."

"From the colonies, how thrilling. M. Oudry, perhaps this

young man can help us with new themes for our paintings." She clapped her hands together and a servant appeared at her side instantly. "M. Oudry, I wish to show my guests our efforts for today." The painter rose from the table and followed the servant out of the room. He returned several seconds later bearing a wooden panel on which had been painted scenes of priests baptizing formerly heathen Chinese. Some pains had been taken to depict the oriental countryside and pagodas.

Oudry held the panel so that everyone could see it. "Her Majesty has just completed this today," he said. All at the table applauded politely and the Queen blushed. "I could do nothing without M. Oudry," she acknowledged. "He draws for me; he mixes the colors and he tells me where to put my brush. But I love it and I love to use what little talent God has given me to depict scenes of His triumphs. M. Oudry knows much about the Chinese landscape but perhaps, you, young man," she turned toward Stephen, "may tell us about the victories of our Holy Mother Church in New France. Nothing violent, mind you. I've heard stories about the sufferings of the martyrs; I could not sleep for weeks afterward. I want only to hear about the good things."

"I will tell you everything I can, Your Majesty."

"Good. Manya, arrange for M. LaGarde to visit us again, especially during our painting lessons."

"Will this painting be installed in your private chamber with the others now?" asked DeLuynes.

"Good heavens, no. Do you think me a fool?" laughed the Queen. "Oudry will paint it all over again and it will be his panel that will be installed. I may love to paint but I also love beautiful things; I have no intention of surrounding myself with inferior works of art."

By this time the Queen had finished her supper and was sipping her wine. "Manya," she said. "I must show our guests the lovely gift His Majesty sent to me today."

The princess went across the room to the gold mantelpiece and returned to the table with a silver inkstand in the shape of a Bourbon fleur-de-lis. "The King noted that my old stand was shabby. It was so kind of him to notice, don't you think?"

DeLuynes stirred uneasily in his chair and looked at the princess, who stood directly behind the Queen. She shook her head at him. Both knew that the King had ignored the Queen's existence for the past several years. She loved him desperately and still hoped for the return of his affections.

But Louis XV was slowly coming under the complete dominance of the woman who would come to control not only him but all of France in the years ahead, the Marquise de Pompadour. The King's new mistress was not hostile to the Queen. In fact, she attempted to cater to her. In reality, both the duke and the princess knew that in all probability the inkstand had come from the marquise in the King's name.

Michal took the gift into his large hands and held it up to the light from the candelabrum. "I'd hide this silver if I were you, Your Majesty," he said. "You remember what happened to Louis XIV's solid silver furniture in the Hall of Mirrors. He melted it down to pay for one of his wars."

The Queen laughed. "Well, my Louis doesn't go to war like his grandfather."

DeLuynes looked at the Queen in surprise. "Aren't you at all disturbed about the situation in Europe, Your Majesty? The Emperor Charles of Austria is nearing the end of his career. His daughter, as his heir, is extremely vulnerable. The King of Prussia has agreed to respect her inheritance but none of us really believes that he will. I believe that the weakness of the Hapsburg heiress will be too tempting for France as well. The King's ministers will urge him to move against Austria. I don't see how we can avoid it. Unfortunately, the English will insist on the balance of power to protect King George's German possessions. They will never tolerate the combination of France and Prussia destroying Austrian power in Central Europe. *Voilà,* you have a war, and one that will span the world."

"Why the whole world?" interjected the princess.

"Because," said the duke, "as this young man from New France must know, when England and France sneeze, their colonies catch cold with them."

"Enough of this talk," said the Queen. "We must discuss only those things that please me. Manya, I've invited your brother here this evening not only to feed a starving student but also to inform him of my plans for you. Michal, your sister is now of an age to marry. Don't you agree?"

Michal opened his mouth to say that he thought her a bit too young at seventeen, but he never got the words out. The Queen went right ahead with announcing her plans. "My father, King Stanislaus, and your mother were brother and sister. With the death of your parents, I feel responsible as the head of the family to provide for your well being. I've decided that Manya could have no better match than to align herself with the family of my dear friend, the Duc De-

Luynes." She smiled across the table at the duke. "I have arranged for the marriage of my dear Manya to Louis DeLuynes, heir to the duchy. Manya will be the future Duchess DeLuynes."

"I hope she will be patient about the title, Your Majesty," said the duke, "considering that the only way she will attain it is by my departing this world for the next."

The Queen laughed. "I'm sure Manya will be very, very, patient, Your Grace."

While the discussion between the Queen and the duke continued, Stephen looked at the princess' face. She seemed totally disinterested, but on Michal's face a storm was brewing. He began to speak in Polish. The Queen looked at him in surprise and Manya seemed genuinely dismayed at last.

The Queen responded to him in French. "Michal, it is extremely impolite to speak in front of my guests in a language they do not understand. In addition, your remarks were offensive. The decision concerning Manya's future is for me and His Majesty to make. Both of you are our wards. I feel it proper to consult you, as Manya's older brother, and to discover your opinion. But I do not seek your approval."

The Duc DeLuynes glanced at the prince in some annoyance and Michal responded to the Queen's anger by lowering his head. It was a gesture of momentary embarrassment but not of surrender. The room fell into an unsettling silence. Finally, the princess came from behind the Queen's chair and sat down at the table. "My brother wishes only what will make me happy, Your Majesty. I'm sure that once he knows how happy I am at your news he will be as delighted as you and the duke are now."

Michal sighed but said nothing.

"Good," said the Queen. "Then it is settled. My Manya will become Louis DeLuynes' bride after the Christmas holidays. Now we must have music. Manya, will you play the harp for me? Something from Poland. And, my somber Michal, you will sing."

When Stephen and Michal returned to their room that evening after supper, the prince tossed his clothes into the corner of the room in disgust and collapsed on his bed naked. Stephen did not know if he should speak to him, but Michal solved the problem by sitting upright and looking at Stephen. "Christ," he said. "She did not have to rush this thing."

"I understand your feelings about your sister and Louis, Michal, but there doesn't seem to be much that you can do about it, especially since Manya has no objections. In fact, she appears delighted with the prospect."

"There is simply no way I can agree to the marriage. Louis is not right for her. Manya is a wonderful girl who is fast becoming a beautiful woman. She deserves someone who will worship at her feet. Louis DeLuynes is concerned only with himself, with his own self-worship. He will never be worthy of her."

Michal got up from his bed and began to pace about the room. "Damn it," he said. "I'm never going to sleep tonight." He went to the corner where his clothes lay in the heap into which he had thrown them. "Let's go out to the tables and play some cards," he said.

Stephen begged off, claiming he was too tired. In fact, he was unwilling to tell his friend that he did not have enough money to gamble. Had he told Michal his real reason for not going, the prince would have laughed. He had no money at all. But he did have connections.

Stephen spent the next days in the Queen's private apartments. Maria Leczinska painted in a room even more intimate than her private sitting room. It had the same white paneling, but the gilt furniture was upholstered in blue and white, the same colors as the drapes. Almost the whole of the room could be reflected in the magnificent mirror affixed to the wall above a black marble fireplace. The room had no natural lighting and so the crystal chandelier burned throughout the day's lessons. This seemed to disturb neither teacher, Oudry, nor pupil, who seemed less intent on the naturalness of color than on the piety of the scene depicted.

Stephen spent hours describing the natives of his homeland and in particular the Abenacki. He told both the Queen and Oudry how the Indians looked, how they lived, what they ate. But it seemed to make very little difference. In the Queen's paintings their huts continued to resemble poorly constructed pagodas, while the Abenacki themselves somehow turned into Chinese with red skins.

Most times, however, Stephen was left alone to speak with Manya, who, although always at the Queen's side, buried herself in her needlework and rarely checked on Her Majesty's progress unless specifically requested to do so by the Queen. Stephen asked her about Poland and was surprised to learn that she remembered almost nothing about it. After her uncle had been chased from the throne, the entire family had moved to the Duchy of Lorraine until Louis of France had married Maria of Poland. Then they moved to Versailles.

"It's strange that you remember nothing about your homeland, yet Michal, who is only two years older than you, remembers so much," said Stephen.

Manya laughed. "Michal remembers no more than I do."

"But I have heard him sing with such feeling about his country."

"One doesn't have to know Poland to love it," responded the princess. "It becomes part of your soul, particularly for exiles. Perhaps we love our country more than those fortunate enough to live there. Maybe we romanticize it and ignore all its faults and problems. No, don't be fooled, Etienne. Michal remembers very little. He can sing of Warsaw nights because he listened to my uncle, King Stanislaus, talk about the beauties of his capital. But even then the King was living in the Hotel Webber in Wissenbourg."

"Still it must be nice to think of your homeland, to cry about it and to dream of returning there."

"Don't you feel the same way about New France?"

Stephen thought for a moment. "I know very little about New France. I have lived only within one walled city, Louisbourg. Now ask me about the city or about my island, which we call the Royal Island, and I could go on forever. Most of all, it is the sea. The sea is everywhere. You can't escape the sound or the smell of it. The forest-covered hills fall into the sea. From the walls of my city, I see the ocean. When I fall asleep at night I can hear the sound of the surf against the rocks of the beaches. If I look inland, I see a different type of sea, an ocean of green, a forest stretching as far as the horizon. I smell the odor of pine and balsam."

"I think you love your home just as much as my brother loves his, Etienne. But tell me more of Louisbourg. Tell me of its social life. After Louis and I are married and he receives his commission, I may sail to your Royal Island. Would I be happy there? Would I outshine the governor's lady?"

Stephen looked at her adoringly. "You would outshine anyone, Your Highness."

She laughed, leaned over and kissed him on the cheek. "Dear Etienne," she said. "Call me Manya."

Stephen's face went crimson. "I don't know very much about the social life in Louisbourg, Manya. I was raised in the Jesuit house. But I have heard talk of great balls at the citadel for the governor and the naval officers and their ladies."

"Good, I shall order Louis to hold a ball in my honor and I shall demand that you come."

The Queen interrupted them. "Manya, dear, come look at my Aba . . . Aba . . . what do you call these creatures, dear boy?"

"They are called Abenacki, Your Majesty."

"I can't imagine why," said the Queen. "M. Oudry, look at these hovels that these poor Christians are forced to live in. I must do something for them. I must divert some of my almsgiving from the Chinese missions to these people. Etienne, who runs the missions for the Abe . . . Abenacki?" She smiled, pleased with herself for getting it right.

"The Society of Jesus, Your Majesty."

"Oudry, make sure a special grant is made to Father DesGouttes as a Christmas present for their Abenacki missions."

The painter frowned.

"Oh, you terrible Jansenist, Oudry," said the Queen. "You are so imbalanced when it comes to the Jesuits. You even poison the mind of the King about them. I'm making the grant to the Indians, Oudry, not the priests."

"We are no more imbalanced toward them, Your Majesty, than they were toward us under the former King, when the convent of Port Royale was closed and the works of men of genius like M. Pascal were attacked."

"But we are all Catholics," said Manya, "and the Jesuits do so much good. Look at the colleges like the one that Etienne, Michal and Louis attend. Look at their work bringing the word of God to the savages and at the way they have suffered for their efforts. Think back to the heresies of the Reformation days. My own Poland would have succumbed had it not been for the Jesuits."

The painter attempted to control his temper. "These priests blind everyone to their evil," he said hotly. "They subvert morality. They compromise the uncompromisable. They encourage evil means to achieve a moral good. They are far worse than the heretics. With the Protestants you know your enemy; he stands boldy before you. But the Jesuits—they subvert the church from within with their moral rot."

Stephen bristled as the painter carried on his diatribe. "You don't know what you're talking about, sir," he said. "I've lived with the Jesuits all of my life. They have housed me and fed me and educated me. They didn't have to do any of those things. They did it for the love and the greater glory of God."

102

"You're naive, boy. They did it because you're the bastard of a French nobleman of importance. Had you been the bastard of a serf, they would have spit on you."

"That's simply not true," said Stephen. "I'm—" He caught himself; he had almost said that for all he knew he was the bastard of a serf—or at least of the American equivalent, an indentured servant. But Stephen's protection of his secret was interpreted by Oudry as his inability to respond to an obvious truth.

The Queen, however, was annoyed. "I don't feel like painting any more, Oudry," she pouted. "And I will not resume my lessons unless they can be held in an atmosphere of kindness and charity. You must apologize for bullying dear Etienne and, for that matter, for bullying your Queen."

The painter realized that he had gone too far. He bowed deeply to the Queen. "My most sincere and humble apologies, Your Majesty. I did not mean to give offense."

"Well, you did. Now go. You may return tomorrow. But now I have grown very weary of these Abenacki. I think we should return to our original theme." She turned to the princess. "Manya, I'm going to take a nap. You run along with Etienne. But first send in my maid."

Stephen and Manya left the Queen's private apartment, walked through a small corridor and emerged into the public apartments of the Queen. With the exception of the guard room, the public apartments were empty at this time of the day. Stephen was still awed by the magnificence of the rooms and furnishings. Manya laughed at him as he gaped at the ceilings. "Etienne, you are such a bumpkin at times. If you must gape, gape at something truly beautiful. Come with me."

She led him into the green-walled room in which he had first seen her and then through another door, into the most breathtaking scene Stephen had ever beheld. It was obviously the Queen's formal bedchamber. The canopied bed stood against the far wall. The bed coverings and the canopy were white, with delicately embroidered roses of pink. The whole bed was set off from the rest of the room by a gold balustrade. Again Stephen's eyes rose to the ceilings. "The four paintings," Manya explained, "are depictions of our Queen's outstanding virtues—charity, abundance, fidelity and prudence. The portraits over the mirrors at each end of the room are the portraits of the Queen's parents, the King and Queen of Poland." The princess stood with her back to the alcove formed by the green- and rose-colored drapes and the floor-to-ceiling windows. Light from the setting sun was reflected against the wall by the spray from the great fountains in the garden in tiny dots of orange and yellow light. Manya's dress was white lace with a low-cut bodice that revealed the curve of her breasts; Stephen stepped over to her. He reached out and touched her face and drew her to him. She smiled at him and he kissed her gently on the mouth. She responded instantly, kissing him back passionately. Then she pulled away from him. She brushed back a strand of her blond hair with her hand.

"You naughty boy, Etienne," she said, somewhat flustered by her own reaction to his kiss. "I don't think we should be found kissing in the Queen's bedchamber."

Stephen too was flustered. "I didn't mean to take advantage of you, Manya. But you are the most beautiful woman I have ever seen."

"Etienne, you are practically a monk. You've seen almost no women at all. Your compliment is hardly a compliment. And you are still a boy."

"I'm as old as you."

"But I'm a woman who knows precisely what she wants and you are still a boy. Besides, I am marrying Louis DeLuynes shortly and I don't intend to allow anything to interfere with that."

Now Stephen was sure he would do anything to stop this girl from becoming Louis' wife. "Michal doesn't want you to marry Louis."

"Michal is not marrying Louis; I am," she responded. "It is none of his business."

"Don't marry him, Manya. Wait for me instead." Stephen shocked himself with this outburst. To this very moment he had not understood how he felt about her. He did love her. She was so beautiful. He had never known anyone so beautiful.

But the girl looked at him incredulously. "You are a nice boy, Etienne, and I think you are far more attractive than Louis. But you see, he shall become a duke and you will always remain someone's bastard—a nobleman, true, but a bastard nevertheless. Please don't hate me for saying that. You see, my brother and I are both orphans and exiles, but we respond very differently to our plight. Maybe it is because he is a man and I am a woman. He dreams romantic dreams of liberating Poland from Prussia, Austria and the Elector of Saxony, maybe even of becoming King himself. I may be

Polish but I am no romantic. I will become a French duchess—no matter what the price to me—and I will be the mother of the next duke and I will be rich. I'll never again live off the dole of a generous relative."

Stephen was growing angry. "Louis DeLuynes is not worthy of you," he said. "Michal and I will stop this marriage."

"Etienne, you are becoming a bore. I don't think we should spend any more time together. Goodbye." She turned away from him and started to leave through the door into the green salon.

Stephen repented his words and called after her. "You promised to tour the gardens with me before the ball. Will you still meet me?"

Manya stopped and then smiled at him. She nodded and then rushed out the door. His heart soared.

The Marquise de Pompadour had just been installed in her new suite of rooms at Versailles, directly above the formal chambers of the King. Louis had easy access to her by a small stairway, but his love of machines had led him to talk of installing a small lift from his private chambers to hers.

She was a handsome woman, some would say beautiful. Certainly Louis thought her beautiful. Others might say her face was too long and her lips too pursed, but those who belittled her looks were mostly those who were jealous of her influence with the King. Increasingly, however, she was doing more than influencing him. She was coming to dominate his thinking, not just on how to run this massive household at Versailles but even on appointments to high office, the very life blood of the Chateau. In a few short months she had risen to dazzling heights and she had every intention of staying there.

There were certain rules to obey. Never humiliate the King. Many thought him stupid and lazy; she knew better. He was shrewd and frequently vigorous. But he seemed physically incapable of assuming responsibility and duty. She would do that for him; even to the point of controlling his ministers. It could be privately understood that she did this but the King's pride must be protected.

The second rule was never to become jealous of the King, never to become sexually possessive. She would use her charms as long as the King found them charming. As soon as he began to lose interest, she would find for him the most beautiful women in France—and the stupidest. She would control him through them. She did not want to dominate the King's body. She wanted very much to control his mind and through it to control France.

Her third rule was to stay clear of the Queen. Maria Leczinska was the daughter of a king, the wife of a king and probably the mother of the next King of France. Every courtesy must be extended to her, and Pompadour would see to it that Louis did not offend or openly embarrass his wife. Maria was no threat to Pompadour, nor would Pompadour be a threat to the Queen. Pompadour was a very clever and very ambitious woman.

Madame du Hausset, Pompadour's maid, scratched politely on the door. "The Marquis de St. Contest is here to see you, madame."

Pompadour rose from her chaise to greet her new friend. "Monsieur le Marquis," she acknowledged.

"Madame la Marquise," he responded with a deep bow.

"Come, join me over by the windows. I have a view of the Parterre du Nord. It will be lovely in the spring and summer when the flowers are in full bloom. But even now the greenery is so fine. Hausset," she called, "some chocolate for the marquis and myself." The maid came to the door, bowed and disappeared again.

"We have some moments now to speak freely," said Pompadour. "That Hausset is always listening at the door and she is such a gossip."

"Why keep her, then?" asked St. Contest.

"Because she is useful. She listens at everyone's door and comes rushing back to tell me the secrets. For instance, she told me all about a certain nobleman who aspires to become foreign minister and who brings his bastard son to court. Then he has him worm his way into the Queen's confidence and never tells his best friend and constant supporter a word about it."

St. Contest threw his hands up in exasperation. "That brother of mine. I assure you, madame, that the boy is not my son."

"Then he belongs to your brother?"

"Jean? Hardly. There was never a truer Jesuit than Jean LaGarde; he keeps his vow of chastity. No, for some reason or other Jean wanted the story spread about the boy that he was my bastard. His superiors wanted the boy at Louis le Grand and they didn't want protest from the other students or their parents. Only the offspring of the very best families are admitted to the college. I had no idea that Jean would bring him to Court until just before they arrived, or that the boy would take up with Her Majesty's Polish coterie. I assure you again, madame, I do have bastards, but this boy is not one of them."

"How interesting," said Pompadour. "I wonder what the Jesuits are up to and I wonder who the boy really is?" She sat back in her chair and sighed. "But it is not fascinating enough to deter me from discussing our main piece of business. I am going to try to convince His Majesty to appoint you as his minister for foreign affairs."

St. Contest smiled appreciatively.

"You know me well enough, my dear St. Contest, to know that I do not do you this favor out of pure generosity. You must do me a service in return, a service that D'Argenson, your predecessor, has refused me. I want a voice in determining the course of action that France will take on the stage of Europe."

Again the marquis smiled. "I do not feel in this case, madame, that there will be any conflict of interest or that I will be serving two masters, since both you and His Majesty seem to speak with one voice."

There was a slight noise at the door, and Pompadour warned St. Contest with her eyes. "You must give me a lesson in the current state of affairs abroad. I feel like such a fool when His Majesty discusses things that I know nothing about." She raised her voice. "Hausset, you may bring in the chocolate now."

The small woman entered with a tray, on which were two steaming cups of fine china. She set the tray down on the tiny lacquered Chinese table. They did not resume speaking until the maid had left the room.

"I know her habits," said Pompadour. "She will not listen again for the rest of the day; she fears I may be on to her. But by tomorrow curiosity will get the best of her again. We must continue. I was not entirely playacting in my remarks about my ignorance, Monsieur le Marquis. How do things stand in Europe today?"

"It is all very tense, madame. I believe we have settled the Polish affair only temporarily. The Russians and Germans will never be satisfied as long as a power vacuum exists there."

"There are some rumors that Poles of influence have been speaking to the Prince de Conti."

"Madame is not as uninformed as she led me to believe. The foreign minister himself did not discover what the King and prince plotted for Poland until very recently, and then only by accident."

"I would think that Austria and Russia would have some difficulty with the thought of a French prince of the blood sitting on the Polish throne."

"They would resist it. But I don't think the spark of conflict rests in Poland. I have no doubt in my mind, madame, that England and France are moving inexorably toward a world wide confrontation. One of us will emerge from that conflict as the world's greatest power for the next century. And I have some serious doubts about who will be the victor. When the stage was strictly European, France's population, her wealth and her military might gave her the greatest advantage. But that has begun to change, as we saw in the last wars of Louis XIV. We are now involved in a struggle for worldwide empire. Both England and France have adopted economic policies of internal self-sufficiency, and both are determined to accumulate wealth. We become wealthy by having everything we need and many things that others need from us. They must buy from us, but we do not need to buy from them. Thus their gold finds its way into our treasury. Both England and our country have created overseas empires by colonization and conquest in the West Indies and in North America. The colonies provide us with things that we can not produce in France. But since they belong to us, it is just the same as if the colonial goods were the products of the mother country."

"I begin to see the problem," said Pompadour. "It is more difficult for us to defend colonial products than to defend those grown right here in France."

"Precisely," said St. Contest. "As long as the struggle remained on the continent of Europe, France was more than a match for England. But move the stage to America, and then the British navy becomes a dominant factor."

"But the King has spent millions on the navy."

"We need to spend even more. We need to defend our possessions in the West Indies. Fabulous wealth comes to France from them. And we cannot ignore New France. The fur trade there is a major ingredient in our wealth."

"Monsieur le Marquis, I can see how the navy can defend our spice islands in the seas, but I fail to see why it is needed in New France. I have looked at the maps of the region. It is huge, and when you add our territory of Louisiana, we occupy most of the continent. The English, on the other hand, possess only a thin line of settlements along the Atlantic coast."

"Your maps can deceive you, madame. Our possessions are extremely vulnerable. English settlers far outnumber ours, and our whole empire could be reduced to nothing by a shrewd admiral. The whole of the fur trade—from the far western mountains down the rivers into the great inland freshwater seas like Huron and Ontario—narrows into what could be compared to a funnel—the great St. Lawrence River. That river is controlled by two geographic points, both of them accessible to fleets. In the west end of the river is the island of Montreal. Ocean vessels can not pass beyond it because of the river rapids, and all the small boats and canoes coming from the west and north come to this one spot to meet the ships that will carry their furs across the ocean. Downriver from Montreal is our capital in New France, Quebec. From its heights overlooking the river, its guns control entry and exit. No one can proceed to threaten Montreal and the fur trade via the St. Lawrence while the walled fortress of Quebec stands."

"It all sounds very secure to me, Monsieur St. Contest."

"It was, until recently. When our enemies were a handful of savage Iroquois or half-savage Puritans from New England, we had no real concern. But the nature of warfare in America is changing. It has gradually become more European. There are more professional soldiers involved, more heavy siege guns and mortars, more military engineering. And as a European-type fortress, Quebec is fatally flawed. Its walls are built on solid rock. We could not afford, nor did the Ministry of Marine see the need, for blasting into the rock to build outer defenses. There is no stone or mortar strong enough to withstand direct hits by heavy siege guns. You must have outer walls, ditches, covered ways and great sweeps of earth sloping upward to deflect cannonballs away from a stone wall. This is the way we have been constructing our European fortresses since before the time of the great Vauban. Quebec has none of these, and if the enemy should climb with guns to the plains in front of the town, those walls will fall and fall quickly."

"What can be done?" asked the marquise.

"Nothing, madame. It is too late to do anything and it is still too expensive. If we blast into the rock now, we bring down the existing walls. No, we can do nothing at Quebec itself. We came upon another solution. Two decades ago, during the regency of the Duc d'Orleans, the government decided on a new course to protect Quebec, Montreal, the St. Lawrence and our vast empire in New France. We constructed an entirely new fortress guarding the entrance to the Gulf of St. Lawrence. We have spent millions on it. It is the fortress of Louisbourg on Isle Royale. Its function is very simple. On the marshes next to a large bay on the Atlantic side of the island we have constructed a European-style fortress with all the outer fortifications that Quebec lacks. It is impregnable from land assault. But we have built defenses to protect it from sea attack as well. And we have stationed ships of His Majesty's navy at the base. The point, madame, is this. No one would dare enter the St. Lawrence and threaten Quebec and Montreal, knowing that the ships of the French navy in Louisbourg could seal them off once they entered the river. It cannot be bypassed; it must be attacked. And we have made the attacking of Louisbourg too costly a venture—too costly in money and in lives. It is the Gibraltar of North America."

The marquise had been listening to the diplomat very carefully. "I see the point," she said after some moments of silence. "Louisbourg is in fact the key to New France. If Louisbourg falls, then all the rest will follow. If it stands, then France's empire is safe."

"Precisely."

"But does it not then follow that Louisbourg will draw the English like a moth to a flame?"

"That is our intent."

"Then it is imperative that the fortress be as strong as you claim it to be. Is it?"

"Military operations, madame, are the sphere of interest of other ministries. I can only tell you the theory. The practice ultimately belongs to the generals and admirals. In time of peace we have an unfortunate habit of ignoring them and tolerating profiteers, especially when many of them can be found dancing in the Hall of Mirrors with us this evening."

Pompadour laughed. "Monsieur, how unsubtle of you to remind me of how late the hour grows and that we both have many preparations to make before we appear in public this evening."

St. Contest was flustered. "I assure you, madame, the thought never crossed my mind. I would not end our conversation in this manner."

"No matter," said the marquise, "it is true. The hour does grow late and I must thank you for the history and geography

110

lesson." She rose from her chair and St. Contest immediately rose and walked to the door by her side.

"I must say," said Pompadour, "that I have some mixed reactions to what you have told me. It is comforting to me to understand how strong we are in Europe, which, of course, will always remain our main concern. But I believe that we are terribly exposed in New France. Can we remain the world's greatest power without our empire? I am not sure how to rectify the situation. I did not achieve my current stature, Monsieur le Marquis, by failing to obey common wisdom. I do not ignore the old adages. I have not placed all my eggs in one basket. The King is good to me, and that I please him is a source of great joy to me. But should he no longer find me pleasing, I would be disappointed, but I would still be comfortable. Do you understand my meaning, sir?"

St. Contest hesitated to reply.

"Well, then, let me apply the analogy. In building the fortress of Louisbourg, you have placed all your hope and the entire future of France's North American empire into one basket. If the wolf—or should I say the lion—seizes the basket . . ." She shrugged her shoulders and did not finish her statement.

"That is why it is imperative that additional funds be found to continue to strengthen the fortress," said St. Contest.

"Money would have to be taken away from our European funds or from building projects His Majesty has initiated at this very chateau. You don't really expect Louis to give up a building project at Versailles for something he will never see or appreciate, do you? For if you do, you do not know your King. You will have to hope the fortress is strong enough, monsieur."

"I only hope that it is," said St. Contest. "In addition, we must continue our policy of Indian raids on the English settlements. We must keep them pinned down if we hope to prevent them from using the advantage that their numbers give them. Or they may also begin to venture away from the coast into the interior, where the real wealth of North America is to be found. Very soon we will begin to explore in the Ohio Valley, closer than ever to the English settlements. And for the fostering of this policy, madame, we need men like my brother and the Jesuits."

"Ah, back to the Society of Jesus."

"They have many enemies, madame. But they are true sons of France. Their missions have provided the assault forces that have kept the heretics on the defensive all these many

111

years. Yet there are those in France and in Rome who would destroy them. We must not allow this to happen. We must protect them."

"And not expose any of their little plots?"

St. Contest smiled and repeated, "And not expose any of their little plots. The one you refer to, madame, is of small importance. It is a minor embarrassment from the perspective of this side of the sea. In New France it may have appeared of greater importance."

"Who is the boy?" she asked.

"His parents were English settlers killed on the frontier by some of my brother's mission Indians. The Society decided to adopt him and raise him as a Frenchman, for his own benefit and theirs. My brother has become very fond of him. He is like a son to him."

Pompadour pulled a cord next to the door and summoned her servant to show St. Contest out of her apartment. "I thought the story would be of greater interest," she said finally. "But the truth is safe with me."

The diplomat left, and the King's mistress called to her maid in an angry tone. "Hausset, you silly woman, hurry in here and get me dressed. The King will not be at all amused if I arrive at the Christmas celebration late."

When Hausset appeared, Pompadour placed her finger over her lips and waited until she was sure that St. Contest had left the outer apartment.

"Hausset," she whispered, "I want you to keep alert. I want to know everything about this boy LaGarde. You are to keep me totally informed, and the minute DuLuynes' son arrives at Court you are to send him to me."

"He has already arrived," answered Hausset.

"I will see him immediately, then."

Pompadour sat down before her mirror and smiled at her own image. She was not sure what the Jesuits were up to, but there were to be no intrigues at Versailles unknown to her. She knew about the Queen's plans for her niece and she knew of the nephew's objections. Now this Jesuit brat was courting the princess. Were the Jesuits behind it all? Were they involved with Louis' plans for the Prince de Conti and the Polish throne? Or was it all as innocent as St. Contest had said? In either case the Queen would have her way. She, Pompadour, would see to that.

Stephen sat in the wooded grove to the left of the great fountain of the sun god. The leaves had long since left the great oaks that surrounded him, and the barren trees stood gaunt against the gray winter sky. He had been sitting alone for over half an hour, and he had begun to wonder if Manya had changed her mind about meeting him.

He rose from the stone bench and began to pace the path that ran between the trees toward the fountain. He heard her footsteps creeping up behind him, but rather than turn around, he decided to play her game. Her small hands reached around his face and covered his eyes. He stood still. "I think my captor is the Princess Wroblevska," he said. "She has the softest hands of all of my women."

She giggled. "How do you know it is not the great Pompadour?"

"Because she wouldn't giggle."

"Oh, you are mean to me, Etienne," Manya cried with a mock pout.

He turned around and looked at her. The anger that had flashed in those eyes earlier was gone, and he liked what had replaced it. "You're not angry with me any more," he said.

"It is difficult to remain angry with someone for saying that he loves you. But you have to understand why I must still marry Louis."

"No. I can't see it at all. I think you love me as much as I love you."

"Even if I did, I would still marry Louis," she said softly.

He started as if she had slapped him.

"Don't make this any harder, Etienne."

"I will make it harder. You love me—marry me."

"No, Etienne. I want to be a French duchess and I want to live in my own chateau when I'm not at Court. All you can offer me is a wilderness."

"I can also offer you gentleness and understanding," he said, smiling at her. He placed his arms about her waist and she responded by placing hers about his neck. They stood facing each other, searching each other's eyes. They did not speak for some moments.

Finally she pulled away from him. "You weaken my resolve, Etienne. I cannot stay with you any longer. I look into your face and all I can see is the hurt little boy looking for someone to love him. I find myself wanting to mother you. It may be what you need, but it's not what I want for myself. I'll give up any kind of love to have security."

"I don't need a mother," said Stephen defensively.

"I think you do. You've never had a woman love you."

"There's Sister Marie Louis." Manya looked at him in

113

puzzlement. "A nun in Louisbourg. She nursed me as a child and she has been my friend ever since. She has been like a mother to me since I was a little fellow."

"I'm glad you had her, at least, Etienne. But I'm not going to be the sister of this part of your life."

He was hurt and his hurt showed in his eyes.

She looked at him and knew she had to leave. It had been a mistake to meet him here. He could win her heart and she did not want her heart won. "Goodbye, Etienne," she said.

She left him there alone, with only the sound of the winter wind creaking in the bare oaks for company.

The Hall of Mirrors was alive with light for the royal feast. Stephen and Michal arrived early before the room became overcrowded, and they had the opportunity to observe it closely. Stephen was struck first by the overwhelming array of lights. The room was well over two hundred feet long and ran along the whole front of the Chateau. The magnificently painted ceiling, depicting the glories of Louis XIV, rose to a height of forty feet. Windows, twenty feet high, in groups of three, ran along the west wall. From them in late afternoon one could see the gardens, fountains and the grand reflecting pool of the Chateau in the light of the setting sun. Opposite the windows was the feature from which the room took its name—a series of floor-to-ceiling mirrors that reflected into the hall the magnificence of the outside of the Chateau through the opposite windows. But at night, when the windows were draped, the mirrors served a different purpose. At night they reflected the light of the candelabra placed atop a series of lofty gilt statues of maidens and cherubs. Three series of enormous chandeliers hung from the ceiling. The flickering light of all these candles bounced from mirrors to polished wooden floor to marble walls and back into the mirrors again.

There were richly embroidered stools and chairs along the walls and a podium for musicians. The room was decorated with greenery. Yew trees in large pots had been brought indoors. From their branches, plums and oranges and nuts from Spain, Portugal and North Africa had been hung as favors for the guests.

At each end of the Hall of Mirrors there were large salons, the Salon de la Guerre and the Salon de la Paix. Each of these rooms contained tables with enormous quantities of food and chairs for all of the invited guests. There were seventeen different types of roasted meat and fowl. Cheeses of every description, along with wine from all the regions of

France, loaded down the tables. There were platters of exotic fruits, similar to those that hung from the trees of the Hall of Mirrors.

The rooms were filled with people now, and Stephen and Michal had difficulty forcing their way back from the salon into the hall. The orchestra had begun to play music for dancing, although no one would have dared begin until after the King had arrived. There was a scurrying of people in the Salon de la Paix as the Marquise de Pompadour, in a hooped gown of dark rose and a high wig with dark pink roses intertwined in it, entered. The value of her favor was now clearly recognized by those seeking power.

The orchestra played a flourish, and the King, in white satin with a simple gold sash, and the Queen, in a gown of gold lace, arrived together in the Salon de la Guerre. Stephen pushed his way through the crowd of guests to get a better look at the King and Queen, but even more important to him, to get a glimpse of Manya. He saw her standing behind the royal couple. She was in a gown of blue, and she looked more beautiful now than ever before. He pushed forward to try to reach her, but as he approached, he halted abruptly. Standing next to her and exchanging smiles with her and formal greetings with the other guests was Louis DeLuynes.

The King, shortly after entering the hall, signaled to the orchestra and, bowing to the Queen, took her hand and began to dance the formal steps of a minuet to the accompaniment of violins. The crowd pushed back against the walls of the gallery to make way for the dance. According to strict court etiquette, the children of France, princes of the blood, dukes, counts and chevaliers with their ladies, joined in the dance until the whole room seemed to swirl in time with the music.

The dancing and eating lasted well into the evening. As the hour grew later, more and more people crushed against the windows and awaited the climactic moment of a royal fete at Versailles. Servants appeared at each draped window in the hall; another liveried and wigged attendant approached the King, bearing a lance. Louis XV took it into his hand and balanced it with familiarity; he was a renowned hunter with all types of weapons. The servant then went to the center window of the hall. The crowd backed away to make a path for him. He threw open the window and as he did so, the other servants pulled back the drapes at the other windows. Louis approached the open window. The attendant reached for a candle from the gilt candelabrum to his right and with it he touched the tip of the King's lance. It burst into flames.

The King waved it above his head and playfully made feints at some of the male courtiers; then he stepped up to the open window and, with a mighty heave, hurled the flaming lance far into the dark night. Instantly the gardens and fountains of Versailles came alight with fireworks. The whole of the Basin of Apollo, with its statue of the god astride his chariot emerging from the waters, was illuminated with colored lights. The whole audience gasped.

Stephen had an excellent vantage point to view the display, primarily because he had barely moved all evening. He had remained standing by the draped windows, watching Princess Wroblevska joyfully take part in the revels. He had danced with no one and he had spoken to no one. As the illumination began to fade and the admiration of the crowd waned, Stephen left his vantage point and strolled into the Salon de la Paix. He saw Michal standing by the wine table talking to Louis DeLuynes. Michal, it was clear, had been drinking heavily and was very angry. As Stephen approached, he heard the prince call his intended brother-in-law a French pig who was totally unfit to join with a Polish sow, much less a Polish princess.

Louis would have ignored the insult if no one else had heard it, but by approaching them Stephen had complicated the matter.

"Michal," said Louis, "you are drunk and your sister will shortly become my wife. I think you should go to bed and sleep it off. We will discuss this in the morning. LaGarde, take our friend to his rooms."

When Michal heard Stephen's name spoken, he spun around to face him and almost fell down. Stephen grabbed him and held him on his feet. "Etienne," said the prince, "you've come just at the right time. I was telling Louis what a pig he is." He started to laugh. "We must get Manya over here so that we can tell her too."

"Michal, I'm warning you," said Louis.

"Oh, the pig grows threatening. Perhaps he is really a wild boar. Whatever he is, he is no proper husband for my sister. Etienne will marry Manya. That is my decision."

DeLuynes sneered at him. "Fine decision for a brother to make, Wroblevski. Let your sister marry a penniless bastard instead of the son of a duke."

Stephen ignored the remark and started to walk away, but Michal would not allow DeLuynes to remain unchallenged. "You can't call my friend a bastard," he shouted.

"Well, I have and I have done it in public, and what is

116

more, he *is* a bastard. I will give your friend the opportunity to have satisfaction any time he wishes to call me out."

There was dead silence about them. Clearly a whole host of courtiers had heard the invitation to a duel. This was a development that Wroblevski, even when sober, had not foreseen. All eyes turned toward Stephen, who stood quite thunderstruck.

"Of course," said DeLuynes, "your friend is still a boy, and an affair of honor is for men, not for boys. But then again, boys should not go about attempting to steal away the affections of young women from their betrothed."

Stephen's face had gone red. He stepped toward Louis. Michal tried to step in his path. He was suddenly very sober and realized that he had placed his friend in mortal danger. But it was no use. Stephen pulled away from Michal and flung the contents of his cup of wine into Louis' face; then he turned away and walked slowly out of the salon. When he found the stairs leading to the courtyard, he raced down them and out into the evening air. By the time he had reached the front door of his quarters, he found to his dismay that he was running and that his whole body was shaking with tension and fear.

Word of the challenge and the impending duel spread throughout the whole Court by the next day. Stephen asked Michal to act on his behalf. The Pole attempted to talk him out of the whole affair; he pleaded with him—he was too young; it was really Michal's argument; he had not the right to become involved. Stephen remained immovable. He was frightened; he knew that Louis was a master swordsman and a good shot, while he had just begun instruction in fencing at the college. He was himself an excellent shot with a musket, but he had never fired a dueling pistol in his life. But at Louis le Grand they taught a code of ethics that, while it did not endorse dueling, nevertheless stressed the question of a nobleman's honor. Stephen was well aware that he could never belong to the college if he attempted to avoid Louis DeLuynes' challenge. And Stephen was determined to belong.

Manya sent a note to him begging him not to continue with the affair. She sent an even stronger one to Michal, blaming the situation on him and warning him that if anything happened to either Louis or to Stephen, she would hold him responsible and their relationship would be forever blighted. Then she turned to the Queen. But, although she found much comfort there, she found no practical advice. When she went

117

to see Louis, he merely shrugged his shoulders and said that if Stephen were willing to back down he would accept an apology, but as matters now stood he had no alternative but to accept the duel or lose his honor.

Stephen had no one to act as his second except Michal. At first the prince refused but, realizing Stephen's dilemma and the impropriety of his acting on his own behalf, he finally accepted. He met with the Duc DuLuynes, who acted for his son, and arranged a meeting on a dueling ground three miles from Versailles, on the road to Paris. The weapons were to be pistols and the time, dawn of the next day, the day after Christmas.

Christmas day was not the most joyous one that Stephen had spent in his young life. It was normally the happiest day of the year for him. It was not only a religious feast but also the day the Jesuits had assigned as his fete day. As far as he was concerned, it was his sixteenth birthday. But he was in no mood to celebrate. He sat in his room gazing into the small fire. Michal was lying on his cot. Neither of them had partaken of the Christmas festivities that were going on all around them.

A knock at the door startled Stephen out of his reverie. He had not heard a knock at any door since he had come to Versailles. Michal rose from his bed and opened the door. It was Father LaGarde.

The priest stepped through the door before Michal could invite him in, and he walked directly toward Stephen. "Etienne, I have just heard what has occurred. You must withdraw from this affair and put an end to this nonsense. It goes too far. I did not bring you to France to have you killed. I brought you here to get you educated."

Stephen did not even look up at his mentor. "Part of the education, Father, and a part greatly emphasized by Father DesGouttes, is respect for the code of honor."

LaGarde's face became very flushed. "Etienne, this is impossible." He turned to face Michal. "Your Highness, would it be possible for me to have a few minutes with Etienne alone?" Without a word the prince picked up his jacket and left the room.

As soon as the door had closed, Stephen got up from his chair and walked away from the fire and the priest. "I know what you are going to say, Father. That I'm not a nobleman and not bound by their code, that there is no sense in getting myself killed for something that is of no concern to me. But it is of concern to me. I love Manya and I don't want her to marry DeLuynes. Even if the code is not mine, you sent me to the college and they taught it to me."

"I sent you to the college, Etienne, so that you might be educated and become a better priest."

"But I fell in love instead."

"Silliness," said LaGarde. "You're sixteen years old. You are not in love. You are infatuated with the first pretty girl you've ever laid eyes on. You have a vocation in the Society, Etienne. I know it; I'm certain of it."

"What about my feelings for Manya?"

"What about them? They prove to me that you're normal. We wouldn't want you if you did not have normal human reactions. God will give you the grace to fulfill your vocation and not to follow through on your very normal reactions to a beautiful woman."

The priest sat down in the chair that Stephen had just vacated. "Etienne, I'll be honest with you. I'm frightened. I'm going to lose you no matter what happens. DeLuynes will most likely kill you. But even if you should win the duel, the mere fact that you have injured another human being in a duel will be enough to bar you from the Society of Jesus."

Stephen looked at the priest in dismay. For as long as he could remember, he had lived his life with the Jesuits. To him they were all heroes. His feelings for Manya had confused all of his emotions to the point that he no longer understood what he wanted. LaGarde rose from his chair and walked over to Stephen, whose face clearly displayed his anguish. He took the boy's hands into his own and squeezed tightly. "Listen to me, my son," he said. "Leave with me today for Paris. I will have us on the next ship bound for New France, away from this place of temptation."

"I wish I could go home, Father, but I can't abandon Manya."

"Etienne, forget the girl. She doesn't want you. She wants to marry DeLuynes. You simply have got to face that fact and so does her brother."

Stephen's face saddened and his eyes filled. "Yes, I think you are right about that. I must learn to accept the fact that she does not want me."

"Good. Then I will prepare our passage to Paris."

"I'm still not going with you, Father. I will not appear a coward."

LaGarde was frustrated by his obstinacy. "Etienne, regard this as a test of obedience. If you were a member of the

Society of Jesus, I could command you to leave with me for Paris."

"If I were a member, Father, I would obey you. But I'm not a member. If you recall, my admission was delayed by your superiors."

LaGarde withdrew his hands and walked back toward the fireplace. He sighed. "If you must go through with it, you must. But kneel; I must hear your confession. I will not have you going into this danger without clear title to God's grace."

When LaGarde left Stephen, he went to his own suite of rooms and sent word to his brother's clerk that he wished an audience with St. Contest. He had expected a summons to the marquis' office and was surprised when his brother scratched politely on his door.

"Reverend Father," greeted St. Contest.

"Must we be so formal?" responded the priest.

"I think we must, because if the rumors I hear all over Versailles are true, then our meeting is a business meeting and not a family gathering to celebrate the Lord's birth."

"You are quite correct, Monsieur le Marquis."

St. Contest smiled.

"I see no way out of this impasse unless the King can be persuaded to intervene," said LaGarde.

"Why should he become involved?"

"Because Etienne is no nobleman—despite some of the things that have been said about him."

"You mean despite the stories that you and your confrères have told of him and that you personally asked me to dignify by ignoring."

LaGarde was annoyed but in no position to defend himself. "As you would have it, brother."

"Ah, I must have scored well for you to be bringing up that relationship."

"My God, will you stop fencing with me," said the priest, his anger now clearly showing.

"All right, Jean, calm down. You are too involved."

"I'm very involved. I don't want that boy killed, and if he goes through with the duel he will be killed. The King must call a halt to it. He must be informed that Etienne is an imposter. Once that is known, it will be impossible for DeLuynes to go through with it without losing face."

"I don't have the King's ear, Jean. I'm only deputy minister. D'Argenson, the minister, would have to bring this information to the King, and as you know, he is no friend to your order. He would make much of the duplicity of the Society."

"There are other ways to get to the King," said LaGarde.

St. Contest smiled. "I know you don't mean the Queen."

"The marquise could be asked to interfere, and I believe she is inclined to protect the Jesuits," said the priest.

St. Contest agreed. "She must know that Her Majesty is distressed by the affair, and Pompadour is determined to do the Queen favors and thus solidify her own position. Yes, I believe that the marquise is the solution. What is also distressing is the thought that she may also have been the source of the problem. It has come to my attention via a very talkative maid in the marquise's own service that Louis DeLuynes visited Pompadour before the ball at Pompadour's own request. I believe that she is playing games with us. She will do anything to secure her position with the King, even if it means making our silly Queen as content as a cow. Your ward was upsetting the Queen's plans for the Princess Wroblevska, so Pompadour set out to eliminate him. Either he fights Louis and gets himself killed, or he runs away from the duel and is thus removed from the scene, or we are forced to reveal that he is not of noble birth. She gave us our options and then sat back and watched us try to work our way out of her trap. In any case she wins. The princess will marry Louis."

"But why would she bother with a petty matter like this? Is she not deeply involved with the affairs of state?" asked LaGarde.

"She will eventually run this nation, brother, because she understands that at Versailles these petty matters are the true affairs of state. But in any case, the problem and the solution rest with Pompadour. I will see her immediately. She will require a very exacting service from me as foreign minister in return for this favor, but rest assured that the story of Etienne's humble birth will be all over the Chateau before long."

Stephen rose well before the assigned hour. Michal was awake and already dressed.

"Do you want any breakfast?" he asked Stephen solicitously.

Stephen shook his head; his stomach was knotted with fear. He dressed quickly and silently. When they descended the stairs from their room to the courtyard, they found a small carriage waiting for them. They got in and the driver guided

121

the horse through the courtyard, out the main gate and onto the highway toward Paris.

Neither Stephen or Michal spoke for most of the ride to the field of honor. Finally Michal broke the silence. "I'll never forgive myself, Etienne, if anything happens to you."

"Of course you will, Michal. There is too much life in you for you to remain sad for too long."

"But it is all my fault."

"That is also true," said Stephen. He was in no mood to humor the prince, not when he was fairly sure he would be dead or wounded within a matter of minutes. There was no more conversation.

The Duc DeLuynes and his son were waiting for them when they arrived. Michal and the duke went immediately into conference with a third man, who would serve as the referee. Michal returned to Stephen's side after the conference.

"You are to stand twenty-five paces apart," he said. "You may fire as soon as the referee gives the signal. But if you fire and only wound or miss, you must stand in place until the other side has returned the fire or has been judged incapable. DeLuynes has insisted that some blood must be spilled to satisfy honor. If you both miss, you will have to do it all over again. I've checked both pistols. They are identical and both are loaded and in good working condition. May Our Lady bless you, my friend." He was close to tears.

The referee signaled the two opponents to come forward. "Gentlemen," he said, "I would like to take this one last opportunity to avoid bloodshed. If apologies are extended, honor will be satisfied and we may halt these proceedings."

Both Stephen and Louis remained silent.

"Very well. Your positions have been marked. Please go to them."

Stephen found his spot. The sun had just risen and the daylight had improved visibility. He could clearly see the grim but confident expression on Louis' face. He knew that his opponent was determined to kill him.

"Are you ready?" called the referee loudly.

Stephen shouted, "Yes," his voice cracking.

Louis answered also.

Stephen raised his right arm and aimed the pistol. His hand shook terribly and as he sighted down the barrel, he knew that he could not kill Louis. He sighted lower, toward the calf of his right leg. The wait seemed interminable and his shaking grew worse; the weight of the pistol increased with each passing second.

"Fire."

Stephen pulled the trigger and the gun seemed to explode in his hand. He knew instantly that he had missed altogether and that Louis had not fired at all. He wanted to turn and run, but he would not. He had to stand and face his opponent. He wanted to be sick, but he would not allow himself that either. His eyes moved to the left and he saw that Michal had turned his head away and burst into tears. He turned back and looked straight ahead—into the eyes of Louis DeLuynes.

Louis still held his pistol out in front of him, sighting, it seemed to Stephen, directly at his heart. Off to the right, he could hear the sounds of horses moving toward them at a full gallop.

"Monsieur," said the referee loudly, "you must not prolong this cruelty. You must fire."

"Hold your fire," a voice shouted. "In the name of the King, halt these proceedings."

Louis lowered his pistol, his face clearly showing his dismay.

"The King commands that you desist," said the now-dismounted captain of the guard. "If anyone disobeys, I have orders to place the offender under arrest."

The captain, the referee, Michal and the duke huddled together. When they had finished, Michal came toward Stephen. "We can return to Versailles now," he said. But in his words Stephen felt a chill.

LaGarde tried to console Stephen. Michal had not spoken to him again and had left their room, taking his few possessions with him. Stephen had remained alone, confused and angry. He had lived up to everything that was expected of him. He deserved better. If he had not been born a noble, he had at least behaved like one. How could they have expected anything more of him? And why had they made him an outcast?

The priest came to him as soon as he heard that he had returned. He took Stephen into his arms and allowed him to rest his head on his shoulder. The boy was struggling to hold back the tears. Finally Stephen broke down and began to sob. "Why don't I seem to belong anywhere, Father?" he cried.

"You do belong, Etienne; you belong to us. We are your family, and to us you are a very noble young man—worthy to be one of us. We will return to Louisbourg as soon as it is possible. It was a mistake to bring you here. We almost lost you."

V

1743

"This is a joyous occasion, Father LaGarde," said Demarais. "I always feel great happiness when one of our young men takes vows."

The two men sat in LaGarde's sparsely furnished room in Louisbourg, sipping a wine that the provincial had imported from France for the celebration. Demarais sampled the wine after savoring the aroma. An expression of pure pleasure crossed his face. "But I have come this spring not only for the ceremony," he said.

"I suspected that you had other reasons," answered LaGarde.

"Jean, I want to discuss with you the staffing of our new mission to the Oneida."

LaGarde broke into a smile. "They have agreed then, finally, to accept a priest."

"It is the breakthrough we have been waiting for," answered Demarais. "We must credit this success to our people among the Mohawk and Seneca. It is an extremely important mission and I want you to provide the staff from this house."

"I would be most honored if you would select me for the post," said LaGarde.

"No, I need you here, doing what you do best. You are an excellent pastor and spiritual guide. You are to remain as superior of this house."

"As you will, Father," said LaGarde.

"But I do need your advice on just who should go," said Demarais.

"If you except me and Father DeGanne, who is too old for the task, it leaves Gregoire, Lalonde and Mercier. I could not recommend Gregoire. His mind is in the stars. I think we would need a more practical man."

"What about Mercier?"

LaGarde thought for a moment. "I have no doubt that he would succeed, but I hesitate to suggest him. He is the chaplain for the garrison and there is much tension at the citadel. The pay of the troops is behind again. Mercier speaks German and has great influence with some of the Catholic mercenaries. If he is withdrawn, the governor will lose a valuable ally."

"His Excellency might try paying his troops on time and he would not have to call on God so often to aid him."

"You are probably right, Reverend Father, but that is a political matter and we must try to stay uninvolved."

Demarais made a noise in his throat that sounded very much like a growl. "That leaves us with Lalonde."

"Father Lalonde has been in this house for four years. He has served primarily in the hospital and as confessor to the sisters. There are times when I feel that I do not really know the man. His manifestations of conscience to me are very straightforward but there is something distant about him."

"Has there been any recurrence of his old problem?" asked Demarais.

"He has never tried to hide it from me. Certainly, he knows that you warned me about his drinking before you sent him to this house. I am quite sure he has overcome it. For that I must commend him. I think that these past four years indicated that he is ready for another chance. I think it should be Lalonde."

"I must trust your judgment, Jean. We will send Lalonde as superior of the mission."

"He will need a lay brother to assist him," said LaGarde.

"I disagree, Father. I would like him to have more support than a brother can provide. He will need an assistant—a catechist—a teacher for both the children and the converts among the adults. What about Brother Etienne?"

"But he is just taking his vows tomorrow, Father," said LaGarde. "He has hardly begun his education."

"He has time, Jean. A spell in actual mission work could prove invaluable. In addition, you have informed me in your reports that he is excellent in Indian tongues."

"He speaks Abenacki, Rene, not Oneida." Demarais waved his hand as if to dismiss a petty problem. "If he can learn one, he can learn the other."

"They are not related languages, Father," said LaGarde. "But I had always thought that when the time came he would return to St. François—to the Abenacki."

"I want the boy to go, Jean."

"I see," said LaGarde with a sniff of annoyance. "You have already made up your mind. I thought you came here to seek my advice."

"Jean, old friend, don't be angry. You are too involved with the boy."

"Etienne is a fine lad. There is real goodness in him and he hasn't fully recovered from the experiences he had in France two years ago."

Demarais interrupted him. "You mean you haven't recovered, and you are not ready to give him up, Jean."

LaGarde hesitated. "You are right; I am indulging myself. But I love that boy as if he were my own son." LaGarde was quiet for a moment; then he spoke. "Thank you for admonishing me, Father Provincial. With your permission I will confess my fault to the community in the refectory this evening."

"You have my permission, Father," said the provincial.

For some moments the atmosphere between the two men was strained. Finally, Demarais leaned toward LaGarde and spoke in a low tone. "The boy still knows nothing of his origins?"

"I have told him nothing."

Demarais took another sip of wine and looked at LaGarde. "I did not write you at the time, but the Bastonois has been in contact with me in Quebec again. He knows the boy is here and has threatened again to make his whereabouts known to the family."

"When was this?" said LaGarde, his eyes wide with surprise.

"At the end of last summer."

"After all these years he still plagues us. I fear for Etienne's safety with that man around. I think I understand better your desire to see Etienne off to the Oneida, Father Provincial."

"I thought you might see the point, Jean. We have protected this secret for a long time. Perhaps it would have been better to admit fault at the time and turn the boy over to His Excellency for repatriation. But we agreed to protect ourselves and our work, and now we have no choice but to continue to do so, in spite of this person Pierce. The boy goes to the Oneida."

The two years since he had first put on the Jesuit habit had seemed to fly by for Stephen. They had been years of hard work, days on end of cleaning pots and pans in Brother Richard's kitchen and more days over the hot tubs in the laundry. The only opportunities he had to rest were the occasional times he had to cover for Brother Porter in his lodge and when he sat in Father LaGarde's room studying the rules of the Society and the significance of the vows he was to take. Rarely was he able to leave the house.

He still carried bread to the sisters, and Marie Louis became his contact with the rest of the world, except for fleeting moments of conversation with Karl on the ramparts at dawn. There were no more hunting excursions with Socono, and Stephen saw the Indian only when he visited the house to consult with Father LaGarde.

But now the great day had arrived—vow day. It began the same as any other. Stephen delivered the bread to Sister Porter at the convent. She said very little to him, not wishing to interfere with his thoughts on this day. He reminded her that she was to attend the ceremony in the citadel chapel. She needed no reminder.

When he returned to the Jesuit house, the kitchen door was locked and he was forced to enter by the front door. At the porter's lodge all the fathers and brothers were waiting for him, dressed in their best black habits, birettas and capes.

Stephen found a newly tailored habit draped over the desk in Brother Porter's room. Father Demarais gestured to the novice to enter the lodge and dress himself in the new habit.

"It is a gift to you from the brothers, Brother Etienne," said the provincial. "Father Rector and I, along with the priests who have been your teachers all these years, have our own gift." Demarais held out his arm and Father Mercier handed him a fine black cape with a silver clasp.

Stephen stepped into the lodge and quickly removed his stained and worn habit. He rubbed the tops of his shoes across the back of his stockings. He had polished them last night, but the streets had been wet and muddy in the morning. He put on his new habit, tied his sash and stepped back into the foyer. Obeying the provincial's gesture, he faced away from him, while Demarais placed the new cape over his shoulders. Father LaGarde offered him his new biretta, a three-cornered clerical hat. Stephen placed it on his head sheepishly. He started to laugh. It all felt so strange.

"Father Rector," said the provincial. "I believe that your candidate for final vows is properly attired for the procession and ceremony. I am not sure that his present mood of levity is appropriate for this solemn occasion but I suggest that we begin before Brother LaGarde breaks out into uncontrollable laughter."

127

Stephen took the good-natured admonition more seriously than it was intended and attempted to look solemn. The brothers, led by Brother Porter, led the way out of the front door, followed by Stephen. The priests, with Father Rector, and Father Provincial last in line, followed the candidate.

They walked for one block along the broad street that ran at the base of the harbor walls. Then at the corner where the intendant's house stood, they turned left up Rue St. Louis.

The few residents of Louisbourg who were in the streets at this early hour stopped as the procession passed them. The men tipped their hats, while the women bowed their heads.

After two blocks the street opened into a large courtyard, which was the King's garden. Across the courtyard stood the citadel—the governor's residence. Two of the Swiss guards snapped to attention as the little procession passed between them and entered the building.

They turned down a corridor and Brother Porter swung open the double doors at the end of it. As they entered the chapel, the choir broke into the opening lines of the Kyrie Elieson of a solemn high mass. While the provincial, the rector and Father Mercier vested themselves for mass at the side altar, Stephen and the rest of the Jesuit community walked down the center aisle of the chapel to the front pews.

On the right side of the chapel, in his customary place of honor, sat Jean Baptiste Louis, le Prevost, Seigneur du Quesnel, de Changy et d'autres lieux, Governor of Isle Royale; next to him was François Bigot, intendant of the colony. Behind them sat the leading military officers and merchants, the mother superior of the convent of Ste. Ann and the rector of the Recollet missionaries. All of the luminaries of Isle Royale turned out when the Jesuit provincial issued invitations.

Behind all this glitter, however, in the middle of the chapel where one would normally expect to find the family of the candidate, there sat one Indian, dressed in breeches and shirt, the buckskin moccasins on his feet betraying the one concession he refused to make to Father LaGarde. Next to him, splendid in his best uniform with his recently earned corporal's stripes proudly and prominently displayed on his arm, sat Karl Stiegler, clearly ill at ease in this religious setting. Finally, next to the aisle, was Sister Marie Louis, grinning from ear to ear and nudging Karl painfully in the ribs with her needle-sharp elbow as Stephen took his place in the front of the congregation.

The mass proceeded with all of its solemn Latin ritual. Father Provincial, his back to the congregation, bent low over the bread and wine. *"Hoc est enim corpus meum,"* he whispered just loudly enough for his two assistants to hear. He genuflected, then raised the Body of Jesus on high and knelt again. Similarly he consecrated and elevated the wine.

Stephen tried to concentrate on the mass. On this day of all days he should be preparing himself for the reception of the Body and Blood of the Savior. But images kept forcing their way into his mind—images of his days as a boy in this walled fortress. He pictured the flour-covered Savard, dead these past eighteen months and now replaced by his equally flour-covered son. He thought of his meetings with Karl on the harbor walls each dawn, halted two weeks ago by Karl's promotion and the end of his morning sentry duty. He thought of Sister Porter and their frequently irreverent jokes. With his vows and new assignments, he wondered if he would see much of her in the days ahead. And he thought of Socono, the Indian with the unexplained scar, the extraordinary dignity and the hidden knowledge that Stephen had promised himself never to try to learn. He thought of those months at school in Paris—of Michal, Charles and even Louis DeLuynes. And he thought of Manya, beautiful Manya, forever beyond his reach.

Stephen left his pew and entered the sanctuary. He climbed the steps toward the altar and knelt before the three priests. They turned to face the congregation, with Father Provincial holding the sacred host in front of him. Stephen began to recite the words he had first memorized months before. He promised to spend the rest of his life in poverty, never again to claim any worldly possessions as his own and to give up his right to inherit any material goods. He promised to live his days a celibate man, to give up forever the comfort of wife and children. And he promised to hear, in the voice of his superior, the voice of God and to obey that voice. When he had finished, he closed his eyes and prayed quietly for a moment. Then he opened his mouth. Demarais placed the host on his tongue. Stephen rose from the altar step, turned and walked back to his place in the congregation.

After mass Stephen and his closest friends retraced their steps to the Jesuit house in the company of the Jesuit community. After breakfast Father LaGarde left the refectory with Father Lalonde. One half hour later he summoned Stephen to his room.

"Come in, Etienne," LaGarde said as Stephen opened the door to the rector's room after knocking. Since Lalonde sat in the room's only other chair, Stephen remained standing.

"I have just informed Father Lalonde that Father Provincial has decided to send him as superior to our new mission among the Oneida. And I have informed him that you are to be his assistant. You will leave for Montreal next Monday aboard the monthly supply ship. In Montreal you will contact Father Beaussier at Caugnawaga. He will see to it that you obtain guides to the Oneida villages. Father Lalonde will fill in the details for you, Etienne, but I feel I must stress to you the importance of this work. The heretics already have a strong foothold in their villages. You will not have an easy task in showing them the true path to God. You must devote yourself with all zeal to the undertaking. Today, Etienne, you promised to obey your superior as the voice of God on earth. From this moment, Father Lalonde is your superior. Now I suspect that you two will have much to talk about. I will leave you."

Stephen had not had an opportunity to say a word, nor was it expected that he would have anything to say to LaGarde. The command had been given. All that was left to him was to obey.

Lalonde motioned to Stephen to sit in the now empty chair. "Well, Brother LaGarde—excuse me, I forgot; after this morning's ceremony the proper title is Mister LaGarde—we have only three days to prepare for our task."

There was an air of efficiency about Lalonde that Stephen had never noted before. Gone was the laconic smile; he no longer seemed to sneer his words. "We will have to sit down frequently with Brother Michel over these days. He served in the Mohawk missions for years and he knows the Mohawk language. The Oneida speak a dialect that is quite similar to Mohawk; Michel can teach us basic words. Many of the Oneida have a rudimentary knowledge of English. You may be of help there."

"It has been years since I spoke English, Father," interrupted Stephen.

"You knew it once. You have studied it with us. You will use it among the Oneida."

"Yes, Father," Stephen replied.

"LaGarde, I have often thought you a stupid boy. Maybe you are; maybe you're not. But I will not allow you to interfere with the task that Father Provincial has given me. I will not fail. I have waited too long for this chance. You will help me or I will break you. I will accept no excuses and I will tolerate only blind obedience."

"Yes, Father," Stephen repeated.

"Good. Now that we understand each other, let us get down to work."

Father LaGarde found Socono sitting alone in the kitchen. He had reverted to his normal dress.

"I am glad you waited for me, Socono. I have something I must tell you. Etienne has received his first mission assignment. He is to join Father Lalonde as missionary to the Oneida people."

Socono said nothing. He rose and started for the kitchen door.

The priest called to him. "Socono, don't leave. Let me explain. I had no choice. Father Provincial insisted that I send him as far away as possible. His uncle is once again using the boy to secure favors from the governor. He was in Quebec last summer."

"Blackrobe, you promised me that the little brother would return with me to my people. Now you send him away to the Oneida. The Oneida are snakes. They will kill him."

"That's not true," LaGarde said testily. "The Oneida have asked for a priest."

Socono smiled. "The Mohawks asked for blackrobes too and they killed them."

"That was years ago," said LaGarde.

"A snake is still a snake." Socono started for the door again but hesitated and turned toward LaGarde. "Ten years ago, Blackrobe, I committed a terrible sin. I got drunk and the toothless devil marked my face. In my pain and anger I caused the deaths of innocent people and caused the little brother to lose those who loved him."

"Socono, I told you then and I tell you again now that the death of Etienne's father was not your fault. You know and I know that if you could have stopped the others you would have."

"That is not good enough, Blackrobe. When I became a Christian, I promised myself I would not kill except to defend my people. I am responsible for the little brother. I left my home and came to Louisbourg to be with him, to help him, to protect him. I understood when you sent him to the college in France. It was so that he might be a better priest and better aid my people. But as long as he and I are both alive, I will not leave his side again. I gave up the search for the toothless one in order to be with the little brother. You promised me that you would send him to live with the Abenacki and then I could return to my people with him. Now you send him to live with snakes. I will go with him."

"Socono, you can't. The Oneida will kill you."

The Indian looked whimsically at LaGarde. "The Oneida will not even know that I live among them. I will build my lodge in the woods near their village. They will not see me. But I will see them and if they try to harm the little brother, I will be there."

LaGarde thought for a moment, absentmindedly pulling at his beard. "Perhaps in the long run, Socono, that would be best. You could also keep me informed on the behavior of Father Lalonde."

"The blackrobes will have to find other spies," said Socono.

LaGarde was surprised by his remark. "I have never known you to refuse to do the work of the Church before, Socono. What has come over you?"

"I have never known the blackrobe not to keep his promise to me before either," replied the Indian. "Some things change, Blackrobe." He turned and left the house.

The supply ship *Attlante* set sail with the tide after sunset. Stephen, who had come aboard at noon with Lalonde and Demarais, stayed on deck rather than miss the excitement of the sailing. He stood by the starboard railing looking up into the rigging, where he could barely see the sailors who had climbed up to make sail. Across the deck, on the port side, the fire of the lighthouse in the harbor entrance shone brightly.

Socono stood next to Stephen, awed but much too dignified to gape as Stephen did.

"Aren't you glad we were ordered to Montreal by sea, Socono, rather than overland?"

"You were ordered, little brother. I am just going home in ease."

Stephen was relieved that Socono was with him, if only for part of the journey. Departure from Louisbourg had been hard. The strained handshake with Karl, tearful hugs from Sister Marie Louis and a blessing from Father Rector had all brought him close to tears. The presence of his Indian teacher had steadied him.

The moment *Attlante* left the security of Louisbourg harbor and began to ride the Atlantic swells, Stephen was convinced that it was not only his confidence that needed steadying. His head began to reel and his forehead broke into a sweat, despite the evening chill. He remembered the awful sickness of his trip to France and fought back waves of nausea. Even Socono lost his air of indifference and clung to the sides of the ship.

Stephen decided to remain on deck and went below to find Lalonde and inform him of his decision. The priest was lying in his bunk. "Are you asleep, Father?" Stephen asked. The priest merely moaned. "Are you ill?" He approached the bunk and forgot his own discomfort when he saw just how sick the priest was. Too dizzy to make his way to the chamber pot in the corner, Lalonde had vomited on the floor of the cabin and then collapsed into the bunk.

Stephen obtained a pitcher of water from the galley and began to clean up. He placed a cold compress on Lalonde's forehead and then, getting down on his hands and knees, he scrubbed the deck clean. After placing the clean chamber pot within the priest's reach, he beat a hasty retreat to the deck and to fresh air. Socono stood where Stephen had left him, still uncomfortable but now in control.

"Father Lalonde is very ill," Stephen informed his friend. "I will have to look in on him frequently, but if it is all right with you, Socono, I'll share your blanket on deck tonight. I don't think I could spend the night in the cabin."

"The night will be cold," said Socono. "Wouldn't you be more comfortable in the other cabin with the chief black-robe?"

"No," said Stephen. "I certainly would not. Jesuit scholastics like me do not move in on their provincials. I would definitely be more comfortable with you. We'll be fine with your blanket and my cape."

Stephen and Socono huddled against some coiled ropes at the base of one of the masts. Several times during the night, Stephen braved the cold night air to check on his superior. He found him flushed and moaning, but he was no longer sick. Stephen replaced the compress and returned to the makeshift bed he shared with Socono.

A brisk wind from the northeast drove *Attlante* steadily southward during the night, and dawn found them approaching the straits of Canso. In more protected waters, the stomachs of all of the passengers settled down. Father Demarais said mass and Stephen assisted him.

At noon *Attlante* passed within cannon range of the English fort at Canso and saluted the English flag with one round from the small nine-pounder in her bow. The English responded and *Atlante* sailed on. Twenty-four hours of northwesterly sailing found them off the eastern point of Isle St. Jean, heading for the Magdalan Islands in the Gulf of St. Lawrence. Here the winds still blew favorably and the sea, in the protected gulf, remained fairly calm.

Now that Lalonde was back on his feet, Stephen had little time to sit and talk with Socono. Lalonde was determined to master basic Iroquois vocabulary. Using the phrasebook compiled by the Jesuit Mohawk missionaries, he insisted that Stephen test him, and he in turn quizzed his assistant. Stephen learned quickly, while Lalonde, to his disgust, had to struggle long and hard with the strange-sounding words.

Socono listened to their efforts and smiled broadly.

"Mister LaGarde, why is that Indian laughing at us?" demanded Lalonde.

"What's wrong, Socono?" Stephen asked in Abenacki.

The Indian placed his hand on Stephen's arm. "I do not mean to mock your efforts, little brother, but the Oneida are Iroquois. They put much stock in words. I think the black-robe would be much mistaken to attempt to address the Oneida in their own tongue. They would laugh at him. He should speak to them in French and find someone to translate for him."

Stephen repeated Socono's warning to Lalonde.

Lalonde glared at Socono, but he finally said, "Well, the savage is probably right. I will have to speak to our people at Caugnawaga when we arrive there."

Socono turned on his heel and walked away from the two Jesuits.

"What is wrong with him?" asked Lalonde.

"He is probably offended, Father."

"For God's sake, why?"

Stephen hesitated to respond but then thought better. "Father Lalonde, Socono is a Christian and has been one for almost fifteen years. He understands French and he does not like to be referred to as a savage or a heathen."

Lalonde's mouth opened in surprise. "Well, of all the gall. Who does he think he is, a noble at Versailles?"

Stephen was angered by the priest's response. From his own experience, he knew Socono to be a man superior to any of the nobles he had met at Court. But there was no sense in antagonizing Lalonde, and so he held his tongue. "Perhaps I should go after him, Father?"

"He can go to hell for all I care," answered the priest.

Stephen was sorely tempted to respond that it was the duty

of a priest and pastor to care about the salvation of those under his charge. But again he kept quiet. He turned from Lalonde and followed Socono.

Two more days of fair sailing weather in bright sunshine brought the ship within sight of Gaspe, and another day brought them to the mouth of the St. Lawrence River. Once the ship was in the river and fighting its currents, their pace slowed. The winds turned contrary, and it took them a week to reach Quebec. *Attlante* did not stay long in port at the capital. Father Demarais now made his residence at the Jesuit house there, and so his journey was over. Some of the supplies from France were unloaded but most were destined for the great fur trade center at Montreal; twenty-four hours after making port at Quebec, *Attlante* pushed out into the river and again fought the current.

The winds remained contrary and the ship was forced to tack within the confines of the St. Lawrence. Progress was slow.

Socono had not gone below decks for the whole voyage. Stephen realized that their journey together was drawing to a close, and after a particularly frustrating session with Lalonde and the phrasebook, he went on deck looking for his friend.

The scenery on both banks of the river had changed from the rugged mountains downriver from Quebec to lower cliffs with broad mud flats at their base. When Stephen reached Socono's side on the port railing, he found the Indian intently watching the south shore.

"We are very near your home now, aren't we, Socono?"

The Indian pointed toward a break in the tree line on the south bank. "That is the mouth of the St. François," he said. "My people should be there waiting for me."

Stephen tried to appear as unconcerned about their separation as Socono. But then the Indian turned to look him directly in the eyes.

"Little brother, I am not happy about what you are being asked to do. It would be much better for all if you were to leave this ship with me and come to live in St. François."

Stephen started to speak but Socono hushed him.

"I know you well enough," said the Indian, "to know that what I suggest is impossible and that you will obey the blackrobes and go to live with the Oneida."

"Socono, I have no choice in the matter."

"I know that, little brother. But before I go, I want you to listen to me carefully. I know you love the blackrobe La-Garde. He has been like a father to you and you have even

135

taken his name. But he has not always been a good father to you. In addition, the blackrobe Lalonde will get you killed if you do not watch him carefully. He is wise in the ways of the whites. He is good at cheating and lying. He should get along well with the Oneida, but before long they too will tire of him and kill him. Protect yourself."

He reached out his hand and gently touched Stephen's face, tracing with his finger the scar that ran through the boy's eyebrow. Before Stephen could ask him to explain his cryptic remark about LaGarde, he slipped over the side of the vessel and lowered himself down the boarding ladder into the bottom of a canoe, which had glided unseen up to the side of *Attlante*. Stephen waved at the departing figure of his friend as the canoe sped quickly away from the ship and into the mouth of the St. François.

Several hours after Socono's departure, Lalonde joined Stephen at the railing. "Where is the Indian?" he asked.

"Gone," said Stephen.

Lalonde looked relieved. He gazed toward the south shore. The tiny village of Sorel was just barely visible ahead of them. Again canoes pushed out from the shore.

"Isn't that a priest in the lead canoe, Father," said Stephen.

Lalonde shaded his eyes with his hand and stared in the direction Stephen pointed. He did not answer for some moments but finally agreed. "It's Father Beaussier from Caugnawaga."

The lead canoe came toward the ship at full speed. As it neared *Attlante*, Stephen could hear the Indian paddlers grunt with each stroke of the paddle. Beaussier hailed the ship when he was within one hundred yards, and the pilot swung about in order to ease the approach of the canoes.

"*Pax Christi*, Father Lalonde," said Beaussier as he climbed up onto the deck.

"*Pax Christi*, Beaussier," Lalonde returned. "This is my assistant, Mr. LaGarde." The two men exchanged greetings in Latin.

"We expected to meet with you in Montreal or in Caugnawaga, Beaussier," said Lalonde.

"Your plans have been changed," said Beaussier. "Oneida guides arrived in Caugnawaga two weeks ago and accompanied me to Sorel to intercept your ship." He pointed to a tall, well-muscled Indian who had climbed aboard from the canoe and joined them on the deck.

"This is Dagaheari, your guide from Kanowalohale, the main Oneida castle."

Dagaheari was a very handsome man with high forehead, jet black hair and black eyes. His nose was flat with flared nostrils, indicating some African mix in his Indian ancestry. He wore nothing but a loincloth and moccasins. He acknowledged their greeting by running his black eyes over them individually, evaluating their potential as warriors. He said nothing.

Beaussier broke the awkward moment of silence. "Father Lalonde, Dagaheari has told me that he wishes to leave for his home immediately. You must load your belongings in the canoes. One is Dagaheari's; the other is mine. I will lend you the canoe and two of my Mohawks for your journey."

"Thank you, Father," answered Lalonde. "We could not have carried everything in one canoe."

"That's what I told Dagaheari, but he is a warrior with no patience for baggage. Also, I would watch him; I don't think he is a supporter of a mission among his people," said Beaussier. "My Mohawks speak French, so they will act as interpreters for you, but once you are in Kanowalohale, you are on your own. Hurry now—we must not keep Dagaheari waiting."

Twenty minutes later, Stephen sat in the center of one heavily laden canoe and Lalonde in the other. Dagaheari and his Oneida companion paddled Stephen's canoe, while the two Caugnawaga Mohawks paddled Lalonde's.

They sped across the shallow waters of Lac St. Pierre and into the mouth of the Richelieu, passing the village of Sorel on the left bank. They paddled against the current of the river for the rest of the day and camped only after sunset.

Darkness had not yet set in, but the early evening chill had. One of the Mohawks began a fire and Dagaheari and his companion disappeared into the woods that lined the riverbank.

Stephen sat with Lalonde before the fire, trying to warm himself. The priest stretched his hands out closer to the fire. "My God, I'm exhausted," said Lalonde. "I don't think I can take another day like today. I thought they would never stop. Every time I moved, one of those savages would yell at me. Perhaps Dagaheari will stay here and rest for a few days, if I ask him."

"I don't think that would be wise, Father," said Stephen. "He is anxious to be home and I don't think he is all that happy about having us with him. If we give him the slightest excuse, he will leave us behind and we will have failed in our duty."

Lalonde looked annoyed. "It's fine for you to talk about duty. You're younger than I and you're half savage yourself. All-day canoe travel should be one of your specialties."

Stephen resolved not to offer Lalonde more advice, but the priest said nothing to the Indians about a delay.

Darkness set in quickly; it was nearly impossible to see the riverbank from where the two white men sat. Dagaheari stepped out of the underbrush and into the light of the fire, carrying the carcasses of two wild ducks. He threw them at the feet of the two Jesuits.

"I think he wants us to clean them and prepare them for the fire," said Stephen.

"We are not his servants," said Lalonde indignantly.

"I suspect that he plans to treat us that way."

"I will protest," said Lalonde.

"To whom, Father?" asked Stephen.

Lalonde had risen to his feet to carry out his threat, but he sat down dejectedly when he saw the sense of Stephen's question. "You clean them, Etienne," he said. "I have never done anything like that. You have experience in kitchen work."

Stephen picked up the first bird and began to work. He plucked quicky and was halfway through the preparation of the second duck before he noticed Dagaheari staring at him from across the fire. He turned his back on the Indian and quickened the pace of his work. Finally, he skewered the ducks on a sharp stake and placed them over the fire to cook, all the while feeling the intense glare of those two black eyes burning into his back.

They rose before dawn, ate the remains of the evening meal and set out on the river again. For the first several miles of the day's journey, Stephen watched the banks of the river and the effect of the rising sun's rays on the trees that lined the shore. Later, however, he gave this up and stared straight ahead at the mesmerizing motion of the muscles of the Oneida's back and shoulders. As the day grew warmer and the current swifter, the paddlers had to work harder. Stephen watched with fascination as the little rivulets of sweat trickled down the back of the paddler in front of him. So hypnotized was he by the monotony of the motion that he failed to hear the rush of water until they were at the very foot of the rapids. He was startled by Dagaheari's yell to the canoe in front of them. Then he saw Lalonde's canoe turn sharply between two rocks and head for the shore.

The current rushed down at the fragile canoe, but in a glance Stephen saw that it was in no trouble. The Mohawks knew the river well; they headed for the normal landing beach used for carrying canoes around the Chambly Rapids. But neither the Mohawks nor Dagaheari had counted on the reactions of Father Lalonde. When his canoe turned for shore and presented its side to the white water, some of the swiftly rushing water leaped over the side of the craft and poured into the bottom. Lalonde, shocked by the coldness of the river and frightened that the craft was about to swamp, panicked and jumped to his feet. The canoe flipped over immediately, throwing one of the Mohawks against a rock and dropping the other paddler, Father Lalonde and all the baggage into the river.

Stephen reacted instinctively. He realized that only the Mohawk clinging desperately to the rock was in real danger. The others were in shallow water and could struggle to their feet. He slipped over the side of the canoe into the water as Socono had taught him. Dagaheari steadied the craft and prevented it from swamping, once he realized what Stephen was trying to do.

Stephen struggled against the rapid current as it pulled on his cumbersome habit. At first he feared that he would be swept past the injured Mohawk. But at the last second, he reached out and caught hold of the Indian. The Mohawk lost his grip on the rock at that instant, and the two were washed downstream. Stephen kept his arm under the Indian's chin. The Mohawk held tightly to Stephen with one hand while the other hung uselessly at his side. A sharp splinter of white bone had broken through the forearm. Stephen reached for the bottom of the river with his toes but failed to make contact. His head sank beneath the white water. The Mohawk went under with him and started to flail about with his legs and good arm. The boy held on with all of his might, cutting off the Indian's breathing and forcing him to struggle all the more.

Stephen felt his strength leaving him but he held on to the Mohawk as a last tie with life. The waters swirled about them and pulled the two men along like bobbing corks. They swept by another rock into an eddy of calmer water. With one last effort, Stephen again thrust his foot toward the bottom and this time he struck hard rock. He placed his other foot down and regained his balance. Dragging the injured Indian behind him like a sack, he struggled against the rush of water toward the riverbank. He grabbed a sapling and pulled himself and the Mohawk up onto the mud. He lay there, gasping for breath.

Dagaheari's canoe glided swiftly to Stephen's mudflat. The Oneida jumped out and knelt beside his almost drowned companions. He muttered something in Oneida, which Stephen was too weary to hear even if he had understood the language. Stephen felt himself being lifted and placed in the canoe, then the Mohawk was placed on top of him and the craft shot out into the white water again. The two Oneida paddled into the current on an angle toward the far bank. Rather than risk the white water upriver, they landed the canoe farther down from the normal carrying place and pitched camp. A very wet Father Lalonde and the uninjured Mohawk carried their ruined goods to Dagaheari's campsite.

Dagaheari was enraged, and when he was angry, he cursed the Christian God in English, the language he had learned from the Protestant missionaries as a boy. "Christ's bloody crutch. What the hell do we do now? The goddamn Mohawk has broken his goddamn arm. I should leave the goddamn blackrobes here in the middle of the woods to rot for all the trouble they have caused me. Paddle two large canoes with three paddlers. I won't do it. We will leave one behind or it will take us a month to get to Kanowalohale."

Dagaheari's Oneida friend stared at him blankly, not understanding a word he said. Stephen, resting by the fire, listened to the Indian's diatribe. Then he said to the Mohawk in French, "Tell Dagaheari that I can paddle a canoe, and by tomorrow morning I will be fit to take my place." Again Dagaheari stared at Stephen for some moments and then nodded assent.

Both of the Jesuits had removed their habits and hung them to dry before the fire. Stephen sat wrapped in Dagaheari's blanket. Lalonde had thrown Stephen's cape about his shoulders and sat with his head in his hands. After some moments he looked up at Stephen.

"Etienne, we have begun badly. We have lost everything."

"Not so," answered Stephen, "all the goods were with me and are untouched." Stephen had not meant the remark to sound like a rebuke, but Lalonde's head snapped up and he hissed at Stephen.

"I suppose you blame me for all this. It doesn't seem to

bother you at all that I nearly drowned today. A great deal of help you were. Instead of coming to rescue your brother in Christ, you go off after the heathen."

"You were in no danger, Father. And the Mohawk is no heathen. He is one of us. He is a Catholic."

Lalonde was subdued by the vehemence of Stephen's response. The boy had never spoken to him like that before. He sat and pouted for a few more moments and then reverted to his original thought. "But we have lost all the mission supplies. I have lost my supply of sacred bread for consecration. My mass vestments are ruined."

"That is tragic, Father. But I had the Iroquois dictionary with me and we can use Indian bread for mass, can't we?"

"If we must," said Lalonde. "If we must."

The next morning the injured Mohawk, the baggage and the canoes were carried around the rapids to Chambly. The priest at the fort at Chambly offered Lalonde and Stephen the hospitality of his small rectory, but Dagaheari was impatient to be off. The injured Mohawk was placed in the care of the priest. The canoes were relaunched and they continued their journey up the Richelieu. One Mohawk and one Oneida paddled Father Lalonde's canoe, while Dagaheari and Stephen paddled the canoe carrying their supplies.

That afternoon, as they moved against the now lazy current of the river, they passed the French settlements of St. Jean and Iberville, on opposite sides of the river from each other. These were the last French communities that they would see. They camped that night on Isle aux Noix in the river. Two days later the river broadened into an inland sea. Stephen was awed by the expanse of water several miles across, and even more awed when he realized that the far shore of the lake was not really the far shore but a great island in the middle of the lake. As their canoes passed between Valcour and Grand Isle, the lake reached its broadest point, some thirteen miles across.

They continued to paddle south. Lalonde wanted to switch canoes. He was bored speaking with the Mohawk, who merely grunted replies in an incomprehensible French. He wanted to travel with Stephen. But Dagaheari would not hear of it. Stephen was surprised by his own reaction to the Oneida's rejection of Lalonde. He had enjoyed the days of paddling in the warm sun. The first day he had removed his habit and paddled in his shirtsleeves, only to be admonished by Lalonde. From then on he had remained properly attired. Now the prospect of having to listen to Lalonde chatter all day, as well as listening to him in camp at night, revolted Stephen. He was delighted when Lalonde was turned down. His days of silence, of hard paddling, of sweating and peace would continue.

With each passing day the lake narrowed, gradually at first and then rapidly. Finally it appeared to be not much wider than the Richelieu had been. Four days from Chambly, in midafternoon, Dagaheari broke from the center of the lake toward the right shore and guided his canoe into a creek. Several miles upstream the creek broadened into another lake.

Stephen marveled at the beauty of the scene. There was no breeze and the waters of the lake reflected the afternoon sun like a mirror. On all sides, the mountains, their peaks defined clearly in the crystal air against a deep blue sky, seemed to drop into the waters of the lake.

That evening Stephen asked Lalonde if he knew where they were. The priest retrieved a worn map from Stephen's baggage and studied it. "This must be Lac St. Sacrament," said Lalonde. "The one the English call Lake George."

"It is an extraordinarily beautiful place, isn't it?" said Stephen.

"I was too tired to notice," said the priest.

With the passage of each day Lalonde grew more restless, and his complaints about his discomforts grew louder. Stephen had taken to smearing his exposed skin with bear grease, provided by the Indians, which helped to ward off the mosquitoes. But Lalonde could not stand the smell and the thought of grease on his skin set it to crawling. By now his face was a mass of bites. Each evening Stephen listened to his litany of complaints, and although he felt truly sorry for his superior, he grew weary of him.

The next morning they again carried canoes inland away from the lake. After a trek of about two miles, Stephen heard the sound of falling water. They came to a high waterfall. Below the falls Dagaheari ordered the canoes launched into the river, and they continued rapidly southward for about ten miles. A small creek flowed into the river that they traveled, and Dagaheari headed for it. For the rest of the day they paddled against the current of this stream until it narrowed and grew too shallow to support even the tiny draught of the canoes. Again they carried the craft and trekked through some dense woodlands along a well-marked trail. They carried for ten miles and finally, exhausted, they reached the banks of a slow-moving but deep river.

The Mohawk dropped his end of the canoe, walked over to the river, knelt down and drank deeply from it. "This is the river of my people," he said. "I have not seen it since my father took me to Caugnawaga. It is good to be home."

Kanowalohale, the main village of the Oneida, was about 150 miles west of the point where the mission party first encountered the Mohawk River. It consisted of about twenty-five longhouses containing several families each. The village was surrounded by a wooden stockade fifteen feet high.

Dagaheari led the party through the main gate. Stephen could feel eyes staring at him from the door of every longhouse. No adults came forward to greet them, but naked children halted their play in the streets to stare wide-eyed at the two blackrobes.

The chief walked the Jesuits to a small house, about twenty feet long, on the far side of the village from the main gate. There were no other dwellings on this side of the stockade. The Oneida gestured toward the house, and the Mohawk translated his words into French for Lalonde.

"The house is yours while you stay with us," said Dagaheari. "I must see Skenandon, the sachem. He will summon you when he is ready to speak with you."

Lalonde pushed aside the skins that covered the entrance to the house and stepped inside. Stephen followed him. The house was built with wooden frame posts about five feet apart and joined at the top by saplings, giving the roof a rounded effect. The frame was covered with cedar bark. The floor was dirt, pounded hard by much use. In the exact middle of the structure, there was a fire hearth beneath an opening in the roof, which allowed the smoke to escape. On either side of a central aisle and raised above the floor, there were two tiers of platforms made of wood poles and bark. This shortened longhouse had not been used in some time and was extremely dirty. As Stephen looked up at the roof, he saw the masked eyes of two raccoons observing him from their roost among the rafters. The empty house had become their lodging and from their chatter, it was clear that they resented this intrusion.

"It will take us a week to make this place livable," said Lalonde in disgust.

After leaving the Jesuits, Dagaheari went to the lodge of his sachem. He sat on some skins opposite the council fire, which burned in front of Skenandon's platform.

"I gather that my cousin has had a successful trip," said Skenandon.

"I have brought the blackrobes as you requested," responded Dagaheari.

"Good. How did they fare on the trip?"

"The chief blackrobe is a fool. He was of no use on the trip. He nearly caused the death of our Mohawk cousin. Even when on his best behavior, he did nothing but complain. The younger one is better. He is strong, says little, keeps quiet in a canoe and paddles well. He is also shrewder than he appears. He knows English but he never used it with me."

Skenandon suddenly looked interested. "How do you know this to be true?"

"He understood me when I spoke English. He knows the language."

Skenandon laughed. "You must have been very angry indeed if you spoke the white man's tongue, Dagaheari."

"If I were you, my cousin, I would knock the older blackrobe over the head today. The younger one you could spare and send to the English at Albany."

"But you are not me, Dagaheari," said Skenandon. "I was chosen sachem by our esteemed aunt, not you. And she chose me precisely because you would follow your instincts instead of your head and murder the blackrobes and bring down the wrath of Onontio on us."

"Onontio, the French governor, is far away and we can have the protection of the English against him whenever we ask for it," Dagaheari interrupted in anger.

"Will you ever learn, Dagaheari? Once we are forced to accept the protection of the English or the French, we will be destroyed. We must keep both sides guessing. Never let either be sure of us. Only then will the Oneida and all the Iroquois be safe."

"If you mistrust the English so much, why do you let the snake Wiggins come to our village to trade?"

"Wiggins is not an Englishman," said Skenandon. "He sides with none but himself."

"He should be banned from our villages," said Dagaheari with vehemence.

"He sells us guns," said the sachem.

"He sells us whiskey too," responded Dagaheari.

"The warriors demand both."

Dagaheari rose in disgust. "Now I hear you have approved the marriage of our clanswoman Gonwatsijayenni to Wiggins."

144

"It is good business and sound politics," said Skenandon.

Dagaheari turned to leave. He looked back at the sachem. "One warrior with a gun is worth ten with bow and arrow. But one hundred drunken warriors with one hundred guns are not worth one bitch in heat."

"So you say, Dagaheari," laughed Skenandon.

"When will you see the blackrobes?"

Skenandon thought for a moment. "There is no hurry," he said. "Let them worry about it for a while."

If Lalonde fretted about not meeting the sachem during the next few days, Stephen surely did not have time to join him in his worries. His first task was to drive out the original tenants of the house. He found a large stick on the ground outside the house and, using it like a warclub, he chased the protesting raccoons down from the rafters, up onto the top platforms and finally out the front door. They came to rest in the lowest branches of the maple tree that shaded the priests' house. There they sat staring angrily at Stephen.

"Now stay out," said Stephen, breathing heavily from the exertion of the chase. Behind him he heard giggling and turned to see a group of young girls, who looked about fourteen to sixteen years of age, watching him and laughing behind their hands. He smiled at them and bowed his best Versailles bow. He walked toward where they were standing. They ran away—all but one, a girl of about sixteen. She stood her ground as Stephen approached. He greeted her; she smiled but did not respond. Her smile was very beautiful, even if the girl was not. She was very thin and small. She seemed to consist mostly of bones housed uncomfortably under tightly drawn skin. If it were not for the outline of her young breasts, it would have been extremely difficult to tell that she had begun to mature. Her face bore the scars of the dreaded smallpox. She nodded to the young Jesuit and, turning her back to him, she walked to where her companions had regrouped. Stephen shrugged and returned to his work.

Recovering his stick, he tied twigs to the end of it and made a makeshift broom. The accumulated dust and animal droppings in the house took a whole afternoon to remove. With the approach of evening, Stephen went to look for Father Lalonde. He found him sitting by the stream that ran by the village. He was reading.

"Father, I have finished a fast cleaning of our house and I would like to start a meal, but we have no food."

"Surely our hosts will bring us some."

Stephen sighed. "I don't think they wish to treat us as guests, Father. I think they expect us to feed ourselves. If you would break open some of the trade goods, I will try to find food in one of the longhouses."

"You know where the trade goods are," said the priest. "Get them yourself and then get us something to eat."

Stephen returned to their house and withdrew a beaded necklace from his baggage. He really did not know where to begin his search, but he decided to try the largest of the houses. He walked across the central square. He passed a raised platform and entered the doorway of the longhouse boldly.

Stephen looked about him in amazement. The house was nearly four times as large as their own, and although the structure was almost the same, this house was actually lived in. There were four fires burning and at least thirty people in the building. Warriors sat on the platforms at the sides. Children ran naked on the dirt floors, playing games of war. Women were tending the cooking pots over the fires and, hanging from the rafters and piled on platforms near the cedar roof, were seasoning carcasses of animals and clay pots of dried corn and beans.

The appearance of the black-clad white man brought an instant silence, which spread like a shock wave. Where pandimonium had reigned before, all was quiet. Almost immediately Stephen felt he had been wrong to come unbidden into this place but, having erred, he felt that at least he should make the most of it and not come away without food. He walked toward a gray-haired woman who seemed in charge of the first cooking fire. Stretching out his hand with the beads, he pointed first to the stew in the pot and then toward the beads. He spoke the Mohawk word for "trade." The old lady screwed up her toothless face and turned her back on him.

From out of the recesses of a platform to Stephen's right, a voice broke the silence of the longhouse, speaking English. "Among our people it is considered bad manners for guests, even uninvited ones, to offer to pay for their food." The girl Stephen had seen earlier in the afternoon stepped down from the platform and stood before him.

"Please excuse my manners, then," said Stephen awkwardly in schoolroom English. "I did not mean to be rude. The priest and I have hunger and no food. I thought to buy it."

"Sit on my platform," the girl said. She walked to the cooking pot, spoke quietly to the old woman, scooped some stew out of the pot with a wooden bowl and returned with it to the platform where Stephen now sat. Life seemed to return to normal in the longhouse, except that the children came to stand before Stephen and the girl. They said nothing; they just stared.

"You eat it with your fingers," she instructed him. He reached for a piece of meat. "Careful. It's hot," she warned too late.

He dropped the meat and shoved his burned fingers into his mouth. Three of the longhouse dogs began to fight for the chance to eat the remains of a late companion. He tried more gingerly for a second piece.

"*Merci*—thank you," he corrected himself. "I do not know how you are called."

"My name is Gonwatsijayenni. But the whites can not say it. They call me Molly."

"Where did you learn English?" he asked.

"My little half-brother Joseph—Thayendanegea—attended the missionaries' school. Mr. Wheelock teaches many Mohawk boys. My brother taught me to speak English and now I am to marry an Englishman, a great man among his people, named Wiggins."

"You are not an Oneida then?"

"No." She looked offended. "I am the granddaughter of the great Brant—sachem of the lower castle of the Mohawks. I live with the Oneida only until Wiggins comes for me here. He is trading furs with the Seneca. Skenandon and Dagaheari are my kinsmen, members of my clan, the Turtle. My cousins entertain me until Wiggins arrives."

"I don't understand," said Stephen. "How can the Oneida be your kinsmen when you are a Mohawk?"

"Our families extend across tribal lines. This helps to bind together the council fires of our confederation."

Stephen nodded as if he understood and did not continue to question her on the politics and kinship patterns of the Iroquois. He ate another piece of meat and smiled at the small group of children in front of him. As if directed by an unseen hand, they all smiled at the same moment back at him. Stephen and Molly both laughed.

He turned to look at her more closely, but he saw that she noticed his stare; he looked away quickly, embarrassed. "Are you looking forward to your marriage?" he asked.

"If Wiggins is good to me, I will stay with him," she responded. "I don't care what he looks like, but they say he is very ugly."

"You have never seen the man?"

147

"No."

"Then how will you love him?" asked Stephen.

She grinned at him and pointed between her legs. "With this," she said.

Stephen became flustered. He ignored her gesture. "Your family has arranged this marriage, I gather."

"Yes. I must start having sons. Brant is growing old. Soon the women of our family will be called upon to name his successor as sachem. We will need boys growing to manhood and babies to become boys. That is the way it has always been."

Stephen had finished his food, but he was fascinated by the girl. He had not spoken to anyone other than Lalonde in weeks. Stephen put the wooden bowl back on the floor, and instantly one of the longhouse mongrels grabbed it and raced away. He lunged for the dog and missed. Molly laughed a second time; Stephen liked the sound of her laugh. He realized that she was laughing at him and that he must appear something of a fool, not knowing how to handle a mere dog. Again he tried to bring the conversation away from his embarrassment.

"What will happen if you don't like this Wiggins?" he asked her.

"I will leave him and find another man," she responded.

"How can you do that if you are already married to him?"

"Mohawk women live with many men until they find the one who is worthy to be the father of their children," said Molly.

"But that's immoral," objected Stephen.

She shrugged her shoulders. "That's what Wheelock says too. White men have strange ideas." She looked at Stephen and a sly smile began to appear. "How about you, Blackrobe? Do you have a woman?"

"No," said Stephen. "I am not married."

"Why not?" she asked. "You are old enough."

"I am a man of God," he said. "I will not marry."

"Wheelock is a man of God and he has a wife."

"He is a Protestant—a heretic," explained Stephen. "True men of God, like us blackrobes, do not have wives."

She stared at him for a moment and then her smile changed into a broad grin. "Ah, I know what you are. The other blackrobe—he is your mate. You are lovers of men, you blackrobes."

Stephen rose angrily from his seat on the platform. "Not at

all; you are wrong," he protested. He realized he should not be so angry with her. She had meant no harm and he was being extremely impolite. Once again a hush had descended upon the longhouse. Everyone was staring at him. He sat down again. "I am sorry for my rudeness," he said.

"No, it is I who must apologize. I have given you offense," she said.

"Among my people to be a lover of men is to be guilty of a great sin," said Stephen.

"I am truly sorry, Blackrobe; I have insulted you."

"No, you did not know." He was quiet for a while and the level of noise in the house grew again. "Molly, I would like it very much if we could be friends. While you await Mr. Wiggins, could you teach me the ways of the Iroquois? I would like to learn to understand your customs and language. Would you help me?"

"I will be your friend, Blackrobe," she said.

"One more thing, Molly," said Stephen. "I need some food for the other blackrobe and I must get back to him. He will be very cross with me."

The next morning, after Lalonde had said mass for Stephen, Dagaheari entered the Jesuit house. He looked about him in amusement at Stephen's feeble efforts to clean up. He said to Stephen in English, "Tell the priest that the sachem, Skenandon, wants him to attend a council of the chiefs tonight. He will be allowed to address the council and tell us his plans for his visit with the Oneida."

Without waiting for Stephen to translate or for a reply, the Indian left the house. Stephen converted Dagaheari's "visit" to "stay" and took much of the sting from the Oneida's comment. Lalonde took quill and ink and paper to his place by the creek to work on a sermon for the council, leaving the house to Stephen.

Stephen began to work immediately. First, he tore out the platforms from the sides of the longhouse. The poles that had constituted the platforms he placed on end in holes in the dirt floor, dividing the house into four compartments: a bedroom for Lalonde; a bedroom for himself; a common room, where the fire would remain directly under the roof opening; and the rest of the house—by far the major portion of it—he left undivided. This would be the chapel. Again using the platform wood, he constructed a series of low benches for the congregation and a wobbly table to serve his superior as a desk or an altar, as the occasion demanded. By the time he had finished his work, it was late afternoon. He was tired, his shirt was soaked with sweat and he was hungry. He had not eaten all day, but there would be food at the council; maybe Lalonde could convince the Oneida to give them their daily bread.

The drums began to beat with the setting of the sun, a slow, rhythmic beating. Stephen stepped to the door of his longhouse to see the beginning of the council ceremony. Lalonde, dressed in his best habit and cape, joined him. Across the village square, before the ceremonial platform, two fires had been lighted. Beyond the great longhouses, on the far side of the square from the Jesuit house, a low, moaning chant rose into the crimson sky. First it was slow and dirgelike, then it grew faster and became almost cheerful. Its mood followed the beating the the drums. From out of the longhouse Stephen had visited earlier walked the sachems of the Oneida, not only those from Kanowalohale but those from Stockbridge and Brothertown as well.

The only person Stephen recognized was Dagaheari, and even he was hard to pick out, dressed in his finest deerskins and bedecked with feathers. The sachems approached one of the fires in the square and formed themselves about it in a large semicircle. The chanting grew nearer and louder. From behind the great longhouses the rest of the Oneida appeared. They were dancing in a slow shuffle in time with the drums. Many were accenting the drumbeats with the gourd rattles they held in their hands.

First came the warriors, all naked except for loincloths. Their bodies were oiled and already glistening with sweat. Behind them danced the women, and the children brought up the rear. The leading dancers reached the Jesuit house and signaled to Lalonde and Stephen to join them. The Jesuits went to the front of the procession without trying to copy the shuffle step of the march.

As the front of the line reached the semicircle of chiefs, an Indian in the center of the circle, splendid in feathers and paint, motioned the two white men to leave the line and join the chiefs. Lalonde was led to a place of honor at the head of the circle, while Stephen was guided to his seat near the end of the line.

The dancers and chanters, crowding together, closed the semicircle about the fire. Dagaheari rose from his place.

Taking a large pipe from the sachem next to him, he filled it with tobacco and presented it to Skenandon. The sachem rose to receive it from his cousin. Night had settled quickly upon Kanowalohale, and beyond the council fire nothing could be seen.

Skenandon lit the pipe. He blew the smoke toward the black sky and passed the pipe to Lalonde. The Jesuit took some smoke into his mouth and, copying the Oneida, he blew it out with a slight cough. The pipe made its way down the line of chiefs until it reached Stephen. He allowed some of the smoke to enter his mouth and blew it out quickly. It tasted harsh; he wanted to spit out the taste of the tobacco, but he resisted the temptation.

Skenandon rose again. The drums and the chanting ceased.

"My brothers," he said, "I welcome you to Kanowalohale. We have come to council to listen to the blackrobe sent to us by Onontio in New France. He has come to tell us about the French Jesus and he will live with us and bring peace between ourselves and Onontio. Let us listen to the blackrobe." He nodded toward Lalonde and took his place before the fire.

Lalonde rose. The only sound that could be heard was the cracking of the burning wood in the fire. One log collapsed and sent a column of sparks into the dark night.

"People of the Oneida nation." Stephen translated Lalonde's French into English, which most of the Oneida had no difficulty in understanding. "I have come from Onontio, the governor, and from our great chief and father, King Louis, to bring to you the word of our God. I bring to you the love of Jesus and the love of His servants, the governor of New France and the King of France. If you will listen to the words I preach and come to the longhouse where I live, I will bring to you eternal life with Jesus in heaven. I know that others have come to you and told you that they could bring you to Jesus. But the English preachers are liars. They have left the longhouse of Jesus and have tried to light a separate council fire. It is they who have killed the true Jesus. But He has risen from the dead and He has sent me to you so that you may know Him and not be fooled by the English."

There was a stirring in the audience as Lalonde's attack on the English began. Many of the chiefs from Stockbridge and Brothertown had been educated by English missionaries, and it was clear to Stephen as he translated Lalonde's words that his companion had lost the support of a large number of his listeners. But he could not alter Lalonde's words, nor could

151

he stop the priest from the course he had taken. Across the firelight he could make out the face of Dagaheari, and he saw that the Oneida was smiling.

Lalonde was falling deeper and deeper into a trap. For the next ten minutes he continued to attack the English and to antagonize the Protestant-trained Oneida. Skenandon looked angry. When Lalonde had finished, the sachem had regained control of himself and he rose to thank the priest.

"The blackrobe has spoken from his heart about his Jesus. We must study his words carefully." Stephen never had time to translate into French; one of the sachems from Brother-town rose.

"I have no need to study his words. The blackrobe is a liar." There was a stirring in the crowd and murmurs of agreement from some of the other chiefs.

"We will not comment on the speech of the blackrobe, my brother," Skenandon interrupted. "We are Iroquois. It is not our way. We must meet among ourselves tomorrow before we give answer to our friend. Now we will dance and prepare a feast for our guests."

As soon as he had finished speaking, the drums began to beat again and the warriors broke from the circle and began a frenzied dash toward the second fire. Stephen was staring at the dancers and did not notice the women as they brought platters of cornbread and venison to the semicircle of chiefs. He could not tear his eyes from the dancers; their bodies, contorted and leaping, looked like black shadows outlined in the flames of the fire. It was not until Dagaheari touched his shoulder that he broke his stare.

"We must join Skenandon and the priest," he said. "They wish to talk." Stephen knew that the Oneida was pleased with the way the council had gone. But then he had never counted Dagaheari among the friends of the mission.

"Well, Etienne," said Lalonde when Stephen joined him at the head of the fire. "It went well, didn't it?"

"I hope so, Father."

"Oh, I'm sure of it," said the priest. "Now I want you to tell Skenandon that we will be needing food, firewood and water carried to our house every day. That is, if he wishes to keep us here in this village. Tell him that I grow weary of the poverty he forces upon me."

Stephen relayed Lalonde's demands to Dagaheari. The Oneida laughed. "He really thinks he will be staying among us after tonight. Your friend is an ass, Blackrobe."

When Dagaheari told Skenandon of the demands, the

sachem, who was furious with the Jesuit for his stupidity, displayed none of his emotion. "Tell the priest that he will receive what he needs," said the sachem.

"In that case," said Dagaheari in anger, "he will receive a tomahawk in his skull."

"No, my cousin. Tomorrow I will smooth over the Frenchman's blunders with the chiefs. He will stay among us, but we will minimize the damage he might do. We will feed the two of them and keep them warm, but we will not allow them to preach among us. We will forbid all to go to their ceremonies. The Oneida must remain united. We cannot allow an English party or a French party to exist among us. It is bad enough that the English have so many friends among us already."

Dagaheari grunted assent. He had hoped for more, but tying the Frenchmen's hands in this way was enough for the present.

When Lalonde heard that his demands would be met, he smiled glowingly at Stephen. "I have succeeded beyond my fondest hopes this evening, Etienne. Come, let us eat and enjoy our triumph."

Stephen, surprised by Lalonde's victory, began to wonder if he had completely misjudged what had happened. "Perhaps Father Lalonde is right," he thought. "I don't think I will ever understand these people."

The leaves of the maple tree by the Jesuit house were scarlet and yellow. The nights turned bitterly cold.

Lalonde sat at his desk before the fire in the common room, his cape draped about his shoulders and gloves on his hands. Stephen entered the room carrying more kindling and logs for the fire.

"It is freezing out there tonight, Father," he said. The priest did not respond but continued to stare into the fire. "Molly says we will have snow any night now."

Lalonde gave a start. "Are you back already, Etienne? What did you say?"

Stephen threw another log on the fire. "I said that Molly is predicting snow."

"You saw her again today? I gather that her husband-to-be has still not arrived."

"I see her almost every day now, Father. She tells me that my Mohawk is now better than her English."

The priest returned to staring at the fire.

Stephen felt sorry for Lalonde For weeks now he had said his morning mass in the presence of Stephen alone. He had prepared his first sermon and showed it to Stephen, to give him a chance to translate it into a language his flock could understand. The sermon remained undelivered. No one came to mass. The children ran from Stephen if he approached them. Only Molly would speak to him. When Stephen attempted to learn from her what was happening, she avoided his questions or claimed ignorance of Oneida ways. Every morning the old woman whom Stephen had first seen in the great longhouse at the cooking pot delivered a basket of food and a pile of wood, enough for the day. Other than that, they communicated with none of the Oneida.

The skins covering the front entryway of the longhouse were pushed aside, allowing a blast of the evening cold to fill the chapel. Stephen, feeling the temperature change, pulled back the skins that divided the common room from the chapel. Standing, looking at the strange arrangement of the benches, was the sachem, Skenandon.

"May I be of service to you?" asked Stephen in dialect.

Skenandon nodded. "I wish to see Lalonde," said the sachem.

Stephen motioned him to enter the common room. The boy spread his cloak on the floor to make a proper seat for the chief and pulled down a haunch of venison, cut off two strips and began to heat them over the fire.

Lalonde greeted the chief formally. They had not seen each other during the long and disappointing summer.

"My brother, the blackrobe, is well?" asked Skenandon.

Stephen hesitated over some of Skenandon's words but they were close enough to Molly's Mohawk that he was able to translate for his superior.

"As well as can be expected under the circumstances," responded the Jesuit.

"The blackrobe is unhappy with his circumstances? Have we not given you a house and food?"

The Jesuit threw his hands into the air. "Look at our circumstances. We live in a wretched and drafty hovel. We eat leftover food and no one—not one of your people—has come to our services in the chapel. Every morning I say mass for Etienne and for him alone. Our mission is a failure. I feel I must write to Onontio and tell him that I have failed and that the Oneida are not his brothers."

"It would not be good if the blackrobes left Kanowalohale. It is winter. You would never make it back to New France."

"Well, freezing could be no worse than dying of boredom here," responded Lalonde.

"The blackrobe has lost his patience. We Oneida believe in patience."

Lalonde ignored his charge. "I cannot believe that no one came to seek my message. They were forbidden to come, weren't they?"

Skenandon smiled. "The blackrobe is shrewder now than he was at the council. The only way I could get the chiefs to agree to let you stay with us was to forbid any of our people to visit you. But now I watch you grow restless. I do not want the blackrobes to grow tired and leave us."

"So that is important to you after all," said Lalonde sarcastically. "You do fear the power of Onontio."

"The Oneida are not fools. Onontio speaks with the power of the great king, Louis."

Lalonde smiled.

"But the English governor in New York, he speaks with the power of the great king, George. We must worry about him too."

"You cannot serve two masters, Skenandon."

"We serve no masters," said Skenandon fiercely. "That is the way my people will survive. We will not suffer the fate of the Narragansetts, the Nipmucks and the Pequots."

"Onontio does not murder his red brothers. It was the Bastonois who murdered the people of those tribes."

"True, Onontio's friends were the Hurons. We do not meet many of them on the trails any longer."

Lalonde gasped in surprise. "It was the Iroquois who were responsible for that. It was your people who destroyed them and murdered my brother blackrobes too."

Skenandon laughed. "Lalonde knows too much for me. True, we destroyed the Hurons. They refused trade. They grew greedy. Onontio told them not to trade with us but to bring all their beaver to him in Montreal. The Hurons became more French than the French."

Lalonde stared angrily at the sachem. Stephen, who had been translating the words of each man, took advantage of the pause to take the deer meat steaks from the fire and place them on platters. Skenandon pulled out a bottle of whiskey from under his robe.

"This will take some of the night chill from our bones," he said. He pulled the cork from the bottle and took a long drink from it. He passed the bottle to Stephen. Stephen looked at Lalonde, who nodded his approval. The young Jesuit followed the model of the chief and took a mouthful of whiskey. He passed the bottle to Lalonde, who politely refused the offer. The Indian sat silently while eating his meat. When he had finished he rose to leave.

"Lalonde will have some Oneida to preach to if he will promise to remain in Kanowalohale," said the chief as he stood before the door of the common room. "Will he stay?"

"He will stay," said the priest.

The chief left.

Stephen watched him walk through the chapel and out the front of the house. As he turned to speak to Lalonde, he noticed the bottle on the table. "Skenandon has forgotten his whiskey, Father. I will run after him and return it."

"You need not do that, Etienne," said the priest. "Leave the whiskey with me. I will return it to him. Go to bed now. I will see you in the morning."

Stephen picked up his cape; he would need it to keep warm this night. After he left, Lalonde continued to stare into the fire. After some moments he held his head in his hands and began to sob softly. Slowly his arm reached for the bottle on the table.

The snow came the next day. Driven by howling winds, it whirled in the alleys between the longhouses and rushed headlong across the open square of the village. It piled against the sides of the palisade and the longhouses in great drifts.

Father Lalonde had overslept and mass had been delayed. No food had been brought to the Jesuit house and Stephen decided to spare the old woman who brought their rations her trek from the great longhouse. Throwing his cloak about his shoulders, he stepped out the front door.

The wind grabbed his cloak and he had to grasp it, pulling it closer to his body. It was impossible to see across the square. There was no path to follow. The snow was already piled at least a foot high everywhere. Putting his head down into the wind, he set off in the direction of the great longhouse.

Stephen trudged through the snow, skirting the drifts. The outline of the longhouse loomed darkly out of the white, but before he could reach the entry, he tripped and fell into a drift. When he rose, brushing snow from his cloak, he saw a dark form almost completely covered with snow at his feet. He had fallen over a body. He brushed away the snow and turned the body onto its back. He could barely recognize the frozen features of the toothless old woman whom he had first approached for food and who had brought the food for the Jesuits every morning since the council.

156

Stephen lifted her and hoisted her body over his shoulder. He pushed aside the skins blocking the longhouse entrance. Dagaheari was the first to come to his side as he laid the old woman down on the blankets on Molly's platform. The girl was not in the house.

"I found her lying in a drift near the entryway," said Stephen. "Is she alive?"

The woman lay face-down on the blanket. Dagaheari stuck his hand beneath her to feel for her heart. "She is alive," he said, "but barely."

"Do you know anyone who might take care of her?" asked Stephen.

"She is my aunt," said Dagaheari. "I will look after her. She complained this morning of a headache. But she is old and always complains of aches. No one paid much attention to her."

The Indian turned her over onto her back. As the light from the fire fell on her face, Dagaheari gasped and leaped back. Her face was covered with red, pus-filled eruptions. "It's the pox," he shouted. "Get her out of here." He turned to Stephen. "And get yourself out of here."

Stephen looked up at the Indian in amazement. "What's wrong?" he asked.

"It's the pox. Get her out of here or we will all get it."

"Where can I go? Where do I take her?"

"There is a hut about one half mile down the creek. Go there. There is wood for a fire. We will send food. Now get out of here."

His shout had sent most of the inhabitants of the house racing toward the rear of the building. Step by step, Dagaheari backed away from Stephen and joined the others. The young Jesuit was left alone with the old woman. He wanted to protest. He wanted to ask for help. But all he could see in their faces was panic. He picked the woman up again and went out into the night.

There was no path to follow, only drifting mounds of snow to avoid. He found the heavy, barked walls of the village and groped ahead of him like a blind man. The old woman began to slip from his shoulder and he had to stop to shift his burden. He followed the palisade around the perimeter of Kanowalohale until he came to the gate of the town. He knew that he was now at the dangerous part of his mission. He must go in a straight line to the creek. If he missed it, he would never find the hut and he and the old woman would die in the snow.

The wind whipped his face, caking his eyebrows with blown snow and freezing the moisture in his nostrils. He was breathing heavily as he trudged through the drifts. He could not avoid them by veering to the right or the left for fear of missing the creek. He could not feel his toes or the tips of his fingers. With each step the woman seemed to gain a pound. Even in the numbing cold, Stephen could feel the clamminess of the sweat forming on his skin beneath his habit.

He could not see shapes ahead of him; he could only determine relative shades of light and darkness. At one point his surroundings seemed to grow whiter, and he was about to assume that the snow was falling even harder when his foot broke through the snow into water. Then he realized that the whiteness was only the absence of the trees' shadows. He had entered the meadow that lined the banks of the creek. He had not lost his way.

He dared not leave the water. He would find the lean-to if he followed the course of the stream. His shoes were already filled with the numbing water. Any damage he might suffer from wet feet had already been done. He waded shin-deep, peering into the whiteness on the right bank for signs of a hut.

After walking about three-quarters of a mile, he decided that he must have missed it. He felt he could not continue. He dropped to his knees on the shoreline. The body of the Indian woman fell forward from his shoulder onto the ground. Her fall was cushioned by more than two feet of snow. Relieved of his burden, Stephen fell onto his face, gasping for breath. He knew he must rise and continue. He knew that if he lay where he was, he would die, but all he wanted to do was sleep. He shook his head to drive the sleep away. Above the riverbank and some way behind him, he saw the light of a fire. He would summon up the strength to make one last effort. He could not pick up the woman again, but he could not leave her behind. He grabbed her buckskin tunic and dragged her behind him through the snow.

The fire grew larger and Stephen called out. No use. His voice was lost in the howl of the wind. He fell down again; he began to laugh. What a joke, he thought. I'm going to die in the cold a few hundred feet from a fire. As he slipped into unconsciousness he felt a hand touch him. He saw a face lean over him.

When Molly returned to the longhouse, Dagaheari was waiting for her at the entrance. Before she had time to brush the snow from the blanket she had wrapped about her, he had thrust a large bundle into her arms and was aiming her toward the outside. "It is our aunt, clan mother of the Turtles; she has the pox. The young blackrobe has taken her to your wedding hut. You must go there and care for them. Do not let the blackrobe return to the village. He is infected. If he returns we will all die."

Instinctively Molly touched her scarred face—the dread smallpox—the scourge that had robbed her of her beauty. She knew why Dagaheari had selected her to nurse its victims. The disease had not killed her; she had triumphed over it and it could harm her no longer. Without saying a word she took the bundle and left.

She had none of Stephen's hesitancy about finding the hut. She had built it herself in anticipation of Wiggins' return and her long-delayed wedding. When she arrived, she constructed as large a fire as she could in the hearth and pushed back the skins of the entryway so that the fire could be seen from outside. Wrapping her blanket about her more closely, she went back out into the storm to look for signs of Stephen and the clan mother.

She had expected them to approach the hut from upstream, not realizing that Stephen had bypassed her. She waited for some minutes in the cold. Fearful that the fire might be extinguished, she returned to the entryway of the hut. Then she heard what sounded like a cry above the noise of the wind. It came from downstream. Maybe it was only the wind. She was about to reenter the hut, but instead she decided to search the area downstream. She found Stephen in the snow, almost unconscious but still holding the old woman's tunic with his clenched fist.

When Stephen opened his eyes, he was lying close to the fire, bundled in furs. His cape, habit, shirt, breeches and stockings were hanging from the rafters. Molly was leaning over her aunt, attempting to spoon broth into her mouth. Stephen could see her face in profile, lighted only by the flickering lights and shadows of the fire between them. He knew immediately that it had been her face that he had seen and that it had been she who had found and rescued them.

He looked at the ashen face of the stricken woman. Her chest heaved in and out, and he could hear a rasping sound in her throat as she breathed.

"How is she?" he asked.

Molly turned her head toward him and smiled. "You're

159

awake. She is not good at all. She has a raging fever and the exposure did her great harm, I fear. She is having trouble breathing. Add this to her age and I think there is little hope."

"I'm sorry," he said. "Maybe if Dagaheari had allowed us to stay in the longhouse, it would have been better."

Molly shook her head. "Dagaheari is a brave warrior but against the pox he is like a frightened child. All my people are, except for those of us who have survived it. He was right not to let you stay. Even bringing her back into the longhouse was a mistake. But he should have led you to this place himself or awaited my return. You might have died as well."

"You are sure she will die?"

"My aunt has been a great power among our people. She has named sachems, including Skenandon, and she has given or withheld her assent to wars. She has given birth to many warriors. She has given pleasure to many brave and wise men. In her last days she has fed her people. She was the nourisher from the beginning of her womanhood to the very end of it. She only gave life; she would never steal it away. She had seen the pox come to our people many times and always she escaped it. Not this time. She knew she had it. I am sure she lay down in the snows to die and to spare the rest of us."

Stephen stared into the fire. "And I brought her back into the house," he said.

"You did what you thought was right. You could not have known. I would have done the same." She turned to face the old woman again and placed her hand behind her aunt's head. She brought the bowl of broth to her lips. Most of it ran down the woman's chin onto her chest. She made no effort to swallow.

"Have you ever had the pox, Blackrobe?"

"No," he responded. "You think I will be next?"

"Yes; it is rare that it spares one so directly in contact with it."

"What should I do?"

"Pray to your Jesus to spare you. You will have to stay here for the next few days. I will ask the other blackrobe to come to you."

"No, don't do that. Father Lalonde must not be infected. If he dies the mission ends."

"If you die, the mission ends for you," she responded. "All right, I will stay with you."

He was fully awake now and comfortably warm under the

furs. He was also quite aware of his nakedness. "I should get dressed."

"No, your clothes are still wet. Leave them hanging until morning."

"I must find something to cover myself with if I am to be up and around."

"Why?" she asked. "It is warm enough in here so far. You have nothing to hide. I saw when I took your clothes off you. You are well formed."

Stephen was flustered by her bluntness. It had not occurred to him to think of how his clothes came to be hanging from the rafter, and the idea of the young girl undressing him was mortifying. He lay back again in the comfort of the furs and was quiet, listening to the strained breathing of the old woman and the rush of the winds through the branches of the pines that surrounded the hut on three sides. The wind's intensity was less now. The snow had ceased to fall but the wind continued to blow the already fallen snow into great drifts.

"I suppose I should be afraid," he said, breaking the silence.

"The blackrobe is a brave man. All in Kanowalohale know how you saved one of my people on the way here. Now the Oneida will learn of your courage in bringing my aunt to this hut."

"Those were instinctive things, Molly. One doesn't think about saving a drowning man. But now I must be brave just lying here, just waiting. What are the symptoms?"

"I was a child when the pox struck me but I remember pain—headache and pain under my arms—and then fever," she answered.

The clan mother began to cough. Molly raised her upper body from the bed to ease her breathing, but the coughing continued—a racking cough that shook her frail body. She mumbled some words that Stephen could not understand and Molly, bending over her, whispered into her ear. The old one smiled, closed her eyes and the rasp of her breathing ceased.

"She is gone," said Molly. Stephen made the sign of the cross and prayed while the Mohawk girl lifted the fur covering and placed it over the old woman's face.

Stephen was quiet for several minutes. "What did she say to you before she died?" he said finally.

"She asked me if I planned to sleep with you," she answered. "Please forgive me. I told her yes. I knew it would please her."

This time Stephen was more puzzled than embarrassed. "Why would that please her?"

"Because you are brave and she thought we might make strong sons and wise daughters together."

Molly wrapped her aunt's body in furs and tied the furs in place with rawhide. Then she dragged the body toward the entrance. Stephen rose instinctively to help her but sat down again to cover himself.

"I must bury her body in the snow," said Molly. "We will be in this hut for the next few days. She will begin to smell if she stays here. I will mark the place with wood and after we leave here I will bring others to help lift her body into the trees, away from animals. Then we will give her a respectful funeral."

Molly left the hut, dragging the fur-wrapped body behind her. Stephen got out from under the furs and reached up to feel his clothing. His shirt was dry but everything else was still wet. He walked over to the fire and threw on another log, noting that there were not too many more, and then he returned to the warmth of the furs.

Molly reentered the hut. "It's getting very cold outside," she said.

"We don't have much wood left," said Stephen. She nodded. "I hope you don't think me rude, Molly," said Stephen softly. "I seem to be most rude when I don't understand your customs. But you seemed to have been very close to your aunt, yet I see no signs of mourning now that she has died."

"I barely knew the clan mother. She was an Oneida and I am a Mohawk. I have known her well only for these few months that I have waited for Wiggins. But even had she been my own mother, I would not have cried for her. She had a full life. She loved, she served, she nourished and she died."

She poured some broth from the cooking pot into two bowls and offered one to Stephen as she sat down next to him. Stephen drank the soup hungrily and she poured him a second bowl. The winds lessened even more, but through the cracks and seams of the hut the bitter cold seeped in. Molly placed the last log on the fire. Night had come but they had not noticed. The darkness outside had merely become a bit darker. Stephen lay on his back, staring at the shadow of the flames as they formed grotesque shapes on the ceiling of the hut. He did not notice when Molly slipped out of her deerskin dress and climbed naked under her fur blanket. The shadows from the flames grew shorter and shorter but before he could see them disappear altogether, Stephen fell asleep.

He was not sure if it was the cold or the sound of the girl's weeping that awakened him. He reached over to touch her shoulder with his hand. "Molly, are you all right?"

She turned to face him, wiping the tears from her face with her hand. "I'm sorry," she said. "I'm not as brave as I thought. I was weeping for my aunt and I suppose for myself."

"Why for yourself?" he asked.

She smiled at him and took his hand in hers. "I'm lonely. I should be married by now but this Wiggins stays on and on with the Seneca. He should have returned a month ago. Perhaps he has heard that I am ugly. Perhaps he will never come for me. Am I that ugly, Blackrobe?"

"Of course you're not ugly," said Stephen. He raised himself on his elbow and looked down into her face. "You are beautiful."

She reached up and touched the scar on his eyebrow and traced her fingers gently along the lines of his face to his chin. She put her arm about his neck, drew him down toward her and kissed him. Stephen started to pull back but he knew he wanted her. He returned her kiss and put all doubts out of his mind. He lifted the furs that covered her body and joined her under them. He reached for her breasts, cupping one in his hand and covering the nipple of the other with his mouth. As he sucked her breast, she reached for his already erect penis and began to stroke it gently.

He raised his head again and looked into her face. "I've never done this before. You'll have to help me," he said. She started to laugh but checked herself when she saw the pained look on his face. She reached for him and guided him into her. He was very excited now and moved rapidly. He placed his face in the grove of her neck and shoulder. She ran her hand across his shoulders and back, which were covered with sweat. He moved even more rapidly. She could feel his body grow more and more tense. Just at that moment Stephen stiffened. He raised himself off her body with his hands and then with a low, drawn-out moan he collapsed on top of her.

They lay joined together for some moments, Stephen's face again hidden in the groove of her neck. He said nothing but then she realized that he was sobbing. She did not ask him why. Instead, she held him tightly until the sobs stopped and the regular breathing of sleep began.

Molly entered the crowded chapel of the Jesuit house. On both sides of the room the benches that Stephen had built were filled with Oneida. They were dressed in their finest and even the children, who normally ran naked and wild in the longhouses, were dressed and respectfully quiet. Father Lalonde was completing his morning mass. He turned and blessed his congregation. Molly sat on the last bench and waited until the congregation had left the chapel. Then she followed Lalonde into the common room after he had finished unvesting.

"May I help you, girl?" said the priest, who was eating some bread and standing at the one table in the room.

Molly did not understand his French, but she handed him the note that Stephen had labored over that morning.

Dear Reverend Father, Pax Christi.

As you have been told, I am under a quarantine. This morning I am feeling not at all well. My head hurts and I believe I am feverish. I must see you because I fear that I am in grave danger of death. I want to receive the last rites of our Mother the church. I wish to make my confession to you. I have sinned greatly and I desire to make my peace with my creator before I meet him. I know I should not ask you to come. But I am afraid. Perhaps you can hear my confession without entering the hut. Please come, Father, please.

Etienne LaGarde, S.J.

As Lalonde read the note the hand in which he held it began to tremble. He sat down at the table and pondered the paper for some moments. He looked up at Molly and spoke the Mohawk word for "sick." She nodded and repeated the word. He rose and went to the chest that stood in the corner of the room. He opened it and began to rummage through its contents until he finally found paper, ink and a quill and returned to the table. Molly waited patiently for his response.

Dear Mr. LaGarde, P.C.

I am sorry to hear of your illness. I think it most ill-timed of you to request me to come to hear your confession. To do so would put me in grave danger of contracting the smallpox. I have no fear for myself, but my death would cut off the work that we have been ordered under holy obedience to perform. For the first time since we arrived here last summer, many Oneida are coming to our services. Although I cannot preach to

164

them, since I do not speak their language, nevertheless their presence at the sacrifice of the mass will do much to spread divine grace in this community.

I cannot come to you at this time. The disease is confined to the one longhouse and even Skenandon has more concern for the future of the mission than you. He will let none of the Oneida from the affected house attend our services. I am sure that you exaggerate the seriousness of your danger and your sinfulness. I will ask Skenandon to have someone look after you. Rest comfortably and then hurry back. We have much to do.

Paul Lalonde, S.J.

He folded the paper in quarters and handed it to the girl. She took it from him but continued to stand before his desk. Stephen had told her to guide Lalonde to the hut. Finally he pointed to the door and told her to leave. She hesitated but then, realizing that he did not plan to accompany her, she walked quickly from the house.

She stepped across the square to the great longhouse where she lived. As she entered she knew that something was wrong. The house smelled foul. It was not the usual smell of thirty to fifty people cooking and living, but a sick smell. The house had been divided in two by animal skins hanging from the rafters. Dagaheari greeted her as she entered.

"What is wrong here?" she asked him.

"The pox is spreading. We have about ten cases in this house, but it has not yet spread to any other. All those showing symptoms are being moved to the back of the house."

Molly walked to the middle of the house and pushed aside the deerskin barrier. She stepped through to the other side. On the dirt floor were strewn the bodies of the sick. One old man lay totally naked near the barrier. He was not dead but he was too weak to move. He had not been able to crawl to the corner of the house to relieve himself and his legs and the floor about him were covered with excrement. He rose to one elbow when he saw Molly, and his other arm reached out toward her in a gesture of desperation. Two children abandoned by terrified parents sat huddled in the center of the room, crying. Their bodies were a mass of sores. The smell of the room was overwhelming. Molly placed her hand over her nose and mouth. She turned and allowed the skins to fall back into place.

"I must return here," she said to Dagaheari. "I can not stay with the blackrobe when my own people suffer so. Perhaps I can bring him here also."

"When so many suffer, one more should not make a difference," Dagaheari replied.

"When was the last time any of the sick were fed?" she asked.

"They have not been fed," he responded. "No one will go in there to feed them."

"Why didn't you at least leave food for them? You did not hesitate to come to my hut with food and wood for the blackrobe."

Dagaheari looked astonished and hurt at the same time. "I have not been near your hut," he said.

"Who fed us then? Every morning there has been a bundle with enough food and wood for the day left outside the hut. I assumed it was from you."

"I have been too busy here," said Dagaheari. "Perhaps it was the other blackrobe."

Molly had strong doubts, but if it was Lalonde, then she was prepared to think better of him. "Dagaheari, get the women to heat some water and cook some food for the sick," she ordered. "Bring all the blankets and furs that belong to the sick to the other side. I must make them all as comfortable as possible." She pulled aside the skins again and reentered the sickroom.

As soon as the blankets had been delivered, she placed them on the empty platforms and made up a pallet for each of the victims. Most of the sick could walk with some help. She offered her arm to them and brought them to their beds. She placed the two children together. They clung to each other, and she had not the heart to separate them. She left the old man until last. As soon as the hot water arrived she sponged his body clean. He could not walk and she could not carry him, so she made up his bed on the floor where he lay.

A large pot of stew was delivered to the edge of the barrier by two women. Molly ladled portions of dog meat into bowls. Those that could feed themselves did so; those that could not, she fed. One by one she spoke to each of the sick. They would get well, she told them, if they kept covered until the fever broke. On the foreheads of those with high fevers she placed cloths dipped in cool water. When she came to the old man, she saw that he was dead. Much of the soothing effect of her presence was lost when she dragged his body past the beds of the others, out the rear entryway, out into the snow.

The wails of the sick accompanied Molly's work. She opened the entryway again and allowed the cold air to enter briefly and drive out the foul smell. Using a large wooden platter as a shovel, she scooped up the waste, from both humans and dogs, that littered the floor. It took her nearly five hours of work. When she finished, it was time to feed her patients again.

When all had been fed a second time, Molly, her blanket thrown over her shoulders, stepped back into the front of the longhouse. All the Oneidas moved away from her. She walked toward the front entrance. Dagaheari, obviously steeling himself, approached her. "Will you be back?" he asked.

She nodded. "I must bring the blackrobe back with me."

Her head was reeling when she stepped out into the cold air. To her it seemed as though a lifetime had passed since she had left Stephen in her hut that morning. She walked through the village gate and toward the creek. Approaching the hut, she noted that no smoke rose from the chimney hole. As she hurried closer, she saw several sets of tracks in the snow, leading to and away from the hut. She tensed and covered the rest of the distance quietly. Drawing back the skin of the entryway, she could see, even in the dim glow of the almost burned-out fire, that the hut was empty. She stepped inside and looked about for signs of a struggle. There were none. Molly went outside again and followed the tracks that led away from the hut. At first there were two sets of footprints. One was Indian; his moccasin tracks were clear. The other set belonged to a white man—Stephen. They were not so distinct. He was dragging his feet. Then halfway to the creek, Stephen's tracks disappeared and the Indian's sank much deeper into the snow. She followed the single set of tracks until they entered the creek and disappeared also.

For several days after they had made love, Stephen had had difficulty looking at Molly, much less talking to her. It was not that he blamed her for what had happened. To the contrary, he blamed himself exclusively. He was in despair. Never before, when he had failed to live up to his ideals, had he been left alone. He wished that Father LaGarde were with him to console him, to hear his confession or even to whip him for his sin. But there was no one.

As the days of his quarantine progressed, his despair grew. He was sick and he knew it. His head pounded and he was feverish. There was no alternative but to turn to Lalonde, a

167

man whom he did not respect but a man who was his religious superior and the only source of consolation to him for hundreds of miles.

It took nearly all his strength to compose his note to Lalonde, and he was too exhausted and feverish to notice when Molly left with the message in the morning. His skin felt as if it were on fire. He threw off the furs Molly had so carefully placed over him before leaving. His eyes stung, and it was not just the normal sting from the wood fire in the hut. They ached with fever. He looked down at his naked chest and stomach; even with his blurred vision he could see the beginnings of the pox eruptions.

He slipped off into a restless sleep. Once again he saw the flame-engulfed open mouth approaching him. The flames leaped from the mouth and formed figures of red. There was the form of a naked woman, covered with open sores. A second form was that of a man, his back turned toward the woman. A third form of grey blotted out the other two; it was a face, coming closer and closer, an ugly but friendly face. It was Socono. Stephen awoke, but the form in front of him did not disappear.

"How are you, little brother?" said Socono.

"I am sick, Socono. Help me. Take me to Father LaGarde before I die."

"You are not going to die. I will take care of you. The disease is spreading in the Oneida village. I don't think your nurse will return. I must take care of you myself. Can you stand?"

"Yes, I must stand."

"Where are your clothes?"

"Yes, if I had put on my clothes, it would never have happened."

Socono realized that Stephen would not be of much help to him. He found the boy's breeches and shirt. He threw the habit into the corner and grabbed a heavy blanket and the Jesuit cape. Stephen could not dress himself, and Socono had to struggle to get his limp arms and legs into the clothes. He stood Stephen on his feet, wrapped him tightly in the blanket and threw the cape over his shoulders.

Socono placed his arm about Stephen and led him outside into the bright sun. He knew that someone would come for Stephen eventually and would be able to follow their tracks. He had taken enough of a chance already, coming this close to the Oneida village every morning to provide Stephen with food and wood. He did not want anyone to discover his hiding place. He made for the river to hide his tracks. Only a few steps into their journey, however, Stephen started to collapse. Socono caught him before he fell and lifted him into his arms. Then he stepped into the river.

Ice had not yet formed, but the current moved sluggishly. Socono moved against it to a point where a small stream joined the creek. He followed the stream away from the larger creek into the deep woods. After fifteen minutes of sloshing through the snow-clogged stream, he stepped out of the water onto some rocks and followed them into a grove of evergreens. Here he rested for a moment, placing Stephen on the pine-needle-covered ground. The snow had drifted against the lowest branches of the fir trees and had created a wall, allowing no winds to penetrate and drive the snows onto the forest floor under the pines. Then, fairly secure that his trail would not be traced, the Indian picked Stephen up again, left the protection of the evergreens and launched into the heavy snows.

He trudged through the snow for half an hour, all the while keeping the great hill to his north as a landmark. By the time he reached the foot of the hill, he was breathing heavily; his arms ached from Stephen's weight, but he began the climb without stopping to rest. Near the top of the hill Socono halted and laid Stephen down in the snow. He pushed aside one small spruce to reveal the entrance to a cave. He picked Stephen up again and placed him within the cave entrance and then rearranged the snow around the spruce at the entry. The front of the cave was large enough to stand up in. Socono carried Stephen toward the rear, where the remains of a good fire were still glowing in the darkness. The smoke escaped through a narrow exitway that led out to the back of the hill. Socono placed Stephen on a bed of furs and picked up a bowl of stew made from the meat of the black bear whom Socono had challenged for proprietorship of the cave. He began to feed his ward.

Stephen's fever broke two days after Socono brought him to the cave. Some days after that, his sores crusted, formed scabs and began to fall off. He had been more fortunate than Molly. Few of the scars would be on his face. As soon as he awoke from his delirium, he began to question his friend. But Socono could be frustratingly evasive, and Stephen got little out of him.

He had been in the cave for almost two weeks, and he was feeling better and stronger. He sat across the fire from the

Abenacki, eating a piece of bear meat. "I wonder what they think has happened to me," he mused. "I wish I could get some word to Molly and Father Lalonde."

"You do that, little brother, and the Oneida will be having me for supper."

"I have never seen them eat anyone."

"Then you have never seen them torture a prisoner," said Socono. "Among my people eaters of men are shunned and thrown from our villages, but the Iroquois—they are disgusting people."

"If you find them so disgusting," interrupted Stephen, "why did you decide to live so close to them?"

"I told you before, my friend, I came to keep an eye on the mission. And don't be so ungrateful. What do you think would have happened to you if I had not come to watch over you?"

"I don't mean to be ungrateful, Socono. I appreciate the care you have given me. But I should have waited for Lalonde. I was sick and I wanted to make my confession. If I had died without the last rites . . ."

The Indian started to laugh. He reached across the dying fire and touched Stephen's knee. "Little brother, you are one of the blackrobes now. Jesus will welcome you into heaven when you die."

"Blackrobes sin too," was his response. "The girl Molly and I . . . we . . ."

At first Socono looked surprised but then he started to grin. "The little brother has become a man."

"Socono, you know it is forbidden to me. It is a sin."

Socono tried to stop grinning. "For you, I guess, it is a sin. Not for me. For me it is pleasure. Did you enjoy it?"

"No," Stephen lied. "At least . . ." He paused for a moment. "I enjoyed making love to Molly while I was doing it. I did not enjoy the guilt I felt afterwards."

Socono shook his head. "I do not understand you blackrobes. I knew that you had the equipment to be men, but up to now I had not understood that you had the desire to be men. But why do you deny yourselves?"

"For the greater glory of God," said Stephen.

Socono did not respond. Stephen reached for his cape and wrapped it around him. He stretched out before the fire. Socono stirred the embers and threw a large log on top of the freshly stirred flames. The wood was dry and the fire was very hot. Within a few seconds the log began to make cracking noises as the flames consumed it. Stephen's eyes were smarting from the smoke in the cave. He was very tired and he fell asleep quickly.

Isaac Wiggins moved rapidly across the snows. He was very much at home with the awkward gait required by snowshoes. He traveled alone and unburdened, carrying only his musket, powderhorn and a small pouch containing food and shot for the rifle. He was dressed in fur coat and fur hat.

He had left Gathtsegwarohare, a Seneca castle, a week before. Considering the snows, he had made excellent progress. He was not in any hurry to reach Kanowalohale and the Oneida. But now that he approached the village, the thought of a willing bride, warm fire and available whiskey quickened his pace.

He had been delayed in the Seneca towns far longer than he had anticipated. Originally he had planned to reach the Oneida towns before winter set in. At first the French authorities at Niagara, when they heard that an English trader had come to deal with the Seneca, had attempted to use the Jesuit priests against him. He had no fear of them. Pierce could always fix it for him. The Indians at first shunned him, but when you offered the average Seneca trapper rum, along with shot and ball for his musket, he soon forgot the whining of the men in skirts. But the French had surprised him; they had sent a party of soldiers to Genesee Castle, his headquarters. He had escaped with no time to spare and lost his entire cache of furs. He fled to Gathtsegwarohare, across the Genesee River and several miles away. For six weeks he had done nothing but use up what was left of his rum and try out a different Seneca woman every night. Then the snows came. He was without rum, without furs, without money and without bride gifts.

Pierce had ordered him to marry the Mohawk princess and he had ordered him to Kanowalohale while he was in Genesee. Pierce's message had explained that the Nowell brat, the kid he was always so worried about, was now in the Oneida village. Wiggins was to go there to marry and to keep an eye on the boy. He was sorely tired of taking orders from Pierce and getting so little in return. The French commander at Niagara obviously had not heard that Pierce and his agents were supposed to operate freely in that area. Wiggins had delayed going to the Oneida purposely. But now, since he was dead broke, he would have to obey, if only to get his pay.

He had never approached Kanowalohale overland from the Mohawk before. He rarely traveled long distances in the winter. Dusk had already settled in, and he had some doubts that he would reach the Oneida castle before nightfall.

He walked with a sure, steady gait, his eyes fixed straight ahead to help him avoid any branches that might bar his way. He would never have seen the smoke from the mountaintop, but Wiggins was a man of keen senses. He smelled the smoke. He stopped and looked about him.

"Damn me," he said. "I'm too far from the town to be smelling its smoke. I have to skirt the hill before I'm even in eye range of the place." As he looked up at the hill blocking his path, he caught sight of a puff of white smoke against the darkening sky. He puzzled for a moment. Should he continue to Kanowalohale or should he investigate the smoke? "If they're friendlies, maybe I can camp with them," he decided. "They may even have some rum. If they're hostiles, wouldn't do me no harm to know it and warn the Oneida. They might overlook my poverty if I could bring them a few scalps." He smiled his toothless grin and, having made up his mind, he started to climb the hill.

The north slope of the hill was far steeper than the south face, the side Socono had climbed carrying Stephen. It was dark before Wiggins reached the smoke hole. He approached it quietly and, even though the smoke burned his eyes when he peeked over the edge into the opening, it was not thick enough to block his vision. In the gloom of the cave below he could make out the forms of two men sitting before the fire. Both were wrapped in Indian blankets and they were speaking in low tones. Wiggins strained to hear their words. They were not speaking an Iroquois tongue. They were hostiles.

He slipped away from the edge of the hole and retraced his steps down the steep face of the mountain. He increased his speed the farther away he got from the hole. He lost control of his gait. His snowshoes caught on each other and he tripped. Cursing, he brushed the snow from himself as he rose. He would have to slow down. The moon had not yet risen and the night was very black. But if he slowed his pace and walked carefully, he would reach Kanowalohale with his news before two hours were up.

Stephen awoke with a start. The fire was almost out and he knew several hours had slipped by since he fell asleep. Socono was not in his normal place on the opposite side of the fire, but his blanket was there. Stephen reached over and felt the blanket. It was still warm from the Indian's body. Stephen rose to his feet and began to walk toward the front of the cave. From the shadows a hand grabbed his arm and pulled him to the floor. It was Socono.

"Make no sound," commanded the Indian. "The Oneida are outside. They have blocked off the rear way as well."

"How could they have found us?" asked Stephen.

Socono shook his head in dismay. He looked Stephen directly in the face. "I will not be taken by these snakes, little brother. I will not let them burn me and make me scream."

"Don't talk like that, Socono. I know these people. I know the sachem. I have risked my life to help them. I'll speak with them and ask them to let you go."

"It will not work, Blackrobe."

"Please, Socono, don't shed any blood and don't throw away your life for no reason. Trust me. I can work it out."

The Indian stared at Stephen. He did not believe that the boy could save him, but a plea from this one person not to shed blood could not be disobeyed. The boy's look of anguish was enough to force him to agree to surrender. He knew what it meant for him; something he had always dreaded would now surely be his fate. He resigned himself to it. Now that he knew he would die, he prayed not to the Christian god but to the gods of his own people—to Glooskap and to Malsum, the wolf. His face lost expression and he withdrew into himself. Again Stephen pleaded. Socono merely nodded assent.

Stephen went to the entrance of the cave and hailed. The sound of his yell had barely ceased to echo when he was shoved to the ground. As he fell he could see the blur of black forms racing past him. He was held to the ground with his face in the snow. He had not the strength to resist, even if he had wanted to. He could not see Socono but he had to assume that the same was happening to him. Finally his captor allowed him to stand and shoved him back toward the rear of the cave.

There was now enough light from the fire's glow to see the face of the man who had held him. Stephen was shocked to see that his captor was a white man—an ugly, horrible man. He was grinning and he had no teeth.

Stephen twisted in Wiggins' grip to catch sight of Socono. What he saw frightened him. At first Socono stood passively in the grasp of Dagaheari; his eyes seemed to see nothing. But as Stephen twisted, the glow from the fire fell on Wiggins' face, and his toothless grin was revealed to Socono. Socono's eyes widened and then bulged in their sockets. His passive expression disappeared and was replaced by rage. With all his strength he pulled away from Dagaheari, who had been lulled

173

by Socono's original passivity. He tore across the cave and leaped at Wiggins. As he grabbed his enemy by the throat, the two of them fell to the ground. Wiggins' initial shout of surprise was cut off into a gurgle by the force of Socono's grip. Dagaheari recovered quickly and jumped across the fire to where the two men struggled. With the flat of his tomahawk he struck Socono on the back of the skull. The Indian's body went limp and his grip on Wiggins' throat eased.

"What got into him?" said Wiggins, his voice a hoarse rasp. He turned to Dagaheari. "Why the hell couldn't you hold the ugly bastard? He damned near killed me."

"If he had," answered the Oneida, "I would have rewarded him with a swift death instead of the death by fire that awaits him now."

"You're goin' to burn him, then," said Wiggins, smiling now. "I want to be around for that."

"Dagaheari," interrupted Stephen. "Please listen to me. Socono, the Abenacki, is my friend. He meant no harm to the Oneida. He came here to watch over me. He was nursing me through the smallpox."

"Jesus," shouted Wiggins. "You got the pox?" He backed away from Stephen.

Dagaheari turned to look at Stephen. "Your friend is an Abenacki, Blackrobe, and he was spying on our village. He has been here for some time. He is our enemy and he will die the slow death. We will burn him. He will cry out for his death."

"But I saved your aunt. Doesn't that mean anything?" argued Stephen.

"My aunt is dead, Blackrobe."

"I saved the Mohawk when we were coming here," said Stephen in desperation.

Dagaheari bent down and tied Socono's hands behind his back.

"Doesn't that mean anything to you?" repeated Stephen.

Dagaheari looked up from his work. "Go to the Mohawks for a reward," he laughed. "But the Abenacki dies."

They marched down the side of the hill toward the village. When they arrived within a few hundred yards of the front gate, Dagaheari halted the party and, lifting his face up into the night sky, he howled. From the village came a high-pitched response and an instant beating of the drums. The party renewed its march at a quicker pace, covering the distance to the village rapidly.

When Stephen entered the front gate, he saw that the entire

174

village was up and the whole town glowed with fires. The women had formed two long lines that faced each other, stretching from the gate to the great longhouse. They were carrying sticks, switches and heavy clubs.

Socono was stripped of all of his clothing. He was still somewhat groggy from the blow on his head but he was able to walk without assistance. He knew what was expected of him, and when Dagaheari shoved him toward the rows of yelling and cursing women, he broke into a trot, darting first to the right to avoid a blow from a club and then to the left, parrying the thrust of a stick with his hand. He made it through the first half of the gauntlet with little damage, but then an old crone thrust her stick between his calves, tripping him. Like a crowd of hungry vultures the two lines closed in on the fallen man and began to beat him with their clubs.

Dagaheari would have intervened to save his victim for better things, but before he could, Stephen rushed down the line, shoving women first this way, then that. He kicked at a hand holding a club just above Socono's head and threw himself on top of the body of his friend.

Dagaheari forced his way through the crowd and ordered the women back. He pulled Stephen off Socono's back and, grabbing hold of the naked Indian's shoulders, pulled him to his feet. Suddenly the crowd turned quiet. The lone figure of Skenandon, the sachem, crossed the square toward the prisoner.

"A prisoner, Dagaheari?" said the chief.

Stephen pulled from the grasp of one of the Oneida warriors and stepped between Dagaheari and the sachem. "I beg the chief to allow the Abenacki his freedom. He is my friend. He is the friend of Onontio. If you kill him, Onontio and King Louis will take their revenge on you."

Skenandon smiled at Stephen. "Does the blackrobe threaten the Oneida? We have always burned our Abenacki prisoners in the past and Onontio has not complained to us."

"This Abenacki is different," said Stephen. "He is a Christian and a very close friend of the blackrobes. You must spare him, Skenandon."

"He is Dagaheari's prisoner," said the sachem. "It is up to him."

Wiggins stepped into the circle that had formed about the Abenacki prisoner. "Burn the bastard," he said. "The scarfaced son of a bitch tried to kill me."

A warrior brought an iron pot to Dagaheari. The war leader took it from him and dipped his hand into it. He then began to smear a black pitch on Socono's chest and face. "He is my prisoner," said Dagaheari. "I paint him black for the fire."

"As you will," said the sachem. "But not tonight. We have time. We will discuss his death and the manner and time of it tomorrow. Take the prisoner, after Dagaheari is finished with him, and place him in the great longhouse." Then he turned and walked toward his own house.

Frightened as he was, Stephen had watched the wily sachem carefully. He was convinced that his threats had hit the mark. Skenandon was afraid of the French governor in New France. He could save Socono if he put even more pressure on the sachem. Socono, still naked but now painted with pitch from head to toe, was led into the great longhouse. Stephen saw Molly standing by the entry as Socono was led in. He walked toward her but halted in his tracks when he saw the white man without teeth take her by the arm and lead her away. He knew then who his captor had been. Perhaps Molly would still help him, but now he was sure that the one person who had enough influence with Skenandon to rescue Socono was his superior, Lalonde. He headed for the Jesuit house.

When Stephen entered the chapel, it was dark. He could barely find his way to the entrance of the common room. Lalonde had placed a vigil light at the front of the chapel before a rough-hewn wooden cross. Stephen groped his way through the awkwardly arranged benches by the flickering of the tiny red lamp. He called out Lalonde's name but received no answer. Then there was a stirring in the common room, and Lalonde's form, outlined by the fire in the hearth behind him, appeared in the entryway, holding back the deerskin divider.

"Is that you, Etienne?" he whispered. "Thank God, it is you," he said as Stephen approached him. "What is happening out there? I was asleep; then there was such a commotion."

"Come into the common room," said Stephen, grasping the priest by the arm and turning him to face the fire. "I must speak with you."

Stephen noted the bottle of whiskey on the table but said nothing. He picked up an unsplit log that lay near the fire and, turning it on end, he placed it on the dirt floor by the table. He motioned Lalonde to sit at his bench while he sat on the log facing the priest. Lalonde clearly resented the air of command Stephen was adopting and determined to return matters to their proper order.

"I would like a complete account of your whereabouts these past two weeks," he said. "And I warn you, if you have been living with that Mohawk woman, I will be forced to write to Father Provincial with a recommendation that you be suspended from the Society."

"I was with her when I first became ill."

"I know. She brought me your note."

"She did deliver it after all," Stephen said.

Lalonde looked away from him toward the fire. "You must understand why I couldn't come to you. The safety of the mission had to be guaranteed."

Stephen was astounded. It had never occurred to him that Lalonde would have failed to give a dying man the last rites. "I could have died."

"Well, you didn't," said the priest with an air of finality. "Obviously my decision was the correct one. Now tell me what has been going on outside."

Stephen put his head in his hands. "It is all my fault. I didn't know it but all the time we have been in Kanowalohale, Socono has been watching over us. Now the Oneida have taken him and they plan to burn him."

"Socono? Your Indian friend from Louisbourg?"

"Yes," said Stephen. "When the smallpox began to spread, he took me to his camp. Somehow the Oneida discovered us and captured him. You have to help him, Father. I talked him into surrendering to avoid bloodshed. I told him I could save him. But they won't listen to me. You must intervene."

"Me?" said the surprised Lalonde. "What can I do? I can't jeopardize our success here, Etienne. People are coming to my mass."

"You must go to Skenandon, Father. He is afraid of you. It all makes sense now. He could have thrown us out of Kanowalohale after the council. The other sachems and the powerful war leaders like Dagaheari wanted him to. He didn't. He let us stay. When it became obvious that our failure to attract potential converts had depressed you to the point that you were considering abandoning the mission, he provided us with a congregation. He wants us to stay. He needs us. If you go to him, you can demand the release of Socono. You can threaten him, threaten to return to New France."

"Give up the mission for an Indian? Are you out of your mind, Etienne?"

"You don't have to give up the mission, Father. All you must do is threaten to."

Lalonde sat quietly for a moment. Stephen saw his eyes dart toward the bottle on the table several times. Then he spoke very softly. "I will not risk the mission."

Stephen rose from his log seat. "Then I'll go to Skenandon," he said.

"You will not," said the priest. "And I hope that I do not have to remind you that you have a vow of obedience and that I am your superior and the voice of God."

"The vow of obedience, Father, was not intended to force me to sit by and allow a moral evil to occur."

"It is not for you, my boy, to decide what is morally evil," shouted Lalonde, rising from his seat. "It is my responsibility —not yours."

"I am going to Skenandon, Father. I will not allow Socono to die."

Lalonde sighed and his body relaxed. He sat back down on his bench. "All right, Etienne, I can't have you going off threatening the sachem. I'll go to him. I think I am more of a diplomat than you are. What do they plan for Socono?"

"He is being kept in the great longhouse tonight. Tomorrow they will decide his fate. But I am sure that Dagaheari intends to burn him tomorrow night at the latest," answered Stephen.

"Well, at least we have time." The priest motioned Stephen to sit down again. He patted the boy's hands. "I don't know about you, Etienne, but I need something to calm me down after all this excitement. Do you care to join me?" he asked as he pulled the cork from the whiskey bottle.

"No, Father, I don't want any and I am not sure we have any time to waste."

"Of course we have time. In the morning I will visit the sachem and try to get him to release Socono."

Stephen would have preferred instant action, but getting Lalonde to agree to act was as much as he had any right to expect. Lalonde poured some whiskey into his cup. Stephen relented.

"I think I will have some whiskey, Father. Maybe it will help me sleep."

Lalonde offered him the cup. "Here, take this to your room with you. You'll need it tonight. You'll find your habit hanging there. The girl returned it to me after you disappeared. I expect to see you wearing it in the morning."

Stephen rose wearily. He picked the cup of whiskey up and cradled it in his two hands. "Good night, Father," he said.

"I'll serve your mass for you tomorrow; then we can call on Skenandon."

"Good night, Etienne."

Stephen carried the whiskey carefully with both hands. He would have spilled most of it if he had tried to carry the cup in any other way; his hands were trembling from fatigue and fright. When he entered his room, he put the cup on the floor and collapsed onto his pallet. He would have fallen asleep as he was but he forced himself to sit up again.

"This will not do," he said to himself. "No matter what is happening and no matter what I've done, I can't continue to allow the sacred order of the day to fall apart."

He should have made his confession to Lalonde. He had not done so deliberately; Lalonde might latch on to any reason for not interfering to save Socono. But at least he would not let his simple duties slide. He slipped off the pallet onto his knees. He had trusted too much to human efforts and he had ignored the real source of his strength. He prayed. He prayed God to forgive his sin—his breaking of his sacred vow—and he asked God to save his friend.

He rose from his knees, removed his clothes and slipped under his blankets. With his back propped against the wall of the house, he picked up the cup of whiskey and began to sip it. When he was half finished, he placed it on the floor and turned on his side to sleep.

After Stephen had left the common room, Lalonde stared at the half-empty whiskey bottle. Then he poured some into his cup. Why had the Abenacki come to Kanowalohale? Was it that the provincial had not trusted him or was Jean LaGarde spying on him? He took a large gulp of whiskey. Unlike Etienne, he had no protectors in the Society. All he had accomplished had been on his own merits. Now this spoiled child was about to force him into foolish risks. He drained the cup and poured himself another. Skenandon could not be bullied. If he tried to save the damn Abenacki, the sachem might bar his people from coming to the chapel again. The mission would fail. Maybe that was just what Jean La-Garde intended—to ruin him, to mark him as a failure and to destroy his career in the Society. If he failed in the Oneida mission, he would never have another chance.

Lalonde swore out loud and reached for the bottle. He poured another drink. He was sure of it—LaGarde had planted his protege in the mission to undermine him and then he had sent the Indian to spy and report back. Why should he save the Indian? His death would upset LaGarde's plans. No wonder Etienne was so insistent. "That young pup," he said aloud. "He has had everything handed to him. Well, not this."

He took another long swig of whiskey, this time directly from the bottle. It didn't burn so much going down now. He was getting drunk again. The boy had not even tried to make his confession to him, even after living alone with that promiscuous woman. He could imagine all the foul things they had done together. He was sure the boy disapproved of his drinking. He had not said so but glances spoke more than words. The hypocrite.

He was drunk now. The fire had gone out and he could barely see to make his way to Stephen's room. He pushed aside the curtain and crossed the dirt floor to where he knew the boy lay. Stephen was asleep. His light snore was the only sound in the room. The priest staggered and kicked Stephen's cup of whiskey, spilling its contents onto the floor. Lalonde steadied himself with his hand, leaning on Stephen's hip. He sat down on the boy's bed.

"Wake up, LaGarde," he said. "You will not ruin me." There was no response. "Wake up." Stephen stirred and turned onto his back. His regular breathing continued.

The priest reached out to shake him awake, but he pulled his hand back. His eyes had adjusted to the darkness, and he could make out the boy's features. He looked very peaceful in his sleep, very beautiful.

Lalonde sat some moments longer staring at the boy. He reached out his hand again. This time his hand moved along the edge of the pallet and under the blankets. He touched the boy's bare leg and waited to see if there was any reaction. There was none. His hand moved upward until he reached the boy's pubic hair. Stephen stirred again in his sleep. Lalonde waited a moment more and then reached for Stephen's penis. He stroked it softly and it began to stiffen. He determined to see what his hand was accomplishing. He leaned forward and pulled down the blankets from the boy's body. He took his hand from the boy's sex and, steadying himself against Stephen's body, he rose to his feet and then slipped to his knees, his mouth inches away from its goal.

"If you touch me again, I'll kill you." Stephen's low, intense voice broke the silence of the room.

Lalonde sat back on his heels, stunned. "You were awake all along," he said.

Stephen raised himself on his elbows. "If I had been, you would not have gotten so far."

"Don't get so high and mighty with me, boy. I'm sure the Mohawk girl and you did as much and more."

"I'm not arguing with you. You reek of whiskey. Just get out of here before I hit you."

"Why be so hasty?" said the priest. "A little kindness to me now and I might be more persuasive with Skenandon tomorrow."

Stephen leaped to his feet and swung his fist at Lalonde's face. The blow struck the priest on the bridge of the nose, snapping the bone. Blood poured from Lalonde's nostrils and he staggered backward, tripping over his own feet and finally falling down. His head struck the ground with a thud.

Stephen checked to see if the priest was still breathing. He was. The boy then sat down on his bed. He had to think. "Damn the bastard," he shouted into the darkness of the room. "The drunken fool." He realized that his plan for saving Socono was finished. Lalonde would seek bitter revenge for the events of the last few moments. He would have to think of something else. His lips started to form the words of a prayer, but he stopped. He had had enough prayers for one night.

First he would need a plan. He and Socono would have to escape, but he knew they could not escape without help. The Oneida's words came back to him in a flash—"Go to the Mohawks for your reward." He knew what he would do.

He rose from the bed and dressed quickly, glancing at his habit hanging on a peg on the wall. The work he would have to perform this night was not suited to it. He pulled his blankets from the bed and, throwing his cape over his shoulders, went out through the common room and the chapel, snuffing out the almost-extinguished vigil lamp on the way.

Kanowalohale had settled down for the night after the excitement of the capture. It was bitter cold and clear. The moon was full now, illuminating the snow-filled square between the Jesuit house and the great longhouse. Stephen crossed the square, skirting the entryway of the house and quietly making his way to the rear exit. The skins were tied in place to keep out the cold air. Stephen pushed his arm between the rough wooden doorframe and the curtain until he found the knots holding the curtain in place. It took him a few moments to untie them; then he crept into the darkness of the sickroom. He could see nothing. Finally, afraid of tripping and arousing the house, he dropped on his belly and began to crawl along the dirt floor. He had to find Molly.

He made it to the platforms on the right side of the house. The first one he searched contained the body of a young man, naked and covered with eruptions. On the second platform an old woman tossed and moaned. Stephen crawled forward, feeling his way with his hand. He froze in place as a shaft of light poured into the darkness of the sickroom from the front half of the house. The divider had been pulled back. Stephen sighed with relief when he saw Molly enter the sickroom—alone.

"Molly," he called softly to her.

She let the skins fall in place and walked toward the sound of his voice. "Blackrobe, is it you? What are you doing here?"

He stood up and reached for her hand. He pulled her toward him and kissed her gently on the lips. She responded to his kiss. "I need your help, Molly," he whispered. "I came here looking for you."

"You were lucky to find me. Wiggins will not let me sleep here. He is afraid of the pox. I have put him in the hut—our hut. I have slipped away, but I must go back there as soon as I finish here."

"There was pox in that hut too, Molly."

She shrugged. "I know that, but he doesn't. He won't catch it. He is a pig. All he ever wants to do is stick his big thing in me. But he has come to my hut emptyhanded and I will not let him have me. I will never marry him."

"Can you help the Abenacki escape?"

She said nothing.

"He is my closest friend. I convinced him to surrender. I will not let Dagaheari have him."

"You ask much of me, Blackrobe. The Abenacki are the enemies of the Mohawk as well."

"Socono is no one's enemy, Molly. Please help me save him."

"Perhaps he will be adopted into the tribe," she offered.

"No," said Stephen. "Dagaheari means to burn him."

"All right," she said. "What do you want me to do?"

"How many men are guarding Socono?" he asked.

"There is only one. The others have gone to sleep."

Stephen pulled at his chin for a moment. "I will need food, clothes for Socono, two pairs of snowshoes and some time."

She smiled wryly. "All but the last are on the other side of the deerskin," she said.

"Can you cut Socono's bonds and lure the guard away?"

"Yes," she said. "I can do that too—for you." She turned to go back to the other side.

"Molly," he whispered. "I may not see you again."

She took a step toward him. He reached for her face and ran his hand across her cheek.

"Do you still think I am beautiful, Blackrobe?" she asked.

"No one ever called me that before."

"As beautiful as this evening's moon," he responded.

She put her arms around his neck and pulled his face down toward hers. She kissed his eyes and whispered in his ear. "Come back to me someday, Blackrobe." Then she broke away from him and was gone.

Stephen waited in the darkness of the room. There were no sounds except for the occasional moans of the sick. In his impatience it seemed she had been gone for hours but in reality she returned after about twenty minutes.

She handed him a large bundle. "Here is the food and clothing. The Abenacki is free. He is a shrewd one—not even a sign of surprise on his face when I cut the ropes and slipped him the knife. How will you get him to come back this way instead of making for the front door?"

"We have a signal," he answered. "With any luck no one will awaken and think it strange that there is a squirrel in the longhouse."

"One more thing," she said. "There is a bow and a quiver of arrows by the entryway. You will have to reach into the house to grab them. I can not bring them back here without arousing suspicion."

Before he could say anything more to her, she left him. He waited some minutes more and then peeked through the skins into the front half of the longhouse. He saw Molly lead a young brave into a platform out of view of the prisoner. Socono seemed to be asleep. Stephen breathed deeply to relax the tension, but it did little good. Very softly he made the sound of the squirrel's chirp and waited, expecting pandemonium to break loose. Nothing happened. Socono did not move a muscle, but Stephen knew he understood. The only sounds in the front of the longhouse were those of the sleepers and now the rather frantic sounds of lovemaking coming from the platform into which Molly and the sentry had disappeared. Finally Socono began to creep away from the spot where he had been bound. He moved rapidly and was through the curtain without being seen. Stephen grabbed him by the forearm. Quietly he handed him a suit of deerskins. When Socono was dressed, Stephen threw a blanket from his bed over the Indian's shoulders. Without a word passing between them, they crawled back out of the longhouse into the snow.

The snow crunched under their feet as they crept through the moonlight toward the front of the longhouse. There, leaning against the doorpost, were two pairs of snowshoes. Socono grabbed both of them and led Stephen into the shadows of the neighboring house. They laced the shoes onto their feet. Socono smiled at the boy.

"Ready," he whispered in Abenacki.

"Let's go," said Stephen.

They strode cautiously toward the front gate of the village. Halfway to the gate, Stephen remembered Molly's words about the bow. He stopped in his tracks. Again he chirped. Socono turned. Stephen held his hand up as a sign to wait and retraced his steps. He reached the entryway of the house in about thirty strides. It too was tied shut. Stephen reached his arm through the tight slit between the skin and the wooden doorpost. He felt blindly to the right for the bow and arrows. Nothing. He pulled his arm out and repeated the process on the left side. This time his hand grasped the bow. Quickly and noiselessly, he pulled it through the crack, placing it in the snow, and put his arm back into the longhouse. The quiver was right next to where the bow had been. He retrieved it just as quickly and noiselessly. He turned and retraced his steps across the village toward the gate.

Socono had moved on toward the gate and had awaited Stephen's return there. He waved as he caught sight of the boy. Stephen started to return the wave and then froze in horror. To the right of Socono and behind him, the figure of a man approached, tomahawk raised. As he crept closer to the distracted Abenacki, he came into full view, bathed in moonlight.

Stephen notched the bow with an arrow. His mind was a maze of contradictory thoughts. He could not yell; he would have to shoot; he must save his friend; thou shalt not kill.

The figure raised the tomahawk higher. Socono, sensing the danger at last, started to turn. Stephen raised the bow, aimed and fired in almost one motion. The arrow sliced through the figure's throat. He dropped his tomahawk and grabbed his neck. He staggered and then began to come toward Stephen. An awful gurgling sound came from his mouth. It was Skenandon. The boy could see the wild look in the sachem's dying eyes. His tongue protruded from his mouth and blood squirted from the wound. He took about ten steps and then fell silently into the snow, his body quivering in death.

Socono moved quickly to where Stephen was standing and

grabbed him by the shoulders, propelling him forward. They pushed back the stockade gate and made their way toward the creek. A wisp of cloud passed over the moon, and the night was suddenly darker. Stephen stumbled when he reached the frozen creekbed. As he fell on his face in the snow, he began to retch. Soon his whole body was heaving, but he could bring up nothing. Except for the whiskey he had drunk earlier, his stomach was empty.

Socono leaned over him. "Come, little brother, we must be out of here. We have a long way to go before we will be safe."

Socono estimated that with any luck they would have a six-hour lead on any pursuers, but only if the Mohawk woman managed to lull the sentry into sleep after lovemaking. They had to use every minute of the head start she had given them. Socono took the lead and followed the course of the creek due north for several miles. He knew that the Oneida would expect him to strike north for the French settlements, but as long as their tracks were visible they would be followed. There was no way he could hide the signs of two sets of snowshoes. Speed rather than stealth was what was called for. He left the creek and set a brutal pace toward the northeast.

Stephen kept up with him for the first several miles but then he began to fall behind. At one point Socono had to stop to allow him to catch up.

"I have to rest a minute," gasped Stephen. The two stood together without speaking. Only Stephen's gasping breathing broke the silence of the soundless moonlit snowscape. "Where are we heading?" he asked.

"First we must get to the river of the Mohawks. If we follow it toward the rising sun, we will find the English settlements. You will be safe there."

"That must be over two hundred miles from here. I don't know if I can travel that far and I know I can't keep up this pace."

"If we are lucky, we will not have to keep up this pace," said Socono. "But now we must have as big a lead as possible. It is our only chance." He reached into Molly's sack, which he carried over his shoulder. "Here, eat some pemmican."

"I'm not sure I can," said Stephen. "My stomach . . ."

"Eat it," ordered the Indian. Stephen obeyed. "Now drink some of the rum your friend provided for us." He pulled a bottle out of the sack.

"That I know I can't take," said Stephen.

"All right, we can save it for later. We may need it if it grows colder."

The Indian turned from Stephen and started out. Stephen followed wearily. Again Socono set the pace and before many strides were taken, Stephen was breathing heavily. Despite the cold, he could feel the sweat pour from his body under his heavy blanket. He tried to breathe deeply but the pain in his chest and in his side only grew worse. He kept plodding on, keeping the blanketed form of Socono in view. The Indian looked behind him every few yards to make sure that Stephen had not stopped or fallen. The pain in Stephen's chest and side spread to his whole body, and then mercifully it eased into a numbness. Still they kept on. They reached the river as the first light of dawn lightened the eastern sky.

All day long the two men followed the course of the frozen Mohawk River, stopping only to allow Stephen to catch his breath and to eat a bit of their food. The day was cold and clear. Socono kept checking the sky and failed to answer Stephen's questions about what he was searching for. At dusk Stephen collapsed. Socono lifted him from the ice and carried him to the shelter of a large spruce, which grew fifty feet from the bank.

The Indian knew that he would have to change his plans. The boy could not keep up the pace. In fact, he doubted that Stephen would be able to move in the morning. They would have to spend the night here under these spruce branches. He knew that the Oneida would not rest this night, and by morning they would be upon them. He would have to meet them. Much would depend on how many of them were in the party and how observant they would be after an all-night trek through the snow. He bundled Stephen up in his cape and blankets and built a fire from spruce branches. At least they would not freeze this night. The fire would burn out before morning and would not warn the Oneida. Then he put on his snowshoes again and stepped out onto the ice of the river. He walked for about a mile and then left the river again by climbing up onto the bank. He returned to his camp through the woods. Then he repeated his journey, this time wearing Stephen's snowshoes. When he returned the second time, he carefully covered the tracks, marking the spot where they had first left the river and climbed up on the bank to make camp. Socono then wrapped himself in the blanket Stephen had taken from the Oneida village and lay down by the fire next to the sleeping boy. He knew that their chances were slim, but he had given them some time; with any luck at all, he might gain even more than time.

Socono awoke with the grey light of false dawn. The fire had burned out hours before and the Indian was chilled to the bone under his blanket. He shook Stephen by the shoulder.

Still groggy with sleep and exhaustion, Stephen asked, "How long have I slept?"

"All night," said Socono. Stephen looked about him in panic. "Don't worry," said Socono. "We couldn't have escaped anyway. We will have to fight them."

"But how? I've held you back. I should have stayed behind."

"I have a plan," said Socono, "and I will need your help. As soon as it is light enough, I want you to put on your snowshoes and walk backward up over the drift to the left of this spruce. You take the bow. If anyone comes into the camp, they must follow those tracks through the woods—across the clearing—to the spruce. With tracks leading to the fire our enemy will not suspect your hiding place. If we bundle our possessions and pile up the snow under our blankets, they will think we sleep by the fire. You put on your cape and I will wear one blanket. We will need them to keep warm while we wait."

"Where will you be?" asked Stephen.

"I will be with the Oneida. So be careful. Don't shoot me."

After Stephen had stationed himself behind the drift and the camp had been made ready, Socono hid behind a drift along the riverbank and waited for the Oneida. About an hour after dawn he caught a glimpse of the first of them. They had traveled at a breakneck pace. In the lead was Dagaheari. With his blanket drawn tightly around him, he trudged along, following the tracks made the night before by Socono in the light snow covering the Mohawk. He missed the place where Socono and Stephen had left the river to camp. A careful tracker would have seen it, but Dagaheari was near exhaustion. He trekked on down the river, passing Socono's hiding place. About fifty yards behind the leader came a second Oneida, and seventy-five yards behind him came a third. Socono smiled. Only three of them had been able to keep the pace.

After the third warrior had passed his hiding place, Socono, dressed in his Oneida-made blanket, dropped down quietly from the embankment and became the fourth warrior.

187

His pace was rapid and within a few strides he caught up with the last Oneida.

The warrior started to turn to greet the newcomer with a look of surprise on his face. He had thought that the rest of his companions were far behind. He looked more shocked than hurt when Socono's arm slipped around his neck and Socono's knife dug into his belly. A second sharp slice and the warrior's throat was cut.

Socono did not stop to finish off the warrior. Instead he increased his pace, following the second one. Up ahead Dagaheari had halted at the spot where the tracks left the river and entered the woods. The Abenacki knew that if Dagaheari waited for his companions or scanned behind him along the river trail before setting off into the woods, all was lost. But the Oneida was impatient with his comrades and annoyed that so few had been able to keep up with him. He strode off into the woods alone. Socono's second victim did not even have the brief warning that the first had. Socono approached the second warrior so stealthily that he never heard or felt anything until he too lay face down in the snow, his throat cut.

Now it was a race. Would Stephen be able to keep his wits and strength together? Instead of following Dagaheari's path, Socono pulled himself up on the bank just opposite the spot where he had killed the second Oneida, hoping to cut Dagaheari off. The third set of snowshoe tracks told him he was too late. Dagaheari had passed this spot already. Socono raced for the clearing. If Stephen was not alert or had fallen asleep, he was as good as dead.

When he entered the clearing, he sighed with relief. In the center, fallen to his knees beside the spruce, was the Oneida chief, the shaft of an arrow protruding from his shoulder. Socono made the loud chirping of a squirrel and waved to the snowdrift, fearful that Stephen would make the same mistake that the two dead Oneida had. He was relieved to see the black-clad figure rise to the top of the drift and advance toward the Oneida. Socono would just as soon have finished him off, but he knew that Stephen would never agree.

Socono approached the Oneida from the rear with his knife drawn. Dagaheari grimaced as the Abenacki grabbed the arrowhead and, none too gently, cut it from the shaft. Stephen held Dagaheari by the shoulders while Socono stepped in front of the Oneida and, placing his knee just below the feathered shaft, yanked it free. Dagaheari made no sound, although Stephen could see that he was in excruciating pain. Socono stemmed the flow of blood with Dagaheari's blanket.

"He won't bleed much more," said Socono. "He can travel slowly but he will be in no condition to follow us. When his stragglers arrive, they will find him. I doubt that they will try to follow us any longer."

Stephen sat down beside Dagaheari. "I am sorry about Skenandon," he said.

Dagaheari spoke through gritted teeth. "You have given great affront to my people, Blackrobe. We would have made you suffer for it. I would dearly have loved to caress you with Oneida fire. And I would surely have had the chance but for the Abenacki and the fact that many of my so-called warriors have grown soft under the peace-loving Skenandon and cannot keep pace with their chief. But we will have our chance yet, Blackrobe. You and I will meet again. In the meanwhile we will practice on the priest."

Stephen looked at the Oneida in surprise. "Why him? He had nothing to do with our escape."

"No matter. We will need a victim. But rest easy; we will not kill him. I did learn some things from Skenandon. We will just make sure that he is very anxious to go home of his own accord."

"Don't hurt him, Dagaheari." The Oneida just sneered.

Socono and Stephen spent no more time than necessary at their campsite. Soon they set out on the ice of the river again. Stephen stared in horror at the blood-soaked bodies of the two ambushed warriors, but he steeled himself and kept up with the pace set by the Abenacki.

Even though Socono moved more slowly now that the immediate danger was gone, Stephen, weakened by the smallpox, still could not keep up with him. After two hours he stopped and begged Socono for a rest period.

"I'm sorry, Socono. I shouldn't have come with you. I am still too weak from the pox."

"We will rest for an hour, little brother."

Despite the cold, both of their faces were wet with perspiration. They wrapped their blankets about them more closely and huddled together. After some moments of silence, Stephen began to shake his head. "My God, what has been happening to me?" he said, his voice a hoarse croak. "Everything I touch falls apart. I am destroying everything. I have broken my vow of chastity. I have broken my vow of obedience. I have struck my religious superior. I have destroyed the Society's work among the Oneida and now I have killed a man. Everything I have ever known and believed in is lost to me."

"Most of what you did, you did for me."

"You are my friend, Socono. I could not let them kill you."

Socono took a deep breath and exhaled with a sigh. "I am not sure I have always been a worthy friend to you," said the Indian.

"You taught me everything you knew; you protected me; you were my friend when I was lonely. I'd say that you were more than a worthy friend."

The wind rose in intensity and grabbed at both their blankets. They hunched lower under the overhang.

"But I did not always speak the truth to you," said Socono. "Even now I am afraid that if you knew the truth you would hate me."

Stephen stared into the Indian's pitch-blackened face. "You have always known more, haven't you, Socono?"

Socono looked back at Stephen. This time his mask failed him. Tears started to pour down his cheeks, some of them flowing into the groove of the ugly scar on his cheek. "I was responsible for what has happened to you. It was my scouting party from St. François that killed your father. You were not found in Acadia but in the country of the Bastonois, on the river of the Connecticut. It was all because of him, the devil Wiggins, the toothless one who captured you in the cave. He did this to my face." He touched his cheek and then wiped away the tears with the back of his fist. "I learned he was to lead you and your parents to your new home. In my pain and anger I wanted only revenge. We struck your party. I killed the scout but it was not Wiggins, only one of his henchmen. I tried to stop the others." His voice began to trail away. "I tried. . . ." He shook his head. "But they were too far away from me. Your father was wounded immediately. I saved you and your father, but he was so badly wounded that he died. You had the cut over the eye. But you eventually recovered." Again tears poured down the Indian's cheek. "I am sorry that I have brought such sorrow to you."

Stephen had said nothing while Socono spoke. He just stared ahead.

Socono continued. "I brought you to LaGarde. He told me that what I had done was very dangerous for the mission. The English governor would complain to the French. The enemies of the blackrobes would use what I had done to take the priests from us. He decided to send you to Louisbourg. He never tried to find any of your family or friends. He never notified any authorities, English or French."

Stephen interrupted him for the first time. "I have a family, then."

"You have a grandfather and an uncle, at least, among the Bastonois."

"How do you know, Socono?" asked Stephen.

"LaGarde told me just before we left Louisbourg. Your uncle has been tracking you down. That is why they sent you to France and to the Oneida. LaGarde and the chief black-robe feared that if he found you at Louisbourg he would cause trouble for them."

Socono fell silent. Stephen said nothing. He could not speak. He opened his mouth but all that came from him was a long, pitiful moan.

Socono picked up the bottle of rum and took a long drink. He grimaced. "I have not tasted any of that since that night," he said. But now that he was certain Stephen could not forgive him, he no longer needed to remain sober.

The air had become warmer as the day progressed. By noon the sun had been obliterated by great, ugly black and gray clouds. Socono halted his march and allowed Stephen to catch up with him. "We have been lucky. It will snow before this afternoon is over. The Oneida will never be able to follow our tracks. They will guess that we head for the north, to Canada. All we must do now is conserve our strength and make it to the river towns. You will be safe there."

Stephen did not feel safe. He was in utter turmoil. His life had been turned around once again. His great, true friend had become the killer of his father, although he had certainly proved himself a friend again and again since then. The priest who had guided his life was a liar; the order that he belonged to and loved was the very cause of his life-long lack of love and his feeling of not belonging anywhere. Maybe it would be different in the English towns. He knew he had no real anger against Socono. The Indian had more than repaid his debt to him. He would insist that Socono return to St. François at last and begin to lead his own life. The burden of guilt must be lifted. But he would never forgive LaGarde, the Jesuits or the French.

When Dagaheari returned to Kanowalohale emptyhanded, the village broke into a frenzy of outrage. Lalonde was seized immediately. They tore his clothing from his body and

191

dragged him to the platform in the middle of the village. He screamed and resisted, but he was dragged and hauled up the ladder to the stage and tied to a stake that rose from the ground through the platform floor. Fires were lighted and hot coals were heated, along with knives and axes.

First it was the women who came to him. They laughed as he cringed in fear when they approached with their razor-sharp knives. They sliced pieces of raw flesh from his inner thighs and chest. He continued to scream until his voice gave out and only a hoarse rasp remained. One young woman grasped his little finger in her teeth and bit. Lalonde pulled against his ropes in agony, but he could not shake her loose. She bit through flesh and sinew into the first joint of the finger and severed it from his hand.

Dagaheari and the warriors were disgusted by the screams and determined to have nothing to do with him. They would leave him to the women. Dagaheari's decision not to kill Lalonde was wavering. The priest was a coward and he deserved to die by the knives of women. He turned away from the scene of torture and walked into the longhouse of the sachem. He found Molly waiting for him.

"My cousin assumes the mantle of sachem of the Turtles before he has been selected by the clan mothers," said the Mohawk.

"How is that?"

"It is clear that you have decided to seek your revenge by the torture and death of the blackrobe. I don't believe the clan mothers will think much of your decision. Dagaheari, if you want to be sachem you must halt the ceremony of caressing before it goes too far. If you kill the priest, you will have blundered and set back the diplomacy of the confedera-tion by decades. Listen to his cries; he is not a worthy victim. The younger one was a warrior; he would have suffered in silence."

"The younger one has a special place with you, Gonwatsi-jayenni, doesn't he?"

"He is a man, strong but gentle, a man with many sorrows but capable of giving."

"He was the murderer of your sachem."

"Oh, how my cousin mourns the death of his sachem. But your tears are false. Let us be straightforward, Dagaheari. You want to be sachem of the Oneida. The Turtle clan mothers will determine who succeeds Skenandon. I can tell you that if you kill the priest, they will never choose you."

Dagaheari stared at her. His black eyes flashed anger; it

was clear that he was struggling with himself. Ambition won the struggle. He stormed out of the house and Molly heard him yell the command that forced the reluctant women away from their victim.

Lalonde's bloody body was carried into the longhouse to Molly. She cleaned him and bound his wounds. He was not seriously hurt, but when she looked into his terrified eyes, she knew that pain and fear had taken control of him.

But she had saved his life. That was not only good politics; it was her gift to the young blackrobe. She owed him a favor. Her monthly flow had not come on time and she knew it was the young blackrobe's seed that had stopped it. She had chosen wisely, as the clan mother had advised her. The young blackrobe was brave; his son would be a proud warrior.

Part Two

The Quest

VI

1744—Spring and Summer

Daniel Pierce sat alone in the Breed parlor. The family had eaten and retired for the night. His wife Betsy and Sarah Nowell had talked incessantly throughout supper. In fact, he had noted how Betsy had been talking more and more with the passing years. The more he ignored her and the lonelier she became, the more she turned to her brother and Sarah for company. Yet Jonathan had become more and more withdrawn, and Sarah was always busy except for the brief supper hour.

Pierce's account book was on the table in front of him. He had begun to wear wire-frame spectacles two years ago for reading, and when he worked on his account books he always wore them low, near the tip of his long nose. This way he could readily identify anyone coming into the room without first having to remove his glasses. The candle on the table fluttered and was nearly extinguished when Hannah, dressed in nightgown and cap, opened the parlor double doors.

"Damn it, woman," he yelled. "Why are you in here? You know I have left strict orders never to be disturbed when I work on my accounts."

"There's a caller," she answered timidly.

"At this hour? Who the hell comes visiting in the middle of the night?" He rose from his book and followed Hannah into the kitchen and then to the back door of the lean-to. The figure of a man blocked the entry of the moonlight through the open doorway. His face was almost hidden in the Indian blanket thrown around his shoulders despite the warmth of the spring night. But Pierce knew him instantly.

"It's all right, Hannah," he said soothingly. "It's one of my runners. You can go back to bed now."

He waited until the woman returned to the small back room

she shared with her husband, then he pushed the visitor aside and stepped out into the night.

"God damn it, Wiggins," he cursed. "Have you lost your wits? How did you know you wouldn't bump into my beloved niece and be recognized? It's not like you to take this type of chance."

"I don't like it any more than you do, Pierce. But I'm doing you a favor, and you and I got a lot at stake. I had to get to you as soon as possible. It's the Nowell kid. I think he's on his way here."

Pierce swung around and faced Wiggins. Suddenly his anger dissipated and was replaced by concern. "How do you know this? Did you do anything to upset the Indians?"

"No," Wiggins lied. "The kid did everything on his own. He didn't need any help from me. He broke with his boss and then he went out and helped a captured Abenacki escape from the Oneida and in the process the sachem of the Oneida was killed. The Indians trailed them along the Mohawk and then lost them halfway down the river. The Oneida think they went back to Canada, but I know how those Frenchies work. He couldn't go back to Canada. He's gonna come here."

"Why here?" Wiggins suddenly became very uncomfortable. Pierce could see it in his ugly face. "Tell me the truth, Wiggins, if you want to continue earning the salary I pay you. Why here?"

"Well, the Abenacki I mentioned. He was the same one who killed Nowell's father. The one I branded."

"God damn it," said Pierce. "Then the kid probably knows everything. When did all this happen?"

"Last winter."

"What?" Pierce shot a look of pure venom at Wiggins. "What the hell took you so long getting here?"

"It was winter," said Wiggins defensively. "I knew he would have to hole up somewhere on the New York side of the mountains until spring. Besides, the Oneida wouldn't take too kindly to my running out on that bloody ugly squaw you hooked me up with."

Pierce calmed down. What Wiggins said was true, and certainly Nowell had not yet arrived in Boston, or if he had, he had not yet found his mother. But now Pierce knew he would have to act swiftly and decisively. He had vowed that if Sarah Nowell pushed him and came close to learning his secret, he would destroy her. Despite all her poking around, though, she had not found out anything, and so he had allowed her to go on living and earning money for him. But now the truth was finding her. Now he would move against her. Pierce looked at Wiggins. He had been responsible for the loss of the father; now he would become the instrument of death for the mother.

A week later Pierce visited Sarah's Charlestown office and told her that fishermen from Newfoundland who had been captured by French privateers operating out of Isle Royale had heard rumors of an orphan boy living in the Jesuit house at Louisbourg. It was only a rumor, but it came from a place where no one had thought to investigate because of its remoteness. Moreover, it was the only lead they had. Sarah was making plans to investigate the story within an hour. And she was determined to investigate personally.

Sarah waited for two weeks for the first company ship to arrive in Boston harbor. As luck would have it, the first to arrive was the *Betsy*. No sooner had the ship docked at her Boston wharf than Sarah arrived at the berth. "William," she announced loudly from the wharf, "I'm coming aboard."

She hiked up her skirts and climbed the steep planking that led from the wharf to the deck. She was giving orders to master and crew before she made it all the way up. "I want this ship unloaded and filled with ballast. Pierce has found and signed on some replacements for any crewmen who are missing and for any who want shore leave and are not prepared to sail immediately. We're taking her out again just as soon as the work is completed."

Vaughan caught her as she came over the railing and pulled her body close to his. "Do you mean we're sailing together again?" he leered at her and kissed her ear.

She pulled back from him and looked into his face. "This is serious business, William. I've had word about Stephen, my son."

"What kind of word?"

"Pierce has uncovered rumors about a boy living with the French at Louisbourg. We're going there to check them out."

"Are you sure you want to do that, to chase after a rumor? You could get hurt. I don't think I could stand to see you hurt again. Besides, the French love to pick on little vessels like ours. We could end up in court for violating French waters."

"Daniel has obtained a safe conduct from the royal governor for us. They won't dare touch a ship with such a letter in the possession of the master."

"Probably true. But I don't like to think that I have to depend on Pierce for anything. When do you want to sail?"

"Just as soon as possible," she said.

"We'll sail with the morning tide—especially if you spend the night on board." He smiled at her and she responded by jabbing him in the ribs with her knuckles.

"You're a vile, over-sexed man, William Vaughan."

"True, and you are a beautiful woman. It is an unbeatable combination." He turned from her and, cupping his hands about his mouth, he started yelling at the longshoremen on the dock.

Sarah smiled at him. He seemed so different from the man she had first seen at the Cromwell's Head—the way he held his shoulders, the smoothness of his body movements. The years had seemed to drop away from him with the passing of time. The longer he commanded, the stronger he became. He was a man she wanted by her side when she confronted the priests again.

"I'm all packed, William, and ready to come aboard. The servants have careful instructions about my father. He can't make the trip with us, although he hates to remain behind. I don't think he could take a sea voyage, even a short one like this."

Vaughan nodded in agreement, although he suspected that the old man could have handled the trip. She was protecting him from the pain of disappointment. He led her by the hand toward his cabin. "I'll have this schooner unloaded and underway before you know it, my love," he said. "You wait for me below. We'll have supper and who knows what might happen after that."

The sail from Boston to Isle Royale normally should have taken three or four days, but warm air flowing over cool northern currents produced massive, dense fogs that were impenetrable. In these fogs the winds died completely, and all Vaughan could do was wait. The captain paced the quarter-deck and stared at the spot where he knew the sails were, even if he could not see them. He tried to curse wind into them—to no avail. Sarah remained below and fretted over the loss of time.

On the evening of their third day at sea, Vaughan stormed into the cabin, tore off his sea coat, threw it into the corner and slumped into a chair before the captain's table. Sarah had been sitting on the bed, staring out the stern window into

200

the gray wetness. "The bloody fog shows no signs of lifting. Damn it all," he cursed.

She rose from the bed and went to his side, placing her hand on the nape of his neck. "He's been there for years now, William; a few more days won't matter one way or the other."

He knew that she was trying to calm him and that she was as upset by the delay as he was. "It's the fog," he said. "Everything bad that has ever happened to me has happened in a fog." He shuddered, thinking of a tragic night off Cape Ann. "Tell you what, love," he said, trying to shake off his mood. "We'll have us a spot of supper. The cook has a rack of lamb that he's been saving for you and me. He's on his way with it now. We'll fix up the table, just like you do at home."

Going to his sea chest, he threw open the top, removed some silver candlesticks from the chest and placed them on the table. He found some short stubs of candles and shoved them into the holders and lit them. Next he produced two pewter plates and two fine silver mugs. He stepped back to admire his work. Just then there was a knock on the cabin door and, after a discreet wait, the cook entered, carrying a small tray with the meat on it, surrounded by boiled potatoes. The aroma of lamb filled the cabin as the cook placed the platter on the table between the candles.

Vaughan picked up the carving knife and started to cut the meat. Sarah winced as the knife sliced through the pink meat and the rose-colored juices dripped from the meat to the platter. "I'm afraid your cook has short-changed us," she said. "The meat is undercooked."

Vaughan looked at her in mock amazement. "Lamb, my love, is properly cooked to a pink color. Anything else is immolation. Try it. This is the way it is cooked in France. It's delicious."

Sarah, who followed the old British tradition that no meat was safe until it had been cooked a dark gray, cut a piece of meat and placed it warily on her fork. Very gingerly she nipped a piece off with her teeth. She chewed the food lightly, bringing air into her mouth at the same time to cool the meat. The lamb was perfect.

"See," laughed William, "you must be willing to try anything."

"So your bedtime philosophy extends to other areas as well," she teased.

201

"But not to every area," he said with a mock-serious air. "For sex, yes; for food, yes; but for a year of my life I tried it with alcohol as well. Had it not been for a remarkable lady, I'm afraid, my darling, my philosophy could have been the death of me."

She leaned across the table and kissed him on the nose. "We have been happy together for these last years, haven't we, William?"

"I've never been happier."

"If the child in Louisbourg is not Stephen," she said thoughtfully, "I believe I shall stop looking for him. He's not really a child any more. If he lives, he is already a young man with his own life. I think I would like to go back to Massachusetts and live with you, Captain."

"I was hoping you would do that in any case, madam." He picked up her hand and brought it to his lips. "I love you, Sarah."

She smiled back at him and put her small hand into his much larger one. "I think I'd like some air," she said.

They rose together. He went to the corner and retrieved his sea coat. "You'll need this," he said, draping it over her shoulders. "Damn cold in that bloody fog."

They walked arm in arm about the quarterdeck. William continually checked the course with the helmsman. In the dense, eerie whiteness that enveloped them, it was impossible to see the wheel. Occasionally a sail would respond to a small flitter of breeze, snapping with a sharp crack, but then the breeze would sneak away and the sail would lie flat against the yardarm. All would be quiet again.

Sarah pulled William's coat more tightly about her. She was shivering. He pulled her closer to his body and wrapped his enormous arm about her shoulders. Suddenly, they heard a loud splash on the port side of the bow and a shout of dismay. Vaughan stopped dead in his tracks. "Up forward, what's that all about?" he yelled. There was no answer—only white silence. "I'd better have a look, Sarah," he said to her. "You go below."

"I'll wait for you here," she said and watched him disappear into the mist. She stood beside the railing and pulled the coat about her shoulders again. She never saw the dark form step out of the gloom behind her, nor could the helmsman some ten feet away see it. The form stopped behind her back and watched her for a few seconds in a calculating way. Then his arm grabbed her roughly about the neck. She tried to scream but the arm tightened, cutting off any sound. The coat slipped from her shoulders and fell to the deck. With it, her locket, its chain broken by the violence of the attack, clattered to the deck as well. She tried to twist around to free herself and see who attacked her, but she failed. Isaac Wiggins, common seaman these last few days, whispered his name in her ear so that she would know who it was who killed her before he thrust his knife through her ribs and into her heart. Then he lifted her body over the railing and allowed it to slip over the side. Sarah was dead before the murky waters of the Atlantic closed over her head.

Wiggins watched her disappear into the fog. He picked up Vaughan's coat and tossed it into the sea after her. Then he noticed the gold locket on the deck. He smiled, picked it up and slipped it into his pocket. He walked quietly off the quarterdeck and found his way back toward the forecastle where the crew slept.

The wagon bounced along the rutted road that ran from Roxbury through the neck and into Boston. The driver made unintelligible noises to his horse but the poor beast, very old and swaybacked, ignored him, the road, and the whole world, as he continued to plod ahead at the same unruffled pace.

Stephen sat in the back of the wagon. After spending the night in a Roxbury farmer's orchard, he had hitched a ride for the last leg of his long journey home. He looked out at the mudflats that lined both sides of the neck of land connecting the peninsula of Boston with the mainland. He was still groggy with sleep; propping his back against the sacks of flour in the wagon, he absentmindedly picked off the white and pink apple blossom petals that still clung to his clothing.

As the wagon continued northward, the scenery began to change. On the right some trenches and a redoubt with heavy cannon in place were grim reminders of the continuing tensions that existed between France and England, especially now that England and Spain, France's ally, were at war. On the left side of the road, the land broadened out, and occasional houses with neat garden lots surrounding them replaced the ugliness of the mudflats. To the northwest and to the west, beyond the houses, Stephen could see the tops of the Boston hills.

Stephen had felt no urgency when he had awakened that morning. Even after eating the last of his food, he had stretched out again to watch the honeybees in the orchard attempt to wring the last drop of nectar from the apple blossoms. But now, as he came closer to his destination and to the truth of his identity, he could feel the tension building within him. Today he hoped his journey would finally come to an end.

The journey had begun frightfully. He and Socono, frostbitten and hungry, had arrived in the little Dutch town of Schenectady after two weeks of struggle along the course of the Mohawk. There Socono had left him. Their relationship, which had been strained by Socono's revelations, had mended during the weeks they fled together. They agreed to meet again after Stephen had found his family.

Stephen made another shorter journey to the large town of Albany on the Hudson. There he found a job in an inn as a kitchen helper, washing pots and dishes and occasionally serving meals, in return for his own food and a small room with a cot off the kitchen. He was promised a bonus of three shillings in the spring if he stayed on.

With the coming of spring Stephen took his bonus, purchased some food and started overland from Albany to Springfield. At first he slept in the forest, but once over the mountains he found hospitality at isolated cabins, where he worked for a meal and a bed in the barn at night. Inquiries in the river towns revealed nothing about his origins. No one in Springfield or Hadley recalled any Indian attack fourteen years earlier. He had nowhere else to turn. Socono had told him that the Jesuits had always referred to his family as Bastonois, but he knew that was a term frequently used to describe all New Englanders. He felt he had no other alternative; he would have to go to Boston.

Once again the scenery about him changed. It was clear that they were entering a large town. The houses were more numerous and closer together. The main road was frequently crossed by other lanes and paths. The traffic on the roads increased; horse-drawn wagons and an occasional lone horseman passed Stephen's driver or crossed his route.

Stephen turned and looked at the driver, but all he could see was his back. "It's not far to town now, I guess?" he offered.

The driver craned his neck partially around in Stephen's direction. "Nope, we're almost there now, son," he replied. "Where would you like me to drop you off?"

"How far are you going?"

The driver had to pull in on the reins as a fast-moving horseman cut in front of him, splattering mud on the side of his old nag. "God damn Anglican—always pushin' people," he cursed.

Stephen smiled. "How do you know he's an Anglican?"

"He's dressed like one," was the response. "Nothing's been right around here since old Governor Belcher quit. He was a proper God-fearing member of the church. Not like this snotty, bepowdered Shirley." He scratched his head, trying to remember what he had been saying before the arrival of the horseman. "Oh, yes, how far am I going? I have to take the flour to market at Faneuil Hall, the new marketplace." He pronounced the name of the marketplace as if it were spelled "Funnel."

"Where's that?" Stephen asked.

"Center of town, near the wharf area."

"I suppose that's as good a spot as any," said the boy.

"What are you looking for?" asked the driver.

"I've been away and I'm looking for relatives. I don't know if they live in Boston or in one of the towns close by."

"What's the name?"

"Nowell."

"Can't say I know of any Nowells in Boston. Used to be some folks by that name over in Charlestown, across the river from Boston. They're all dead now. You should talk to old man Hudson, the ferryman. He knows just about everything that goes on over there. He's been running that ferry of his for years."

"Where do I find him?" asked Stephen.

"Just keep heading north across the mill creek, past the new church and then past the Old North Church—that was Mr. Mather's church before he died. Now there was a God-fearing preacher. Many a time I listened to him blast the devil when I was a young man. It was him that kept me from straying. We don't have men like him no more."

The old man fell silent. Finally Stephen interrupted his reverie. "Where do I go after the old church?"

The driver began to chuckle. "I've been doing that a lot lately, starting out on one road and ending up in a strange alley. After you pass the church, then you come to the docks. Turn left and go on up the hill—Copps Hills. Then you go down to the ferry opposite the burying ground. He'll be there, or coming back from the other side."

They were in the heart of the town now. The houses were closer together and so was the traffic on the road. The driver pulled up before a large, imposing red brick building of the

205

latest design. The ground floor and the streets around it were occupied by the stalls of farmers come to town to sell their produce and by shops of all descriptions. The noise of the market was deafening. Vendors attempted to out-yell each other and attract prospective buyers to their stalls. Wagons, horses, people—all crushed together on market day. It was the largest number of people that Stephen had even seen in one spot since Paris. It was not only the noise that impressed him; it was the smells. Freshly baked bread from the bakers' stalls and fresh fish from the little boats tied to the docks down the street mixed their aromas with the less pleasant odors of the town. The horse droppings that covered the street in front of the marketplace, the unwashed bodies and the accumulated garbage produced a stench that overcame the more familiar and pleasant scents. Stephen could barely hear the goodbye of the driver as they shook hands and parted. He was glad to get away from "Funnel Hall."

Stephen followed the driver's directions, heading due north across the creek and then along Fish Street. The houses on this side of the creek were not as impressive as those in the center of town. Here they were mostly made of wood, one storey with a sloping shingle roof. Some residents had covered the wood with cement and imbedded pieces of broken glass or brightly colored pebbles in it. In the center of town, south of the creek, the houses had been mostly two-storey, many of them brick, using the old English bond: a row of bricks laid lengthwise alternating with a row laid endwise. Many of the second storeys had gables.

But north of the creek, things looked poorer. The streets were narrow and dirty. They were cobblestone, but mud had accumulated to a depth of several inches, especially near the curb and only with difficulty could one tell they were paved.

Fish Street ran into Clarke Street. As Clarke converged with Princess and North Streets, Stephen encountered the church of the renowned, and in some quarters beloved, Mr. Cotton Mather, dead these sixteen years. Stephen had heard of the man, although he had been taught that Mather was the arch heretic of heretics and the cruel burner of witches.

He passed the Old North church and continued down North Street until he came to Charter Street. He caught sight of Boston harbor to his right. It was filled with ships. Some were carefully charting their way through the narrow channels in and out of the harbor; others were tied to the wharves, loading and unloading goods from England and all the colonies in her vast empire. Ahead of him he saw the mouth of the Charles River and beyond it the point of another peninsula of land, on which sat a small village dominated by several large hills. He turned up Charter Street and climbed the hill.

At the top of the hill there was a cemetery, the current resting place of the arch heretic. From the top of the hill, Stephen had an even better view of the town he had just traversed and the broad expanse of its harbor, which was large enough to hold the whole British navy. Below him at the foot of the hill was the ferry slip. The ferry had just arrived from the opposite shore. Stephen hurried down the hill to catch the ferryman before he took off again to Charlestown.

As it turned out, Hudson the ferryman was not at all anxious to return to the Charlestown shore, since there was no one waiting to be taken across. He was universally referred to as "old Hudson," but it would have been difficult to tell his age. He had no hair anywhere on his body. Not only was his head bald, but he had no eyebrows or lashes, no beard or moustache. He claimed that a high fever in his youth had left him bald. He joked about it, saying that he had missed his calling by remaining in Boston as a ferryman. He should have gone west to live on the frontier; he was one of the few whom the Indians would never scalp. His baldness, however, removed from him one of the signs of aging, and one had to look carefully into his face and note the wrinkles and lines about his eyes to guess that he was over seventy. Age had not deprived him of his strength or his garrulousness. When the winds were favorable, he sailed his clients across the strait to Charlestown and back. But if they were contrary, he and an assistant would break out the oars and row across, all the while regaling the customers with the latest gossip from both towns.

"Mister Hudson, sir," called Stephen to the old man as he walked from his boat to the door of the inn's taproom, which stood at the foot of the ferry slip.

"Mister and sir is it?" said the ferryman. "And who might be addressing me in so formal a manner?"

"My name is Stephen Nowell and I'm looking for some information."

"What kind of information?" he said, rubbing his hand across his lips and continuing to walk toward the tavern door and his customary noon mug of ale.

Stephen followed and talked as they walked. "I have been

207

away for some years and I am looking for my relatives. Do you know of any Nowells living in Charlestown or in Boston or in any of the towns around here?"

"Used to be Nowells living in Charlestown. They're all dead now. The last one was the preacher who went out to the frontier. Got himself killed by the Indians."

"Did he have a family?" asked Stephen excitedly. Finally he seemed to be getting close.

"I don't rightly recall. That was a few years back—back around thirty or thirty-one. Oh, yes, now I remember, there was the preacher and his son. The wife, the Breed girl, she survived. Though some say the loss of her husband affected her mind. She went into business here in Charlestown. It created quite a scandal, but she made a fortune. Then she was lost at sea, a few months ago."

"She's dead, too," said Stephen. "Then there's no one left."

"Well, I guess that's right. But there are some Breeds still left in Charlestown. Old man Breed never leaves his house any more, but his sister is still lively. You might try her."

Stephen could hardly suppress his excitement. "Where do the Breeds live?"

"Miss Betsy Breed, her name's Pierce now, she lives up on Breed's pasture—that's the old man's house, on the first hill there above the village." Hudson pointed across the strait as he spoke.

"Can you take me across?" Stephen asked.

"If you have your penny and are willing to wait for me to have my ale, you'll get there. I've been having my noon ale at the Cromwell's Head for as long as it's been standing and I don't see any reason to do anything different today."

The old man entered the inn and Stephen went aboard the ferry to await his return. He had been waiting for years for this moment, but these few additional minutes seemed like hours to him. Three other passengers climbed aboard during the half hour wait, while one wagon driver and a horseman waited ashore at the foot of the ferry slip for assistance.

Promptly at thirty minutes past the hour, the bald-headed man left the taproom and walked down the slope toward the ferry. Before climbing aboard, he took note of the wind and, putting two fingers into his mouth, he whistled shrilly twice. "Wind's died," he said, addressing no one in particular.

From behind the tavern a broad-shouldered Negro, well over six feet tall, came walking toward the ferry, removing a white kitchen apron from his waist as he walked. "Get a move on, Josiah," yelled Hudson to the black man. "Get the wagon on the ferry. You passengers, there, get up into the bow. We'll board the wagon first. That horse can be loaded on last."

Josiah swung open the ferry gate and, grabbing the reins of the team of wagon horses, he skillfully guided them aboard. When all were aboard, Hudson broke out two large oars, one on either side of the ferry, and fixed them in the huge oarlocks. Josiah cast off and ran forward to his sweep. Together the two men dipped their oars into the Charles and pulled. The ferry, groaning under its load, slowly poked her square bow into the river.

The two oarsmen worked long and hard under the hot May sun to cross the Charles River. Both were sweating freely by the time they reached midstream. But Stephen, perched on his spot in the bow, could not take his eyes from the hill above the village and noticed nothing of the strenuous efforts of the boat's operators to reach their destination. He could see the farmhouse from here. Did it look familiar? Yes, it did. But then he desperately wanted it to look familiar. How did it differ from the dozens of New England houses he had seen during the past days?

The ferry touched its Charlestown slip with a heavy thud. The wooden pillars of the slip bent mightily under the blow. Stephen gave his last penny to Hudson and jumped from the bow onto the land.

The village was a small one, without the noise and hustle of Boston. It took him no more than five minutes to walk through it and begin to climb up the slope to Breed's Hill. He could see the house quite clearly now. It had two storeys with a lean-to attached to the back. Smoke was coming from the central chimney. As he drew closer, even more detail became obvious: the small-paned, leaded casement windows, the nail-studded oaken door. All were familiar to him, he thought.

He stood before the door and reached for the great iron knocker. He lifted it and released it, waited a moment, and knocked a second time.

Hannah swung open the door. "May I help you, sir?" she asked.

"My name is Stephen Nowell and I would like to speak with Mr. Breed."

Hannah looked him directly in the face for a moment, and gradually her look of disbelief was replaced by one of astonishment. "My God, it is you." She turned and ran into

209

the house yelling, "It's Master Stephen returned from the dead."

Stephen was left standing at the open door. There was a stirring on the second-floor landing. Stephen could not see what was going on, but he could hear voices. Finally, Miss Betsy, her hair now gray and her face showing some wrinkles, descended the stairs. "Hannah," she called. "What has happened to her? You silly woman, where have you gone?" She approached the open door with a quizzical look on her face and was startled to see Stephen standing there. "May I help you, sir?" she said. "My maid seems to have lost her wits. I must apologize for her behavior."

"No need to apologize, madam," said Stephen. "I'm afraid I startled her. I'm Stephen, Stephen Nowell. I would like to speak with my grandfather."

For a minute Stephen was afraid that Miss Betsy—and he assumed that he was speaking to her—would react in the same manner as the servant. At first there was a look of doubt and then wide-eyed amazement. But she quickly gained control of herself. "Come in, young man," she said. She took him by the hand and led him into the parlor. "Hannah," she called. "Bring us some tea in the parlor and ask Mr. Pierce to join us."

She asked Stephen to sit and he selected the window seat. She sat in the large rocker opposite him and stared. "You must excuse me for staring," she said finally. "My grandnephew disappeared fourteen years ago. He was only a small boy at the time and you are a young man. Yet, it could be. There are striking similarities."

Before she could finish, she was interrupted by the arrival of Daniel Pierce. "Young man, this is my husband, Mr. Pierce." They both rose to greet him. "Daniel, this young man says that he is Sarah's boy—Stephen."

Pierce had extended his hand to greet his guest but as Betsy spoke, he withdrew his hand quickly. He said nothing but only nodded.

Betsy continued. "I was about to ask him his story."

Stephen waited for his aunt to sit down again before beginning. "There is not a great deal to tell, I'm afraid," said Stephen. "I remember almost nothing about what happened to me. I was only recently told the truth. My father was murdered by Indians and I was carried off to Isle Royale. I have been living in Louisbourg and in France for the last fourteen years." He said nothing about the Society of Jesus, knowing that they would never understand his involvement.

"I was told that my family had come to New France searching for me. Instead, now I search for my family."

"You say you remember nothing about your parents?" asked Pierce.

"No, sir," responded Stephen. "The only thing I remembered was my name."

"How then did you learn of your identity?"

"Strangely enough," said Stephen, "from the Indian who was responsible for my father's death."

"Then there is no other evidence to support your claim?"

"No, sir. But I am who I say I am."

"Oh, dear," said Betsy, weeping. "My poor Sarah."

"Betsy, my dear," said Pierce, "I think we have heard quite enough. I think you should show this impostor the door."

Betsy Pierce looked confused. "Oh, my, you think he is an impostor?"

"Of course," her husband responded. "Anyone could see through this blatant attempt to defraud you of your rightful inheritance." He turned to Stephen. "Sir, I demand that you leave this house."

Stephen was shocked by the charge. "I assure you, Mr. Pierce," he said, "I have no such intention. I am merely trying to find the family from which I have been separated for all these years."

"Daniel," said Betsy, "are you quite sure? He seems like such a nice boy and he looks so much like little Stephen."

"Perhaps if I could see my grandfather, Mr. Breed," Stephen suggested.

"That is impossible. My brother-in-law no longer receives visitors. He has left his affairs to me."

"But surely he will see me," said Stephen.

"Leave," Pierce commanded. "If you bother me or my wife again, I will have my solicitor on you."

Stephen rose from the window seat and walked toward the parlor door. He stopped and looked up the staircase. He was determined to see Breed. Betsy broke down and ran crying from the room and up the stairs toward her bedroom.

"Hannah," shouted Pierce. "See to your mistress but first show this man the door." He turned on his heel and stormed out of the room.

Hannah, weeping, did as she was told.

Stephen stepped out again into the afternoon sun. He turned and looked at the house. It did not seem possible to him that he could have approached this same house with such high hopes but a few minutes before. He had found his family, but they had rejected him. His grandfather was inaccessible and his aunt, or rather her husband, feared him.

He started back down the path to the ferry slip and realized that he did not even have the penny he would need to recross to Boston. And even if he made it across, he had no place to stay, no plans. He had placed all his hopes on a reunion with those who had loved him.

He sat down at the side of the path. He needed time to think, time to figure out what he would do. He heard some cannon boom from Castle William, an island fortress in Boston Harbor. He could not see the fort but assumed that it must be some sort of signal gun. He had to see the old man. He would not give up until Breed himself rejected him.

He stood up again. Perhaps Mr. Hudson would let him work for his passage back to Boston. Then there was the Cromwell's Head. He was an experienced hand in the innkeeping business; perhaps he could get a room and meals in return for work. He could take care of himself. And somehow or other he would get to see the old man.

He started down the path toward Charlestown again but was startled to hear his name called out from the direction of the house. He turned and saw an older man running toward him.

"Master Stephen, is it really you?" asked the man as he approached the boy. "My God, it is you. Anyone could see that. It's the eyes—your grandfather's eyes." Tears filled his own eyes as he spoke. "Oh, upon my soul, he must see you after all these years. Hannah, my wife, told me that you had returned and I told him. He wants to see you now." He was crying openly. "Come, keep walking away from the house. I don't want that dried-up old buzzard, Pierce, to see us. We'll go the back way, by the path from Bunker's Hill. Then we'll slip in through the kitchen. By the way, my name is George. I've been servant and good friend to your grandfather for many years."

"I don't remember you, George. I remember almost nothing about the early years. I'm sorry."

"Never you mind, Master Stephen," he said. "We know who you are. Just follow me."

As they approached the kitchen door, Hannah swung it open. Stephen entered and she grabbed him about the neck, hugging him with all her considerable strength. Then she covered his face with kisses.

"Stop it, woman," hissed George. "You'll have Pierce down on us."

"No need to worry about that one. He's gone. Been

212

summoned to Boston, to Governor Shirley's, something about some French raid. The high and mighty prig. He's left and Miss Betsy has taken to her bed, weeping, poor thing."

"Good. We'll have no trouble getting Master Stephen up to see Mr. Breed. Come with me, boy," said George.

They went through the kitchen and into the dining room. It had not changed at all. The heavy oaken furniture and pewterware were the same as on that night fourteen years before at the family farewell dinner.

They climbed the staircase to the second floor. George led Stephen to the door of the master bedroom. He opened it and stepped aside to allow the boy to enter.

Jonathan Breed lay, propped up with pillows, in the large four-poster bed. His face was drawn and sallow. The ruddy complexion of former years had faded utterly. He had lost much weight and his skin sagged from his cheeks and chin, while the skin on his forehead was tight and almost translucent. He rarely left his bed now. He had been dozing but was awakened by the opening of the door.

"George," he called. "Did you bring the boy?"

"Yes, Mr. Breed. He's here." George pushed Stephen gently into the room and over toward the bed.

"Let me look at you, boy," said Breed. "What's my first name?"

"I don't know," said Stephen.

"What was your mother's name?" asked the old man sharply.

Stephen said nothing.

"So you don't know that either, do you? Lean down toward me, boy."

Stephen bent down and put his face directly in front of the old man's. Breed searched Stephen's face and traced the scar over his eye with his thumb. "That's new," he mumbled. He reached up a feeble arm and placed it about Stephen's neck. "You might not know the right answers, but that's a good sign; an imposter would have been prepared for my questions. I know that you really are my grandson. I could no more deny you than I could deny a mirror. I can never forget your face or deny my own eyes." He squeezed and pulled Stephen's head down onto his chest.

"Sarah," he called out, "would to God you were here with me. The boy is back."

Stephen lay limply in his grandfather's arms. All tension drained from him. He had felt the touch of someone who loved him at last.

The old man finally relaxed his grip and Stephen sat upright on the edge of the bed. Breed could not keep his hands off of the boy, however, and insisted on stroking his hand as they spoke.

"You don't remember anything of what happened?" asked Breed. "You weren't an infant when it happened."

Stephen stared ahead. "I remember nothing, sir."

"Call me Grandpa."

"Grandpa. Maybe it was the wound I received. But I can't recall anything beyond living with the Jesuits."

"The God damn bastards. They had you all along. They deprived a mother of her child and an old man of his only consolation. There can't be any lower scum on earth."

Stephen remained silent, not wishing to excite the old man any further. "They did not treat me badly, Grandpa. They fed me and clothed me, and they educated me. But you are right about the suffering they caused to others in order to protect themselves. Tell me about my mother and father—the family—everything."

"George, go downstairs and get my Bible. You know where I keep it."

The servant returned in a few minutes bearing a giant leather-bound book. The old man turned to the pages on which he had listed the family genealogy. He pointed to his own entry. "That's me. Born in 1675, right in the middle of the Indian War. My father was away with the militia fighting the Indians on the Connecticut. That's my sister, Elizabeth," he said, pointing to the next entry. "She's fifteen years younger than me. Would she were fifteen years wiser. She's married to Daniel Pierce now. I'm sorry I allowed it. He helped me search for you, but ever since he married Betsy he's taken over more and more. I hardly feel like the master of my own house any longer. He can't wait until I die.

"That's your mother, Sarah. She was born in 1700. She was my only child, my joy, my greatest love. And she loved you, boy, and she died looking for you. She was lost overboard off the coast of Isle Royale earlier this year."

Stephen swallowed hard. "She would not have found me there."

The old man merely shook his head in sorrow. "This is your father. Samuel Nowell. He was a preacher."

Stephen smiled. "It must run in the family."

"We don't know what happened to him; he disappeared along with you."

"He was killed," said Stephen.

"How do you know? I thought you didn't remember."

"The Indian who was responsible for his death told me. And he told me that I had family in Boston. That's how I came to be here."

"There you be, Stephen," said Breed. "1725, June the 13th."

Stephen smiled. "I've always celebrated my birthday on Christmas day. I'm not as old as I've always thought I was. I thought I was nineteen. Now it appears that I will not be for several weeks yet." He paused for a second. "I have a brother?"

"He died as a babe," said the old man. "There is just you now. I want you to take this Bible with you, boy. It's yours now—and it is your responsibility to keep it up to date, to keep a record of the family. You are the last of my line."

Tears filled Stephen's eyes. At last he belonged. The Bible made it tangible; it was written down. He was Stephen Nowell, born on the 13th of June, 1725, the son of Samuel Nowell and Sarah Breed, the grandson of Jonathan Breed.

The old man reached into his nightstand and pulled out a purse. I want you to take this. It's all the money I have in the house—about £50 worth of silver. You'll need it to live on until I can get my lawyer over here from Boston."

As Stephen bent down to hug his grandfather, the door of the room swung open and Betsy Breed walked in. "Oh, my goodness," she exclaimed.

The old man fixed his eyes on his sister and he swore. "God damn it, woman. Can't you ever learn to knock before you barge into a man's room? If you breathe a word of what you've seen here, you hear me, one word to that creature you're married to and I'll throw you both out of this house. This boy is my grandson, and you two had no right to try to keep me from him. Anyone with eyes could see who he was."

Betsy stood still in the doorway, not knowing which way to turn. Finally, overwhelmed by indecision, she turned and ran from the room.

The old man cursed. "It won't do," he said. "Pierce will have it out of her before the day is through. George, you get word to Mr. Warren, my lawyer, and get him to come to this house. You, my boy, will have to leave here. Go to Boston and stay at the Cromwell's Head; find a man who lives there by the name of William Vaughan. Tell him who you are and tell him that I want to see him. Go now. We have much to do if we're going to settle your life, Stephen Nowell. Before you go, give an old man a kiss and promise him you'll come back. Promise me that I'll never lose you again."

Stephen kissed the old man's cheek and then leaned against his chest. Breed stroked his black hair with one hand and patted his shoulder with the other. "Off with you now."

Stephen rose from the bed and started out the door.

"Stephen," the old man cried.

"Yes, Grandpa?"

"You will come back, won't you?"

Stephen smiled. "I'll never go away again, Grandpa. I've come home for good."

Hudson had no change for Stephen's silver crown, so he accompanied him into the taproom of the inn to allow the innkeeper to change the coin. Stephen followed his grandfather's instructions. He would look for William Vaughan, but first he wanted to register at the Cromwell's Head as a guest; he wanted a hot bath, a good meal and a soft bed for the night.

The innkeeper could provide the meal and the bed. "The bath will have to wait until the wind stirs up a bit." Stephen looked at the innkeeper quizzically, not quite able to connect his bath with the state of the wind. "Josiah heats and hauls the water, but Hudson has first priority on his time," explained the host. "If you don't mind eating dirty, I suspect we can at least get you to bed clean."

Stephen looked down at himself. It was well that the innkeeper had seen his money already or he might not have let someone looking, much less smelling, like Stephen, stay at his inn. He still wore the black breeches he had taken with him from Louisbourg. They were wearing at the seat and the material had already split at the crotch. This last he had repaired himself with the help of a needle loaned him by a kindly farm wife, but the stitching was white and contrasted sharply with the black cloth. His shoes were in decent shape because, after the snows had melted, he had rarely worn them. He had come most of the way from Albany barefoot. His stockings, unfortunately, had not fared as well. Originally they had been white, but now their color ranged somewhere between ivory and gray, and the toes and the heels were gone. His shirt was torn at the sleeve and its color matched that of his stockings. He would have to outfit himself in some good clothes or soon be seized by the constable for indecent exposure. But first he would eat.

Stephen sat at the far corner table of the taproom, sipping

an ale while awaiting his meal. There was a commotion outside the front door. A group of men, some clearly working men and others gentlemen by their dress, came pouring through the door together. One of them noted Stephen sitting in the corner and called to him, "Have a drink with us, boy, and join the toast." He grabbed a mug of ale from the bar. Half of the mug's contents flew into the air as he raised it above his head. "Death to the French," he yelled. "It's war, my lads."

One of the well-dressed men threw some coins on the innkeeper's counter and called for drinks for all. He raised his own mug and called out, "On to Louisbourg." The men sent up a cheer. The landlord called to the kitchen and an enormously fat woman, his wife, came waddling out to help out at the bar.

"There goes my dinner," said Stephen out loud to himself.

The gentleman who had paid for the drinks walked over to Stephen's table. "Won't you join us, young man?" he said.

"I have a drink," Stephen replied.

"Well, join me then in a toast. On to Louisbourg." Stephen raised his mug and touched the man's glass. But he said nothing.

Another man, dressed in a uniform that Stephen did not recognize, approached the table. "Come on, Will," he said. "It's my turn to buy. And we need another toast."

"Well, after Louisbourg comes Quebec."

"That's it," said the uniformed man. "On to Quebec." Again the crowded bar room sent up a cheer.

"You'll join me in that toast, won't you, boy?" said Will.

Stephen was embarrassed by the man's directness and by the presence of several men who had joined Will, standing before Stephen's table.

"The first toast was easy to drink to. But it might be difficult to go on to Quebec. First you must succeed at Louisbourg and that will not be easy."

One of the working men, who smelled overwhelmingly of fish, lunged across the table at Stephen, but his hand was grabbed by Will and knocked aside. "He must be one of those damned frogs, talking like that," said the fisherman.

"On the contrary," said Will. "He sounds like he knows what he is talking about. A sane head admits insanity. Leave the boy alone." The group broke up and several of the men returned to the bar for another round of drinks.

The well-dressed gentleman, whom the others called Will,

lingered, however. "My name is William Vaughan," he said. "I'm sorry if I embarrassed you just now."

Stephen looked up at him in surprise. He rose and shook his hand. "Stephen Nowell," he said. Now it was Vaughan's turn to look at him strangely.

Vaughan sat down at the table. "Do you mind if I join you in a quiet drink? I think I have had enough merrymaking for the day."

"Please do," said Stephen. "This is really quite a coincidence, Mr. Vaughan. I have a message for you from Mr. Jonathan Breed. He wishes you to come and see him as soon as possible."

"I'll make a point of it today," said Vaughan. He was normally a very blunt man, but this time he held back the question that was burning in his mind. Instead he searched the young man's features and concluded that he might well be looking at Sarah's son.

Stephen watched the men at the bar. "I'm puzzled. Why would they celebrate the coming of war?"

Vaughan looked around at the crowd. "For several reasons, I suppose. For one, they are nervous—a bit of bravado to bolster their courage. The war hasn't begun well. War was declared in March, but word was slow getting here. The French are already out; they have seized our fort at Canso. Now only the garrison at Annapolis in Nova Scotia stands between the French and our Maine and New Hampshire towns. I'm a Hampshire man myself." He took a long drink and wiped his mouth with the back of his hand when he had finished. "Another thing, a lot of these men are fishermen. For years the French have been sailing out of Louisbourg and raiding the New England fishing fleets."

"But you must admit, sir, that the New Englanders encroach with impunity upon French territorial waters," said Stephen, who had heard LaGarde discussing the subject many times.

"I'd not admit anything of the kind," said Vaughan. "They are simple seamen looking to earn their living. The Grand Banks have always belonged to all fishermen, no matter what their origins. Now the French simply come out of Louisbourg and take them. Any move to take Louisbourg will be popular with seafaring men in New England."

"As I said before," said Stephen, "that won't be easy."

Vaughan looked at him. "You know something about the place?" he asked.

"I used to live there," said Stephen. "I was captured by the

French when I was a child. I spent most of my life there. I have only just escaped from them."

Vaughan caught his breath. Sarah had been on the right track after all. "My God, you must know the place better than any Englishman alive. You could be of great value to the right people. I'm supposed to meet with Governor Shirley this evening. I would like to spend time with you before I go. Even better, I would like to be able to bring you with me. Would you mind coming with me and answering some questions for His Excellency?"

"I wouldn't mind," said Stephen. "But I will have to buy myself some decent clothing."

"Never mind that," said Vaughan. "It will take days to get a tailor to outfit you properly. I would lend you some of mine but I'm afraid I'm much too big. I have put on a little bit about the middle as well these last few years. You and Graham are about the same size; I will lend you some of his things. But first, I am supposed to be meeting another man here. He also claims to know something about Louisbourg. Perhaps you will stay with me and meet him."

Stephen nodded assent. The innkeeper's wife was still passing out mugs of ale. He knew he would have a long wait for his meal. The celebrants were getting very drunk. The noise in the room was deafening. Several fishermen pushed aside the tables in the center of the taproom and began to dance the hornpipe, to the accompaniment of the raucous singing of the rest of the crowd. Vaughan did not join in the singing and Stephen did not know the song. He remained an observer, laughing when two of the dancers knocked into each other and collapsed into a drunken heap.

The ale was beginning to get to him as well. He lifted his mug and was about to call to the innkeeper for a refill, but the words froze on his lips. Standing in the doorway of the inn was Isaac Wiggins. Vaughan saw Wiggins enter at the same time. He stood and called, "Wiggins, over here. Join us."

The trader saw Vaughan and waved in his direction. He crossed the floor toward the corner. He was smiling his toothless smile but, as his eyes focused behind Vaughan and he saw Stephen, his grin faded and was replaced by a look of disbelief.

"Nowell," said Vaughan. "This is Isaac Wiggins, the man I was telling you about."

Wiggins nodded but said nothing. Stephen suppressed the anger that the sight of Wiggins caused. If Wiggins was going to pretend they did not know each other, he would go along with the fiction—for the time being.

"Have an ale, Isaac," said Vaughan, oblivious to the undercurrents around him. "I've been speaking with Mr. Nowell here about Louisbourg. He used to live there and knows the place well. Wiggins has been telling me about some of the weaknesses and strengths of the fortress. He feels that a surprise landing at night and an attack on the land walls would bring about the best chance of success."

"That's absurd," interrupted Stephen.

Vaughan stopped speaking and looked at Stephen in surprise.

"What's so damned absurd about it?" snapped Wiggins. The malice in his voice was obvious.

Stephen stood up. "Mr. Vaughan, you will have to excuse me. I don't like the company you keep and I would just as soon go to my room."

Wiggins stood up as well. "You didn't answer my question, Frenchie," he said. "What's so damned absurd about it?"

Stephen's anger was about to explode. He was trying desperately to control himself. The noise in the room, the ale and now this hated face staring into his had set his head reeling. Getting hold of his emotions, he responded. "If you must know why your suggestion is absurd, it is because there are no safe landing beaches around Louisbourg. Even a daylight landing will require great care because of the high surf. Secondly, the land walls of the fortress are the strongest part of the defenses. The place to strike is at the West Gate. Heavy artillery will be needed, but those walls will crumble under heavy fire."

"The place is surrounded by swamps. How the hell will you get cannons in front of those walls," said Wiggins.

Stephen's head was pounding but he kept control. "You're right about the swamps, but that's a problem for the engineers."

Wiggins interrupted him. "Vaughan, why are you listening to this pup? I know all about him. He is one of the goddamn Frenchies. He's worse than that. He's one of their priests. I just finished running him out of the Oneida country, where he was undermining King George. You shouldn't be listening to him; you should be hanging him."

Stephen finally let loose. He wanted to get at that face—that grinning face. Wiggins had been responsible for the death of his father. It was Wiggins who had scarred his friend, Socono. He swung blindly.

Wiggins blocked his arm and went for his throat. Stephen fell backward, dragging Wiggins, whose fingers clenched at his windpipe. They sprawled against the wooden table, overturning it and scattering chairs in all directions. Stephen struggled to his feet, but still he could not break Wiggins' hold. He could not breathe. He had to get some air. His lungs ached and he could feel his heart pounding in his chest.

Stephen brought his knee up sharply between Wiggins' legs. Wiggins screamed and let go of Stephen's throat. Bending at the middle, he grabbed his crotch. Stephen's right hand smashed into that hated face with all his might. Wiggins' body was straightened by the blow and he fell onto his back, sliding into the next table, throwing ale mugs onto the floor with a crash.

Wiggins shook his head as if to get his eyes back in focus. He struggled to his feet and pulled a skinning knife from his boot. He crouched on the balls of his feet and, holding the handle of the knife loosely in his hand, he approached his opponent. "I've quit playing with you, little boy," he rasped. His tongue darted out of the space between his teeth to lick the blood that trickled from his nose. "You been bothering me, getting in my way. You fucked my woman and now she don't want nothing to do with me and then you mess up my deal with the Oneida by getting their chief killed. I think you need a cutting."

His knife hand flicked out, too quickly for Stephen to avoid. He darted back, but the breeches on his left thigh were neatly sliced open and blood began to race down his leg.

"Just a few inches to the right now," said Wiggins, "and I'll finish you off by stuffing your cock in your mouth." He was grinning now. He wiped his bleeding nose on his sleeve and switched the knife to his left hand. He did not see the chair raised high over his head, and he was taken totally by surprise when it came crashing down. He fell to the floor with a thud, the knife sliding harmlessly across the wooden floor.

"The man is a dangerous animal," said Vaughan as he calmly replaced the chair against one of the few untouched tables in the taproom. "But he is valuable. Lt. Graham, can you take Wiggins to his lodgings?" Vaughan addressed his uniformed companion of the earlier toasting. "I think he is staying at your inn on Marlborough Street. In any case he's staying in the south end."

Stephen was still trying to regain his breath. "You shouldn't have interfered," he gasped. "He and I have a score to settle."

"Mr. Nowell, I really don't care what exists between you and Wiggins. All I know is that Wiggins has Governor Shirley's ear and I can't allow him to get hurt. Although I think it was more likely that you would have been the one to be hurt. I happen to believe you possess valuable information. You would be of little use to me as a soprano in a boy's choir."

Stephen wiped the sweat from his forehead with his sleeve. His breeches were soaked with blood. Vaughan tossed him a towel from the barman's counter. Stephen pressed it against the cut in his leg. He resented Vaughan's superior air but reasoned that there was much truth in what he said.

"Josiah," called Vaughan. The black man's head appeared from the kitchen door.

"You called, Mister William?"

"Have Nowell's dinner brought to my room. Also bring the hot water for his bath there. We have some business to discuss."

Stephen lay back in the tub, luxuriating in the sensual comfort of the warm water. He had scrubbed his hair clean with a harsh lye soap. Standing in the half-empty tub, he had soaped his whole body, rubbing vigorously except for the tender area of the cut on his thigh. Then he sat back down into the water. His wound reopened in the hot water and began to tint it pink.

Josiah entered the room, carrying two large buckets of water. "I brought the water for rinsing, Mr. Nowell," he said.

Stephen rose again. Josiah poured the first bucket over his head. Stephen gasped. It was not quite as cold as the water in the pool at Louisbourg, but it was not far off. It took his breath away. The second bucket was just as cold. Dripping water, Stephen stepped out of the tub onto the rug. He threw a towel about his body and sat on a stool near the tub. He picked up what was left of his shirt and, using it as a bandage, attempted to stop the flow of blood from his wound.

Vaughan entered the room just as Stephen finished drying himself. He paused; the scene reminded him of another time. Then he went to the chair by the table and collapsed into it with a weary sigh.

"Mr. Nowell, I have a question to ask of you. Are you Sarah Nowell's son?"

Stephen looked at him in surprise. "Yes, I am," he said.

"I think, then, it is important for me to tell you that your mother was the only woman I have ever loved and that I loved her more than life itself. Since I lost her, I have tried to fill my life, but I fear I will never stop mourning her."

"What happened? How did she die?"

"I don't know," said Vaughan, his voice cracking with grief. "I've asked myself that question again and again. One minute she was next to me. I stepped forward from the quarterdeck and when I returned she was gone. We never found a trace of her." He shook his head, as if to banish the horrors of that long, foggy night.

"What did she look like?" Stephen asked softly.

"How can I describe her? She looked a lot like you. Dark hair and skin browned by the sun. She was my only love. I believe you are her son and you are dear to me for her sake. But you, my boy, are going to need help. Your mother made me what I am. When she and old Joseph Moulton found me, I was a drunk, on my last legs. She was the inspiration for my beginning anew. I've never slipped back. My famous toasts today were a sham. I drink soft cider, apple juice. Josiah keeps a supply for me. I've never slipped back because to do so would be to betray her. I don't expect you to feel anything for me, but I want you to know that I will do anything I can to help and protect Sarah Nowell's son."

"I don't quite know what to say. I seem to have gained a grandfather and a step-father all in one day," said Stephen.

Vaughan sighed once again. "I don't mean to be cruel to you, but I have to be straightforward. The reason I asked these questions is that I have just discovered that you do not have a grandfather. Jonathan Breed died this afternoon."

Stephen bowed his head and from force of habit started to make the sign of the cross. The tears began to flow down his cheeks.

"I'm sorry too," said the older man. "He was a good friend to me as well, particularly after Sarah died. I guess we shared a sorrow and could console each other. I shall miss him."

Stephen could barely speak. He was overcome with grief. He had hardly known the old man; his grief was really more for himself. The drifting feeling was taking hold of him again. He still didn't belong anywhere. Once again he was alone.

There was a knock on the door and Josiah entered without waiting for permission. He walked directly to Vaughan. "Mr.

Will, sir," he said. "I found this on the floor of the taproom. I was wondering if it belonged to Mr. Nowell, considering the fight and considering that it has this big N on it."

Vaughan took the locket into his hand. His face was expressionless, but his insides were churning. It was Sarah's. "Stephen," he asked finally. "Is it yours?"

"No, it belongs to that bastard Wiggins. He was wearing it."

"Are you sure of that?"

"Yes," said Stephen. "I must have torn it from his neck during the fight. There is no way that I can be made to be responsible for returning it to him, Mr. Vaughan."

"I don't expect you to return it to him, Stephen," Vaughan said thoughtfully. "I've left my dressing gown on the bed. Once you get yourself fully dry, put it on and go down to your own room. You are exhausted and hurt. I think you ought to try to get some sleep."

"I couldn't sleep now," said Stephen. "What happened to my grandfather?"

"Pierce thinks his heart gave out."

"Perhaps my coming back was too much. Maybe if I had stayed away, he'd be alive."

"George told me what happened, Stephen. You made that old man happier than he has been since you left. Don't blame yourself for what happened. I'm just happy that he lived to see you." Vaughan turned to the black man. "Josiah, show Mr. Nowell to his room and then send Lt. Graham to me."

When Graham arrived he found a very agitated William Vaughan. "Graham, quick, come in and close the door. I've been trying to put the pieces together and I think I've got them all in place."

"What are you talking about, Willy?"

"Sarah, Stephen, the old man—it all fits into a pattern. The key is the relationship between Isaac Wiggins and Daniel Pierce. Why hadn't I seen it before? Every time Wiggins arrives on the scene, someone dies or disappears, and with each death or disappearance, Daniel Pierce advances. Sarah told me it was Pierce who hired Wiggins to guide the Nowells west. Samuel and Stephen disappear. Pierce advances in Breed's eyes. He allows Pierce to marry his sister, something he opposed earlier. Sarah disappears from my God damn ship. Wiggins arrives three months later wearing her locket. As a result of her death, our partnership is dissolved, with Pierce making off with the lion's share. Wiggins arrives in

Boston the very day that Stephen reappears. Jonathan Breed dies before he can alter his will in favor of his grandson. Betsy Pierce is Breed's legal heir."

"Let it rest, Will. It's all circumstantial. You can't prove a thing."

"No, but Wiggins is still here. I think the son of a bitch murdered my Sarah. I'll see him burn in hell for that. And in the meanwhile, I must protect Sarah's son. He'll be the next victim. Sarah put away a great deal of money for him in trust. But since I doubt if he can prove who he really is, he'll probably never get his hands on it. But if he were dead, Pierce could acknowledge him—or his corpse—to gain the money through his wife, who would be Stephen's only living kin. By God, that boy is going to stay alive. John, I want you to take him with you. Take him to Nova Scotia. I'll make up some excuse. I'll give him some kind of job. Just get him out of Pierce's way. Pierce may send Wiggins after him, but we'll be watching them."

After several hours of tossing and turning, Stephen rose and joined Vaughan in his room once again. They had some dinner, and after the meal Vaughan lit a pipe and offered one to Stephen. Stephen was no smoker, as his one experience at the Oneida council had proven to him.

"Well, at least there is one vice you lack," said Vaughan good-naturedly.

Stephen blushed.

"What are we going to do with the boy from Louisbourg? How can we make use of you now?"

"What do you mean?" asked Stephen.

Vaughan took a deep breath, inhaling the smoke from the pipe into his lungs and tossing his head back. He exhaled the smoke toward the ceiling. "I assume that there is some basis to Wiggins' claim that you are a priest."

"Mr. Vaughan," said Stephen, "I was captured as a child by the French and raised in the Jesuit house in Louisbourg. I was deceived by them. They told me nothing about myself, and it should not be a surprise to you that I would try to join the Society of Jesus when I became older. I was not a priest. I was a scholastic in training to become a priest. When I learned the truth about myself, I returned to Boston to locate my family. I have good reason to seek revenge against the French and against the Society of Jesus in particular."

"You really ought to try to check that temper of yours, Nowell," smiled Vaughan. "I did not say that Wiggins should

225

be believed. I just wanted to know the whole story. I believe that you are no French agent. For one, you are too young, and secondly, spies don't go about instigating brawls in inns, making themselves likely targets for castration. If you are a spy, you are either a bloody awful one or the cleverest man in North America. Frankly, I can't think of you as very clever."

Stephen was perplexed. He did not know whether to feel insulted or grateful. Vaughan continued. "Wiggins will spread lies about you to His Excellency. There is little use in my taking you to see him. What you said about Louisbourg makes a good deal of sense. I will be honest with you, Nowell. I intend to try to persuade the governor to send a force against Isle Royale. I am going to head that expedition, and I intend to take Louisbourg. Men like you will be very useful to me. But you can't stay in Boston. Wiggins will look for you and he will certainly get to you."

"I'm not afraid of him," said Stephen with some vehemence.

"Well then, you are a bigger fool than I thought," said Vaughan. "I would be afraid of him, if he were my enemy. You should be afraid of him too."

"I won't run away from him."

"No," said Vaughan. "I am not suggesting that you do anything dishonorable. I am suggesting that you enter the employ of my trading firm, and that as my employee, you accompany Lt. Graham and his scouts to Annapolis."

"What would I be expected to do there?" asked Stephen.

"Not much," was the reply. "Let us say that your presence there would be like a reserve force set aside for when it is needed. You could help Mascarene, the commander there, or you might be of assistance to Graham and his rangers until I get word to you when I need you."

"Mascarene? He sounds French," said Stephen.

"A Protestant. He has been in King George's service for years."

"How much will you pay me?" asked Stephen bluntly.

"Let's say five pounds per annum plus expenses to begin with," said Vaughan.

"That's not very much," objected Stephen.

"You won't need very much."

Stephen finished the glass of claret that Vaughan had placed before him. He was not clear about what his job would be, but he clearly had little choice. He had to trust Vaughan. For now he would have to set aside his anger at Wiggins and the French. Later he might be able to get back at those who had hurt him so terribly and kept him from his family.

"Agreed," he said finally.

John Graham climbed the stairs from his cabin to the deck of the *Massachusetts Galley*. Below deck, sixteen of his twenty rangers were just beginning to show signs of recovery from the seasickness brought on by four rough days on the Atlantic. That morning they had entered the Bay of Fundy and the roll of the sea had lessened.

The galley lay at anchor in mid-bay, awaiting the rush of the tremendous tides before it attempted to enter the narrow channel of the Annapolis Basin. The channel lay one mile to starboard and looked like a slice cut through the hilly shoreline with just enough room for two ships to pass through simultaneously.

Graham saw two of his rangers, Kip and Arbuckle, standing by the railing, looking toward the cut in the hills. He walked over to them. "Are you two feeling better?" he asked.

"Not much," said Corporal Kip. "I truly believe that men were not meant to go on ships. We are land creatures. I damn near puked my guts out below decks."

Arbuckle still looked green. He said nothing in response to the lieutenant; he merely groaned and looked down at the green-gray waters of Fundy.

Graham smiled at both of them and walked on.

"Damn officer," said Kip softly.

"Why, Israel Kip, John Graham is a fine man. You yourself said so when we signed up for this outfit."

"I said he was a good officer. There is an essential contradiction between being a good officer and a fine man. Besides, I'm the one who signed up. You just tagged along. You should have stayed back home and done your planting."

"I've got two boys old enough to do the planting," said Arbuckle. "All my life I've watched you, footloose, coming and going as you please, while I stayed home taking care of my wife and young. Just this once I wanted to be free like you and have some fun."

"Fighting the Frenchies and the heathens can be risky fun, my friend. You could go home with no hair on your head."

Nat Arbuckle started to laugh. Kip always made him laugh. Whenever he returned from some new adventure, they spent the night in front of the fire in Nat's cabin outside of Kittery on the Maine side of the river, talking far into the night. Nat's wife, Mandy, would grow tired and climb into the loft to join the children in bed. But he and Kip would go right on talking, sipping some ale and smoking their pipes. Kip would tell him of the rivers, valleys and lakes of the West, of Indian tribes he had lived with or fought. He'd talk of the girls he had slept with—red, black and white. Arbuckle had made up his mind that this time Kip would not go off without him. He wasn't a ranger and he sure wasn't a woodsman. He was a farmer—plain and simple. But despite four days of puking, he was determined to make this the adventure of his life.

Captain Noble, the ship's master, came on deck a few minutes after Graham, giving orders to make sail and take advantage of the tides. "Break out the sweeps, Mr. Mason," he yelled to the ship's first officer. "I'll be taking no chances with the Fundy Tide."

Seamen began to climb the netting and to inch their way out onto the yardarms to release the sails. Others raised anchor, and still others set the long oars into position in case they were needed.

Stephen sat on deck at the base of the mast. Graham walked over to join him. "Mr. Nowell," he said. Stephen nodded a reply. "You don't sleep in your cabin, do you?"

"No," said Stephen. "This is my fourth time at sea and I know that if I don't remain in the fresh air, I will be terribly sick. Even in foul weather you will find me on deck."

"I'm not a bad sailor," said Graham, "but I can see what the sickness can do to a man. You just have to look at those two by the railing." He pointed toward Kip and Arbuckle. "Or go below and take a look at the rest of my rangers. Right now they couldn't lick a company of toddlers." Graham turned and looked at the gap in the hills. "What are your plans in Annapolis, Nowell?" he asked.

"Mr. Vaughan told me to offer my services to Colonel Mascarene and then to await word from him through you."

"Willy Vaughan has been good to you, hasn't he?"

"Yes, sir."

Graham looked down at Stephen. "Vaughan is a good man and a decent one. But he is also ambitious. He has some delusions about being a soldier. I warn you now; he will never make it. At heart he is a merchant and always will be a merchant. If you have your sights set on following Willy to fame or success in politics or in war, you've targeted on the wrong man. I've even got doubts about his eventual success as

228

a merchant. He's too honest. And he lost most of his soul when Sarah Nowell died. He has never recovered from that tragedy and he never will."

"I'm not a climber, Lieutenant," said Stephen.

"Good," said the ranger. "If you just make a friend of Willy Vaughan, you'll be ahead. He has been a good friend to me."

The galley's sails caught the wind and it began to move with the tide toward the channel. Graham and Nowell walked to the railing of the deck to watch the ship's passage through the channel and into the basin. The ship came so close to the hill at the entrance that Stephen felt he could have reached out and touched the trees. Once free of the channel, the galley swung to port as a wide and deep bay spread out before their eyes.

"What a fine harbor," said Stephen.

Graham shook his head. "It's a pretty sight to look at, but the navy people tell me it's a bad harbor. Too hard to get in and out of. And you have to brave the tides to enter or leave here. They want to give up Annapolis as the capital of Nova Scotia and settle a new site on the Atlantic shore. It makes sense as far as fighting the French navy at Louisbourg goes, but most of the people of this province are French-speaking Acadians living on the Fundy shore."

"At Isle Royale we still spoke of the Acadians as loyal to King Louis."

Graham smiled. "You are probably right. But don't try to tell Mascarene that. He's a great supporter of the concept of Acadian loyalty to the good treatment they have received from the British crown. He believes that they will remain neutral in this war."

"You don't think so, do you?" asked Stephen.

"Time will tell," said Graham.

The winds died again and Captain Noble ordered the sweeps out. The ship was a large one, and even with most of its crew manning the oars, its progress toward the capital was pitifully slow. The fort at Annapolis could now be seen in the distance. It was a timber-supported earthen fort. Above the blockhouse the Union Jack was hanging limply.

"Something's wrong," muttered Graham, who studied the fort through his glass. "Captain," he called, "do you make out anything strange at the fort?"

Noble, who had been conversing with his mate, reached for his glass and trained it on the fort. "There has been fighting, or at least the threat of fighting. The houses outside the walls have been burned."

Graham nodded assent. "Either those houses have been burned by the enemy or Mascarene got some sense and destroyed them himself. He never should have allowed his officers to build their homes outside the walls in the first place. They make an ideal little fort for beseigers. Nowell, go below and tell my sergeant to get the men on their feet. You may have to get the sergeant on his feet first, but we will be at the fort in a few minutes and I have a feeling we must be prepared for anything."

They arrived even more quickly than Graham had predicted. The fickle morning wind quickened again and the sails filled. Noble ordered the sweeps pulled in and stored away. The galley approached the Annapolis wharf, but Noble, taking no chances, ordered the ship anchored offshore, with the decks cleared for action. A gun was fired from the ramparts of the fort; a cheer came up from inside the walls. The gates of the fort swung open and a heavily armed force of about twenty-five men, their scarlet coats torn and stained, came marching out toward the wharf. Noble ordered a gun fired in salute. The fort replied.

The captain sent a boat over the side. Its oars dug into the water, and it glided quickly up to the wharf. An officer from the fort's party climbed aboard and the boat swung around, returning to the mother ship.

As the officer climbed up the sea ladder through the entry port of the galley, Stephen noted that he bore the insignia of a lieutenant, the same rank as Graham, yet Graham must have been twenty years younger. The officer saluted the flag and nodded toward Captain Noble. Then he turned to Graham. "Lieutenant William Sanford presenting Colonel Mascarene's compliments," he said. "The colonel wishes you and your men to report for duty immediately. We have been under siege."

"Sergeant Gibbons," yelled Graham.

"Sir."

"Get the men ashore as soon as possible."

"Yes, sir."

Graham held his hand out to Sanford. "Lieutenant John Graham, New Hampshire Rangers."

Sanford's contempt for colonials was evident. He turned to look at Graham's seasick warriors without offering his fellow officer his hand. "Lieutenant, you must have been expecting the colonel himself to come and greet you. It is not customary

230

to turn out a guard of honor for a lieutenant, even for a lieutenant of the King's regulars."

"That's no honor guard," said the obviously offended Graham. "That's my whole force."

Sanford froze and swung back to look in Graham's direction. "You joke, sir."

"I do not joke, sir."

"Do you mean to tell me that this motley crowd of seasick provincials is all that the governor of Massachusetts could afford to send to defend this colony?"

"I wouldn't insult these men, Lieutenant," said Graham. "They will more than hold their own in a fight. Governor Shirley did not know the French would be here so quickly. He is sending more men later in the summer. As commander of His Majesty's forces in North America, he is totally committed to defending Nova Scotia. How large is the French force?"

"It's not the French," said Sanford, "although no doubt there are some French among them. It is the red devils—the Indians—about two hundred of the buggers. Normally that would be little bother, but this damn fort is in frightful disrepair. It was built to be defended by a force of five hundred. We have just over one hundred actives, and we have over two hundred women and children to protect. There are so many blind spots, so many places where we have only token defenses. We live in constant fear that they will break in and slaughter us all."

As Sanford spoke, his shoulders seemed to sag and his weariness became more evident. The conviction that the galley would offer little help seemed to take the spirit out of him.

Captain Noble came to join the conference. "Lieutenant Graham, your men are now loaded in my boats. As soon as the boats return, it is my intention to sail for Boston when the tide turns." Then he turned to Sanford. "If the colonel has dispatches he wishes to send to Boston, I suggest you go to him immediately and return with them."

"Agreed," said Sanford.

Stephen stepped to Graham's side. "Lieutenant Sanford, this is Mr. Stephen Nowell. He is a civilian attached to my ranger troop as a scout. He is a good woodsman, has some experience with Indians and speaks fluent French."

"Welcome," said the deflated Sanford. "Every strong arm and every musket is a welcome addition." He shook Stephen's hand. Then the Englishman turned and made for the boat.

Graham took Stephen by the shoulder and led him toward the entry port. "Come with me, Stephen, when I report to Mascarene. I want you to meet him."

They climbed down the ladder and jumped the last foot or so into the waiting boat. The oarsmen started to pull the short distance to the wharf. They were greeted by one of Mascarene's aides on the wharf and led along the path to the front gate of Annapolis Royal. Sanford did not wait for them, but ran ahead to report Noble's intentions to his colonel.

News that the ship had brought little relief had spread quickly in the fort. Stephen could see the disappointment on the faces of the regulars and signs of fear among the civilians. They were led to a large house at the far end of the parade ground, which served as the commander's headquarters. Sentries stood on guard before the front door. They made a vague attempt to come to attention and salute when officers entered the house.

Graham and Stephen entered a simply furnished room. There was a small desk in the center of the room and a larger table covered with a plan of the fort in the corner. Standing by the window, looking out, was a man of medium height. His hair was unpowdered but gray. He had developed a definite spread about his middle and looked his sixty years.

"Colonel Mascarene," said Graham.

"Graham, it's good to see you again," said the older man with a faint trance of a French accent. "Although from what Sanford has told me, I wish you had been able to bring more help along with you."

"Yes, sir," responded the lieutenant. Mascarene glanced at Stephen. "Excuse me," said Graham. "Colonel Mascarene, this is Stephen Nowell. Willy Vaughan thinks he may be of use to us." Stephen made a slight bow toward the colonel.

"Mr. Nowell. Happy to make your acquaintance," said Mascarene. Then he addressed Graham. "Why does Vaughan think he can help us?"

"Well," said the lieutenant, "he was raised French."

Mascarene smiled at Stephen. "Well, that is something we share, Mr. Nowell, although at this point I fail to see how that will be a help to either of us."

Graham continued. "He was raised in Louisbourg and could provide valuable advice when we get on to finishing off that place."

Mascarene nodded. "When we get around to that," he said.

"In the meanwhile," said Graham, "he can be used as an extra hand."

"We can use all we can get," said the colonel. He sat down at his chair in back of the desk, sighing unconsciously. "I am sending as many of the women and children as I can back to Massachusetts aboard the galley. Some will have to be left behind. There is no helping it. I am also sending my good friend William Shirley a letter begging for more help. Twenty provincials—no offense intended, Graham—are not nearly enough. We may hold off the Micmacs, but should the French send a regular force against us, there is absolutely nothing I can do."

There was a knock at the door, and the colonel's aide entered the room, handing Mascarene a note. The colonel crumpled the paper and laid it on the top of the desk. "Just a note from my officers demanding that their dependents get places on the galley ahead of the dependents of the regular troops and the civilians."

Graham looked puzzled.

"I know what you are thinking, Lieutenant," said Mascarene. "Of course that is the way it would be arranged anyway. My officers just wished to indicate a lack of confidence."

"I would think that they would have little reason to do so," said Graham.

"It's mostly politics, Graham. Governor Phillips has not been in this colony for years. I am acting governor, as senior member of the Council. In addition, I command the troops. It's a bad mixture—soldiering and politics. Some of my officers are council members and my political opponents. What they fail to understand is that I am too old to be an ambitious man. They can't ruin me. The worst they can do is to have me sent back to Boston to join my children and grandchildren. I long for that." His face hardened and he clenched his teeth. "But I'll not let them give this fort to the enemy without a fight."

"I would like to do my share," said Stephen.

Mascarene relaxed. "Thank you, Mr. Nowell. We can use you. The men are tired. It's the night duty that is important now. Graham, I want your men on the walls tonight. If they can give twenty men a good night's sleep, things will improve mightily around here. Get a musket for Nowell. They are in short supply, but I suspect a spare one could be found."

"Whatever you say, Colonel," said Graham.

"You may be excused now. I have a letter to write."

"Yes, sir," said Graham. He saluted and turned to the door. Stephen bowed slightly and joined the lieutenant.

"*Au revoir, monsieur*," said Mascarene to Stephen. Stephen bowed again and left the room.

There was no moon, and what little light it might have given would have been hidden by the low, heavy clouds that rolled into the basin just before sunset. The rain fell in a slow but steady drizzle. Stephen joined two of Graham's rangers and two regulars to man the advanced redoubt, which jutted from the main fortifications and acted almost as an independent fort, covering the main gate. Stephen, stationed between the two rangers, was huddled in a duffle coat and an Indian blanket, which had been issued to him for the night. He held his new musket under the blanket, trying to keep the powder dry.

"Did you ever kill a man, Nowell?" asked Corporal Kip, who was hunched down behind the earth embankment on his right.

"Yes," responded Stephen, without offering any details.

"Well, it will sure enough be hard to kill anyone with a musket tonight. You won't be able to see the bastards until they are on top of you, and then when you do see them the damn musket will never fire in this weather."

On his left Private Arbuckle belched. "I'm dying," he groaned. "First they stick me on a God damn tub in the middle of the ocean and I puke my guts up, and then we come ashore and they feed me stinking salt pork. The stuff was green, I tell you."

Kip made a sound of disgust. "I know. If I wouldn't get myself shot for desertion, I'd leave this place. And I wouldn't blame Nowell here if he came with me. The two redcoats could stay. They're too stupid to care."

Stephen looked over toward the two regulars manning the opposite side of the redoubt to see if they had heard Kip's remarks. If they had, they gave no indication of it. They continued to stare straight ahead into the blackness of the night.

Arbuckle groaned again. "I was just thinking of Amanda's cooking. I surely would love to have some of the venison that she cooks special for me. I bring home the deer, butcher it and we hang it in the barn till it's seasoned, just to the good side of going bad. Then Mandy puts it on the spit in the fire and bastes it with a sauce she makes—tomatoes, vinegar, some salt and some of those special spices she prizes so much. The meat would melt in your mouth."

Kip looked at him incredulously. "You eat tomatoes—love apples? Any fool knows they're poison."

"I've been eating them for fifteen years," answered Arbuckle, "me and Mandy and the two boys. Ain't done none of us no harm." He appealed to Stephen. "Tell him, Nowell, tomatoes ain't poison, are they?"

"I've eaten them many times, Corporal Kip," said Stephen, "and I have never been sick from them."

Kip snorted, and the three remained silent for a few minutes. Kip checked the flintlock on his musket; Stephen and Private Arbuckle followed his example. Across the redoubt one of the redcoats stirred and whispered to the other. Kip crouched and crept toward the regulars. "Something wrong over here?" he asked.

"Jones, here," said one of the redcoats, pointing to his companion, "thought he saw something moving out by the burned buildings."

Kip stared some minutes in the indicated direction. "I don't see nothing," he said finally.

"That's what I told him. He's daft," said the redcoat. "The savages would never attack on a night like this. They hate the rain. They're all wrapped up in their blankets, snoring, just like we should be."

"Maybe," said Kip. "But keep a sharp lookout just in case." He crept back to his post.

"Israel," whispered Arbuckle, "did you see anything out there?"

"Nope," he responded.

"Good. I knew the redcoat was seeing ghosts." Arbuckle turned his attention to Stephen. "You married, Nowell?"

Stephen shook his head.

"Have you ever had a woman?"

Stephen just looked at him, not knowing how to respond to his bluntness.

"Shut up, Nat," said the corporal. "Don't you have the good sense to know what's none of your business?"

"I didn't mean no harm, Israel," he apologized. "But talking about Mandy got me to thinking about her. I just thought talking about it might help. I sure could use a woman right now."

"I think you are too hard on Arbuckle, Corporal," said Stephen. "I think our friend, the private, is just plain lonely. I think . . ."

The rest of his words were blotted out by the blast of the redcoat Jones' musket and the scream of its victim. It was almost as if Jones had given the signal to attack. On both sides of the redoubt the Micmacs, under cover of darkness and rain, had infiltrated the ditch and made it halfway up the sloped earthen sides. Firing erupted from other sectors of the defenses at nearly the same moment.

Kip rose from his crouched position, aimed and fired into the blackness below, then dropped down again to reload. Stephen and Nat rose together to fire. Stephen could see nothing to fire at. Then, in the flash of a musket below and to the right, he could see the form of an Indian. He aimed and fired, then dropped behind the wall. Arbuckle remained standing, searching for a target. Suddenly, he crumpled at the knees and fell on top of Stephen.

"You hit?" yelled Stephen. He received no reply. He reached up and pushed the limp body of the private off his back, searching Nat's face for signs of life. He placed his hand behind Arbuckle's head to lift him and then pulled it away quickly. Stephen's hand was covered with blood. The whole side of Arbuckle's head had been blown off by a musket ball.

"Jesus," shouted Stephen, half in disgust, half in prayer.

"Get your musket reloaded," Kip yelled at him. "Some of them are trying to get up into the redoubt." He rose and fired quickly.

Stephen shuddered and mechanically shoved the paper cartridge and metal ball into the musket and rammed it home with the rod. He primed the pan with powder from his horn and was ready to fire, all in about ten seconds. He rose. Exactly opposite him, within the sights of his musket, was the painted face of an Indian, contorted, yelling, tomahawk raised to strike. Stephen fired and the Indian fell backward down the deep slope, on top of two companions, who had followed him in an effort to scale the wall. All three bodies fell toward the bottom.

Kip rose again to fire. But as he did, he was knocked down from behind by a Micmac who had hurled through the air and knocked the corporal down before he could fire.

Startled, Stephen turned to the other side of the redoubt. Jones lay clutching his stomach, his mouth moving silently. It dawned on Stephen that Jones was screaming but his voice could not be heard over the noise of the battle. While Stephen watched, the other redcoat was pulled from the walls and hurled down the slope. The boy grabbed his knife from its sheath at his side. He plunged it with all his might into the back of the Indian who was struggling with Kip. He tried to pull the blade out again, but it was stuck in the shoulder blade of the Indian. He grabbed the Indian's tomahawk and whirled to face the Micmacs who were coming over the undefended wall.

He heard and felt the heat of a musket flash from behind his shoulder. Corporal Kip had regained his feet. His ball tore through the throat of one of the Indians who stood on top of the repart wall.

A second Micmac made the mistake of trying to finish off Jones. The blade of his knife had already entered the redcoat's scalp when Stephen reached him. The Indian stood up to meet Stephen's attack. He grabbed Stephen's arm as it descended toward his head. Stephen drove his fist into the Indian's stomach. He bent in half and as he did Stephen brought the tomahawk crashing down into his skull.

Kip came running past Stephen and intercepted a third invader, who was approaching Stephen. The Indian dodged as Kip's knife flashed, severing the muscle of the Indian's right forearm. He was holding his tomahawk in his left hand and he raised his arm to strike Kip. Stephen threw his ax. It hit the Indian in the face just as Kip's knife struck out again. The Indian pulled back, clutching his belly with Kip's knife still lodged there, and collapsed.

The cannon of the fort began to fire. Stephen looked about him. No more Indians attempted to enter the redoubt. He moved over to the corporal. "Are you all right, Israel?" The words barely got out, he was so winded.

"Yes. How about you?"

"I don't know," said Stephen. "Just very frightened, I think."

Jones had stopped screaming now. He was alive, but Kip did not think much of his chances. "Belly shot," he said. "Never live." The corporal walked over to the body of his friend, Arbuckle. "Poor bastard," he said. "Mandy's love apples would have finished him off anyway." He sat down with his head in his hands.

Stephen checked the bodies of the Indians. One was still alive. Stephen tried to make him comfortable and bound his wounded belly. When he had finished, he went back to his post. His head pounded and his stomach was churning. He turned to the side and was sick.

The Indian attack had failed; the closest they had come to breaking through was in the battle of the redoubt. In other sections of the fort, cannon fire had driven them off.

After Stephen was relieved by Lieutenant Graham from the carnage in the redoubt, he returned to his billet in the rangers' empty barracks. He collapsed onto his bunk. There he tossed for fifteen minutes, unable to free his mind of the horrors he had witnessed. He wanted to sleep; he needed to sleep. But sleep would not come.

John Graham opened the door of the barracks and peered into the gloom of the windowless room. "Nowell?" he called. Stephen sat up in his bed and Graham walked over to him. "I thought you might be asleep already."

"I can't sleep," said Stephen.

"The colonel would like to speak with you if you feel up to it."

Stephen put his bare feet on the floor and sat on the edge of the bed, running his hands through his hair. Graham looked down at his weariness with sympathy. The lieutenant bent down and picked up Stephen's carelessly discarded shoes and handed them to him. He held out his hand to Stephen and helped him to his feet.

"It was a hell of a fight," said Graham as they walked across the parade grounds to headquarters. Stephen did not answer him. "Are you sure you are all right?" asked the lieutenant.

Stephen stopped walking and looked at Graham. "No," he said. "I am not all right. How could I be all right? I've killed again. I trained for years to help people, to spread the message of peace, and just a few hours ago, I shot a man in the face; I stabbed another in the back and helped to bring down another by throwing an ax in his face. It violates everything I was raised to believe. No, I am not all right and I doubt if I will ever be all right."

Graham interrupted him. "What you did, you did to defend yourself and your comrades. Any man would do the same and probably not as bravely."

"That's just it," said Stephen. "Any man would have done the same. None of you understand. I was not trained to be just any man, and I find it very difficult to accept the fact that I am just like everyone else."

Graham looked at him quizzically. "Are you sure you are not hurt in any way?"

Stephen shook his head. "No. Forget it. I'm fine."

They entered the colonel's headquarters and the clerk in charge greeted the two provincials with some deference. "The colonel is waiting for you, Lieutenant," he said. The door to Mascarene's office swung open and the colonel greeted Graham and Nowell. "Gentlemen, good to see you. Graham, your men fought well. Nowell, I have had a report on the action in the redoubt. Congratulations."

Stephen nodded his acknowledgment.

"Please sit down, gentlemen," continued the commander. He walked to his desk and pulled open a drawer, taking out a decanter of port and three glasses. "I think some wine is in order," said Mascarene as he filled the glasses. Stephen took the glass offered to him. Graham lifted his glass and unthinkingly offered the normal toast, "To hell with the French." He realized quickly that the toast might be inappropriate but both Mascarene and Nowell joined in the drink.

"I have a scouting report that the Micmacs have withdrawn from their positions and have pulled back into the hills," said Mascarene.

"That is good news, sir. We've beaten them," said Graham, clapping Stephen's shoulder.

"Not quite," Mascarene interrupted. "They have withdrawn, but some of our friends among the Acadians tell us that a force of French regulars from Louisbourg is approaching our position. We shall soon be under heavier and more dangerous siege."

"Damn," said Graham.

Mascarene looked at him with annoyance. "There is no need for profanity, Lieutenant."

"I am sorry, sir," replied Graham.

"Nevertheless," continued the colonel, "I can understand the frustrations that may have prompted your expletive. We have had a rough time. It may be weeks before the *Massachusetts Galley* returns with reinforcements. If the French arrive in great force and with siege equipment, I shall have no choice but to surrender. If they arrive with any force whatsoever, I will be under pressure from my officers to give up. What I must have, however, is information. I must know immediately how strong they are." He turned abruptly and faced Stephen. "This is where you come in, Mr. Nowell. I need you to go among the French. You were raised among the Acadians. Surely you can pretend to be one of them. I need you to be my spy."

"Colonel," interrupted Graham, "I feel compelled to remind you that Mr. Nowell's position among us is somewhat irregular. He is not a soldier and you ask him to place himself in grave danger."

"You need not remind me, Graham. Nor do I feel I need remind Nowell that he is a subject of King George, particularly not after his courageous actions in the redoubt a few hours ago."

Again Graham interrupted. "Sir, there must be an officer who could do the job."

Mascarene exploded. "There is not an officer in the garrison, beside yourself, who is worth a thimble full of pig droppings." He swung back toward his desk, smashing his hand into a pile of papers and scattering them onto the floor. "All I get from them is complaints, demands, pleas that I surrender this glorified privy and let them get back to England."

Stephen placed his glass on the colonel's desk and absent-mindedly twisted the fragile stem between his fingers. "I think I may be of some use to the colonel, John," he said in a low, barely audible voice. "And I think I should have no further illusions about myself. I can be a spy."

"Stephen, the risks . . ."

"Are risks," said Stephen. "If I have to kill again, I'll do it, and if I can be useful as a spy, I'll be a spy. If I have to lie, I'll lie." Stephen stood and faced Mascarene. "I will be your spy, Colonel. What is it precisely that you wish me to discover?"

"Good boy," said Mascarene nervously, not knowing the import of Stephen's outburst. "First of all, I must know the precise strength of the French force that is approaching. In particular, I need to know if they have cannon or if there are any prospects of their receiving cannon. Next, I must know just how many French regulars are in the force and, very importantly, I must know the attitude of the Acadians. Will they remain neutral or will they join the French? We must work out a way for you to get your information back to the fort."

"A meeting in a prearranged spot at a specific time might be the answer," suggested Stephen.

Mascarene nodded his head in agreement. "Graham," he said, "is there anyone trustworthy whom we could send out of the fort at night to meet with Nowell? I would send you, but I cannot afford to lose you, quite frankly."

"What about Corporal Kip?" asked Stephen.

The colonel looked at Graham quizzically. "One of my rangers, sir. Yes, I think he would do nicely. Knows how to find his way about in the woods—a good soldier."

"It's settled, then," said Mascarene. "Corporal Kip will visit the prearranged rendezvous nightly. You, Nowell, will meet him there if you have anything to report. But you must

240

act immediately. I suggest that you slip out of the fort tonight, just as soon as we can find some workmen's clothes for you. Your clothing has the look of Boston about it."

Stephen smiled and slowly broke into the Acadian *patois* he had heard so often in the streets of Louisbourg as a child. "I doubt if the good fathers who raised me would approve of my accent but I think I can make an acceptable habitant."

Mascarene laughed. "That's excellent, Nowell, excellent. You must come back here before you leave. My clerk will give you the passwords that I will work out. You must memorize them and take no copy with you. Kip will also know the code and will bring your report to Graham or me. Good, it's all settled then." He lifted his half-empty glass of wine. "A toast, gentlemen," he said. Stephen and Graham rose and lifted their glasses. "Confound the French, gentlemen."

"Confound the French," they repeated after him.

Stephen walked across the parade ground toward the barracks where his gear was stashed. The wind had risen, slapping at the Union Jack flying from its pole on the ramparts above his head.

"Nowell," called a voice from the shadows of the barracks wall.

Stephen turned toward the voice. He could barely make out the form of Israel Kip. "Why are you lurking about, Israel?" asked Stephen.

"The colonel wants to see me, and if I receive his orders I am going to have to go to him. If he can't reach me, I can do what I should be doing—getting old Nat buried proper. You want to come along? Being as you and me were the last persons he ever spoke with, I think that would be fitting."

Stephen agreed and the two men slipped behind the barracks building and out a sally port, across the open field, past the charred remains of the officers' cottages.

The burial ground was fenced with a low split-rail fence. A group of New Hampshire Rangers surrounded a small mound of earth. Beside the mound was a long sailcloth bag containing the body of their companion. Across the yard, standing at stiff attention, in spotless precision, their metal accouterments highly polished and their white cross belts accenting the brilliant red of their coats, stood a contingent of the garrison's regulars beside two sailcloth bags.

The chaplain began to speak the prayerbook service for the dead. "I am the resurrection and the life, saith the Lord: he

241

that believeth in me, though he were dead, yet shall he live, and whosoever liveth and believeth in me shall never die."

The wind from the Bay of Fundy, blocked only by the grassy knolls that separated the treeless graveyard from the sea, whipped at the surplice and stole of the clergyman and blew the pages of the prayer book violently from back to front. Beyond his wind-strewn whisps of straggly white hair, the black, rain-laden clouds dashed across the bay toward them.

"I will lift up mine eyes unto the hills, from whence cometh my help." A flash of lightning streaked across the sky from north to south, followed almost instantly by a crack of thunder. One of the redcoats, perhaps lulled by the softness of the chaplain's prayer, forgot discipline completely and swore out loud. His sergeant's withering glare made the skin on his back crawl. He would feel the sting of the lash across that same skin before the day was over and he knew it. A feeling of weakness in the pit of his belly spread through his thighs to his knees and he had to struggle to remain at attention.

"Unto Almighty God we commend the soul of our brothers departed, and we commit their bodies to the ground; earth to earth, ashes to ashes, dust to dust."

With one redcoat holding the feet and the other the enshrouded shoulders, the bodies of the two Englishmen were placed on wooden platforms and as the minister continued the prayer, the platforms were lowered on long ropes into the same grave, one on top of the other. The pallbearers returned to their ranks. The chaplain closed his prayerbook and, bending over, he picked up a handful of dirt and dropped it into the open grave. The sergeant barked out a command. There was a clatter of metal as muskets were raised toward the menacing skies. Before the sergeant could complete the words of the next command, the roar of the muskets overpowered the sound of the wind's rush. Then, as if the muskets themselves were a command to the elements, the rain began to fall in a torrent.

The New Hampshire men huddled more closely together about the grave they had dug for their friend. The chaplain offered to read some prayers for Arbuckle. "Nat Arbuckle may be roasting in hell for all I know," said Kip. "But he were never no Church of England man while he was alive and we ain't going to bury him as one." He rubbed his nose with the back of his hand. "I ain't one for making speeches and I

242

sure ain't much of a praying man, but we can't just drop old Nat here in the ground. Something ought to be said."

The rain was slashing across the burying ground now and Kip had to shout to make himself heard by his companions. He turned to Stephen and clasped his shoulder. "You are one of us, boy, and you've been educated. You say something for poor Nat."

Stephen was startled by the request. He pushed a sopping wet lock of his black hair off his forehead and tried to dry his face with the sleeve of his drenched shirt. He had to shout over the roar of the wind. "I just met Nat Arbuckle a day or so ago and I spoke with him only for a few minutes before he died. But since I was standing next to him when he died, I guess fate threw us together. What I remember most about him was the way he spoke of his wife and family, how much he loved them. And I'm sure that love was returned. Any man who has that has everything." He stopped speaking. He felt he should say more but before he could think of what to say, Kip and another ranger, thinking that he had finished, picked up Arbuckle's body and lowered it into the grave. They could not hold it all the way to the bottom and had to let go. The body splashed into the pool of water that had already begun to form at the bottom of the grave. Quickly the rangers began to shovel the mud onto the body of their fallen friend. The rain came down even harder.

Stephen moved with as little noise as possible through the woods beside the main trail that led from the northern Acadian towns toward Annapolis. He could have been more careless had he wanted to. He had been trailing a wagon team guided by a man and a boy for three hours now. They made so much noise as they tried to urge on their ox every time the wheels of the wagon sank into the trail that they would not have heard him if he had tripped over a log and fallen flat on his face. But he saw no harm in being cautious. He had seriously thought of revealing himself to the Acadians and trying to pump them for information, but he was not as sure of his accent as he had led Mascarene to believe. He hoped that merely by eavesdropping he might pick up valuable information. He was wrong. Thus far he had learned from them only that the ox was lazy and that the boy was of dubious parentage and should work harder and help more.

Stephen knew that he would have to speak with the Acadians if he was to learn anything about their mission. Just at this moment the harness linking the ox to the wagon gave way with a loud snap. The ox lurched forward and fell to its knees and the wagon, groaning loudly, turned and fell onto its side.

"God damn," yelled the man in exasperation.

The ox struggled to its feet and lumbered up the trail, with the boy in pursuit.

Stephen stepped through the underbrush and hailed the man. "May I be of help to you, friend?" he said. "You look to be in some trouble."

The man was startled by his appearance. "Where'd you come from, stranger?"

"I've been walking in the woods along the side of the trail. Keeps the mud off my boots. I've come all the way from Louisbourg. I am hoping to join up with the army moving against Port Royale," he said, using the French name for Annapolis. "What's your name and where are you heading?" asked Stephen.

"Jean Marie. I'm bringing grain to the army from Midas. We should be in front of the fort this morning."

"In Louisbourg it is said that the Acadians of Midas Basin are now subjects of King George and will sell their food to Mascarene."

The man grunted. "They must think us fools in Louisbourg, then. Mascarene is bottled up in his fort. The French army is free to roam Acadia, especially with the Micmacs loose. Do they believe that we would risk having the red devils pay us a visit? Mascarene is a good man and King George leans less on us than King Louis did in the past, but who can afford to take the chance and remain neutral now that the French army is here? One of these days, we will be destroyed by these wars. Many of the young men have joined the French army because the martyr came to our village."

"Who came to your village?"

"The martyr," repeated Jean Marie. "You know, the priest tortured by the Iroquois. He comes from Louisbourg. Surely you know of him."

"Oh, yes. But we do not refer to him as the martyr," Stephen bluffed. "What was he doing in Midas?"

"He came two weeks ago to replace the visiting chaplain we are allowed by the treaty that ended the last war. He told everyone about his mission to the Oneida and how the English undermined it and finally how they had him turned over to the savages after his work had been betrayed. He showed us where they had burned and cut him. They even cut off his fingers like they did to the sainted Father Jogues years

244

ago. It is said the Pope will allow a dispensation to Lalonde to say mass—even with his missing fingers—like was done for Jogues."

Jean Marie leaned closer to Stephen to impart a deeper secret. "They say that the Indians cut off his balls too, although since he's a priest, I guess that is not as bad for him as it would be for you or me—eh, friend?"

Stephen tried to hide his shock from the Acadian but he was not successful.

"What's the matter? Afraid the Indians will get your balls too?" he laughed. "You people of Isle Royale lead too tame a life. Don't worry about the Micmacs. They are French Indians. They will murder only women and children, as commanded by the good fathers like Lalonde."

"You don't approve of priests?" Stephen asked him.

"They come into our villages and tell us we must fight for King Louis. But where will they be when the fighting is over? They will be safe in their houses in New France or maybe in France itself. We will be left to face the ire of the English alone."

"Do many feel as you do?" asked Stephen.

"No. They are fools. The young men in particular have been inflamed against the English by Lalonde. He preaches like a madman. I swear he has a devil. 'Kill the English,' he says. 'Murder them in their beds. Drive them from the sacred land of Acadia. Purify the defiled land with their blood.' Those are no words for a priest, a holy man. After he left our village, he went on to another and another and the young men marched off to fight the English."

The boy appeared, leading the ox. "Ah, Robert and that poor excuse for an ox have returned," said Jean Marie.

"May I help you with the wagon?" asked Stephen.

"It will take more than you and me and even the ox to right it," the Acadian sighed, running his fingers through his gray hair in exasperation.

"Then I will go on ahead. When I join up with the army I will send help back for you. I am sure they will want your grain to bake bread for the troops."

"That would be good of you, friend," said Jean Marie.

Stephen left them sitting by the side of the muddy trail, the ox busying himself searching for some edible grass or choice leaves. They would have a long wait.

Jean Marie's words had shaken Stephen. He had not thought to confront Lalonde again. He had given no thought to the man since that night on the frozen Mohawk when he

245

learned the truth about his origins. He had been so intent on saving Socono's life and so angered by Lalonde's advances toward him that he had given no thought whatever to the priest's fate. Skenandon had been the mission's only supporter and Stephen had killed him. Dagaheari's revenge on Lalonde must have been brutal. Stephen shuddered. As much as he despised Lalonde, he had not intended him to suffer so terribly.

Stephen stepped off the muddy trail into the woods again. Yesterday's rain was still clinging in little droplets to the needles of the pine and balsam trees, and each time Stephen pushed a branch aside to clear his path, a small shower fell on him.

He realized that he was completing the final arc of a great circle, begun in last night's storm. First he had headed north and east, searching for either the French army's whereabouts or at least a clue to where to begin to look. He had traveled several miles before striking the well-worn trail. The rain had washed away any tracks, but it was obvious from the condition of the trail that a large body of men had recently marched along it. Then he had discovered the wagon team and followed it south. Now he was striking west, with Annapolis, his starting point, as his destination.

The Micmacs who accompanied the army would be infesting these woods, and Stephen thought it wiser to turn back to the open trail. In the open he could play the role of an army recruit straggling along but more than willing to join up.

The sun finally broke through the clouds just as Stephen found the trail again. He sank to his ankle in the mud and cursed. The mud seemed to suck his shoes down. With each step he was forced to pull his foot from its grasp. He moved along in this slow fashion for half an hour, then he sat down along the side of the trail to remove his shoes. The heat of the sun grew intense, warming the rain-soaked earth.

Sticking one's bare feet into ice-cold mud was not Stephen's idea of a pleasant experience but now, warmed by the sun, he could save his shoes and perhaps move along a little faster. With his back to the underbrush, Stephen did not see the small body of soldiers step from the edge of the woods toward him. But for all their stealth, he heard them. He was prepared for the shock of the cold metal muzzle of a musket when it was placed on the bone behind his ear.

"Don't make a sudden move or I'll blow your head off," a voice said in French.

Stephen sat quietly, not daring to move a muscle.

"Now stand and slowly turn and face me."

Stephen obeyed the command. He turned to face three heavily armed soldiers who spoke French with the strong accent of the Swiss. One of the men stepped behind him and roughly searched his clothes and body for weapons. When he found nothing, he grabbed Stephen's arm and twisted it up behind his back. Stephen grabbed his shoulder in pain and started to turn to face his tormentor, when another of the soldiers grabbed him by the shirt collar and swore into his face. "Who are you, you little shit, and what are you doing sneaking up on the rear of the army?"

"I've come to join up," Stephen stuttered.

The soldier turned to the companion, who still had his musket pointed at Stephen. "Another of these bumpkins come to play soldier," he said. "Call the corporal. May as well get him sworn in and into the front ranks. Get enough of them as shields and we may come out of the campaign with most of the real soldiers alive." He shoved Stephen away from him. The soldier to the rear let go of his arm but as Stephen fell backward, the soldier stuck out his leg, tripping Stephen, who landed with a splat in the mud.

"What's going on here?" said a voice from behind the soldiers.

"Nothing, Corporal. Just another of the local pigs joining up," laughed the man with the musket.

Stephen started at the voice. The soldiers stepped aside to make way for the corporal, and the hulking form of Karl Stiegler stood above the mud-covered form of his old friend.

"Well, I'll be damned," he said. "Here, give me your hand." The corporal reached out toward Stephen and helped to pull him to his feet. "Bullinger, get over to camp and get a set of dry clothes for the new recruit," Karl said to the soldier with the musket.

The soldier hesitated. "The lieutenant will not approve of a weakening of the flank guard. Suppose the English should sally."

"You just do as I order and get your ass over to camp," shouted Karl.

The soldier soon disappeared from sight; his companions wandered back toward their positions. Karl waited until they were alone before he spoke.

"My God, Stefan. What are you doing here? Do you know you are an infamous person in Louisbourg? All we heard from Lalonde was about the Judas, Etienne LaGarde. Although you might be interested to know that they refer to you

247

as Noel again. All he could talk about was how you had betrayed your vows and the Society, how you had betrayed the church and your God and how you had betrayed him, the martyr. If he gets his hands on you, your life will be worth nothing. He'd have you burned at the stake in the governor's garden. It's a good thing that none of my men recognized you, but they have all heard your name."

"Has everyone in Louisbourg turned against me?" Stephen asked.

"If you are thinking of Father LaGarde, I have not spoken to him since you left, nor to Sister Louis either," Karl answered.

Bullinger arrived, carrying well-worn parts of various uniforms. Stephen took the clothes from the Swiss and followed Karl off the trail and into the woods. They came to a small clearing, where the soldiers were camped. Stephen stripped off his muddy clothes and tried to wipe the mud from his body. Karl offered him a slice of sausage as Stephen finished dressing and sat on the ground next to Karl. "I guess you are waiting for my side of the story before you decide what to do with me," said Stephen.

"Hell, no," interrupted Karl. "Lalonde is a bastard and a Frenchman. He got everything he deserved."

"When I left, you hated only French officers. I see that your hatred has spread to French priests as well."

"I hate all Frenchmen. They treat us Swiss like dirt in Louisbourg; they steal our pay, feed us garbage and then shove us into frontal assaults on forts to turn us into fertilizer. I hate the bastards. If you did them dirty, I'm glad. You're safe with me."

"If you hate them so," said Stephen, "why continue in their service?"

"Where else do I go? I'm a soldier," said Karl. "The other side could be just as bad and besides, they're heretics."

Stephen chuckled. "Since when did dogma become important to you? Half your Swiss contingent are Calvinists."

"Sure," shrugged Karl. "The Geneva boys. But at least they're Swiss—even if the French-speaking kind."

Stephen reached over and touched his friend on the arm. "Karl, I'm working for the English army. I have been sent by Colonel Mascarene to scout this army and to tell him what threat it presents to Annapolis. Join with me and when the war is over, we can get some land from the government and be our own men."

"'Tis a tempting offer, Stefan. But I'm a soldier and not a

248

farmer. Besides, I don't think much of switching sides in the middle of the game."

Stephen reacted to what he took as criticism of his own behavior by quickly withdrawing his hand.

Karl noticed the look of offense. "I'm not making reference to you, my friend. You are English. You just found your proper loyalty."

"But how can you remain loyal to France and let me go free?" asked Stephen.

"Stefan, don't misunderstand me. My first loyalty is to my comrades—the Swiss troops in this army. We are agreed among ourselves that there will be no attack on Annapolis by us. The officers know it and for all I care you can tell it to your colonel. If he leaves us alone, we'll leave him alone."

"What do your leaders plan then, Karl?"

"I don't know; they don't tell me. But if I were in command of this army, I would try to bluff the English into surrendering. If I were determined to attack, I would get hold of some loyal troops rather than unhappy mercenaries and I would get me some cannon."

"You have no artillery?"

"Nothing heavier than a miniature swivel gun. Couldn't dent paper with it."

"Now that is important information, Karl."

"If it helps us avoid a battle, you're welcome to it."

Stephen did not respond. It was not to his advantage to tell Karl that the English garrison was as disaffected as the Swiss mercenaries. Information that the French lacked siege guns, however, might stiffen the English will to resist.

Bullinger stepped between Stephen and Karl. "The Micmac scouts are returning and they have a prisoner," he said.

"Damn," said Karl. "Now they will want to have a burning. Bullinger, get over to the main camp and tell the lieutenant that the scouts are here and that if he wants a prisoner in condition to answer some questions, he had better hurry his tail."

"I'll put it just as you did, Corporal."

"Yeah, I'll bet you'd like to." He turned to Stephen. "This could be nasty, Stefan. You had better be armed. Take one of my pistols." He reached into his knapsack and handed a loaded pistol to Stephen; he stuck its twin into his own belt. Just at that moment five men entered the bivouac area, four of them Indians and the fifth a white man. His tattered red uniform indicated that he was from Annapolis, probably a deserter, and his bloody face indicated that he had received rough treatment at the hands of his captors.

"Thank God," muttered the captive through swollen lips when he saw the French soldiers. "Help me."

Stephen moved toward the Englishman, but Karl grabbed his shoulder and held him back. The scouts had been drinking and reeked of rum. Karl signaled a welcome to one of the Indians, whom Stephen assumed must be the leader of the scouting band. The leader snarled a welcome back.

"King Louis' brothers have captured one of his enemies, I see," said Karl. "I have sent word to Lieutenant Bertier and he will be here shortly to question the prisoner."

"No. The white prisoner belongs to us," said the Indian. He turned to his comrades and spoke rapidly in a language that Stephen could not understand. Some words were related to Abenacki but the relationship was distant.

The Indians began to rip the clothes off their prisoner. The redcoat started to yell. Again Stephen moved to help and again Karl held him back.

"The bastards are drunk, and when they're drunk, they're extra dangerous. One move from you to help the prisoner and we will both be dead," said Karl. "When Bertier gets here, he will save your countryman, if he cooperates."

The Indians stripped the captive naked, dragged him over to a young maple tree and bound him to it. One of the Micmacs produced a large-bladed hunting knife from his buckskins and, with a quick stroke, sliced off the prisoner's right ear. Blood spurted from the wound and poured down the side of his face and onto his shoulder. The maiming had happened so swiftly that the victim did not realize what had happened to him until he saw the blood. He screamed, a long, miserable wail.

The Indian with the knife then grabbed the Englishman's scrotum and stretched it out, brandishing his knife. The victim fainted from shock and fright. The Micmacs began to laugh. They fell to the ground holding their stomachs, tears running down their painted cheeks. One pointed to the captive's thighs and calves where the Englishman had messed himself, and they roared even louder.

"Karl, I've got to do something for him," said Stephen, pulling at the corporal's grip.

"If you are still given over to that sort of thing, I would suggest only prayer, Stefan. I would rather stick my head into a bees' nest than touch a drunken Indian's prisoner without his permission."

Suddenly the Indians became very serious. A horseman dressed in the white uniform of a French infantry officer entered the small clearing. The Micmac leader walked toward the man, whom Stephen assumed to be Lieutenant Bertier.

"My brothers have done well," said the Frenchman. "Captain Duvivier will be pleased to hear of your capturing an English soldier. He must be brought to the captain for questioning."

As riotous as the Indians had been only moments before, so were they now the epitome of dignity. Standing tall, with no sign of the influence of rum, the leader rejected Bertier's assumption. "The prisoner belongs to us," he said as Bertier dismounted.

Karl moved quickly to hold the reins of his officer's horse.

"But if you burn him, Nomo, he will never answer the questions we need answers to. Unless, of course, you and your warriors already know the answers to the questions."

The Indians looked at one another sheepishly.

"Of course the captain would never expect you to surrender so valuable a captive and to give up the pleasure of making him suffer without some sort of reward."

The Micmacs perked up at the mention of a reward. The leader turned to his companions and spoke to them in their own language. The others responded and they began to haggle among themselves. Finally Nomo turned to Bertier. "The Englishman is yours, but each of us must receive a musket and rum."

"Agreed," said Bertier.

Stephen moved to release the prisoner.

"Not yet, soldier," said the lieutenant. He walked toward the bound Englishman. "I see that Nomo and his playmates have already done some work on him. I'm afraid that I'll have to go a little further with him. Nomo," he called. "Build a fire next to the prisoner. We must convince him that his only salvation is to tell me everything I want to know. Corporal, how is your English?"

"I don't speak it at all, sir," Karl responded. Karl looked at Stephen but received only a blank stare.

"Well, I guess my poor efforts will have to do," said Bertier. "I don't expect the poor bastard will know any French. You, soldier," he said, pointing at Stephen, "get something to stop the bleeding."

Stephen reached for the muddy shirt he had abandoned earlier. The tail had been tucked into his breeches and had not been dirtied by his fall. He tore it into a strip and gently wrapped it about the prisoner's head.

"Corporal," said Bertier, "get some water and wake him up. Nomo, put some knives into the fire and make some torches, just as if you were going to burn this poor fellow."

Karl splashed water into the prisoner's face. He came to with a start and looked about him. His eyes grew wide at the sight of the fire blazing at his side; he started a low moan, which gradually grew in volume.

Nomo, carrying a torch menacingly in front of him, approached the bound deserter. The prisoner's moan turned into a screech of anticipated pain. The Indian poked at the prisoner's face, singeing the hair that fell over his eyebrow and removing part of the eyebrow as well. The Englishman threw his head back against the tree trunk to avoid the fire. Nomo then plunged the torch into the prisoner's armpit, extinguishing the flame but not before his victim shook the forest with his scream.

Bertier stepped between Nomo and the prisoner. "My good man," he said in heavily accented English. "You must be aware by now that you are about to die by the fire. There is only one way I can save you. If you tell me everything I want to know, I may be able to convince these savages that you are a valuable prize whom my commander will want to question further. Evade my questions and I can do nothing for you. The leader—the one picking up the heated knife—he speaks your language as well as I do and so you will have to be very truthful and very convincing."

The Englishman nodded assent. "Yes, Your Lordship. I will tell you everything you want to know," he gasped.

"How many men does your commander have fit for duty to defend the fort?"

Without any hesitation the soldier blurted out the figures as best he knew them.

Bertier nodded to the Indian next to the fire. He approached the Englishman, his knife's heated blade held in front of him.

The captive's eyes widened with fear. "Your Lordship, you promised. You told me to tell the truth. I swear on the bloody bible—on my mother's grave—that I told you the truth. We've only got one hundred men and most of the officers want to surrender. Keep that savage away from me," he screamed. "Please, Your Honor. I'll tell you the passwords. I'll tell you how to get into the fort without being seen. Anything you want to know."

Bertier turned to the Indian with the heated knife and extended his hand. The Indian looked toward Nomo, who nodded his head. The lieutenant took the knife and cut the captive's bonds. The Englishman slumped to the ground, his back still resting against the tree.

"Get to your feet," said Bertier. "You're coming to camp with me. If you try to escape or are less than truthful with my captain, I'll turn you back over to my friends here. Corporal, lend this prisoner some breeches. I can't have him walking into camp stark naked."

Stiegler threw Stephen's muddied pants at the prisoner, who was grateful for some covering, no matter what its condition.

"Two of you come with me," Bertier ordered. "The rest of you remain here for the night. You will be relieved in the morning."

Karl took Stephen by the arm. "You stay here, Stefan," he said in a whisper. "There is no need for you to risk entering the camp and having someone recognize you. I'll be back for you in the morning or maybe even later tonight. We can decide then what we should do."

"Lieutenant," he then said in a normal tone to Bertier, "I suspect the Indians will want to keep an eye on the prisoner. I think they will stick to us like glue until they receive the muskets and especially the rum. Once they get the rum, every scout in these woods will join them. We can forget about any scouting tonight. The enemy will be free to prowl at will."

Karl looked back at Stephen to see if he had understood the import of his words to the lieutenant. With a slight nod, Stephen indicated that he had.

Kip sat with his back resting against the charred remains of a doorpost. The houses constructed outside the fort's defenses had been burned by the English themselves, but only after they had been used by the Micmacs as temporary forts against the main ramparts. The fact that they had been constructed at all was an indication of the laxity that had grown in Annapolis during the long years of peace from 1713 to 1744.

The moon had not yet risen, and the darkness in the shadows of the burned houses was profound. He was not at all sure what he was doing here. He had the password and orders to come every night to this spot and wait until he made contact with Nowell.

Since Nowell had left Annapolis only the night before, Kip had little thought that contact would be made tonight. Although Mascarene had emphasized the importance of his new duty, Kip could not help but think it beneath the dignity of a corporal of the rangers. He was little better than a messenger boy and he resented it. He had crawled out of the sally port when darkness had first set in and had been sitting now for two hours, listening to the night sounds.

Mosquitos were everywhere and Kip slapped at himself several times. "Damn rain yesterday must have washed away a good deal of my natural smell. Damn skeeters don't seem to shy away." Somewhere in the charred remains of the house closest to the fort where he sat, a cricket had survived the burning. Its song combined with the lonely shrill of a locust. When both stopped their music, Kip could hear the distant sound of the bay's surf, whipped into angry breakers by the intensity of yesterday's storm.

It was the silence that alerted him to Stephen's presence. He gripped his musket tightly and called the code word, "Shirley."

A black form emerged from the shadows at the corner of the house and gave the proper response, "Mill Creek.'"

"You're damn good, Nowell. I never heard you coming. Not many men can come up on old Israel like that."

"I think you're getting a bit hard of hearing," laughed Stephen, "because I'm out of practice. I haven't spent much time in the woods recently. In fact, I feel like a bull moose trampling down the underbrush."

"Moose, hell, Nowell. You're good and you know you're good. You didn't learn how to move in the woods at night living in Boston."

Stephen failed to respond and Kip did not push the matter.

"I didn't expect to meet with you so soon. You get some word for the colonel?"

"Tell Mascarene," said Stephen, "that the French are here in force, about four hundred regulars from Louisbourg. In addition, large numbers of Acadians are joining the French. The Micmacs are out in force too. They're expecting a lot of scalps and plunder when the fort falls."

"Do you have any good news?" quipped the corporal.

"Matter of fact, I do," answered Stephen. "The regulars with the French are their Swiss mercenaries. From what I can learn they have no intention of making an assault on the fort and their officers know it. They won't even try. In addition,

254

they have no siege guns. Tell the colonel to hold firm and the fort is safe."

"That's easy said, Nowell. Them officers is awfully determined to get out of this fix. Last night, right after you left, they came in delegation, right while I was in the colonel's office, and demanded to know his intentions. It's easy for the officers to surrender. They'll be looked after by the French officers. No one is going to look after no corporal. Who's going to stop some redskin from lifting my scalp after I surrender my musket? Certainly no French officer. No, we will fight if we have to."

"I don't think you'll have to," interrupted Stephen. "Just tell Mascarene to hold out and not let the French bluff him. You might even spread the word, among the officers especially, that the French can't control the Micmacs. That might put a little steel into their spines. You can say that they burned a deserter they caught yesterday."

"Did they?"

Stephen shook his head. "No, but they would have if the French had not interferred."

Kip smiled. "No harm stretching the truth on that score. Why don't you come back to the fort with me? Seems to me you got Mascarene the news he wanted."

"No," said Stephen. "I think I can learn some more of the French plans if I stay out."

"Suit yourself," said Kip. "Will you be coming in again soon?"

"Keep showing up here, Israel. But I think it may be some days before I can get information on French plans. My sources are not very high-ranking and don't get the orders until just before they are to be carried out."

Kip turned to look at the fort, where a sentry's call disturbed the peace of the night. When he turned back to face Stephen, he was gone. "Son of a bitch," Kip muttered. "He is good."

Stephen retraced his way across the open field and made it safely into the underbrush just as the rim of the moon appeared over the hills behind him. He moved cautiously through the woods, fairly certain that Karl's comment that the Indians would be too drunk to scout this evening was accurate, but he was still not willing to take any unnecessary chances. When he returned to the small clearing where Karl's guard was camped, the fire had diminished to glowing embers. Stephen crawled on all fours to his bed and quietly rolled himself in the blanket that Stiegler had loaned him.

255

"Where have you been, Stefan?" Stephen heard his friend's voice from behind the log to his right.

"I had to relieve myself," he responded.

"I see. I hope your news was consoling to your friends."

Stephen lifted himself up onto his elbows and stared into the night. He could barely make out Karl's face. But when he heard his friend's soft chuckle, he relaxed and lowered himself back onto the ground. He closed his eyes and gave in to his weariness. He slept.

Karl shook Stephen's shoulder roughly. "Wake up, soldier," he said in a loud and rough tone. "God damn Acadians, ain't much good for anything but sleeping."

The other soldiers, in various stages of dress, laughed. Stephen sat up and pushed his unruly hair away from his face.

"Come on, bumpkin," Karl joked. "Get your ass out of bed. We've orders to get into camp."

Stephen rose to his feet. He took water from the water skin that Karl offered to him and splashed it into his face. He took some into his mouth, swirled it around a bit, and then spit it out into the ground.

The four guards set out ahead, as ordered by the corporal. "The Acadian and I will clean up the camp and make sure that nothing is left behind," called Karl as the four Swiss set out for the main camp without much semblance of military order. "Service under the French is ruining a lot of good soldiers," Karl said to Stephen. "Look at them; you'd think they were off to a picnic." He lowered his voice. "Why did you come back last night, Stefan?"

"I have more to find out," was the reply.

"I think you shouldn't have come back, and if you're smart, you'll take the opportunity I'm giving you now to take off and return to English lines."

"Karl, I have a job to do and I need your help. I need to know your commander's plans."

"I've already told you. His plans don't count for much. We are not going to attack. Duvivier has got the Micmacs all worked up making fire arrows, and the Acadians are busy building scaling ladders. But that's all for show. He knows he can't attack with us Swiss and he can't attack without us. It will be some time before he gets any more troops from Louisbourg."

"Who is Duvivier?" asked Stephen.

"He's the commander of this expedition, the same one who

256

captured the fort at Canso at the beginning of the war. He is the best man they have among the French officers—which is not saying much."

"I'm going to camp with you, Karl."

"You're a fool, Stefan."

"You're probably right. But why all this sudden activity? Why the summons to camp?

"There's to be a parley today. Mascarene has agreed to meet with Duvivier, and the captain wants every available body on display to impress the English with the size of our force."

The two men followed the trail toward the main French encampment. The captain's headquarters were on a knoll within sight of the fort. The tents of the regulars were arranged in neat precision on the lower ground in the depression at the foot of the knoll, where a stream flowed to the west. Farther down the stream from the tents of the regulars, the campfires of the Acadians were easily identifiable by the total lack of order in their camp. Only the Micmacs, who lounged about smoking, drinking, and busily painting themselves for the parley, could have made the Acadians seem military by comparison.

"This is dangerous, Stefan. If someone should recognize you . . ." Karl did not have to finish his sentence.

Lieutenant Bertier intercepted them as they entered the camp. "Stiegler, get to your men and form a line of march. We are to meet with the English, halfway between the fort and our camp. You," he pointed at Stephen, "get over and join the other ruffians among the Acadians—and try to look like a soldier."

The drums were beating steadily now, and the camp was in a turmoil as men rushed to and fro, looking for their units. Stephen walked casually toward a large, broadshouldered man in homespun, who seemed to be in charge of the Acadians. "I'm a new recruit, sir," he said.

"Where are you from, son?" the man asked, his speech slurred by the pipe clenched firmly by his teeth.

"From Isle Royale," answered Stephen.

"I don't think we have any among us from that far north. Most of us are from Grand Pré. But you are welcome to stay with us. Fall in at the rear of the column over there. They're short a man, I think."

With the regulars marching to the beat of their drums, led by splendidly attired, mounted officers, and with the Acadians and the Indians more casually bringing up the rear, the attacking forces of the King of France marched across the fields toward the fort of Annapolis Royale before they had reached their destination, halfway between fort and camp, the great gate of the fort swung open and the squeal of the bagpipes could be heard. A much smaller delegation of redcoated men marched in precision toward the chosen meeting place. In the lead was the heavy gray form of Paul Mascarene. Mascarene had obviously chosen the opposite course of action from Duvivier—the English commander had wished to hide the small size of his garrison by sending only a delegation, while the rest of his men packed the ramparts facing the French.

When the French forces reached the appointed spot, they halted and awaited the arrival of the English delegation. Lieutenant Bertier rode to the rear, down the line of Acadians. Spotting the contingent from Grand Pré, he rode up to the giant militia leader. "You there, get your columns up front. The captain wants Mascarene to know that the Acadians have answered the call of their king." The lieutenant then swung his horse around and galloped off toward the front of the column again.

"Damn," said the man standing next to Stephen. "Mascarene has a memory like an elephant. He won't forget that it was Grand Pré men who stood in the forefront for King Louis. He'll take it out on our hides when this war is over." Stephen tried to look glum, but he was delighted to be within earshot of the negotiations.

By the time the Acadian contingent had reached the front of the line, the English delegation had arrived and proper salutations and gifts had been exchanged between the leaders. A table and two chairs, facing each other across the table, had been put in place. With a sweeping bow Duvivier gestured to Mascarene to be seated. The colonal returned the bow and sat down.

"It is my greatest regret," Duvivier began, "that we meet, sir, for the first time under such circumstances and that it is my duty to demand of you the surrender of Port Royale to His Most Christian Majesty."

Mascarene addressed him in English. "I presume, Captain, that if I do not surrender, then you will bring forward your cleverly concealed siege guns and blow my fort to pieces."

Duvivier waited for Bertier to translate his opponent's words for him. He was too clever a man to attempt to bluff Mascarene on the matter of guns. "The guns have obviously not yet arrived, Colonel. Nor have all my regular troops. I am, however, expecting reinforcements from Louisbourg at any moment."

Mascarene frowned. Lieutenant Sanford, who served as his aide and who was standing behind him, leaned over and whispered into the colonel's ear. Mascarene's frown turned into a look of disgust but he remained silent.

"The arrival of these reinforcements will give us more than enough men to take the fort," continued Duvivier. "In addition, I regret to tell you that the Indians who have accompanied us on this mission are not really under my control. I suspect that they will obey me if they can expect a reward. But should some of them lose their lives in an attempt to scale the walls, then I will never be able to stop them from taking scalps, no matter what terms we might later arrive at."

Mascarene rose to his feet. "Captain, your last remark was unworthy of a gentleman and an officer. If you cannot control your own forces, you have no business being in command. I suspect that we should terminate this parley immediately."

The color drained from Duvivier's face. "Colonel, I had not expected a Frenchman to be so rude—even one who fights for his country's enemies."

Again Sanford whispered in the colonel's ear.

Mascarene returned to his chair. "Captain, you amaze me. Surely you would not want a heretic like me serving in the French army. Some sixty years ago good King Louis XIV made it very clear what he thought of our country's Protestants. But let us not fight ancient battles. We have one of our own at hand. Lieutenant Sanford," he sneered, "reminds me constantly that I must do my duty and find out what terms you are prepared to offer me."

Duvivier had calmed down also. With a smile he returned to his seat. "I offer you the full honors of war, sir. You may keep your battle flags and weapons. You will be detained until the arrival of my reinforcements. The two supply ships I am expecting momentarily will take you and your men under truce to one of your New England ports—say Portsmouth."

"These are indeed generous terms, Captain," said Mascarene. "I am at a loss to explain your generosity. Perhaps you are just a man possessed by greatness of soul. I am sure my officers and men will be pleased to know that they face so generous an enemy."

"But, *mon ami,* I cannot remain so generous for very long."

"Captain, I have already discussed this matter with my officers and we have agreed. I accept your offer."

Duvivier was startled. Before he could say anything, however, Mascarene continued.

"But since we must wait for the arrival of your supply ships before anything more can occur, I must insist that we sign the capitulation of the fort to take effect when your ships arrive. Until that moment the fort remains the possession of His Majesty, King George."

Stephen smiled when he saw the disturbed faces of Duvivier and Bertier. Now it was they who were in a bind. To refuse the English offer of surrender without a fight would be hard to explain to their superiors in Louisbourg. But if the ships did not arrive, then no surrender could be expected from the English.

Duvivier pondered for a moment. Then he rose. "I must consult with my officers, Colonel."

"Quite proper, Captain," said Mascarene. "It is always wise for a commander to consult with his brave comrades." His voice dripped sarcasm. "I presume that this conference is over until you send me word of your decision." The colonel rose from the table. "Sanford, we must return to our duties."

The two officers strode to the head of the column. The piper struck up a Scottish air and the British contingent marched back over the knolls toward the fort.

Duvivier slammed his fist down on the table. His orderly brought his horse to him. He mounted and rode off in the direction of his headquarters.

"Your colonel did well today, Stefan," said Karl as he sat down next to his friend at the campfire of the Grand Pré men.

"Not so loud, Karl. I know you regulars think all the Acadians are stupid, but they are not that stupid."

"Maybe not, my friend, but they are asleep," said the corporal, craning his neck to glance at the blanket-wrapped forms lying about the center campfire. "Duvivier has left himself in a difficult position. He cannot reject his own terms, and even if he demands instant surrender, your colonel will reject it and then we are stalemated. My officers know that our men will not make an assault, and the Indians have already tried and failed. They are in no mood to try again— and your friends here are not capable of an assault. No, Stefan, Duvivier has worked himself into a corner. All he can

260

do is accept the conditional surrender and hope that the supply ships will arrive. They won't. Duvivier will sit here all summer before the masters of the *Caribou* and the *Ardent* will leave Louisbourg for anyplace other than France or the West Indies. No profits in sailing here.."

"What will happen then? Nothing?"

"Exactly," said Karl, "nothing. Oh, I expect that after some weeks, Duvivier will try an attack here or there—but nothing concerted and nothing serious. And then we will all go back to Louisbourg before winter sets in. Unless, of course, you English send reinforcements, and then we shall go back to Louisbourg even sooner."

"Karl, have you thought at all about what I said when we first met?"

The corporal frowned and then looked away from Stephen. "My comrades are here and at Louisbourg, Stefan. I won't be a deserter, even to join up with you, my friend."

"Then let me return to Louisbourg with you. I want to talk to your comrades. The English will never leave Louisbourg alone. Governor Shirley is already making plans, and the man I work for, Mr. Vaughan, is determined to attack. Perhaps together we can convince your comrades to surrender the fortress without a fight and together we can claim lands from the English king. I'm not going back to Boston, Karl. My family is gone, except for one aunt, who is in no position to act like family. You are my family now—you and Socono and Sister Louis. You are the only ones in this world that I have ever cared for and who have cared for me. You and I will be brothers. What is it that the Abenacki do? Socono told me about it. They mix their blood and become blood brothers. Let's do it now."

Karl frowned for a moment, then laughed quietly. "Very well," he said. "I always wanted a little brother."

Stephen reached for his hunting knife and, with a fast slash, he cut the vein on his wrist and watched as the blood began to run down his arm. He reached for Karl's hand, but the Swiss playfully pulled away.

"Are you crazy?" he laughed. "Do you think I'm going to let you slit my wrist? Here, I'll do it myself." He took Stephen's knife and very gingerly pricked his vein with the point until some blood appeared. They held their wrists together and allowed the blood to mingle. They looked at each other and both became very serious. It was clear to each that what they had just done—although very boyish—was important to them both.

"Now we return to Louisbourg as brothers," said Stephen finally.

"Stefan, don't be crazy. If you return to Louisbourg, you're a dead man. Lalonde will be there. LaGarde and the whole Jesuit community, any number of residents of the town, will know you by sight. You would be arrested within an hour after you entered the west gate."

"I'll let my beard grow," said Stephen.

Karl laughed out loud and grabbed Stephen's cheeks between his fingers. "You call that fuzz a beard?"

"Ah, listen to the old man," said Stephen, knocking his friend's hand from his face with his arm. "You must be all of twenty-one now. Seriously, Karl, I can disguise myself. I can be safe and together we can free you and your comrades from the corruption and the arrogance of the French."

"I can't say I wouldn't like that, Stefan. Things have gone from bad to worse these last few years. I have had no pay for the past half year, and as a corporal I'm treated better than most. I don't think we would have any trouble starting a mutiny. But it will have to be timed with an English attack, or else we will all hang."

"Good, it's settled then. I'll return to Louisbourg with you. It is early enough for me to get a message to Mascarene tonight."

"I'll go to the picket line with you, Stefan, and wait for your return. I wouldn't want anything to happen to you before we even have a chance to launch our little plot. Although I'm not sure why I am so happy about launching it at all. I should go right this moment to Lieutenant Bertier and tell him that I suspect that you are the Judas, Noel. Knowing that I had done that, you wouldn't dare come back. You would flee to Port Royale and remain there—safe."

"We're going to Louisbourg together, Karl, and when we're finished there, we will start a new life."

The two stepped out of the light of the fire and walked toward the darkened tents of the regulars, on their way to the picket lines of the French army. As they left the camp of the Acadians, the prone figure closest to where they had been sitting and talking stirred. He raised himself on his elbows and watched the two conspirators disappear into the darkness.

VII

1744-1745—Fall and Winter

Stephen rolled as close to the large campfire as he could. The chill night air crept into his blanket and froze his backside, while the leaping flames roasted him in front. He turned his back to the fire and tried to even things out. He was too uncomfortable to sleep.

His mind roamed over the events of the past days. The besieging army was now reduced to the Swiss troops. The Indians recognized a lost cause for what it was, and all but a handful had faded away into the forests. The Acadians had gone home even before the Indians. Each would now have to invent a story of how he had remained neutral—a story convincing enough to save him from the wrath of the English governor of this soon-to-be-secured province of Nova Scotia. The final blow fell just two days before. A supply ship had appeared in the basin. It was from Boston, not from Louisbourg. Governor Shirley had come through at last and Annapolis was safe. But still Duvivier refused to withdraw what remained of his army. With winter coming on, however, he would have to face the inevitable before long. The nights were colder, and although the sun warmed the forests in the daylight hours, it shown down on an ever-increasing array of yellow, red and brown leaves.

Stephen shivered as a gust of icy wind blasted his face. The light of the fire cast long shadows into the woods and Stephen could see falling leaves whirling in the grip of one gust and then another.

Stephen tossed back into his original position with his back to the wind. He caught sight of Karl scurrying from a far campfire toward Stephen's. "My God, where have you been, Karl? I'm freezing my ass or roasting it. Why don't you turn in and block off that wind from me?"

"To hell with you, my little brother," laughed the corporal. "I've been making contacts with my comrades. There seems to be strong support for taking some action, but not until we are back at the fortress. If we desert now and simply surrender to the English, we will be treated as prisoners of war. None of us wants to spend the rest of the war rotting in some English prison. The men agree; we must get back to Louisbourg. We'll organize those who were left behind and we'll wait upon the English. If they attack, we will strike from within and turn the fort over to them in return for a subsidy and a safe passage to our homes."

"You've worked well," said Stephen. He thought a moment. "Perhaps I should have returned to Annapolis and worked my way back to Boston to set all this in motion."

"You had your chance for that, Stefan. It's too late now. The men are not going to take my word for it that the English will strike. I need you with me. You are a well-known English spy—or so Lalonde has painted you. When I whisper your name to my friends, they take my plans more seriously. When we get back to the fort, I will need you to help me convince the others."

Now doubts began to replace Stephen's earlier conviction. "But I have no guarantee that the English will attack. There was only talk of it when I left Boston."

"Oh, they'll attack," interrupted Karl. "It is the logical thing for them to do now that Annapolis is saved. They will grab the initiative. And even if they fail to follow through, we will have lost nothing, because we will do nothing ourselves until the whole damn English navy is outside Louisbourg harbor."

Karl turned his back to Stephen and mumbled a good night. It seemed to Stephen that his friend began to snore only seconds later, but Stephen could not sleep. The fire died down. Now instead of alternately freezing and roasting, Stephen felt only the night wind. He crept closer to Karl to try to use his body as a shield, but that did not help. He could not keep his mind quiet. In broad outline Karl's plan was feasible. Just how they would seize the fortress would have to be worked out. But he was sure that a disaffected garrison could accomplish it. If the English were at hand at the time of the mutiny, it would all be simple. Late at night, however, he could not suppress his doubts and a terrible sense of foreboding. He had begun to grow a beard but still he knew many people in Louisbourg. Surely someone would recognize him. The very reason Karl gave for the necessity of his presence in the fortress could prove their undoing. He was still awake worrying about the future when the first light of dawn colored the sky.

Karl had not stirred from his original position or ceased to snore throughout the night. Finally he rolled onto his back and opened his eyes. "Good morning, little Jesuit," he said to Stephen and laughed when Stephen's eyes opened wide with panic. "Don't fret so, Stefan. A man would have to have keener hearing than your old friend Socono to overhear me. There's no one around. Christ, I'm hungry." He sat up. "Bullinger," he shouted. "Roll your arse out of your blanket and get a fire started. Me and my friend here want some coffee."

Bullinger stirred in his blanket on the other side of the burned-out campfire. "You and your Acadian friend can get your own fire and your own coffee," he murmured.

"Doesn't he know about me?" asked Stephen.

"Bullinger talks a good fight," responded Karl. "I've never seen him actually fight, mind you. One thing I do know about him is that he has a head full of mush where he should have brains. He'll join the mutiny as long as he thinks it's going to succeed. But I would never trust him with any information. As I said, he talks a good fight but mostly, he talks."

Stephen decided not to risk Bullinger's ire and started to make his own fire and brew his own coffee. Within ten minutes a good blaze was burning and Stephen breathed in deeply the heady mixture of crisp morning air and brewing coffee.

Several of the men seated about the fire rose halfheartedly when Lieutenant Bertier came to the camp. He glared at Karl. "Corporal Stiegler, when there is an officer present, it is your responsibility to bring your men to attention."

"Yes, sir," Karl responded in an exaggerated tone. "Men," he shouted. "Attention."

All leaped to their feet, including Stephen.

"Prepare for inspection," shouted Karl with even greater exaggeration.

"At ease, Corporal," said Bertier. "I just wanted to make sure that proper discipline did not break down."

"You may rest assured of that," said Karl stiffly. "Proper discipline will not break down."

"Good; now get your men ready to move out. We are withdrawing to Louisbourg this morning." He turned and left the campfire.

The soldiers dropped down to the ground again, several of them making obscene gestures, not only at Bertier but at all officers.

"You heard the lieutenant," said Karl. "It's back to Louisbourg."

Juneau, a tall, bearded Swiss who rarely said anything, began to curse. "Back to that fogbound, cold, hellhole for another winter of no pay, no women and no drinks. I don't think I can take any more of this, Karl. What you were talking about last night—when do you think it will happen?"

Karl pointed at Stephen. "You ask him. He's in charge of that matter. He has the ties with our friends in the south."

Juneau looked at Stephen. "Are you really the man he says you are?" he asked.

Stephen saw that Bullinger was out of earshot. "I am if he told you my name is Stephen Nowell."

"You are the one who sold the priest to the Iroquois?"

Stephen squirmed a bit, not knowing quite how to answer.

"Don't fret. I'm from Geneva. I wouldn't care if you sold the whole lot of them priests to hell. Will the English come?"

"In the spring," answered Stephen, hoping that no one would ever accuse him of lying because of his response.

The French army lingered even longer in Nova Scotia, but the contingent to which Stephen was attached made a forced march to Canso. After a brief rest in the captured English fort, they crossed the straits to Isle Royale.

Once on the island, Stephen relaxed. Despite the fact that he approached danger, the familiarity of the countryside put him at ease. These were the woods he had explored with Socono. Every rock, every stream evoked a memory. He knew his way in these woods.

They emerged from the forest onto the shores of Gabarus Bay, south of the town. Stephen and Karl walked together along the beach until they came to the spot where the stream that flowed from the pool merged with the surf of the bay.

"The English will have to land here," said Karl.

"Isn't the surf too rough?" questioned Stephen. "Won't it upset their boats?"

Karl shrugged. "Some of them," he responded. "But this is the smoothest beach. The rest of the points jutting out into the sea are too rocky. It will have to be here."

"How will we get that information to them?"

Karl scratched his chin. "As soon as we have them sighted,

I guess we'll have to smuggle you out of the town and hope you can reach your friends."

They pushed back into the woods, following the course of the stream to the pool. Then they struck out from the pool directly toward the town via Green Hill and the West Gate. From the summit of the hill, Stephen again saw the fortress that had been his home. The autumn sun struck the spires of the citadel and the hospital, turning them golden. Although he was sweating from their hard march and the long climb up the hill, Stephen shuddered as if chilled when he caught sight of the city.

Karl threw his arm around Stephen's shoulder when he saw that his friend was frightened. The confidence built during the day dissolved in the face of the real dangers they would have to confront. "Come, Stefan," said the corporal. "We must go down to the town. We have work to do."

The cold winter fog pervaded everything. No one ventured out into the streets unless the task was essential. The windows of the houses frosted over, making it impossible to see out of them—although nothing could have been seen through the murk. The residents of the town huddled in front of their fires and waited for the winds that would blow the fog away. Yet even these winds would bring no real relief. They would roar out of the north and west, out of the snows of Quebec and Labrador, pass over the frozen plain of ice that was the Gulf of St. Lawrence in winter and descend upon Isle Royale and Louisbourg, chilling the people to their bones. Then the true winter would begin.

Stephen lay huddled in his bunk, his dufflecoat and campaign blanket pulled tightly about him. Karl, Bullinger and several others of the Swiss contingent sat before a stove sipping black, thick coffee from mugs whose steam mixed with the steam of their breath.

"Christ, it's cold," said Bullinger, rubbing his hands on his coffee mug, trying to wring some permanent warmth from it. "What a rotten Christmas eve this is going to be."

"We need more wood for the stove," said Karl, looking at Bullinger.

"Don't look at me. I got the last load. Get your Acadian friend out of his bed and let him freeze his ass off getting wood. He hasn't stepped out of this room except for morning review since we got here."

"Bullinger, what do you call the insignia on my arm?" asked the corporal.

"It's called a reward. You get it for kissing some French officer's behind."

Karl said nothing. There was absolute quiet in the room. Even Stephen, who had been in a semi-doze stirred, disturbed by the silence. He sat up to see what was wrong. Karl stood and faced Bullinger, who also started to rise. Before he could, however, Karl, with a quick snap of his wrist, flipped the contents of his coffee mug onto Bullinger's lap. The soldier yelled in surprise, but as the hot coffee began to soak through his breeches, his yell grew into a roar of pain. Quickly he tore open the buttons of the pants and pulled them down below his knees. Lifting one leg off the floor, he attempted to pull his foot through, but the material caught on his shoe. The other soldiers began to howl with laughter as Bullinger hopped on one foot, naked from the waist to the knees. Finally he tripped and went sprawling to the floor, face first. He turned over and, sitting with his knees spread as far apart as his twisted breeches would allow, he tenderly examined the reddened skin of his inner thighs.

"You could have ruined me for life, Stiegler," he shouted.

"I doubt if the garrison whores would have noticed it, even if I had," laughed Karl.

"You shouldn't have done that to me, Corporal," Bullinger said in a lower voice, still rubbing his scorched skin.

"The only reason I shouldn't have," said Karl, "is that now I will probably have to send someone else out to get the wood."

"I'll go," said Stephen, dropping his feet over the side of the bunk onto the floor.

Karl looked at him and gave him the look that Stephen had come to call Karl's I-don't-think-it-is-wise look.

Stephen decided to ignore him. He dropped his blanket onto his bed, pulled his coat collar up around his throat and stepped through the front door, out into the fog. The winter's wood was stored in a roofed shed, open on three sides, whose only wall was the side of the barracks. Stephen piled five heavy quarter logs in the cradle of his arms and started back toward the barracks entrance.

"Who is that?" said a voice from out of the gloom. "You there, stay where you are. I need someone to guide me."

Stephen recognized the voice, and his whole body froze. The man drew near enough for Stephen to make out his form. "Good, you're one of the soldiers. Guide me, my good man, to the chapel entrance. I am Father Lalonde. I am to say mass for His Excellency this morning."

Stephen dared not speak. He shifted the wood to one arm and pulled his neck down farther into his collar; he prayed that the beard he had grown since fall would help disguise him. Stephen offered Lalonde his arm. "This way, Father," he said in an exaggerated Acadian accent and led him in the direction of the main entrance to the King's bastion. Stephen could not help but think of the last time this man had touched him and, despite the damp cold, sweat began to trickle down his spine. They walked across the snow-covered garden area to the main door in silence. The sentries at the door came to attention as they saw the priest.

"Thank you," said Lalonde loudly to Stephen. Then he reached over, grabbed Stephen's collar and whispered in his ear. "Etienne, you look superb in a beard, but your accent does no justice to your upbringing."

Stephen stopped in his tracks; he did not know how to respond. Then Lalonde was through the door of the bastion.

Stephen stared at the doorway into which Lalonde had disappeared. The wood he carried in his arms seem to grow heavier. After some moments he turned and started to walk back toward the barracks. As he came closer to his destination he broke into a run.

The scene in the barracks had not changed greatly in the few moments he had been gone. Bullinger was still rearranging his breeches while Karl and the other men sipped their coffee.

"You're slow," said one of the soldiers to Stephen. Karl, however, after glancing quickly at Stephen, rose from his seat and took several of the logs from Stephen's arms.

He led Stephen to his bunk and out of earshot of the others. "What's happened?" he asked in a whisper.

"I've seen Lalonde."

"Did he recognize you?"

"Worse, he spoke to me. I don't know what his game is, Karl. He could have turned me over to the sentries right on the spot. Perhaps he is at this moment denouncing me to the governor and the intendant. I've got to get out of here."

"You're right about that. But we mustn't panic."

"Everything we have worked for these past weeks will be lost if we are discovered," said Stephen. "Where can I hide?"

"We're not ready to take over yet," said Karl. "The men are angry but they are still afraid of hanging."

"You are the only person in Louisbourg I can trust, Karl. I don't know where else to go."

"What about the old nun?"

"But wouldn't that put her in danger?"

"Stefan, I don't think you have much choice. Lalonde knows you're in Louisbourg. He hates you more than any person alive, except maybe for a few Oneida. If he knows you are here and he hasn't given you away, then he knows he has you in a trap; he is playing with you. He'll destroy you and, for that matter, me too—but all in his own sweet time."

"Maybe he doesn't know anything about our plans. If he did he would see a mutiny as my means of escape," said Stephen. "There is a way out. I must go into hiding and you must set the mutiny into motion as soon as you can."

"It will take a few days, Stefan, and you know we will fail," said Karl. "Without an English army present to take advantage of our troubles, it will be for nothing."

"We've botched this badly, haven't we, Karl?"

"Speak for yourself, Bastonois," said Karl. He tousled Stephen's already unruly hair and slapped him hard on the knee. "Just get out of here. I will know where to find you."

"When you come looking for me, Karl, the signal that all is well is to tell Sister that you seek the Archbishop of Paris."

He grabbed his blanket from the bunk, pulled his coat collar about his throat and stepped through the barracks door without looking back. The streets were still fogbound, yet Stephen knew his way to the covent door.

Lieutenant Bertier walked down the row of carefully made bunks with Karl Stiegler immediately behind him. His inspection was as careless as usual. He failed to notice Stephen's absence. When he had finished, he nodded absentmindedly at the corporal and made for the front door.

"Is that all, sir?" asked Karl.

"Yes, Corporal."

"But, sir, it has been customary on Christmas Eve for the Officer of the Day to provide a little brandy or English rum for the men."

"We haven't any this year," interrupted the officer, "and besides, we are at war. We've little to celebrate this Christmas."

Bullinger, who stood by his bunk at attention, muttered under his breath.

"Corporal Stiegler, put that man on report." The lieutenant

walked up to the private and looked him squarely in the face. "You were saying, Private?"

The private's fist slammed into the officer's gut, bending him in half. Bullinger's knee then crashed into Bertier's jaw. Blood squirted from the officer's mouth and his eyes rolled back up into his head.

"And I ain't had no God damn pay in nine months," spat out the enraged soldier, standing over the form of his unconscious officer.

"That starts it," said Karl. "Spread the word to the other barracks. No one is to leave the barracks until I give the signal. If we can get hold of the governor and hold him hostage, we may have a chance yet."

"Why don't we all just rush the citadel?" asked Bullinger.

Juneau shook his head. "The marines are on guard. They'll mow us down without a thought."

"We have to sneak in and grab him," said Karl. "Juneau, you and Ernst know what to do; you come with me—you too, Bullinger. I don't want to let you out of my sight."

"What about the marines?" said Juneau. "We planned this for a night when we would be on guard duty."

"We have one man among them who is with us," said Karl.

"I've never heard of a Swiss among the marines," said Juneau.

"He's not Swiss. He's French," said Karl.

"I don't trust no God damn Frenchman," yelled Bullinger.

"Shut that clown up," hissed Karl. "We have no choice but to trust Michel. Let's move."

The four soldiers filed quietly out of the barracks and passed through the governor's garden. The fog still hung over the city, and it was impossible to see the sentries on duty in front of the governor's residence. Karl whistled the arranged signal. There was no response.

"I don't like this, Stiegler," whispered Bullinger. "Let's forget it. Maybe we should make for the gate and the woods."

"And then what? Freeze your ass off in the snow? What's happened to your nerve? You were pretty quick to flatten Bertier."

"He's a prick and I've been wanting to do that for four years," was the reply. "But hell, Karl, where's your man? Doesn't he know your signal?"

"I don't know where he is," answered Karl. "But we don't

271

have any choice now but to go through with this." He began to creep toward the gray stone building that loomed out of the fog in front of them. There were no sentries on duty at all, and the gates were wide open.

"I'm not going in there," said Bullinger. His two companions nodded in agreement. "It's a trap. They've set it for us and they'll spring it on us just as soon as we're inside."

"We needn't wait even that long," said a voice from out of the fog to their right. Duvivier stepped from the mist, with three naval officers carrying muskets immediately in back of him. "The mutiny is over, my friends."

Bullinger swung his bayoneted musket around to face the officers, but before he could raise it to fire or lunge, Duvivier's sword flashed out of the darkness and pierced the private's arm. Bullinger screamed and dropped the musket onto the cobblestones with a clatter.

A young officer of marines stepped forward and saluted Duvivier. "I've posted my men at the front and rear of all the barracks, sir. The Swiss scum are locked in."

"Thank you, Lieutenant. Now take these other three away." He turned to Karl. "Corporal, you will come with me. His Excellency and the good Father Lalonde have some questions to ask of you."

The surprise had been complete. Except for Bullinger's pitiful defense, the mutiny had been a farce. Karl stared at his captors. The only thing that could save Stephen now would be his silence. He could do nothing to save himself.

The officer led him down the long corridor toward the chapel. Just before its massive doors, they turned into a room on the right. The room was warmed by a large fire in the hearth. Karl recognized the Jesuit, who stood looking out the window into the impenetrable fog. He turned as the door opened and looked at Karl and his captor. A faint smile flickered across his lips; then he turned back to the window.

The man seated behind the cluttered desk in the center of the room was the new governor, the Chevalier Duchambon. Beside him stood Isaac Wiggins. The governor never raised his head as the captain escorted Karl into the room and forced him to stand on the small, square rug facing Duchambon.

"Corporal," said the governor, looking up for the first time, "you have plotted against His Most Christian Majesty. You are guilty of treason. Have you anything to say for your-self?"

Karl remained silent.

The governor turned to Duvivier. "Take him out and shoot him," he said.

"Your Excellency," Lalonde interjected. "Let us not pro-ceed too hastily. Obviously this man deserves shooting, but not before the other ringleaders, especially the English spy, are found. I have no doubt that if the corporal here cooper-ates with us and the traitor Noel is found, you might reconsider your verdict."

"The priest is right," said Wiggins. "The Englishman must be seized."

"You are right, Father. You, Stiegler, where is the English-man?"

Karl continued to remain silent.

"Don't try my patience, bastard," Duchambon yelled. "We know the Englishman is in the town. We have known what you both were planning from the very beginning. Our agent, Wiggins, who is in the employ of the most important spy in New England, has had you spotted since the Englishman joined you before Port Royale. We know that Noel works for the English and for that traitor to King Louis, Mascarcne. Since you entcred the city we have watched every move you have made. We know all. You may as well confess and give the Englishman over to us. He cannot escape. There is nowhere to go."

"The corporal seems determined to remain silent, Your Excellency," said Lalonde, walking from the window toward Karl. He placed his hideously deformed index finger under Karl's chin and raised his head with it. "I think you should let M. Wiggins and me take him downstairs to the cells. We have some friends there who might begin his tongue wagging. In fact," his voice turned to ice, "I have been able to teach these friends a thing or two about inflicting pain—thanks to that scum friend of yours."

Karl pulled his head away from the priest's hand.

The governor grimaced but Wiggins chuckled. "Duvivier," said Duchambon, "take the Swiss below. Find out where the Englishman is and come back with him in irons."

Duvivier led Karl out of the room. Two marines waited for them in the hall. One of the marines pulled Karl's arms behind his back and tied them tight enough to cut off the circulation of blood. "Get moving, scum," said the other.

"François is waiting for you. A little fire, a little iron and you will talk."

Karl's mind went numb. He had no thought of escape. All he hoped for was to keep silent. He would endure whatever they handed out to him; he would not talk. They reached the end of the corridor and he was shoved through a doorway to the left and down a flight of stone stairs. They were below the surface of the ground now, and the walls were covered with ice. What little light there was came from two candles embedded in wall niches.

The stairway curved around to the right and down into a large hallway. On both sides of the hall, iron doors lined the walls. Karl was pushed past these. At the far end of the hallway, there stood a great oaken door. As the party of men approached, it was swung open and Karl was grabbed by three more men. His hands were retied in front of him; a chain was looped through his bound hands and, before he knew what had happened, he was hoisted up, his hands high over his head, his feet eight inches off the floor. With a quick tear his shirt was stripped from his back and then yanked completely off. Another tug brought his breeches down to his knees and then off.

A large, muscled man walked around in front of the soldier, examining him. "Corporal Stiegler, my name is François. We are about to get to know one another very well. You are a large man and this may take some time. I truly hope it does."

Karl tried to look away. Two men grabbed his legs and fastened them to hooks in the floor.

François reached into a brazier and brought out a small branding iron. "Since you are guilty of treason, Swiss pig, I've a little mark reserved for you."

"No more than is necessary, François," said a voice from the doorway behind the prisoner. Karl recognized it as that of the Jesuit, Lalonde.

"Yes, Reverend Father. Stiegler, tell me where the English spy is?"

The iron was thrust under his nose and Karl could smell the terrible heat of it. He clenched his teeth. François waited a second and then plunged the hot iron into the strained muscles of Karl's stomach. The air was filled with the hiss and the stench of burning flesh. Karl screamed and then grew silent. Sweat began to flow down his sides.

François smiled. "Yes, Father. No more than is necessary, but I think this is going to take a while."

Stephen approached the porter's door carefully. The fog blotted out all familiar landmarks and Stephen had to feel his way along the stone wall of the cottage. He did not see the door until he was close enough to touch it. He knocked softly. No answer. "There's no avoiding it," he whispered. "I'll have to ring the bell." He tugged violently at the rope, hoping that if he made it loud enough she would hear him the first time. He heard a shuffling of feet inside.

"Who's there?" said an old, familiar voice. The top of the Dutch door swung open. Sister Marie Louis stood before him, holding a lantern in front of her face. "Speak up, whoever it is. I can't see through the fog."

He grabbed her wrist and swung the lamp up to his face. "It's me, Etienne."

"My God, child, it is you." She lunged for him and pulled him to her, hugging him. "Why are you here, Etienne? It is dangerous. The Jesuit, Lalonde, has told terrible stories about you. If they catch you, they will kill you. You must leave."

"I've no place to go, Sister. May I stay with you?"

"Come in out of the night. We must talk," said the old nun.

He stepped through the door just in time to miss being caught between the two halves as Marie Louis swung them shut.

"Damn the fog. I ache from the chill in my bones," she muttered to herself.

Stephen started to speak but she hushed him. "First we have something warm. Then we talk." She shuffled back to her cupboard and returned with a bottle of rum. "I've taken to stronger stuff than warm milk since you saw me last, boy. There is no sun outside to warm me and so I'm forced to pour a little sun into me to get the chill out." She poured a cup for each of them.

She looked into his face, clearly straining to see him better than her tired eyes would allow. "I never believed what they said about you, Etienne. You were always a good boy, a generous boy."

"Thank you, Sister," he said. "My life has changed and I have done things I'm not very proud of since we last spoke. But for much of it I had reason."

"You still talk like a Jesuit," she laughed. "By the way, the great lady doesn't believe what they say about you either."

Stephen looked puzzled.

"The Polish lady, Madame DeLuynes."

"Manya? Manya is here?"

"She came to see me just about the same time that Lalonde started to spread those awful lies. She said that you had told her about me. She said you thought of me as your mother. We must notify her. Perhaps she can help us."

They talked on into the night. He told her of the mission; with some embarrassment, of Molly; of the smallpox; and of Socono and the flight onto the frozen Mohawk. He told what he had discovered of his origins. He told her of his grandfather and his aunt and his mother, of Father LaGarde's perfidy and Lalonde's perversion.

When he had finished, she sat stunned. She poured herself another cup of rum, tears streaming down her face. "Lalonde is a wicked man, Etienne; many of us have seen through him. He has suffered, no doubt, but he hates those who hurt him. Some call him the saint, the martyr. But he is a devil. It is Father LaGarde who is to be pitied, Etienne. I think he really loves you."

"He never loved me," Stephen hissed. "If he loved me, why did he rob me of my family—of my very name?"

"Etienne, do not make the same mistake Lalonde has made."

"I can't help it," he shouted.

She put her finger to her lips. "You will have Mother Superior over here if you keep that up. We must figure out what to do with you. You can spend the rest of the night here."

"I hope my friends in the barracks will solve the problem of what to do with me before very long," offered Stephen, but not with a great deal of conviction.

Stephen slept on the floor of the porter's lodge that night, and the next morning he took refuge in the large cupboard. Twice Sister Marie Louis left him alone, once to attend early mass and a second time to bring the morning Jesuit bread to the convent for breakfast. Stephen grew more and more impatient waiting for word from Karl. There had been no sounds of fighting during the night and in the morning everything seemed unchanged.

Sister Marie Louis returned from the convent for the second time and busied herself in her small kitchen, making a breakfast for herself and Stephen.

"You must eat quickly and then we must do something about you," she muttered. Stephen knew something was wrong. The old woman seemed flustered and ill at ease.

"What is it, Sister? What's wrong?"

"It is the army. There is something wrong at the barracks. The soldiers are all locked inside, and cannon have been set up outside the doors. Some soldiers have been arrested and taken to the citadel."

"We've failed, then," said Stephen.

"They are looking for you, Etienne. The whole city has been alerted. Soon they will come to question your friends. Mother Superior has already asked me about you. I lied to her. That is the first time I've lied to a superior in fifty years of religious life."

"I will have to leave here," said Stephen. "Have you been able to get word to Manya?"

"There has been no opportunity," she responded.

"I must do without her help, then. If they catch me here, it will go hard for you."

What can they do to an old reprobate like me?" she chuckled. "The order will take this job away from me soon. You may not have noticed it, but I do not see and hear as well as I used to."

"No, I had not noticed." A weak smile was all that he could manage.

He had no idea of where he could flee. He was a good woodsman, but the worst part of the winter was about to set in. Making it into the woods, however, required getting out of the city. Now he had little chance of escaping, with every loyal man in town looking for him.

The nun placed a large bread knife and a loaf of warm bread in front of him, along with a pitcher of milk. She patted his cheek and sat at the table next to him. Just at that moment, there was a soft knocking at the door. Stephen froze.

"What is it?" the old woman asked him.

"Someone is at the door."

"Then it must be one of your people. Anyone looking for me would certainly know I could not hear a knock. They would have rung the bell."

Stephen rose from his chair and picked up his musket.

The old woman put her hand on his and shook her head. "No violence, Etienne."

Without her noticing it, he slipped the bread knife off the table and into his hand. He stepped to the right of the door so that he would be hidden from view when it was opened.

There was a second knock at the door, this time a bit louder. Stephen signaled the nun to wait before answering it. He really did not know what to do. If it was Karl, then he should draw as little attention as possible to the porter's lodge and not force him to ring the bell. If it was not Karl, then he should not give his presence in the room away. But he had to act. He nodded to Sister Marie Louis to answer the door.

"Who's there?" she called out.

A low voice responded, "The Archbishop of Paris."

Stephen's heart sank. The response was right but the voice was wrong—worse than wrong. It was Duvivier. He was trapped. Perhaps if he could get them into the lodge, he could break for the clear from behind the door and lose them in the narrow streets. It was his only chance. He grasped the latches for the upper and lower halves of the Dutch door, swinging both open at the same time. There was an instant rush of men through the doorway. Stephen slammed the upper half shut with all the strength of his arms and ducked low through the open lower half, barely managing to escape being entangled in a mass of legs and arms. He heard a pistol fire. He was out in the street. He straightened himself and looked down the alley to his right. He could see a troop of horsemen mounting. He turned around to his left and stood face to face with the grinning face of Isaac Wiggins, standing beside Lalonde. He could feel the cold metal of Wiggins' pistol against his belly.

"Why, Etienne, it is so good to see you again; we seem to be running into each other all the time," said the priest. "I'll just take the knife from you. That way you won't get hurt."

For a moment Stephen was speechless. He felt he had stumbled into a nightmare. The faces of Lalonde and Wiggins leered at him out of the fog.

Duvivier appeared at the doorway of the lodge.

"Father Lalonde, you must come quickly. The old sister has been shot."

Stephen rushed back into the lodge. At first Lalonde thought he was trying to escape and called to Wiggins to fire. But Stephen was back inside the porter's lodge before Wiggins had a chance to respond.

Marie Louis was lying in the middle of the floor. Blood pumped from a wound in her chest. Her black habit was already soaked through and a pool was growing around her on the floor.

Stephen rushed to her side and knelt down. Picking up her head, he held it in his lap and rocked back and forth. A low moan escaped him. He sobbed. "Get a doctor," he yelled at Duvivier. But the captain had been soldier long enough to know a mortal wound when he saw one.

"She needs a priest, not a doctor," was his response.

Lalonde stepped into the lodge and handed Stephen's knife to Duvivier. "I will not grant that woman absolution—not after she has harbored a heretic and a traitor," he said.

Several of the officers and marines began to whisper to each other. "Father," said Duvivier, "the sister is dying. Surely you will give the last rites of Mother Church."

"Don't question me, Captain, in matters of ethics. I don't question you in matters of military discipline."

Stephen barely heard the exchange. He still cradled the nun's head in his lap and rocked.

She opened her eyes. They were filled with pain. But when she saw Stephen's face, she smiled. She reached up to touch the scar on his eyebrow. "Such a nasty wound on so pretty a little boy," she said. She continued to move her hand down his face and felt the tears streaming down his cheek. "Don't cry, little boy; Sister will be your Mama." She gasped. "Oh, Etienne, I think I will need a priest."

Stephen looked up at Lalonde, who turned away from them and walked out of the door. Marie Louis followed him with her eyes. "No matter," she said, "I have always done what I thought was right. My god will understand that, even if his won't. Come down here to me, boy." He bent his head and placed his wet cheek next to hers. "If you can get away, Etienne, go home to your people or to the Indian girl you talked of so much. Have no more to do with this place. Forget revenge and violence." Before he could respond, she was dead.

He sat in the middle of the floor, surrounded by her blood, for some minutes. Duvivier finally walked to him and placed his hand on his shoulder. "M. Noel, I must place you under arrest for spying and for mutiny. You will come with me."

Stephen nodded acknowledgment and rose to his feet after gently allowing her head to slide from his lap to the floor. He started to leave the lodge but turned back and looked at her again. He opened his mouth to speak but the captain turned him away.

"Come along; Mother Superior has been notified. She will take care of everything." With two marines holding his arms, he was led out of the lodge and into the sunlight. The fog had lifted at last.

For three days Stephen was kept in isolation in a cell deep within the citadel. No one came to question him, and his food was brought to the cell while he slept. He had hours to think of what he had done wrong. If he had remained in Boston or even at Annapolis, his two closest friends might have survived. Sister Marie Louis had died because of him, and he was sure that Karl was either dead already or had very little time to live. He himself probably would not live much longer either. It seemed that everything he touched—every person he loved—withered and died. Again and again, however, he returned to Isaac Wiggins. What was he doing here? What was his relation to the French? The door of his cell swung open and Father LaGarde stepped inside. "I'll come and get you when you call," said a voice from the hallway.

"Thank you, François," said the priest. "Hello, Etienne."

Stephen looked away.

"You don't have to speak to me if you do not wish to. I realize that you must hate me for all that I did to you. I have no excuse—other than the fact that I did what my conscience and my loyalty to the Society told me to do. I tried to make it up to you in other ways—by guiding you, by showing you the path of righteousness, by bringing you to God. . . ."

"I don't believe in your god," said Stephen. "Your god is Lalonde's god. Your god allows you to lie and cheat. He allows men like Lalonde to prosper and he kills good people like Sister."

"It seems to me, Etienne, that you were as responsible for the death of that good woman as anyone. Let us not attempt to excuse ourselves by placing the blame on God."

Stephen put his hands to his ears. "Get out of here. I don't want to listen to any more of your drivel. Why have you come here—to lecture me about the failings I already know I have?"

"No," said the priest. "I will not lecture you. I've come to tell you that I have been trying to help you. I have considerable influence with the governor. I am still the religious superior of the Society of Jesus in this fortress."

"I thought that Lalonde was cock of the roost," interrupted Stephen.

"I'll ignore your rudeness, Etienne. Lalonde has gained some prestige in the community as a result of his sufferings at the hands of the Oneida. He has lost much of it in these past few days as the story has spread of his failure to tend to the dying. There are many who will not forgive him for that."

"Will you, Father?"

LaGarde smiled. "Is this a test, Etienne? Yes, I'll forgive him if he asks forgiveness of me. But, as you know, he will have to do penance. However, I have come to speak of your fate, not Lalonde's. I have spoken with the governor about you. In fact, His Excellency and I had some very heated words. It seems he wanted to hang you, but I insisted that he could not. He could hang you if you had been guilty of mutiny, but of course you're not in the army and therefore not subject to military discipline. He could also hang you if you were a spy. You would be a spy if you had come into the city of Louisbourg with the purpose of giving our secrets to the English. I assured him that there is just as much evidence that you were a member of the Society of Jesus returning—by a long and circuitous route, mind you—but returning nevertheless from a failed mission. In short, you are one of us and I have claimed you. He can't have you."

"Neither can you," said Stephen.

"I am sorry to hear you say that," said LaGarde, "but I had thought as much. Duchambon is no fool. He knows the reason for my arguments. He knows I plan to have you set free. There is little he can do about it; you have vows. He can complain to Father Provincial, which most assuredly he will. He can banish you from the colony and he can keep you locked up until he finds a means to get rid of you. But he cannot not hang you. He won't keep you here long. He will want swift punishment of the guilty parties and then a quick settlement of all grievances. You will be a reminder of the mutiny as long as you're kept around. I think he will let me arrange your departure with the English prisoners from Canso who are due to be released shortly. I will write to Rome to release you from your vows. The dispensation will be granted. You may regard yourself free of them on the day you sail for Boston."

"I have regarded myself as free of them ever since Socono told me of your lies."

"The Indian grieves, Etienne, and he is often drunk. You should not take out your animosities toward me and the Society against a good and decent man."

"On that point you are correct," said Stephen. "I have made my peace with Socono. But he is the only one."

"Does the name Isaac Wiggins mean anything to you?"

Stephen looked at him in surprise. There were times he felt this man knew him so well he could read his thoughts.

"From the look on your face, I gather you know the man. He is the one who notified the authorities here of your plot. He followed you here from Port Royale. He pleaded for your death with the governor in the name of one who has much influence in New France. You have special reasons to be afraid of these men."

"I suppose I should thank you," said Stephen.

"If you feel gratitude, Etienne. But I would prefer your forgiveness."

"Do you ask it of me, Father?"

The priest looked at his hands and murmured, "I do."

"If I say yes," said Stephen through clenched teeth, "then all you will have to do is do a penance. No, I want no part of that game any more. You ask your god for forgiveness. You will get none from me."

"François," the priest called. "I'll be leaving now. Please let me out."

As the door to the cell swung open, the Jesuit turned to look at Stephen. "You will be transferred to the cell with the prisoners of war today." He turned again to leave but paused at the door. "Another thing I thought you would want to know. Your friend Karl will not be hanged either. It seems that the governor is too short of soldiers to kill them off during wartime. He is to be flogged today and then put back in the ranks as a private." LaGarde turned and left before Stephen could say anything.

After the cell door closed, the priest opened the small viewing hole and watched Stephen through it. He stared for several minutes. Finally he turned away from the door and walked slowly down the dungeon corridor.

Stephen had dozed off and was not awakened by the clang of the iron door of his cell. Once again François ushered a visitor in ahead of him. This time, however, the jailor remained in the cell. Manya Wroblevska dropped the hood of her cloak to her shoulders and tried to adjust her eyes to the gloom of the cell. "Etienne," she called when she made out his form lying on the floor. She rushed over toward him and knelt on the stone floor by his side.

He awoke with a start when her hand touched his face. "Manya?"

"Yes, I heard what had happened and I had to come."

"Louis let you come to see me?"

"He doesn't know."

"He will now. You should have stayed away."

"I had to make sure that you were all right."

"They will be releasing me and exchanging me with the Canso prisoners. I'll not be harmed. But it's Karl I'm worried about—my friend the Swiss corporal. They will try to make an example of him. You must help him, Manya."

"He is to be flogged, Etienne. The whole town knows. It will be soon. They are making preparations for a public punishment. Everyone in Louisbourg will be there. I'll not be able to do anything until afterward. I'll visit him, bring ointments for healing, make sure he is properly fed. For your sake I'll try to bring him back to health."

He was worried but deeply grateful. She had changed. He remembered their last meeting and her vehement refusal to mother him. Now for his sake she was willing to nurse a man she did not even know.

"Has Louis been good to you?"

She averted his eyes and bit her lower lip. She would not answer him. She changed the subject.

"I heard about Sister Marie Louis; I am terribly sorry. She was a wonderful mother—even to me—here in your wilderness. I shall miss her desperately."

"Princess," called François. "I promised you this brief time. You must leave now. They will be coming for him. It must not be known that I got you in here."

"I paid you well."

François merely leered.

"Manya, you must go. Take care of Karl. I'll be back for you both."

"Etienne, don't begin that anew. I had to know that you were safe, but that was all. I don't love you enough to give up what I have for you. I'll help your friend. Come back for him but not for me."

She rose from his side, pulled the hood over her blond hair and followed François from the cell.

Stephen watched her go. His heart sank.

A few minutes later, the door to Stephen's cell opened again, and he was led by a guard out of the hall, past the cells with the iron doors and outside into the courtyard of the governor's garden. The garden was filled with marines and sailors from the ships of the King's navy in the harbor. No Swiss regulars were in sight. In the center of the garden one single post had been erected, with two iron rings near the top of it. "We wait here. The governor says you're to view this ceremony," said the guard to Stephen.

Commands were yelled and the marines and sailors fell into formation. A drum began to beat, and four heavily chained and well-guarded men entered the garden. Stephen recognized them immediately as his former bunkmates. The last one in line was Karl. Stephen tried to catch his eye but Karl just looked away and stared toward the post.

"Karl," called Stephen.

"Shut your mouth," yelled the guard, shoving him with the butt of his musket.

Karl, walking with an awkward, painful shuffle toward the whipping post, did not respond.

The drum continued to beat its soft tapping. When the four prisoners reached the center of the garden, each was stripped to the waist. The first two were to receive fifteen stripes each with the cat. Each was screaming before the third stripe was laid on and each had fainted before the end of his ordeal.

Bullinger was the third to suffer. He began to scream and beg for mercy before his wrists were fastened to the rings of the post. He began to curse as the cat tore the flesh of his back. "It was all Stiegler's idea," he yelled. "He and that Englishman." But the cat showed no mercy. At the count of fifteen Bullinger too was quiet, but still the strokes were laid on. At the count of twenty, the sweating marine sergeant halted and Bullinger was cut down from the post.

Now it was Karl's turn. The marine was replaced by an enormous, heavily muscled man. As Karl was brought out of the shade of a tree to be fastened to the whipping post, Stephen gasped. He was already a mass of oozing sores. His shirt had been torn from his back, ripping open semi-healed wounds. Even the guard next to Stephen whispered, "Jesus, will you look at his hide. François has already worked him over and now he is going to get it again."

Stephen looked away as the count began. Each slash of the whip was followed by a loud grunt from Karl. It seemed to go on forever—the slashing, the grunting. But soon there was only the slashing. As the count reached twenty-five, the governor ordered a halt. Stephen looked up. His friend's back was covered with blood and pieces of torn flesh. Karl had sagged against the post and was not moving.

One of the naval doctors was asked to examine the prisoner. He pushed back Karl's eyelid and listened at his chest. "He is still alive," he called to the governor.

Duchambon waved to François. "Finish the count."

François smiled and began anew. Twenty-six, twenty-seven, twenty-eight, twenty-nine. It was like beating a log. Stephen began to yell for them to stop. Only the butt of the musket crashing into his skull silenced him.

Stephen awoke in a strange cell on a mattress made of straw. Someone was sitting beside him. As he opened his eyes he heard a voice speaking English. "Captain, this bloke's coming to now."

"Thank you, Corporal."

Stephen started to sit up but the ache in his head was enormous. A face appeared suddenly in front of his eyes. Except for a scraggly beard, it was a very handsome face—blue eyes, sharp nose, high cheekbones and soft, blond, wavy hair that grew down over the collar. The stranger touched his shoulder. "Don't be too quick to move. You have a nasty bump there. My name is Bradstreet—Captain John Bradstreet—senior ranking officer of the prisoners of war here." He held out his hand. Stephen shook it.

"Mine is Nowell, Stephen Nowell of . . ." He hesitated a moment but then added, "of Charlestown, Massachusetts."

"Gentlemen," called Bradstreet, "we have a Yankee in our midst."

"I could have told you that before—from the smell of him," said a voice from the other side of the room."

"You're the prisoners from Canso," said Stephen.

Bradstreet stood and, giving an exaggerated bow, said, "At your service, sir. And you are one of the young men involved in the mutiny. How did you avoid becoming part of this morning's entertainment? We all took turns viewing the spectacle from the little airhole they keep referring to as a window."

"I don't know how I avoided it," Stephen lied. He did not know if he could trust these men, but he was sure they would not trust him if they knew of his past. "What happened to the men who were beaten?" he asked.

Bradstreet chuckled. "Oh, they will all survive without much wear and tear to show for it. All but the last one, that is. They really gave him a going over. He was the ringleader, I understand. I suspect he too will survive, but it will take him a long time to get back to normal, if he ever does. Prison grapevine has it that he has been released already."

Stephen looked startled.

"Yes, some big chief among the local priests around here has taken him into their house to recuperate. I guess he will get good care there. All in all, I'd say he was pretty lucky. Had he tried that sort of thing in the British army, short-handed or no, he would have swung.

It must be LaGarde, Stephen thought to himself. Maybe Karl will have a chance after all.

"Our guards tell us that you will be accompanying us back to Boston," said Bradstreet. "We will be leaving at any time now. A ship has arrived from Boston and the ice has not yet blocked the harbor. If we stay one more week, we won't get out of this pesthole until May. I gather you have nothing to pack."

Stephen smiled. "The only things I have I'm wearing." He tried to stand but was still dizzy.

The captain offered him his hand and pulled him to his feet. "MacGregor," he called.

"Sir," responded a voice from the dark side of the room.

"Give Mr. Nowell a swig of MacGregor's special brew."

"But, Captain," said the squat Scotsman who stepped out of the shadows, "I've only a few swigs left of the blessed stuff and it has to last until we get to Boston."

Bradstreet laughed. "Mac, the man is drowning. Surely even a Scotsman will throw him a bit of rope."

Grumbling, MacGregor went back into his corner and returned with a battered Army canteen. "One small swig now, my man, and don't try nothing funny."

Stephen took a swallow and started to gag. The liquor burned all the way down into his belly. But at the same time the warmth of it began to flow from his gut to his limbs.

"He only gagged a wee bit. There may be some hope for this Yankee yet," purred the Scot.

"Either that or he's already a confirmed drunk like yourself," said the captain.

"Captain Bradstreet," called the man who seemed to be stationed at the door.

"Yes, Mason."

"There's a bunch of Frenchies coming down the hallway." Mason stepped away from the door and in a few seconds it swung open.

"Gentlemen, your dinner," said the huge man who entered with a crew of five, three to pass out plates and two to hold muskets on the prisoners. Stephen recognized the huge man instantly as Karl's tormentor.

"Today, my good friends," he said in heavily accented English, "I have brought you the specialty of the chef."

"Gruel," said Mason, sticking his spoon into the ugly whitish-gray mess on the plate handed to him.

"You mean you do not appreciate what my chef has prepared for you? We worked so hard to please you."

"Up your ass," yelled MacGregor.

"Captain Bradstreet," said François, smiling, "I think that

286

your men are too angry to eat." He turned to his assistants and ordered them to stop distributing food. Once the prisoners realized what was happening, they started to advance menacingly toward the door.

"Captain Bradstreet, I warn you," said François. "Hold your men back or I will be forced to order the soldiers to fire."

"At ease, men," yelled Bradstreet. The men backed off, and the French scurried out the door, which was then slammed with a bang.

François called back into the cell from the hallway. "Next time, Captain, ask your men to behave themselves if they want to eat. That is, if there is a next time."

"Son of a bitch," mumbled Bradstreet. "I would like to kill that man if I could get my hands on him."

Stephen looked the captain in the face. "You'll have to get your hands on him before I do, because he'll be dead when I'm finished with him."

They were released the next day. Duchambon himself came to the cell and read to the prisoners the terms of their parole. They would return on condition that they not take up arms against France for the duration of the war. Each was then required to come forward and sign the roll, indicating acceptance of the terms. As Stephen's name was called, Duchambon interrupted. "He is not to sign," he said to the clerk. "He is a civilian. We will not dignify him with a soldier's sense of honor."

They were marched out of the cell in single file, down the hallway and up a flight of stairs into the governor's garden. A large number of marines and sailors from the ships were sent along the route to act as guards, but so delighted were the English with their release that they would have certainly walked to the ship without any guards.

Shopkeepers and street ruffians lined the way to the wharf, where the English merchant vessel sent under truce from Boston awaited them. One boy scooped some muck from the gutter and hurled it, striking Bradstreet's once-red coat with a resounding smack. The crowd cheered. Bradstreet turned and bowed toward the crowd but behind his back MacGregor made an obscene gesture. They cheered again.

Stephen walked next to Mason. As they passed the house of the intendant and turned to the right toward the Jesuit house, he strained to get a glimpse of it. He thought he saw a black-cloaked form in the upstairs window. As he drew closer to his old home, the face of his enemy became clearer and clearer in the window. Their eyes met. Stephen shivered. Karl might be in the tender hands of LaGarde, but he would not be safe, no friend of Stephen's would be safe, as long as Lalonde was alive.

They boarded the vessel, *The Charles River*, out of Boston. On board the men stripped down, throwing their ragged remnants of uniforms into a great pile. The ship's pumps had been rigged up on deck to provide showers for all, despite the cold. The released prisoners whooped joyfully in the spray. Strong brown soap was passed around. Mason sat on the deck, his head covered with lathered soap, frozen solid.

Clean sailor's pants and shirts were handed out to all and a hot meal was served. Toward dusk the tide was right for sailing. The ship's master gave the order to let go the lines that held the ship to the wharf. *The Charles River*, ever so slowly, drifted away from the dock. Sailors scampered into the rigging to set a few sails and take advantage of the slight breeze blowing across the harbor from beyond the Grand Battery.

As the ship moved into the channel, Stephen looked back at the town. The sun had already fallen behind the western hills, but its rays still struck the metal spires of the churches and the hospital.

"Goodbye, Sister," Stephen said. "Hold on, Karl; I'll come back for you."

He turned his back on the town. The ship slid between the Island Battery and the Lighthouse Point. One of the battery's great guns saluted. On the port side one could see the small form of a man climbing the circular steps leading to the lighthouse platform. Soon the fire would be lighted, showing the way out to those who left and the path home to those who would return.

VIII

Spring, 1745

Stephen jumped the last few feet from the gangway to the wharf. He looked to the left when he heard his name called and recognized the richly dressed William Vaughan. Boston's harbor front was jammed with people, some in carriages but most crowded together on foot. Some were here to greet returning loved ones, others merely to catch sight of men who had been in French prisons. Stephen walked quickly to Vaughan and grabbed the hand offered to him.

"Good to see you back, lad."

Stephen nodded in response.

"You weren't supposed to try to take Louisbourg by yourself, boy. I panicked when we lost track of you in Nova Scotia."

"Wiggins didn't lose track of me, though, sir. He was in Louisbourg working with the French."

"You've smelled the same scent I have, Stephen. But I hope you have more evidence than I."

"I've no more than what I've told you," said Stephen.

Vaughan turned away and cursed; then he calmed down. "The governor's in his carriage at the end of the wharf. I want to introduce you to him and then I want you to join us at his residence for a conference this evening."

Stephen caught sight of Captain Bradstreet as he walked down the gangway, somewhat unsteady on his feet after a hard bout with seasickness on the voyage home. "Bradstreet," he called, waving his arm. "I want you to meet Mr. Vaughan." Stephen introduced the captain to Vaughan.

"Welcome to Boston, Captain," said Vaughan. "I presume you will be attending the conference with Governor Shirley this evening."

"So I was told aboard ship," said Bradstreet.

"Both of you come with me. I want you to meet Shirley."

Vaughan began to walk briskly toward the end of the wharf, with Bradstreet and Nowell following.

The governor had stepped out of his carriage before the three men reached him. He was not a big man, but he was impressive-looking. He was dressed in a coat of royal blue with a white sash, on which was pinned a variety of colorful ribbons and decorations. His breeches were a brilliant white. His wig was powdered.

"Sir William." Vaughan made a slight bow as he greeted the governor.

"Mr. Vaughan. It is no surprise to see you here. Gaining more information for your Louisbourg scheme, no doubt?"

"You know me too well, Your Excellency," Vaughan smiled. He turned then to Stephen and Bradstreet. "I want you to meet two of His Majesty's loyal subjects just recently released from the prisons of Isle Royale—Captain Bradstreet and Mr. Stephen Nowell, who is in my employ."

"I believe that Captain Bradstreet and I have already met," he said. "Mr. Nowell, it is a great pleasure to meet you." Stephen bowed.

"Captain Bradstreet has already been invited to this evening's conference," said Vaughan. "I would like your permission to bring Mr. Nowell along with me."

"Mr. Vaughan," said Governor Shirley, "the conference is a military one. I have invited you because the plan to be discussed is yours. What can Mr. Nowell add to the discussion?"

"I assure you, Your Excellency, that he has information vital to our cause."

"Your cause," corrected the governor. "Your cause."

"My cause, sir," acknowledged Vaughan, "which I hope after this evening you will make your cause as well."

"That depends on the chances of success, Vaughan. I never lose, and I never lose because I never act unless the odds favor me. Bring your Mr. Nowell. This evening at eight sharp."

The governor turned and reentered his carriage. A crowd of released prisoners was being led to the end of the wharf. They had already received back pay and had come to give three cheers to the governor, who had anticipated their needs and thus won their loyalty. Shirley nodded solemn acknowledgment of their cheers from within his carriage and then gave orders to his driver to take him home.

Vaughan watched the carriage disappear and turned to Stephen and Bradstreet. "Well, that's step number one."

Stephen looked at his employer incredulously. "I thought we had gotten a lot farther than that."

"We have. We have a great deal of support. But we have not yet convinced Sir William. I am counting on the merchants of this town to sway him; he needs their support politically. But Shirley fancies himself a soldier. He is, after all, commander-in-chief of His Majesty's forces in North America. If he does not see a possibility—an excellent possibility—of winning, it will be much harder to convince him to take the risks. That is where you come in. You must convince him that the fort can be taken."

"It can be taken," interrupted Bradstreet. "Nowell and I have gone over the plan again and again. My only regret is that my parole will prevent me from helping out."

"I have taken rooms for you at the Cromwell's Head in the north end, Stephen. Do you have a place to stay, Captain?" asked Vaughan.

"No, I thought I might find a nearby inn."

"Nonsense," said Vaughan. "If Stephen does not mind, his quarters are big enough for two. You can stay with him."

Stephen lay on the soft, down-filled comforter. He had bathed and Josiah, the innkeeper's helper, had shaved him and cut his hair so that it could be tied neatly in the back. Josiah was now in the process of doing the same for Bradstreet. Stephen had dressed himself in all but the jacket of a new suit of clothes, which Vaughan had sent around to him. Governor Shirley had sent some captain's second uniform to Bradstreet so that he might be properly dressed for the evening conference.

Stephen had almost dozed off when he was startled by the sound of a knock on the door. He rose from the bed, straightened his breeches and cravat and opened the door.

A conservatively dressed man stood in the doorway with a surprised look on his face; the door's opening had caught him with fist upraised to knock again. "Are you the young man who calls himself Stephen Nowell."

"My name is Stephen Nowell."

"My name, sir, is Eben Warren, solicitor to Mr. Daniel Pierce. I would like a few words with you." Looking into the room and seeing Josiah and Bradstreet, he added, "in private."

"I'm afraid we will have to go down to the taproom. I don't know how private that will be," said Stephen.

"As you say, sir," said Warren.

The two men descended the flight of stairs to the noisy noon-hour crowd in the taproom. They found a table in a relatively quiet corner.

The innkeeper's wife approached. "May I order you some refreshment, Mr. Warren?" asked Stephen.

"No, sir, I'm here on business."

Stephen ordered a mug of ale.

As soon as the order was taken, Warren began to speak. "I have come to inform you, sir, that my client, Mr. Pierce, has become aware that his late father-in-law, aided by two rebellious and disloyal servants, who have since been dismissed, paid you certain sums of money. I am told that the total is in excess of fifty pounds. Since this money was paid by Mr. Breed just before his death, when serious doubts about his coherence could be raised, Mr. Pierce feels that if you are a gentleman, you will return the sum to him."

"Mr. Warren, the money was given to me by my grandfather and I regard it as merely partial payment of my rightful share of my grandfather's estate."

"My client," said Warren, "has acquainted me with your assertions of being Mr. Breed's grandson. I'm sure you must have documentation to support your claim."

"No, I don't. But my aunt and George and Hannah have all recognized me."

"Ah, the two servants again. Very clearly, sir, I can see that this is a plot to defraud the Pierces of their proper inheritance. Their nephew, Stephen Nowell, and his father were killed by Indians fifteen years ago."

"I am their nephew," said Stephen angrily.

"Really, my good man, if you persist in this claim, my client will have no alternative but to bring charges against you with the Suffolk County sheriff. You are to cease using the name of Stephen Nowell and you are to return my client's money." Warren stood up as he made his demands and, without waiting for Stephen's response, he turned and stormed out of the inn.

Stephen sat at his table alone. His ale arrived but he felt in no mood to drink it. That old bastard, Pierce, must have kept his eye on every farthing in Grandpa's accounts, thought Stephen. How else could he have discovered his generosity?

Stephen's thoughts were interrupted by a booming voice. "Young man, you are sitting in my accustomed place."

Stephen looked up and saw the hairless face of Hudson, the ferryman. Stephen rose to make room for him.

"Now I didn't say you had to leave, young man. I merely

said you were sitting where I have been sitting for the past fifteen years for my lunch. If you will give me my chair, I will be happy to have you set and keep me company until the next ferry is due to leave."

"I do have business elsewhere, Mr. Hudson, but perhaps you could do me one favor."

"If I'm able," was the response.

"Do you know the whereabouts of George and Hannah, who used to be servants to Mr. Breed and have been working for the Pierces?"

"I not only know where they live, but being that they live in a set of rooms in Charlestown, I will take you there myself right after lunch, provided that you have three half pennies."

"Three half pennies? It was a penny last year," said Stephen.

"That was before the war began," said Hudson. "Everything has gone up. My lunch costs me more and this highway robber of an innkeeper charges me more for his helper's muscles when there be no winds."

"I think I can manage the extra half penny," smiled Stephen. He sat down again and finished his ale.

Stephen followed Hudson's directions carefully until he faced a door covered only faintly by traces of chipped green paint. He was in the most run-down portion of the village of Charlestown. He knocked and the door was swung open almost immediately by Hannah.

"Mister Stephen, is it you again? George, Mr. Stephen is here," she shouted and almost immediately began to shed great tears.

Stephen stepped through the doorway. Directly across the room but off to the right and out of the chill of the open door, he saw a man in bed, the wasted form only vaguely resembling the robust man who had greeted him a year earlier.

George raised his arm in greeting, but dropped it wearily to the bed. Stephen walked over to him and took the hand in his. He turned his back on George and looked quizzically at Hannah. She began to cry even harder. "He's been like this since just after we was let go. We worked for the Breeds for seventeen years and they threw us out without a penny," she said between sobs.

"Mr. Stephen," said George hoarsely, "I'm sorry. Me and Hannah failed you."

"Why did Pierce do this to you?" asked Stephen.

"He's a brute, Mr. Stephen," interrupted Hannah. "He locked my poor Miss Betsy in her room and threw George and me out. We have enough money to pay the rent, but that's all. Now with George took sick I don't know what we will do."

"I suspect Pierce of the worst, Mr. Stephen," said George. "Mr. Breed's death was too convenient. You must stop him from doing anything to you."

"Don't worry about me," said Stephen. "It's you that needs caring for."

"Aye, if it hadn't been for that Indian friend of yours, we would have starved. He brings game to us regular like clockwork," said George.

"Indian? Socono is here?" said Stephen.

"That's his name," said Hannah. "Never can remember those heathen names. But despite what he is, he has been mighty Christian to us."

Stephen did not bother to tell her that Socono was a Christian. "Where can I find him?" asked Stephen.

"We don't rightly know," said George. "He never told us where he lives. But he always comes back when he says he is coming, and he is due here tonight." George started coughing and could not continue. Hannah rushed to get him a drink from the pitcher on the night table by his bed.

"Hannah," said Stephen. "I want you to do me a favor."

"Yes, Mr. Stephen."

"When Socono returns here tonight, you are to tell him that I am staying at the Cromwell's Head—just across the river at the ferry slip at Copp's Hill. Tell him to meet me there tonight. He will have to wait for me until I return from Governor Shirley's, but I want to see him tonight."

"Yes, sir, Mr. Stephen," she said.

Stephen turned to George, who seemed to have grown even weaker during the few moments Stephen had been in the cottage. "George, if you and Hannah are willing, I want you to consider that you now work for me." He made a fast calculation of how much of the fifty pounds that his grandfather had given him remained and how much Vaughan owed him for a year's service. "I think I can pay you enough to cover your rent and your food."

"You're a good man, just like your grandfather," wept Hannah.

George looked disturbed. "What do you expect of us in return? I'm in no shape to be of much service to you."

294

"What I expect of you is that you get well," said Stephen. "I have one great task ahead of me, which may take me some time to achieve. But when I return, I will want to set up house and I will want you two to do it for me."

"Will you stop and have supper with us?" asked Hannah.

Stephen was hungry but he could not bring himself to eat any of the few provisions his friends might need later on. "Sorry, Hannah," he said. "I have to catch the next ferry back to Boston. It will be a busy evening for me." He shook hands with George, kissed Hannah on her cheek and left.

There were at least ten carriages lined up in front of the governor's residence, as the powder-wigged Vaughan, an uncomfortably uniformed Bradstreet and the simply clothed Nowell approached the front gate. Footmen were scurrying in every direction.

"Obviously, Sir William has had a dinner party to which we were not invited," quipped Bradstreet.

Vaughan looked disturbed.

One of the footmen took their names and showed them to the governor's study, asking them to wait.

Vaughan and Bradstreet sat down in two of the more comfortable chairs in the room. Stephen wandered about, checking the volumes that filled the bookcases. Within a few moments they heard voices outside the double doors. Suddenly the doors swung open and the governor, brilliantly attired in the uniform of a general in the British army, accompanied by five richly dressed men, entered the room. Stephen barely saw the splendor of the governor because his eyes were riveted on the face of the man to the governor's left. It was his great-uncle—Mr. Daniel Pierce.

Pierce saw Stephen as quickly as Stephen saw him. His face registered surprise but he said nothing.

Shirley moved behind his desk. "Please, gentlemen, find yourselves chairs and be seated. We have some serious matters to attend to."

The double doors swung open again and servants entered with glasses of wine and pipes of tobacco. "I think you will enjoy the Madeira. I had several kegs especially shipped in just before the war began. French privateers are making a mess of the Portuguese wine trade, but so far I have not suffered. I don't know if you all know each other. You all know Mr. William Vaughan, but I doubt if any of you know Mr. Nowell or Captain Bradstreet, who have just returned from His Majesty's service in Nova Scotia." He turned to

Bradstreet and Stephen. "Gentlemen, I want you to meet Mr. Brattle, Mr. Pierce, Mr. Usher, Mr. Hutchinson and Mr. Pepperrell—all of them leading men of business in this town. The men shook hands, but Stephen and Vaughan avoided Pierce.

When all were seated again, Daniel Pierce spoke to Bradstreet. "Captain, can you tell me where you have been serving?"

"I was at Canso, sir, when war broke out. I was captured and imprisoned at Louisbourg. I really didn't see much fighting, unlike Nowell here. He was at the siege of Annapolis."

"Oh, was he?" smiled Pierce.

Shirley interrupted. "It is about the course of the war, gentlemen, that I would like to speak with you. I need your advice. Mr. Vaughan has, for months now, been advocating an expedition against Louisbourg. I've resisted his plan so far because it first seemed imperative to save Nova Scotia before taking the offensive. In addition, there are past examples of this colony taking up arms against Canada on its own—with disastrous results. Sir William Phips' expedition against Quebec and Montreal took place over fifty years ago, but many of the families of this community remember that fiasco with bitterness. Louisbourg has a fabled reputation as an impregnable fortress. Yet Mr. Vaughan says it can be taken. In fact, he insists it must be taken."

"Yes, Your Excellency, I do insist," said Vaughan. "Ever since the end of the last war, the French have been building the fort. Privateers sailing from its port have made a shambles of the fishing fleets of this colony and my New Hampshire. That trade will never return to its former prosperity until the French are forced off Isle Royale."

"There's a lot of truth in what Vaughan says," interjected Pepperrell. "We Maine men are of one mind with New Hampshire on that point."

"I'm sure I need not remind you, of all people, Mr. Pepperrell, that what you refer to as Maine is nothing more than part of my jurisdiction of Massachusetts."

"No, sir, you need not remind me. We in the eastern counties are glad indeed to be part of this great colony, especially with you as governor and commander-in-chief combined. We expect that with you in charge something will be done about the French, who are constantly breathing down our necks and sending their redskinned devils to burn our farms and murder our women and children. We have

296

every expectation that you, Sir William, will drive them out of Louisbourg. I'm with Vaughan on this."

"As am I," said Brattle.

"Agreed," said Usher.

"Hutchinson," said the governor, "what do you think?"

"I would rather hear more of the argument before I commit myself," said the slim, dark-haired merchant-politician.

"Always cautious, Tom," laughed Shirley. "Pierce, what do you think?"

"Your Excellency, I believe that all of us are probably agreed that it would be desirable to drive the French from Louisbourg. The question remains—just how are we to do it? What plans does Mr. Vaughan have for us?"

Vaughan stood up and began to pace the room excitedly. "We have a plan, gentlemen, one that will work. It involves raising an army of volunteers. I'm sure that Massachusetts alone could provide 5,000 men."

Pepperrell interrupted. "We could get three thousand from Maine . . . eh . . . the eastern counties." He smiled toward Shirley.

Vaughan continued, "We will appeal to Connecticut and to New Hampshire and perhaps even to New York for more men."

"Forget about New York," said Brattle. "No New Yorker is going to take up a New England cause."

"You forget, I have some influence in New York," said Shirley. "Continue, William," he said to Vaughan.

"We'll assemble the army here in Boston and sail in early spring for Canso. The French have abandoned it now that their siege of Annapolis has failed. Once the icepack around Isle Royale breaks up, we'll land our troops at Gabarus Bay. We'll approach the fortress by the west side and place our guns on the hillocks overlooking the west gate. It's in terrible repair, and we can force the walls from that side."

"Impossible," Pierce blurted out.

"Sir?" said Vaughan.

All eyes turned toward Daniel Pierce. "My informants," he said, "tell me that the land between Gabarus Bay and the fortress is all swamp. It would be impossible to bring siege guns, which by the way we don't have, across that swamp."

"You forget, Pierce," said Vaughan, "that I'm a New Hampshire man, and we have swamps that will compare with any on Isle Royale. We harvest timber in those swamps and drag loads heavier than the heaviest siege gun through them on sleds. Our New Hampshire men will get the guns to the hills."

"Governor Shirley," said Pierce, "I think that Vaughan's scheme is harebrained. Louisbourg will not be taken by a formal siege. We have no men trained in siege operations— no military engineers. The French will sally from the fortress and destroy all our amateurish efforts."

"That they will not do," said Bradstreet. "The garrison has just mutinied. Nowell and I were there to view it. The officers will never trust those Swiss bastards of theirs outside the walls. They'd never get them back inside again."

"That may be true," argued Pierce, "but I've an alternative plan. We land at night, make our way as lightly loaded as possible through the swamps and storm the citadel by surprise. I believe this course offers us a much better chance of success."

Shirley looked pleased. "Daniel, I think your suggestion is an improvement on Willy's plan," he said. "What do the rest of you say?"

"I've heard that suggestion before," Stephen said softly. "Made by a snake called Wiggins. It was lunacy then and it is lunacy now."

Pierce looked as if he had been slapped in the face. "Your Excellency," he said, "I know this man. He calls himself Stephen Nowell and pretends to be my wife's nephew. He's a liar, an imposter and I have good reason to believe that he's a spy." Stephen made a move toward Pierce, but Bradstreet grabbed his shoulder.

"Gentlemen," said Shirley. "Let us try to behave in the manner in which I have just addressed you." He turned to Pierce. "Daniel, those are very harsh accusations."

"I have proof, Your Excellency. Let him deny that he was raised a papist; that he lived in the Jesuit house in Louisbourg; that he took vows in that hideous organization and that he has worked as an agent of the French government among the Oneida."

Shirley looked dumbfounded. "Mr. Nowell, what do you have to say to these accusations?"

Before Stephen could respond, Vaughan interrupted. "Your Excellency, I brought Nowell here and vouched for him. He is one of my most trusted agents. In the course of his duties in my employ he has filled many roles and has used many names. I give you my word he's trustworthy."

Shirley was clearly torn by indecision. Finally he said, "I

trust you, Willy. You've never failed me before." Pierce's belligerent expression sagged.

"But," said the governor, "I'm determined to implement Mr. Pierce's plan. We'll land at night and take the fortress by surprise. For that we need no siege guns and no long and expensive siege."

Vaughan looked glum, while Bradstreet and Stephen merely shook their heads. Shirley did not notice their reactions. Usher and Brattle had both agreed with the governor loudly.

"Good," said Shirley. "We will take Louisbourg. Now all we need is a leader."

"Why, you, of course, sir," said Pierce to the governor.

"I would like to, Daniel," responded Shirley, "but my position as commander-in-chief requires that I remain here in Boston to receive orders from the ministry. What about you, William?"

Vaughan's face brightened and then immediately he scowled as he realized that the governor was not looking at him but at William Pepperrell.

Pepperrell looked shocked. "Me, sir? I have never held military rank."

"Agreed, William, but you're an excellent organizer. You have good ties with the mercantile community and can expect to raise some funds there to pay for the cost of the venture. When word is out that you're leading, I suspect a lot more of your Maine men will join up."

"I think Pepperrell is an excellent choice," said Usher.

Shirley turned finally toward Vaughan. "What's your opinion, Willy? We've heard nothing from you."

"I believe Mr. Pepperrell will do an excellent job leading your forces, Your Excellency," said Vaughan finally but none too vigorously.

"Good, then it's settled. Pepperrell will command."

"Thank you, Sir William," said the Maine merchant. "I'll do my best."

"Surely, William," said the governor, "you can work up a more positive attitude than that." Turning to Hutchinson, Shirley smiled. "Cat got your tongue tonight, Thomas? You haven't said two words all evening."

"Perhaps, Your Excellency, it's because I have not been able to believe my ears. I don't know when I've heard anything more farfetched—a proposed siege without siege guns. That's like skinning a bear before you trap him. You plan to storm the strongest fortress in North America by

299

surprise and at night, as if it were some little blockhouse in a frontier town. In fact, it is so farfetched, it might work. The French just won't believe what is happening."

"Ah, we are now to be the butts of a little Hutchinson sarcasm," said Shirley. "You know, gentlemen, there hasn't been any genuine Hutchinson humor since those dreadful Puritans hanged his great grandmother."

"They didn't hang her," smiled Hutchinson. "She was merely banished."

"No difference," said Shirley.

"Really, sir, may I make one suggestion before we break up?" said Hutchinson. "Write to Newcastle and ask His Grace to alert the West Indian squadron under Commodore Warren. I think the presence of the Royal Navy would be most beneficial to your plans."

"There be your siege guns, Hutchinson," said Vaughan.

"I'll do as you ask, Thomas," said the governor. He rose and held his glass of wine aloft. "Gentlemen, a toast. To William Pepperrell and the capture of Louisbourg." The others rose and drank. "Thank you, gentlemen. I believe that our work for this evening is over. Pepperrell, I leave everything in your hands. Good night."

Shirley left through the double doors of his study followed by everyone but Stephen, Bradstreet, Vaughan and Pepperrell.

"Willy," said the new general-in-chief.

"Yes, sir," said Vaughan.

"I want you and your friend with me. Pierce is an ass and no gentleman. He got rich by taking an old man's money. We will take Louisbourg, but we will take it your way, not Pierce's."

"That is good news, sir," said Vaughan. "But what about Governor Shirley?"

"Governor Shirley," interrupted Pepperrell, "will not be there."

Pepperrell drove Vaughan, Bradstreet and Stephen back to the Cromwell's Head. Stephen saw the others off to bed and entered the taproom by himself. It was quiet, with only a few solitary drinkers in sight. Josiah was behind the counter. Stephen walked over to him.

"Can I serve you anything, Mr. Nowell?" he asked.

"No," said Stephen, shaking his head. "Has anyone been asking to see me, Josiah?"

"No, sir, Mr. Stephen. It's been quiet tonight."

Stephen left the taproom and walked upstairs to his room. He threw open the door and started to call out to Bradstreet, but he stopped in mid-sentence. There in the center of the room, gagged and bound hand and foot to a chair, was his friend John Bradstreet. Stephen saw Bradstreet's eyes try to signal him that danger lurked behind him—too late. A strong arm reached around his face, cutting off his vision, but he caught the sweet, greasy smell of an Indian. Then, just as suddenly, the arm freed him. Stephen turned and looked into the scarred face of Socono.

"Little brother," the Indian said. Stephen put his arms about his friend. The two men stood looking at each other and smiling.

"Aaagh," came the sound from Bradstreet's gagged mouth.

"My God, I forgot about John. Why did you do this to him?" asked Stephen as he began to untie his friend.

"George said this was your room. This man is not you," said the Indian. "If he is not you, then he must be a thief sneaking into your room. I thought it best to keep him here until you returned."

Stephen pulled the gag from Bradstreet's mouth.

"My God, Nowell," said the captain. "Is this creature a friend of yours? He damn near had me crapping in my breeches. What is that heathen tongue you're speaking?"

"I'm sorry, John. I left a message for him to come and wait for me. He is an Abenacki. He didn't understand about you."

"So I gather," said Bradstreet, rubbing his wrists.

"Captain Bradstreet, this is my friend Socono, a wise and brave man, a sachem of his people."

Bradstreet did not quite know how to respond. The Indian made no effort to reach forward with his hand, yet to bow to the blanketed figure in front of him seemed absurd, so he did nothing.

Socono had not understood Stephen's words although he had recognized his name. He needed no introduction. Bradstreet was accepted by Stephen; that was enough for him.

Stephen ordered a late snack brought to their room, and the three men shared a meat pie and a pitcher of ale. He was surprised when Socono drank his own share. Soon Bradstreet grew tired and, although he was somewhat edgy about the news that Socono would be spending the night in the room, he collapsed onto the bed without removing his uniform. He was soon snoring gently. Stephen and the Indian talked late into the night. Stephen told Socono of the Louisbourg plot; of Marie Louis' death; of Karl's arrest and punishment.

Socono surprised Stephen by telling him that he already knew much of Stephen's recent exploits. Father LaGarde had told him and had given him instructions on how to find Stephen. These had led him to George and Hannah.

"I thank you for caring for them," said Stephen.

Just before retiring, Stephen touched Socono's arm. "One more thing, Socono," he said. "It's Wiggins. I've seen him, both in Boston and in Louisbourg. He was the one who tipped off the French about our plans. Now he is in part responsible for Sister's death and for Karl's suffering. The list of his deeds keeps growing and growing. I am working to get proof of his treachery. We must watch him. He will slip, and then we will have him."

Socono did not even blink. It was as if he had slipped into a trance. Stephen stared at him, uncertain as to what to do or say. Finally he got up from the table and fell into bed. The Indian sat for almost an hour without moving while the two white men snored. Finally he smiled, rose from the table and slipped his blanket off his shoulders. He spread it carefully on the floor at the foot of the bed and curled up to go to sleep.

The next morning Stephen was summoned to Vaughan's room. He found his employer still in his dressing gown, sipping his morning tea.

"Have some tea, my lad," he said, pouring a second cup.

"I've already had some," said Stephen.

"Have some anyway. After I'm finished with this meeting, you'll probably need something stronger. I've held back telling you this up to now because I felt you were badly in need of protection. I sent you away because I thought you would be safer out of Boston. When I lost track of you I was frantic and accused myself of betraying a sacred trust."

Stephen was deeply puzzled by Vaughan's words but remained silent.

Vaughan continued, "I want now to tell you of some very damning evidence that I have in my possession. I think you will be safer in the future if you know the truth. I told you when we first met how I felt about your mother. She was the strongest and the best woman I have ever known. She salvaged my life and I owe everything I have become to her. I loved her very much." He took Sarah Nowell's locket from his dressing gown pocket and placed it on the tea table in front of him. "This belonged to your mother."

Stephen looked at Vaughan in utter confusion. "But

how . . . ? I thought it was Wiggins'. He was the one who lost it."

Vaughan pounded his fist on the table, upsetting the tea service. He ignored the spilled milk and sugar. "Precisely, Stephen. It was in Wiggins' possession. How did he come to have your mother's locket? Sarah was wearing it the last time I saw her aboard the *Betsy*. It contained a lock of your hair then and it still does. I'll tell you what I suspect. I believe that Isaac Wiggins is the foul arm of a foul brain named Daniel Pierce. I think that Pierce was responsible for your father's death. I think he arranged your grandfather's death and your mother's death, using Wiggins as his tool—his executioner. I had worked all this out before I sent you off to Nova Scotia; I was sure that you would be the next victim. I thought you would be safer with Mascarene. Then Wiggins left Boston. I had him followed. It was clear he too was traveling to Port Royale. Then I knew I was right. I sent word to Graham to have you protected, but it arrived after you had volunteered to act as a spy. My people lost contact with you. Then we lost all track of Wiggins at just about the same time. Now you tell me that he showed up in Louisbourg itself, hand in glove with the French authorities. He was there to guarantee your death, Stephen, of that I am certain. For once he failed, but only because your priest, LaGarde, was stronger than he was."

Stephen had passed from amazement to rage and then back to cool anger as he listened to Vaughan. At first he wanted to lash out at Wiggins. All thought of waiting to trap him left his mind. He wanted to destroy him as he had destroyed his family. He considered him in the same category as Lalonde and all the Jesuits, in fact, the same as all the French. But then as rage subsided, his anger deepened and became more deadly. The real object of his hatred should be Daniel Pierce, and Daniel Pierce was not a cleric and not French. The American continent, like Europe, was filled with evil men who always seemed to prevail.

"What is it you expect of me?" he finally asked Vaughan.

"I want to get them, Stephen. I want to pay them back for Sarah, for Jonathan and for your father—and for you. And I want you to help me do it. The two of them are joining the Louisbourg expedition. I don't know for sure what their game is, but I have my suspicions. Wiggins shows up working with the French. Wiggins works for Pierce. I think that Pierce is tied in with the French too. That would explain a great deal about his wealth, which just seems to grow and grow in a center that just shouldn't be important in the fur trade. He is advocating a plan of attack on the fortress that is doomed to failure, and a failed attempt on Louisbourg is far more in France's interest than no attempt at all. We'll never convince anyone to try again if we fail this first time. I think Pierce's game is to lure us to Louisbourg and destroy us."

"We're lucky that Pepperrell has no intention of following his plan."

Vaughan rubbed the stubble on his unshaven chin. He thought for a moment. "You're right, of course, lad," he said, "but surely Pierce will attempt to use his influence with Shirley to change the command if he can. Perhaps he feels that the merchant Pepperrell can himself be easily swayed. We will have to watch him carefully throughout the expedition and we will force him to reveal himself. Then we will watch him swing."

"I don't trust the course of justice, sir. I think we should move against them on our own."

The older man smiled a grim smile. He liked this boy very much. If he could not have his Sarah back, at least he could console himself by having her son as his friend. "Then we become outlaws like them, Stephen. No, hold back; we'll trap them."

The invasion fleet assembled off the shore of Nantasket in preparation for sailing to Canso. Stephen and his crew were already aboard. The weeks since his meeting with Vaughan had been filled with preparations. First Shirley had called for volunteers, promising a bounty and plunder. Then he had written the governors of other colonies seeking support. The response had been better than Shirley had expected. Five thousand Massachusetts men signed up, three thousand of them Maine residents. Connecticut sent five hundred men, and Shirley appointed Samuel Waldo of that colony as second in command to Pepperrell. New Hampshire provided one hundred fifty men, many of them rangers and timber men. Even pacifist Rhode Island offered help in the form of a sloop of war outfitted by the Baptist merchants of Providence. Making a liar of almost every man in New England, New York sent a battery of ten heavy guns to aid the colonial effort.

Vaughan's hurt feelings were partially assuaged by Shirley's suggestion that he form a company of volunteer rangers. He threw all his considerable energies into organizing the group. Stephen was commissioned as his ensign and given responsibility for recruiting. Stephen's tasks were made more simple by the sudden return of John Graham's platoon of Gorham's New Hampshire rangers from Annapolis. John Graham became Vaughan's executive officer, leaving Stephen free to roam the taverns looking for recruits.

Stephen found Israel Kip in a taproom in Portsmouth. After two rums, he signed Kip up, along with the other available veterans of the Annapolis defense. Socono sent a message up the Kennebec to the village of Norridgewock, guaranteeing a friendly contingent of Abenacki at Louisbourg to offset any damage that the Micmacs might attempt.

The weeks seemed to slide by for Stephen. He was so busy with his new tasks that he had little time to think. He had not thought of Manya or Marie Louis in some time. Even Molly Brant was becoming a vague memory. His desire to strike out at Pierce was present but subdued by Vaughan's admonition. Even his desire to rescue Karl and avenge his torture faded before the business of the preparations. He did not visit George and Hannah, although their welfare was provided for by Stephen's purse.

Now all was ready. Stephen had never before seen so many ships assembled in one place as now awaited the proper winds and the commander's signal to descend on Isle Royale. Surely if Louisbourg could be taken, it would fall before so mighty a force. Surely men like William Vaughan, John Graham, Kip and Socono would help him free Karl from Lalonde's control and avenge the death of Sister Marie Louis. And they would help him to avenge the murder of his parents and his grandfather. He remembered Sister's warning not to become like Lalonde, but he could not help himself. He also remembered her suggestion that he return to New York—to Molly. She had probably been right. When all of this was over, he would go back to New York and seek her out. Perhaps he was fading from her memory just as she faded from his. Perhaps she had already married someone else. But he hoped she waited for him.

Molly's image may have grown weaker in his mind, but the thought of her brought another image—that of Isaac Wiggins. Wiggins was with the army. Stephen had not seen him, but Vaughan had warned Stephen that Wiggins was acting as a scout for the company that Daniel Pierce had formed. Stephen had mentioned this fact to Socono, but the Indian had said nothing.

Socono sat now, as he had sat so many months ago, against the mainmast of the ship. He was as determined now as he

305

had been before to maintain his dignity in spite of an uneasy stomach. All the others had gone below to avoid the cold. Stephen turned from the rail, from which he had been watching the fleet at anchor. He walked to his blanket next to Socono and sat down on it, cross-legged, Indian style. He grabbed the corners and drew the blanket about him. Israel Kip came on deck and sat down on the opposite side of Stephen.

"When you coming below?" he asked.

"I'm not," said Stephen. "I've been looking at the fleet. It's huge. A hundred transport ships, I hear."

"It's going to be some show at Louisbourg," said Kip. "Ships, rangers and even some Indians—on our side for a change." Kip nodded toward Socono. "This Indian friend of yours and me have been talking."

Stephen looked at Socono, who merely grunted. "It must be difficult for you both," said Stephen. "He doesn't speak English and I'm not aware that you speak anything else."

"No matter," said Kip. "I understand him and he's teaching me some of his lingo. Now this fellow," he said, pointing at Socono, "claims to be a Christian. I've met some praying Indians in my time, like some of those Stockbridgers, but this one don't seem like any of them. They was always shouting hallelujahs and half of them would be drunk on Sunday before the sermon was ten minutes old."

"He's a Christian," said Stephen. "He was converted by the Jesuits years ago."

"That explains it then," said Kip. "He's a papist, and if he's a papist then he can't be no Christian."

Stephen was tempted to launch into an explanation of the Reformation, but before he could say anything, Socono, who had been sitting with his back turned toward them, interrupted. He asked Stephen to translate what Kip was saying. When Stephen had finished, Socono spoke. "This Boston, across the water, is it not the town the blackrobes told me about? Is it not the home of the people they call Puritans?"

"Yes," said Stephen. "I'm told by some that my ancestors, the Nowells, came to Boston in 1630 with the first ships."

This time it was Kip's turn to ask for a translation. "My family stretches back far, too," he said. "They came over to escape the persecutions of papists like old Kings Charles and James."

"These Puritans," continued Socono, "was the man Mather one of their leaders? The one who hanged women for their magic?"

306

"Hey, Indian," interrupted Kip, breaking into Stephen's translation, "are you trying to tell me that you papists are better Christians than me and Nowell here?"

"No," said the Indian. "The little brother is a Christian like me. I don't know what you are."

"Well, I'll be damned," said Kip.

But before he could say any more, the signal gun from shore was fired, its roar reverberating across the angry gray waters of Boston harbor. Without warning sailors appeared from nowhere and began to climb up into the rigging and out onto the yardarms. Lines were tossed, and shouting sailors were everywhere. To an outsider it would seem as if chaos had triumphed.

Kip looked over at the Indian, disgruntled that he could not continue the debate. He tried to speak, but the shouting of the officers and sailors, combined with the thud of canvas filling with wind, drowned him out. The expedition against Louisbourg was underway.

The wardroom of HMS *Launceston*, Commodore Warren's flagship, was jammed with the officers of the colonial army and with those of the royal navy. The New England army had arrived at Canso on the 27th of April, two days before. On this day, the 29th, to the joy of all, Commodore Warren and four great ships of the West Indian squadron had arrived. Pepperrell had ordered a council of war to introduce his officers and those of the king's navy to his plan.

"Gentlemen, I'm sorry that there are not enough chairs for all of us," said the commodore. He was a most impressive-looking man in the uniform of a flag rank officer of the royal navy. His sunburned face was a clear indication that his small fleet was a recent arrival off the ice-bound coasts of Canada. "And since most would have to stand," he continued, "I thought it better that we all stand. The general and I will be brief. General Pepperrell," he said, nodding to the Maine merchant.

"Thank you, Commodore," said Pepperrell. "I want you to know, gentlemen, that we sail for Louisbourg this evening. We should arrive in Gabarus Bay, south of the fortress, by tomorrow at noon. We will land just as soon as we arrive."

"In broad daylight?" interrupted Daniel Pierce.

"In broad daylight, Captain," answered the general.

"But Governor Shirley's instructions call for a night attack. We will lose the element of surprise if we land in daylight."

"Captain," said the commodore, anger beginning to enrich

307

the color of his face, "every scouting report from my sloops indicates that the surf in the bay would prevent anything but a very careful landing in full light. We would lose too many boats and too many men to the sea if we carried out the governor's instructions."

"But that commits us to a formal siege," said Pierce. "We haven't the experience or the guns to carry one out."

Again Warren spoke out. "I have four line-of-battle ships with me, Captain. My sloops are carrying my signals to the six remaining ships of my squadron. I have every expectation that within a week of our landing, I will have ten ships of the line with me. I have more than enough guns and experienced gunners to help you in your tasks."

"What about engineers then, sir?" said Pierce. "Or do you believe the drivel that Vaughan was handing out—that if we strike the West Gate, we can penetrate and that the French will not sally?"

"I believe it," said Warren.

"So it is to be Vaughan's plan," said Pierce. Then in a voice that could be heard only by the officers in his immediate vacinity he said, "My friends, we are undone by treachery." Several officers nodded in agreement with Pierce's sentiments. Stephen heard Pierce's comments and was angered by them. One look at the expression of concern on Vaughan's face kept him quiet, however.

Warren was not accustomed to having his plans subjected to criticism by his inferiors, especially not by a merchant turned soldier for a day. He would have silenced the debate immediately but Pepperrell, also an amateur, knew his men far better than Warren.

"Daniel," he said, "the commodore and I have agreed to far more. It will be one of the army's major objectives to allow the commodore's squadron to enter the harbor. The great walls of the fortress are on the land side. The harbor walls are very much weaker. We must therefore achieve the hills above the West Gate. From there we will attempt not only to penetrate the walls there but also to silence the one major defense on the harbor side—the Circular Battery. We silence that and Warren enters and bombards the town."

"Not as long as the Grand Battery and the Island Battery exist," shouted Stephen over the murmur of approval that had greeted Pepperrell's words.

"Yes, Mr. Nowell," said Pepperrell, "you're right. We know they have to be subdued also."

"What are these batteries?" asked a captain of the Connecticut volunteers, who stood behind Pierce.

"Harbor defenses," answered Pepperrell. "The island blocks the channel of entry. It has about twenty heavy guns pointing across the channel. The Grand Battery is across the harbor from the fortress. It has about twenty guns also, all pointing across the harbor. It commands the inside of the harbor."

"In other words," screamed Pierce, "the navy is never going to get into the harbor until we all get killed trying to take these forts. Your plan is doomed to failure, Pepperrell."

"Captain," shouted Commodore Warren, "if you were under my command you would now be under arrest."

"But I'm not under your command," said Pierce.

"General, may I speak?" said Vaughan.

"I don't want to listen to that man's drivel," interrupted Pierce.

"Daniel, shut up," yelled Pepperrell. Then he turned to William Vaughan and signaled him to begin.

"I know these defenses," Vaughan said. "The Grand Battery looks very formidable from the harbor and no doubt it is formidable. It could probably blast away any ship that tried to enter without the approval of the harbor master. But all of its gun embrasures face the sea. If we get behind it on the hills with our guns, they will have to surrender the battery to us. The island is also like an independent fort. But just across the channel from it is the lighthouse—at a much higher elevation. All we have to do is put some guns there and the island will have to surrender. We'll get our fleet into the harbor and we'll take the fort."

"Here, here," shouted Graham.

"That's drivel you're spouting, Vaughan. I won't take the word of a Jesuit papist," yelled Pierce.

"Hastings," Warren said to the flag lieutenant by his side. "Put that man in the brig." He pointed to Daniel Pierce. Pierce turned to leave the wardroom and several of his fellow officers deliberately stood in Hastings' path, preventing him from reaching the retreating captain. The room was in an uproar. Pepperrell turned toward Warren and spoke to him angrily.

Warren's face broke into a look of disgust, but he called Hastings back. "Leave him be, Adam," he said to his assistant. "The general here doesn't want me to molest his officers. I believe that this conference has gone far enough. I'm calling it to an end. We leave for Louisbourg tonight. God save us."

After the meeting many officers crowded about Pierce, shaking his hand and patting him on the shoulder. Pierce smiled back at his well-wishers and then climbed over the side, descending clumsily to a small boat, to be rowed ashore. It was a brief row from the flagship through the pitch-black night to Pierce's camp on the shore. As Pierce approached his camp, he recognized the profile of Isaac Wiggins sitting before his campfire. Speaking softly, he called to Wiggins to join him, out of the light of the campfire.

Pierce was angry. "The bastards have given up our plan, Isaac. They have decided instead on a formal siege. We'll never succeed now." Then, more softly, he added, "You must give the warning."

A look of surprise crossed Wiggins' face at Pierce's words. Pierce turned and entered his tent. Wiggins remained outside and then turned and walked to his own campfire. He picked up his belongings, stuffed them into his pack and, throwing his musket across his shoulder, he disappeared into the night darkness, heading in the direction of the woods.

But Wiggins did not leave the camp alone. As he melted into the dark forest, another man, who had been observing his movements intently, followed a short distance behind.

Vaughan's rangers were among the first troops to disembark in Gabarus Bay. Vaughan himself took possession of the rudder of the longboat while Kip and Stephen helped the transport's sailors with the oars. Most of the rangers, however, huddled forward, trying to protect powder and musket from the ocean spray as the waves struck with loud slaps against the sides of the boat.

From where he rowed, Stephen could catch sight of the shoreline. He could not immediately locate Fresh Water Cove, the spot Karl had pointed out to him as the best landing site. Just as he would begin to orient himself, the boat would dip into the valley between waves and all he could see was the white tips of the onrushing water. Finally, in desperation, Stephen grabbed hold of Kip's shoulder to steady himself and stood on the rowing bench. Now he could keep a view of the horizon for several seconds longer. To the starboard side Stephen caught sight of a rocky point of land that he recognized with relief. It was White Point. That meant that Black Cape was directly ahead of them. He

310

pointed to Vaughan to steer the boat to port. Fresh Water Cove was to the left side of Black Cape. With any luck at all, they would beach the boat safely in the sandy cove.

Stephen sat down again. He grabbed the oar he shared with Israel and concentrated on pulling. He stared at the bulging neck and shoulder muscles of the sailor rowing in front of him. The noise of the surf smashing against the rocks and then being sucked out between them came to him from the starboard side—his side of the boat. He stood again. The sandy beach of the cove was directly ahead. Suddenly a breaking wave grabbed the longboat and sent it hurtling at breakneck speed toward the shore. Stephen lost his balance and fell backward into Vaughan's lap. The soft scraping of sand against the boat's bottom was a welcome sound. The boat came to a halt with a jerk. Sailors pulled in their oars and jumped over the side to beach the boat more securely. The rangers grabbed their gear and let themselves down easily into the ice-cold, knee-deep water of the bay.

As the other boats followed Stephen's to shore, Graham went from ranger to ranger, checking out equipment and making sure each man had dry powder and blanket. When Graham had finished, Vaughan called his hundred rangers to group about him. "Rangers," he shouted so that all could hear above the roar of the wind and surf, "our first task is to follow Ensign Nowell to the army's campsite and secure it for General Pepperrell and the rest of our comrades." He nodded to Stephen to lead on.

Stephen gestured to Kip to send out flankers to guard against ambush; then he set off along the bank of the stream that gave the cove its name. It was the most direct route to the meadow Pepperrell had picked as his first campsite.

Stephen set a fast pace. He knew these woods well. As the rangers moved steadily inland, the sounds of the sea faded, to be replaced by the chirping of birds or the scurrying of game from the underbrush.

The sun was high in the sky when Stephen reached the trail and broke away from the stream bank. About fifty yards from the stream they came to a large meadow. This was the site selected for the camp. Stephen entered the meadow cautiously, fearing an ambush from the underbrush on the other side. He kept low to the ground and the rangers followed his example.

When he was almost across the meadow, he saw a strange form tied to a tree facing him. He rose to his full height in astonishment and stopped dead in his tracks. The ranger behind him rose also. "Oh, my God," he whispered.

Impaled on a stake was the brutalized body of Isaac Wiggins. He was naked, and blood dripped down his torn chest, from which the heart had been ripped. His fingers and toes had been cut off and his eyes gouged. An enormous pool of blood lay at his feet.

Kip came up and joined Stephen. "What the hell happened here?" he asked. "Are the Frenchies trying to scare us?"

"They've succeeded," said another ranger. Soon most of the rangers were standing about the naked body.

Stephen began to vomit. He had hated this man; he had wanted to see him dead. But face to face with the brutality of revenge, he was sickened.

Lt. Graham, when he entered the group about the stake, wasted no time. "You two," he said, grabbing two of the rangers closest to him, "get that man buried. The rest of you spread out into these woods. I want to be absolutely certain that there are no Frenchies around here just waiting to put a ball in Billy Pepperrell's fat ass when he gets here today."

Stephen started to walk off toward the woods, but Graham halted him. "Vaughan wants you," said the lieutenant, pointing toward the south end of the meadow. Stephen could see that several rangers had already begun to erect a tent for the commander there, and he walked toward the command post.

Vaughan was in an exuberant mood. He grabbed Stephen's hand and then threw his arm around his shoulder. "Excellent progress, Nowell," he said. "We've made the campsite before noon. I've sent word to the general that we're here and I have left guards all along the trail to lead the army to this spot. No ambush—no enemy in sight."

"You've not heard about the body we found?"

Vaughan looked at him with a puzzled expression. "I've just heard some of the men talking. What do you make of it?"

"It was Wiggins, William," said Stephen. "And I'm sure that Socono did it. It was terrifying."

Vaughan slumped into the chair that had been set up for the general. "Don't you start feeling sorry for him," Vaughan finally said. "The bastard killed your mother. I'm sure of it. I'd hoped to finish him off myself."

"He died hard," said Stephen. "Socono was merciless."

Vaughan shrugged his shoulders. "Now all we have to do is trap Pierce," he said. With that he dropped the topic. "Once we settle in here, Stephen, and secure these woods against

312

ambush, I'm going to lead my rangers out of here and into a more advanced post. I'll want you to guide me."

Stephen nodded agreement. He was still shaken by the sight of Wiggins and by the enormity of Socono's hatred and revenge, but he went off to find Kip to help him scout the woods.

There were no signs of any French forces outside the fortress. Warren's ships soon appeared off the entrance of the harbor, effectively blocking off any aid from the sea. One ship of the French navy, *Vengeance,* had attempted to bolt from the harbor, but Warren's heavier ships had blasted it from the water. Most of the crew had been killed or captured. Pepperrell spent the whole first day landing half his men and equipment and marching them off to the campsite established by Vaughan's rangers. Pepperrell himself came to the meadow that first day and took command. He sat there in a canvas sea chair, siping a mug of cool cider. Colonel Waldo had remained behind at the beach to supervise the remaining landings, but a recent message from him had indicated that the surf had lessened and that he expected to complete the landing of men and equipment on the next day. All of the officers who had landed and made it to camp had been called to the command post to share some ale or cider with the general.

Stephen, as a low-ranking ensign, was barely within listening range of Pepperrell's voice, but he could tell from its tone that the general was indeed pleased with himself. Stephen saw his uncle in the inner circle, standing next to Vaughan and very close to the general.

"This is a fine site for a camp, Willy," the general said to Colonel Vaughan.

"You can thank my man, Nowell, for finding it, sir," said Vaughan.

Pepperrell nodded assent and took a long swig of his cider. He smacked his lips together loudly and folded his arms across his belly. "Yes, this was a good first day, but our work has just begun. We must bring the guns from the beach, through the woods and across the swamps to the hills. That will take almost every man I have."

"We will only need two or three heavy guns at first," said Vaughan, "and I have already directed our timber men to start the building of the sleds." Vaughan was quiet for a moment as Pepperrell signed some papers presented to him by his clerk. When the general looked up from his work,

Vaughan spoke again. "I would like your permission to scout the area tomorrow, sir. I would like to scout out the Grand Battery and the Island . . ."

Daniel Pierce interrupted. "I'm opposed to Vaughan gallivanting off from the main army, General."

"Why so, Daniel?" asked Pepperrell.

"With all the rangers off somewhere else, the French will strike out at us from the fort and ambush our men working to bring up the guns."

Pepperrell thought for a moment. "I think," he said finally, "that I can arrange a compromise. We can put out other scouts to tell us if the French sally tomorrow, and they are not likely to do so in broad daylight. First thing tomorrow Colonel Vaughan will lead his rangers on an expedition about the harbor to gain information. He will return before nightfall to place guards about our camp for protection."

Pepperrell was even more pleased with himself now and ordered another round of drinks for all the officers in the headquarters. When the ale and cider had been poured into about twenty waiting mugs, the plump little general rose from the sea chair. "Gentlemen, the King." That traditional toast drunk, the general offered another. "The fall of Louisbourg." Several of the officers began to cheer. The mugs rose almost in unison as the second toast was drunk.

"We'll have much more time to celebrate later," said Pepperrell, "but now we must return to our duties. Good luck and down with the French."

"Here, here," said several of the officers while several others began to applaud. The group began to disperse.

Vaughan walked over to Stephen. "I want our men up and ready to leave before dawn, Ensign," he said. "Tell Graham."

"Yes, sir," responded Stephen, and he sauntered off to find the lieutenant. Tomorrow would be even busier than today had been, and today's action had exhausted him. He knew he would have no trouble sleeping.

In fact, Stephen had very little sleep that night. At sunset a message arrived from Governor Duchambon, asking for a discussion between the two sides. Stephen was summoned to Pepperrell's camp. He was to accompany Colonel Waldo as his interpreter. The two men were to receive a safe conduct into the citadel of Louisbourg.

As he entered the fortress through the West Gate, Stephen was reminded of that day so many years ago when he, Karl and Socono had returned from the holiday in the woods. Although it was now dark, Stephen imagined that he could see the spot where Karl had pushed the stone out of the wall. He hoped that it could still be done.

They were led by a contingent of Swiss mercenaries through the streets of the town. Citizens stared at them. The bravado of last December was gone. Now none dared throw mud at the Englishmen.

They entered the gates of the citadel and were led through its familiar corridors toward the room off the chapel that served the governor as an office. Duchambon sat at his desk; Stephen was startled by the persons who flanked him on either side. On his right stood Paul Lalonde and on his left was Manya. Both of them were equally surprised to see Stephen.

Lalonde's eyes flashed white. He flushed. "Your Excellency," he said in French, "it is the traitor, Noel. He must be arrested and removed from this conference."

"Father," said Duchambon. "This is a parley called by us to convince the English to save lives by withdrawing from this island. These two men are here by my request and are under my protection. As an officer and a nobleman, I can do nothing to harm either one without a loss of honor."

Lalonde looked at the governor with complete contempt. "I obey no code of honor. I obey the voice of God. You must obey his commands as well, sir, or I will turn the people against you."

Seeing Duchambon was clearly unperturbed by his threat, Lalonde stood up and strode toward the door. He turned and smiled at Stephen; the smile broadened into a leer. He threw his head back and laughed.

"The man is completely mad," said Duchambon. "I don't understand why the citizens of this town don't see that." The governor was obviously more shaken by the priest's departure than he appeared to be. It was clear to Stephen that Duchambon had come to rely on the Jesuit's influence with the people.

Stephen stared at Manya and she returned the stare with a slight smile on her lips. He thought her as beautiful as ever.

Waldo was introduced to Duchambon by Stephen, who then took up his duties as translator. "What is it you seek of us, Your Excellency?" asked the colonel.

"I request that you leave this island and that you do so in the name of humanity."

"That is, of course, impossible, Your Excellency. In return

315

let me make a request of you—that you surrender this fortress to His Britannic Majesty and save the lives of the inhabitants."

"This is a fortress town, monsieur. Those who live here have always lived with the threat of a siege. Somehow or other they are all connected with the military. They knew what they faced when they came here."

"You will not reconsider?" asked Waldo.

"Will you?" asked Duchambon.

"No." Waldo turned to leave.

"Before you leave," said Duchambon, "I have a request to ask of you. This gentlewoman is the Princess Marianna, wife of the late Louis DeLuynes, first officer of the *Vengeance*. She seeks a favor of the British navy. Her husband was reported killed in the effort of his ship to escape the harbor. She requests the return of his body, if possible."

"My condolences, Princess," said Waldo.

Stephen translated and added, "And mine also, Manya."

Duchambon looked up at him. "You know the princess?"

Manya answered for him. "The English officer and I met some years ago at Versailles."

"They must have been happier times for you, Princess," said the governor. Manya merely smiled.

Duchambon offered Waldo a glass of wine before he departed. Waldo accepted the offer, allowing Stephen to speak with Manya.

"I am sorry to hear about Louis, for your sake," he said. "I won't try to pretend to you that I liked him."

Manya smiled. "I will not pretend either, Etienne. Louis was an awful husband. You and Michal were right. But I will do my duty by his family. I will try to recover his body and have it buried here in the fortress. But I am both relieved and sorry. I'm relieved to be rid of Louis DeLuynes, and I'm sorry that I did not bear him a child and that I will never become duchess. Now his brother will inherit the title after the duke dies. So once again I'm the penniless, dependent Polish princess."

"Surely the duke will provide for his son's widow?"

"I doubt it," she said. "As soon as I'm free to leave your Louisbourg, Etienne, I will return to Versailles and become the Queen's companion again. My stay has been brief, and I can't say that I have enjoyed it here or that I share your feelings for this country."

"So much has changed for me also, Manya, as you can see. I'm afraid I can't look upon this fortress either without great pangs of sorrow. Do you have any news for me about Karl?" he asked quietly so that Duchambon might not overhear.

"I've not seen him, but I tried to discover his whereabouts. He was taken to the Jesuit house by LaGarde; no one has seen him since. Now with Lalonde in charge, I think you should fear for his life."

"Why was Lalonde here tonight?"

"He is the new Jesuit superior. The people trust him. Duchambon finds it useful to have his support."

"Where is Father LaGarde?" Stephen asked softly.

"He was recalled to France in disgrace because of his actions in your case. He was censured by the Jesuit General in Rome. He has been sent to a house of repentence."

Stephen felt a twinge of guilt over his part in LaGarde's fate, but he felt even more concerned for Karl, now that Lalonde was the rector.

"Where is Michal now?" he asked after some moments of silence.

"In the French army fighting in the Polish brigade against the Austrians. He mentioned you often after you left; he missed you. You must not judge him too hard. When he snubbed you at the end, he was only doing what he had been taught to do. You have more reason to have harsh thoughts against me. I loved to be with you and maybe I even loved you, but I was so determined never to be poor again and you were so poor. I snubbed you too, but not out of any sense of honor. I snubbed you out of greed."

"I don't hate you, Manya. I could never hate you."

She turned from him and walked over to where the governor and the colonel were conversing. Duchambon greeted her with respect. "The colonel has agreed, Princess, to search for your husband's body, and he has agreed to allow you and the other ladies of the military contingent to sail under escort of the British navy back to France." She bowed to Waldo and, without looking back at Stephen, she left the room.

The next day, after scouting in the rear of the Grand Battery, setting fire to some naval stores, and proceeding on to the lighthouse, Socono and his Abenacki warriors arrived to join the English forces.

Vaughan, Stephen, the ten rangers and Socono and his Indians settled down for the night on the lighthouse bluff. The colonel ordered watches stood so that his little force would not be taken by surprise. Stephen sought out a site for the watch just as soon as darkness set in. He found the only landing beach at the foot of the bluff. If the French had spotted them from the island, they would have to land here to attack. Stephen had drawn the first watch and, wrapping himself up in his blanket, he placed himself on the wet sand behind a rock with a full view of the beach.

The moon had not yet risen and it was soon impossible to distinguish the black sea from the black night. The only sound Stephen could hear was the gentle swishing of the harbor waves against the unseen beach. He knew immediately that he was not alone. He had not heard anything; it was just instinct. But before he could even turn around, Socono had wedged his body between Stephen's and the rock to his right.

"Damn it, Socono," Stephen whispered in English. He then switched to Abenacki. "You just scared several years off my life. What in God's name have you been up to?" Face to face, Stephen could make out a grin on the Indian's face and he still smelled of rum.

"I am at peace, little brother, and I have been celebrating. There is something I want to show you." He grabbed a large deerskin pouch at his side and pulled out its contents.

Stephen sank away from it in horror. It was the grinning, toothless mouth of his nightmare. Socono was holding by its hair the severed head of Isaac Wiggins.

Stephen felt the vomit rising into his throat; he fought it back down. "Take it away," he gasped. "Why are you carrying that thing with you? I thought they had buried him."

Socono chuckled. "I dug him up again. I followed him when he left Canso. Wiggins was on his way here to warn the French of your coming. I killed him and I killed him with much pain. He was not brave. But now I will take his ugly face back to my people. I have borne his scar for many years; now his head will sit outside my lodge—to show my people that I have had revenge."

Stephen looked again at the head, still grinning, even in death. There was little he could say. He knew how his friend had suffered at the hands of Wiggins. He knew how his own family had been the victims of Wiggins' cruelty. But coming face to face with the results of an overwhelming lust for revenge had sobered him. He felt no sorrow for Wiggins. Instead, he felt pity for Socono and for himself, that they both could be driven to seek such a revenge.

First light brought a message from Pepperrell, carried by Kip. Vaughan was to return to camp immediately and not await relief, not even from the royal marines.

"Graham told Kip that the general is angry with me for not returning last night," Vaughan confided to Stephen as they shared some ship's bread and dried beef. "I should have gone back and left John in charge here. I want a chance to carry this place, the glory of winning. I've gambled all on it, Stephen." For the first time Stephen understood the depth of Vaughan's ambition and realized that Vaughan, too, was a driven man. Vaughan stood up and walked down toward the beach.

Stephen called after him. "Sir, the French will see you."

"I don't care," answered the colonel. "We'll be leaving this place almost immediately anyway." He disappeared behind one of the boulders.

Stephen realized, also for the first time, just how much he had come to care for William Vaughan, this man who had loved his mother and in a sense was his only link with her.

Stephen turned toward the remaining rangers and Indians to get them underway. Just then he heard Vaughan cry out. Stephen grabbed for his musket and raced down the path toward the beach. He saw the colonel kneeling before something in the sand. The rays of the morning sun struck the object; it flashed brightly.

"Nowell, come quickly and help me dig away this wet sand." Stephen dropped to his knees and started pulling at the sand with his cupped hands. Within a few minutes he had uncovered the barrel of a brass cannon. Meanwhile, Vaughan had hurried off about twenty paces up the beach beyond the view of the Island Battery to another bulge in the sand. It was another brass twenty-pounder.

"My God, Stephen," said Vaughan. "We don't even have to drag a cannon here. The French must have abandoned some guns right here on the beach, months ago. All we have to do is dig them up. They're brass so they haven't rusted. I've got to get back to Pepperrell with this news." He raced up the path toward the bluff with Stephen following closely behind.

The party was smaller now. The Indians had disappeared, but Stephen knew they were about and he need not fear ambush. He set a pace toward the Grand Battery that soon brought them to the scene of their first sighting of the fort. Again Stephen approached the rise overlooking the battery

319

cautiously. He was instantly aware of something different this time. Yesterday morning there had been guards in the towers and smoke rising from the chimney. This morning there were neither. He called Kip to get Vaughan to come forward, but before the colonel could respond, a clearly tipsy Socono walked out of the woods toward the rear gate of the battery. Stephen held his breath. If the French caught sight of him, the Indian was dead.

Vaughan dropped beside Stephen on the hill. "What the hell is the Indian doing?" he asked in wonderment.

Stephen was too frightened for his friend to respond.

"Gonna get himself killed," said Kip, who now stood up to get a better view.

Socono stood in the gateway of the fort. He pulled a bottle from his pouch and brought it to his lips. Then he turned around and waved at Stephen.

"Son of a bitch wants us to come on," said Kip.

Stephen rose to his feet, as did the rest of the small detachment of rangers. "The damn place is empty," Stephen said to Vaughan.

"Then let us enter, by all means," said the colonel, laughing as he began to run down the slope to join the Indian.

The inside of the battery was a shambles—the evacuation had been hasty. Clothes were strewn about the floor. Several cooking pots had been shoved into the far corner. Everywhere along the floor there were little mounds of lead that had rehardened after dripping to the floor. The greatest mess, however, was made by the huge forty-two pounders, which had been tipped from their embrasures and knocked out of their carriages. The carriages themselves had been stacked and burned. The barrels of the cannon had been filled with molten lead to prevent their use by the captors of the fort.

Socono disappeared into the kitchen, while Vaughan entered the powder magazine to see if any charges had been placed to blow up the battery. Socono was the first to reappear. He was not alone. Behind him he pulled a young Swiss soldier, whom Stephen did not recognize from his earlier residence in the barracks.

The boy was terrified by the Indian, and by the time Stephen approached him, he was crying hysterically and calling in French, "Don't let him scalp me. I surrender." He grabbed Stephen about the knees as soon as he could reach him and held on with a viselike grip. Stephen bent down to look the boy in the eye.

"The Indian won't harm you if you tell me all I want to know," he said. "But if you lie to me, we will build him a fire to roast you over."

The boy started to speak, but was prevented by his heaving sobs.

"Has the battery been mined?" asked Stephen.

The boy shook his head. Stephen looked over toward the colonel as he emerged leisurely from the magazine of the fortress and assumed that what the boy had told him was true. "Is there anyone else left behind in the battery?"

The boy shook his head again. "I deserted," he was finally able to say.

"Why did the French abandon this place?" Stephen asked.

By this time Vaughan had caught sight of the interrogation and had joined the group surrounding Stephen.

"My captain saw the smoke from the storehouses and knew that you would be attacking. He wrote to the governor and told him that you were in our rear and that we could not hold the battery against an attack. His Excellency gave permission to abandon after we destroyed our guns." Stephen translated the boy's responses to the colonel.

"They botched the job too," said Kip after he heard Stephen's translation.

Vaughan turned to Kip and walked with him over to one of the big guns, which lay carelessly strewn on the floor. He ran his hand over the smooth metal tube of the forty-two pounder. "They didn't spike them," he said softly.

Kip nodded.

Then Vaughan let out a whoop of joy. "They didn't spike them," he laughed. "The stupid bastards have just handed us twenty big siege guns and a God damn fort to fire them from."

The Swiss deserter caught on to the cause of William Vaughan's delight. "We didn't have time," he said rather lamely to Stephen. "We thought you would be attacking at any minute."

Vaughan sat down on the floor of the battery, pulled a scrap of paper from his coat pocket and reached for his pouch at his side. He extracted some ink and a pen and started to write. The small group of rangers formed a circle around their commander. Finally he stopped writing. "Kip, I want you to take this message to the general." He chuckled again. "But first I want you all to hear it." He stood up and lifted the paper to eye level.

"Grand Battery; Louisbourg, Isle Royale. Honorable W. Pepperrell, Esq.—General." He paused. "I wonder if I have left out any titles," he said.

"Sir," he continued. "By the Grace of God and the courage of . . ." He stopped reading and, pointing with his finger, he began to count the men under his command. ". . . twelve, thirteen . . ." He began to read again, after filling in the missing number. "And the courage of thirteen men, I have taken this place and am awaiting a reinforcement and a flag. Sincerely, W. Vaughan." He scratched his name at the bottom of the letter. "Let them try to ignore this request for help." He folded the paper and handed it to the sergeant. "Off with you, Kip, and make sure you have at least a company with you when you come back—if not more." Kip made a semi-salute to the colonel and disappeared out the rear entrance of the battery.

Stephen left the group surrounding Vaughan and continued an exploration of the Grand Battery. He found the stone stairs that led, by a circular route, into the tower on the south side of the battery. When he reached the top of the stairs, he was confronted by a heavy oak door. He pushed it outward and slowly and cautiously stuck his head through the portal. The breeze was blowing in directly from the sea. Once he determined that the tower contained no hidden dangers—in fact, it contained nothing; the French had managed to remove the small swivel guns normally mounted in it—he walked to the ledge and stared across the harbor to the city. He breathed in deeply the rich smell of the salt air. Pushing back the hair from his forehead, he shaded his eyes from the glare of the sun as it struck the harbor waves. And then he saw them, at first mere specks on the water. But soon, as he stared at them for perhaps two minutes, they grew larger. As soon as he was certain, he turned and raced down the stairs to give the alarm.

"Colonel Vaughan," he shouted. The group of rangers was still standing joking with their leader, and as one man they stared at Stephen when he jumped the last three stairs to the stone floor. "Longboats heading this way from Louisbourg," he shouted. "It's the French. They're coming back."

Instantly Vaughan ordered one ranger to every other embrasure. Each man had about fifteen rounds for his musket, but there were some small quantities of powder and musket balls that had been abandoned in the magazine. At the moment Vaughan was placing his rangers, Socono came up out of the kitchen carrying an enormous ham and a small keg of beer. Vaughan looked at him and started to laugh again. When he saw Stephen looking at him quizzically, he pointed at Socono. "Forgot him. There were fourteen of you," he explained.

Vaughan sent two men to the north tower, while Stephen and Socono climbed back up into the turret that Stephen had just left. The longboats were much closer now. Stephen dearly wished that the French had not taken the brass swivel guns. He did not know how to fire them but he was sure that someone else in the force would. They could have made short work of the French if they had had the cannon.

There were four boats, each with about twenty men in it. Stephen had his musket and fifteen rounds. Socono had the same, in addition to his bow and quivver of arrows. There was nothing for them to do now but wait, as the longboats drew closer to the battery landing beach with each pull of the oars.

Stephen looked over at Socono, who stood about five feet away from him on the other side of the tower. His pouch was gone. Stephen spoke softly to him in Abenacki. "Has my brother finished his celebration?"

Socono smiled and looked at him for some moments. He showed no signs of his earlier drinking. "You did not approve," he said finally.

"I'm in no position to judge you," said Stephen. "You did what you felt you had to do. I'll do what I feel I have to do."

"Killing the toothless one brought no honor to me," said the Indian, "but it did bring me peace. I had completed the task I set for myself on the morning when I awoke to find this on my face." He pointed to the puckered skin on his cheek. "My first effort at revenge brought great sorrow to you. I have tried to make that up to you."

"You have," said Stephen.

"And I have been repaid in kind," said the Indian, smiling. "But now it is over. I will not be haunted by that face in my dreams, and the mark will fade."

Stephen looked at Socono, wondering if he really believed that the scar would go away.

The Indian answered his look. "Not from my face, little brother: from my soul."

Vaughan's head appeared in the tower doorway. "Everything all right up here, Nowell?" he asked.

Stephen nodded.

"I don't think they know we're here yet," said the colonel.

"They're rowing very boldly toward the beach. I think they have come to their senses and have come to reoccupy or to spike the guns. We have to hold them off until help arrives, but our only chance is surprise. You won't be able to hear my command to fire up here, so wait until the men in the embrasures fire before you begin." Vaughan waited until Stephen had translated his orders to Socono before he disappeared back down the stairs.

The minutes dragged on. Stephen was afraid to look over the tower wall, for fear that he might give away his position. But he knew that the longboats were very close. He could hear the sounds of the oars. Vaughan had guessed correctly; the French were not aware of their presence. He could hear them laughing in the boats.

Socono crept from his position on the far side of the rampart and moved toward the turret door and the stairway below. He closed the oaken door quietly and dropped the beam down that locked the door from the outside. Should the battery below fall to the French, Stephen knew that he and Socono could hold out for some time on top of the tower. Before Socono could make it back to his position, Stephen heard the bottoms of the first boats scraping on the sand of the landing beach, followed by some cursing in French and more laughter. Next Stephen heard the sound of another boat beaching and, almost immediately afterwards, the roar of ten muskets firing as one.

There were screams from the beach. Stephen stood to fire his musket. He could see several bodies lying on the path leading from the beach to the battery. He saw an officer drawing his sword and calling to his men to follow him. Stephen's ball struck him in the face and he fell backward into the water. Socono fired and another soldier fell on top of the lifeless form of his leader.

Apparently the French had not bothered to load their muskets on returning to the battery, because it was several moments before any of them could return the fire. Two of the boats had not yet landed when the fighting began. Their oarsmen hung back to await instructions from the officer Stephen had killed.

Socono was busy reloading his rifle and Stephen's while the boy tried to pick out likely targets. The French had fallen all the way back to their boats and were using them for protection. Still they did not fire. Then, on a given signal, thirty men rose as one body and, led by their sergeant, began a desperate charge with fixed bayonets. Stephen and Socono rose together and fired again with deadly effect—two more French soldiers were halted in their tracks and fell backward. Fire from the battery below killed several others, but still the charge rolled on, closer and closer to the gun openings. Now the French had their opportunity; the rangers had fired and would need time to reload. The French raced toward them, trying to reach them with their bayonets.

Socono threw his musket to Stephen to reload. He grabbed his bow and notched an arrow; he aimed carefully and fired. He notched a second arrow and fired again, but he could not kill them all. The sergeant leading the charge reached the embrasures and began to climb through before any of the rangers had finished reloading. Stephen tossed Socono's musket to him. He stood fascinated by the form of the sergeant standing in the gun embrasure, clearly readying himself to leap on someone below him. Instead, there was the roar of a musket and the sergeant was blasted backward, a ramrod piercing his chest.

Stephen ducked down again and began to reload his musket. Socono fired and tossed him the empty musket. Stephen handed him the loaded one and began the reloading again. The minutes sped by. The French were in the battery. The two men in the tower could hear the firing and yelling from below. Suddenly there was a pounding on the tower door. Stephen, thinking it to be some of the rangers trying to escape, moved to open it, but Socono yelled to him to stay put. The pounding continued and Stephen stared at the door. Finally he could stand it no longer. He rushed by the Indian, who stuck his foot out to trip him but missed. Stephen grabbed the beam and shoved it upward. The door crashed open and two men, with limbs intertwined, fell onto the floor of the tower. One was William Vaughan and the other a French soldier. The Frenchman had a grip on Vaughan's windpipe and the colonel's face was scarlet. Socono swiftly replaced the beam, and, with one smooth action, took his hunting knife from his belt and plunged it into the Frenchman's back. A scream pierced the air and the Frenchman loosened his hold on Vaughan's throat. He fell to the floor. Vaughan, pinned to the ground by the dead weight of the man, drew rasping breaths. He tossed the dead Frenchman off him and sat up.

"I'm afraid they have retaken the fort," he gasped. "None of the others are alive down there. I wonder if the other tower has fallen." As if to answer his question, a musket exploded from that direction and the ball splattered against the stone wall behind Stephen's head.

Socono had turned back to the rampart. Looking toward the sea, he spoke to Stephen in Abenacki. "Tell your chief that he has not lost the fight."

Over the rampart Stephen saw that the longboats that had not landed were pulling away. Stephen grabbed Vaughan's arm. "They're retreating, sir," he yelled.

"Where?" said Vaughan, standing to get a better view. Again a musket from the opposite tower fired, but it was badly aimed and struck the outside wall of the rampart. The three targets dropped lower.

Socono crawled to the opposite side to view the landward approach to the battery. Pouring down from the opening in the forest from which they had first seen the battery were the rest of Vaughan's rangers, Israel Kip and John Graham in the lead.

Some of the French surrendered on the spot to Graham; the rest jumped out of the embrasures and began to race to the beach and their boats. Socono stood upright and raised his hand to his mouth. He gave a long, warbling call and out of the brush surrounding the landing beach rose his Abenacki, firing their arrows into the flanks of the French. None of the retreating men made it to the boats.

Vaughan looked down in amazement. "Were those men there all the time?" he asked Socono. The Indian looked at him blankly. Clearly angry now, the colonel turned to Stephen. "Ask the blasted savage if his men were there throughout the whole battle."

Stephen relayed the question to Socono. "Of course they were," said the Indian.

"But why didn't you bring them into the fort to help us?" asked Stephen.

"Because it looked as if you were going to lose. If I had placed them in the fort, they would now all be dead, like all the white men. We are not foolish white men, little brother. We fight when the odds are with us. Otherwise it is better to lie low, to live to fight again at some more favorable time."

"But you stayed with us," said Stephen. Socono merely shrugged his shoulders and turned away.

"Well," said Vaughan, "what did he say?"

"They arrived just before the rangers," Stephen lied.

Vaughan's anger cooled almost immediately. "Please thank him for what he did," said the colonel, now clearly apologetic. He threw open the door and descended the steps into the battery.

Stephen followed. The floor of the battery was strewn with bodies and slippery with blood. Israel Kip walked over to him and grasped him by the shoulders. "Son of a bitch, I'm glad you made it, boy. Looks to have been as bad as the time you and me fought off the band of red devils at Annapolis." He knew that Socono, who had come down behind Stephen, spoke no English, but he glanced toward the Indian nervously. "Come over here, Nowell, there is someone I want you to meet." He pulled Stephen by the arm to the side of one of the upset guns. An enormous figure of a man was bent over, staring at the barrel. As he stood up, Stephen realized just how enormous he was—not tall, but muscular. His neck was barely existent. His head seemed to be set on the enormous muscles of his broad shoulders. The expensive white shirt he wore looked ready to tear under any sudden pressure exerted by his barrel chest, and the muscles of his thighs were clearly outlined under his tight breeches.

"Major Pomeroy," said Kip, "this is Stephen Nowell. Nowell, Seth Pomeroy—the best God damn blacksmith and the strongest man in New England."

Stephen took Pomeroy's offered hand into his own. He could feel the strength of the man in his grip.

"Nowell, I've heard a bit about you from General Pepperrell. You're the young man who knows so much about this place."

"Yes, sir," said Stephen. "I've been serving with Colonel Vaughan. By the way, where is he?"

"Vaughan's in a heap of trouble," said Pomeroy. "Pepperrell is mad as hell at him for not returning with his force yesterday."

"But taking the battery—certainly that should soothe the general's feelings, shouldn't it?" asked Stephen.

Pomeroy laughed. "I would think so," he said. "But Pepperrell doesn't know what he's got yet. All he can think about is that he had to send out his rangers to get Vaughan out of some scrap he could have avoided by coming home when he was told. Told me to relieve him and send him back to camp." Stephen was shocked by the major's words and his face gave him away. Pomeroy clapped him on the shoulder. "Don't be so upset, Nowell. Soon as my report gets back to the general, old Willy will be out of the doghouse."

"I'm glad to hear that, sir," said Stephen. "Colonel Vaughan hopes to take part in the attack on the fortress."

"I'm sure he will, boy," said Pomeroy. "Pepperrell's already got his timber sleds built. We'll be on the hills above the West Gate with our siege guns before too many days go by. Then we'll blast the hell out of the Frenchies. You and Vaughan were right. They haven't dared to set foot outside the fort except to try to retake this place by boat. We've got them hemmed in. In a few days we'll be firing from this place on the city. We'll level it. As of now, only the island stands in the way of our friend Warren's ships and their six hundred guns. But in the meantime, we have more work here than a parson in a whorehouse. I'd appreciate it if you and Kip here would find Lieutenant Graham and get these rangers to work."

Five cannon had now been drilled and placed into position, ready to fire with the first light of dawn. Stephen had climbed up into the tower to avoid the heat of the battery and to try to pick up some of the night breeze. He had been joined by Kip and Socono, who had avoided the heavy work of the past few days by leading his Abenacki on scouting trips. Stephen looked across the harbor toward Louisbourg. It was still an hour to dawn and the city was asleep and dark. Socono snored softly, but Kip was already awake, wrapping his blanket and gear into a small bundle for easy carrying. He finished and sat down with his back against the stone wall, watching Stephen stare into the blackness.

"You must want to get inside that place awful bad," he said to Stephen.

"I do," Stephen responded.

"What then?"

"I go to the Jesuit house and get Karl Stiegler out."

"Then what?"

"I don't know," said Stephen. "Maybe I look for a certain priest and give him what he deserves."

"No, I meant after this is all over. What are your plans? I've been talking to this Indian friend of yours. We understand each other real good now. Don't he have a village somewhere up on one of them Maine rivers?"

"There's one on the Kennebec," said Stephen.

"Fine," said Kip. "That's as good as any of them. Lots of furs to be had in that region. I was figuring him and me would go up there together and trap for a season or two. Fellow could do mighty good trapping beaver. Besides, if you hadn't found me in Portsmouth and brought me on this expedition, I think I would have up and died. Can't take to life in the towns and I be no farmer. Why don't you come trapping with Socono and me?"

"I might just do that, Israel, but first I will have to look for Karl, and from what I saw he may still be hurting."

"A man can get his strength back faster in the woods than anyplace else," said the sergeant.

"You're probably right. But I also have to look after two other people, my grandfather's old servants. They have become financially dependent on me."

"We'll make good money with the furs, Stephen."

"But there is someone else—a girl. I have to go back and see her."

"In Boston?" asked Kip.

"No," said Stephen, "on the Mohawk. She's an Indian."

"A squaw?" said Kip. "Christ, you can have any dozen of them you want among Socono's people. I'm sure he could fix you up."

"She's not just anyone," said Stephen, surprising even himself by the passion in his voice. "I want to go back to her. I want her."

"Well, in your case I figure a squaw would be better than some prissy white gal. Don't figure you to be the domestic type, like my old friend Nat Arbuckle. You'll end up in the woods yet. 'Cept you'll be hauling along your own squaw and papooses."

Socono stirred and was awake. He sat up.

"Good morning, you scarfaced ugly bastard," said Kip affectionately.

"You, morning, Kip, you plenty big bastard," responded the Indian in his own version of English.

Kip laughed and slapped his knees. "See, didn't I tell you, Nowell, that we was getting along?" He picked up his gear and descended the stairs into the battery.

Stephen looked over at the Indian. He slipped into the familiar, confortable sounds of Abenacki. "Are you planning to go trapping with Kip?"

Socono looked puzzled. "Is that what he has been asking me?" said the Indian. "Ever since I've been back he has been making noises at me—loud noises, ugly sounds and gesturing with his hands. I thought maybe he had gone mad and I should honor him. I thought maybe the great spirit had touched him."

"None of those things, Socono. He thinks he is talking to

329

you, even fancies himself speaking Abenacki. He wants you to take him to Norridgewock after this and trap beaver with him."

"Will you come, little brother?"

"Not right away," said Stephen. "First I must settle the score with Daniel Pierce, and then there is someone I must see."

"The Mohawk girl?"

"Yes."

"She is an enemy of my people, but she helped you to save me. I think she must be a noble woman if you love her. I think you should go to her."

Stephen patted his friend's shoulder and the two climbed down from the tower into the battery.

The sun was above the horizon, shining into the eyes of the crews manning each of the five big guns. For the past hour each of the crews had been drilled by Lieutenant Adam Hastings, flag lieutenant to Commodore Warren and former gunnery officer on H.M.S. *Launceston*. Most of the men thought Hastings a pompous ass, but Stephen found him an efficient and knowledgeable officer. He tried to learn everything he could from Hastings about the firing of his gun. Now all was ready. Stephen and his crew were firing gun number three; the first gun was commanded by Lieutenant Graham and the second by Sergeant Kip. Four and five were commanded by crews under corporals.

Hastings disappeared up the stairs to the tower to observe, and Major Pomeroy joined Graham next to the fully loaded first gun. "Whenever you're ready, John," said the major.

"No, Seth," said Graham. "This has been mostly your labor. You fire the first gun." Without further ceremony, Pomeroy picked up the slow match and touched the powder hole of the gun. The whole battery was instantly filled with its roar. Flame belched from the muzzle as the forty-two-pound ball was hurled with destructive force across the harbor toward the town. The gun recoiled backward on its carriage, but the heavy ropes grappling it held. The crew grunted almost as one man as they pushed the gun back into position.

Hasting yelled from the tower, "Short. Elevate 100 yards." The command was carried to the crew by a ranger stationed halfway up the stairs. The process of swabbing out and reloading the first gun was already underway when Kip touched the match to his gun. Again the incredible roar, the fire, recoil, corection of aim and reloading.

Stephen fired his gun—also short. He corrected elevation. Graham's second shot was a near hit.

Kip winked at Stephen. "This one is right on target," he yelled. Stephen could not hear him over the bedlam of smoke, sweating men and noise that the battery had so suddenly become. Kip fired his gun. Stephen waited for the results of Kip's shot before firing. "A hit," came the shout of the ranger on the stairs. A great cheer rose from all five gun crews.

Stephen fired. He overshot the target, but on his fifth shot, Stephen too had a hit. Now three of the guns were on target, and they began to blast away without pause on the Circular Battery. The heat of the Grand Battery became unbearable.

Gun number five still had not found the range. Hastings had given up on voice relay and was sending written messages, but the frustration became too much for him. Still immaculately dressed in the blue coat and white breeches of the Royal Navy, he descended the stairs from the tower and walked to gun number five. He shoved aside the corporal in charge of the crew. "Out of my way, you stupid son of a bitch. I spent all morning showing you clods how to do this and you still can't do it right. If I had you aboard my ship, you'd learn how or you'd be strung up for a taste of the cat." He sighted the gun. "Now load," he yelled. The powder man was about to shove a large cartridge down the muzzle. Hastings drew his sword and lunged at him. The sword pierced the man's palm and made him drop the cartridge. "You stupid lout," the lieutenant shouted. "You want to get us all killed? First you sponge out the muzzle." Another man grabbed the sponge and swabbed out the gun. "Now the powder." The powder man was still holding his bleeding hand. "You," Hastings yelled at him, "you're only scratched. Shove that cartridge home." He did as he was told. A huge cannonball was lifted into place and shoved down the muzzle. Then Hastings touched the match. The cannon roared. Hastings turned to the corporal commanding the crew. "Don't touch that elevation again. That shot was true or I don't know my business."

The crew at the number four gun, terrified by Hastings' action at gun number five, was loading. Stephen saw number four's powder man about to drop his cartridges into the muzzle; the sponge was on the floor, untouched. He yelled and threw himself against the man nearest him, knocking him

331

to the floor behind the protection of the carriage of his own gun. All Stephen felt was a searing heat on his face and hands.

The explosion momentarily silenced all the guns. The overheated fourth gun had blown to pieces, sending metal flying in the enclosed battery. Pomeroy, who had been working on guns at the far end of the battery, raced to the blood-soaked form of Lieutenant Hastings. All four of his limbs had literally been torn from his body by the explosion, and his trunk was riddled with pieces of metal. The whole crew of number four had also been killed.

Stephen rose slowly to his feet. His face and hands hurt, but as he looked over his body, he was happy to see that he had no wounds. Kip sat on the floor next to his gun, blood streaming down his arm from an ugly wound in his shoulder. Stephen rushed to his side and started to lift him.

"Where the hell are you taking me?" Kip yelled.

"Down to the surgeon in the kitchen," said Stephen.

"You mean the butcher in the kitchen. He doesn't put his knife on Israel Kip. Did you ever hear of a one-armed fur trapper?" Stephen had his arm around Israel's chest when he fainted. He dragged Kip into the kitchen.

Seven forms lay stretched out on the floor of the kitchen already, including the lifeless form of the lieutenant. On the kitchen table, held down by four surgeon's assistants, lay one of Stephen's own crew. He was naked and Stephen could see that his leg was smashed, a piece of bone sticking grotesquely from his shin. One of the assistants was pouring a bottle of rum down the crewman's throat. He could not handle the flow and was gagging, forcing the rum out the side of his mouth. The surgeon, a red-faced, foul-smelling barber from Kittery, Maine, was placing his knives and his saw beside the body of the naked gunner. "I'll have to take that leg off," he said in a bored tone.

The gunner started to struggle. He looked over wild-eyed and saw Stephen standing holding on to Kip. "Ensign," he screamed, "don't let him cut me."

Stephen looked at the surgeon. "Can't you save the leg?" he asked.

"No, I can't, unless you want him to die," said the surgeon. "Now get the hell out of here and don't try to tell me how to do my business. What's wrong with him?" he asked, finally deciding to take notice of Kip.

"Shoulder wound," said Stephen.

"Let me look at it."

Stephen let Kip slide down to the floor of the kitchen. The surgeon bent over the sergeant's chest and probed the wound with his finger. "This one is lucky," he said finally. "No broken bones, just a clean wound with a little piece of gun I can take out. He'll be up and about in no time." He took a knife and a probe from his pocket and wiped them off on his coat. "May as well take care of this one while he is out cold. At least he won't do any squirming on me. I want to get the other one a lot drunker before I work on him."

Stephen shut his eyes as the probe went into the wound.

The surgeon fished around for a moment. "There it is," he mumbled to himself. He took a scissorlike instrument and inserted it. Again he probed and finally yanked. He dropped a piece of the number four cannon into his palm. "If I got it all, he should be good as ever. Now for you," he said to Stephen.

"What do you mean, me?" said Stephen.

"Well, for one thing, your face has been burned. You ain't got no eyebrows or eyelashes, and most of your hair is singed. I'll put some grease on your face." He walked over to his cabinet and pulled down a large jar. He smeared grease on Stephen's tender skin. Rather sheepishly, Stephen held out his burned hands for some further medication.

"I've got to get back to my gun," said Stephen.

"If you're up to it," said the surgeon. "Leave your friend here for now, but come back for him tonight. He'll sleep better among his friends. There won't be much sleeping in here tonight."

Stephen stayed with Kip for some minutes, trying to make him comfortable. Finally he stood up and reclimbed the few stairs from the kitchen to the battery. Behind him the low moan of his crewman grew into an inhuman wail as the surgeon began his grisly business. Stephen clapped his sore hands over his ears, but soon the scream was drowned out by the roar of the guns. The fifth gun scored hit after direct hit on the Circular Battery, aimed by a dead man's hand.

The guns of the Grand Battery continued to fire over the next three days without further mishap. Kip survived his wound. No fever set in and he was evacuated to the main camp to recover. On the third day William Vaughan returned to the Grand Battery.

He entered the fort through the rear entry, but as soon as he was recognized his rangers began to gather about him and shake his hand. He smiled broadly and grasped each hand thrust at him. "Thank you," he said again and again, "but

333

back to your work, men. Can't give the Frenchies any respite. Keep those guns firing." He worked his way over to where Stephen was standing. "Infernally hot in this place," he said to his ensign.

"Good to see you again, Colonel."

"Thank you, lad. I've come to rescue you from this hell."

"Rescue?"

"I'm finally back in Pepperrell's good graces. Your work here has just about silenced the Circular Battery, and now the only thing standing between Louisbourg and the Royal Navy is the island. Now Pepperrell remembers my report about the lighthouse. I'm ordered to establish a new battery on the point to neutralize the island and allow Warren into the harbor with his ships. I want you and twenty volunteers, preferably men who have learned something about firing big guns these last few days."

Pomeroy was not happy about losing twenty men but he put no obstacle in the way. Within the hour Stephen and the twenty eager rangers had joined Vaughan on the long trek to the lighthouse.

In the days that followed, Stephen felt as if he were repeating the experiences of the Grand Battery. First the brass cannon had to be located in the sand and mud flats on the beach below the lighthouse. Then they had to be dug up and hauled by rope and pulley up to the bluffs above the beach. The brass cannon were considerably smaller than the great guns of the Grand Battery, and the work of hauling them was carried out at night to avoid small arms fire from the Island Battery across the channel. The nights were cool and the work seemed to go faster. Once the guns were hauled to the bluffs, they had to be placed in carriages and positioned in emplacements dug into the stony soil of the point.

The firing from the hills west of the town continued every day, and the heavy guns of the Grand Battery had smashed the harbor defenses. Now they poured heavy cannon fire into the town itself. At night, while working on the beaches, Stephen and his men could see the southern sky aglow beyond the island, lit by the flames of burning buildings in the town.

Israel Kip arrived at the lighthouse almost two weeks after the explosion in the Grand Battery. Stephen was sleeping in his blanket after a night shift on the beach. The men in the camp rushed to greet him, as did those who were digging the gun emplacements. Most officers would have driven the men back to work, but Vaughan merely smiled at the scene in the camp. Privates who were overjoyed at the return of a wounded sergeant were indications of excellent morale.

Stephen was awakened by the cheers of the men and sat up on his blanket. Kip, his arm in a sling and the heavy chest bandages bulging underneath his shirt, walked to where Stephen sat. Stephen stood up to greet his friend and in deference to his wound took his left hand and clapped him lightly on the left shoulder. Kip dropped his backpack on the ground, unfastened one tie and reached in, withdrawing a quart bottle of rum. He handed it to one of the rangers. "This is for you, men," he said, "but wait until the end of your work shift before you try any of it. I don't want Willy Vaughan down on my back before I'm in camp for less than ten minutes." The rangers laughed and followed the one with the bottle back to the digging. Kip reached into his pack again after the others had left and pulled out a second bottle. "This one is for you and me, Stephen," he said.

"I've missed you, Israel. How are you feeling?" Stephen asked.

"Fine, just so long as I keep away from the doctors. That's the reason I returned to duty so soon. Some dumb arsehole wanted to bleed me. Said it would make me feel a lot better. But it seems to me that if I lost a lot of blood from this here hole in my shoulder and losing that blood made me weak, then taking more blood from me is going to make me even weaker. But do you think I could convince those doctors at the camp hospital of that? They told me I was mad. One of them said I was nothing but a layman and that I had no business challenging one of the basic principles of medicine. So it was either the house for loonies, getting bled or coming back to fight. So here I be. How did you lose your hair?"

Stephen's hand rose to his forehead. He had almost forgotten about the burns he had received. He knew that the skin had peeled from his hands and face, and he presumed that the new skin on his face was as red and tender-looking as the skin on the backs of his hands.

"Same way you got that," he said, pointing to Kip's shoulder.

"But you didn't get that scar on your forehead in that blast. That's a lot older. Funny I never really noticed it before. Your hair used to hang down over it."

Stephen touched the scar. "Got that from the Indians when I was a baby and my father was killed."

335

Their conversation was interrupted by the distant roar of Pepperwell's cannons firing on the town.

"How is the fighting going back there?" asked Stephen.

"They're knocking the hell out of the walls. Big holes is opening up at the gate. You could drive a team of horses through some of them. Pepperrell wants to march in right now and take the place, but that relative of yours—that Pierce fella—keeps making trouble for him."

"What's he doing?" asked Stephen, angry at even the mention of Daniel Pierce's name.

"They had a meeting of the officers last night. Word came back to us that a majority of them had agreed at the council to try to breach the walls tonight. Pierce didn't like that at all. He insisted that it should be a joint attack with the navy. Said too many good men would be killed rushing into the fort without the navy blasting away at the town from the harbor."

"But the navy can't get into the harbor until we eliminate that island down there."

"That's what Pepperrell kept saying."

"So are they attacking?" asked Stephen.

"Nope. Even though the officers voted to attack, Pierce came out of the meeting and began to spread the word that Pepperrell was planning to get everybody killed. Pierce's own company—that bunch of Boston scum—voted and decided not to attack no matter what the general said. Then Pierce's company sent out representatives to all the other Massachusetts companies, explaining things all their own way. Soon the whole army was buzzing with talk about not attacking and waiting for the navy. Just before I left to come here, word was around that the officers had had another of them councils and this time they voted not to attack, being as none of them would have any men following them into battle. It's a hell of a way to run an army, Stephen. God help Americans if they ever had to fight a real war on their own—without the Royal Navy present to pick up the pieces, that is. They clean out the jails and the saloons to put their army together. No sense of discipline."

Kip pulled the cork from the rum bottle with his teeth and offered the bottle to his friend. Stephen took a swig and passed the bottle back. A messenger from the colonel arrived, summoning the two men to Vaughan's tent.

"Good to see you back, Sergeant," said Vaughan. "You couldn't have picked a better time to return. I've been summoned to a council of war aboard the *Launceston* and I want Graham and Nowell with me. You'll be in charge here while we are gone."

"Whatever you say, Colonel," Kip said, flopping into Vaughan's chair just as soon as the colonel vacated it.

Vaughan looked back at him in amusement as he and Stephen walked past the lighthouse and down the path that led to the small landing beach on the ocean side of the lighthouse peninsula, where they were to meet Lieutenant Graham.

"What do you make of this call from the navy?" Stephen asked.

"The word that comes to mind is impatience," said Vaughan. "This is all taking too long to suit the Commodore."

Stephen reported Kip's story of the canceling of that night's planned attack.

"That's what it will be about, Stephen, my boy. Warren must be seeing red."

Vaughan was correct. When they arrived in the wardroom of the *Launceston*, the whole senior officer corps of the volunteer army was already present. Pepperrell was seated at the wardroom table.

Warren stormed about the room yelling, "What kind of farce are you running here, gentlemen? You take votes on whether or not you will attack. You allow the common soldiers to have the final say. Do you think the rabble likes to get killed? You must have discipline. They must be more afraid of you than they are of the enemy. I'm not going to wait for your rabble to do this job for me, Pepperrell. You're to get me into that harbor. I won't ask any more than that from you and your scum."

Pepperrell's face went white. "I resent your remarks, sir."

"I don't give a good God damn for your resentment, you pompous ass of a merchant. Just get me the hell into that harbor."

Pepperrell gained control of his anger. "Commodore," he said softly, "we both have the same objective—the King's service and the capture of this fortress. My men are not professional soldiers and we have a tradition of democracy in our militia structure. We listen to our men and we allow them to elect their officers. Despite this, however, we have not done all that badly thus far."

Warren stopped pacing and turned to look at the general. He said nothing but his anger seemed to cool.

Pepperrell noticed Vaughan standing by the doorway with the other latecomers. "Colonel Vaughan," said the general, "Commodore Warren wants to get into Louisbourg harbor. How long before your work will open the door for him?"

Vaughan stepped forward. "General, my men are working in double shifts as it is now. I will have my guns in place by the end of the week."

"Be more precise, Colonel," interrupted Warren.

"I will commence firing on the Island Battery, sir, at midnight Saturday," responded Vaughan angrily.

"Too long," said the commodore, banging his fist on the table. "It will take another week to silence the battery. I'm not prepared to sit out here sailing back and forth for two more weeks." He turned to Pepperrell. "You will have to do better than that, General."

"Perhaps I can be of assistance," said a voice from the opposite side of the wardroom. Stephen could not see who spoke but he recognized the voice. Several officers stepped aside to allow Daniel Pierce to come forward.

Warren looked at Pierce. He did not seem to remember their last encounter. Militia captains were not important people in the world of a flag officer of the Royal Navy.

"I have an alternative plan to suggest," said Pierce as he reached the table. "There is a landing beach on the island. I'm told it is wide enough for about three or four long-boats to land at one time. I'm willing, sir, and beg the privilege of you, General, to lead a volunteer force to attack the Island Battery—tomorrow night."

Pepperrell looked at Pierce strangely. It was clear to all the army officers that the two men had grown to despise each other. Pepperrell could not forgive Pierce's undermining his authority in the army.

But Warren's reaction was very different. "Now that's more like it," he said. "We've been getting nightly fogs and there is no moon tomorrow night. Perfect time for a surprise landing and attack. Captain? . . ."

"Captain Pierce, sir."

"Captain Pierce, you take the island tomorrow night and the next day I will sail into the harbor and fire broadsides from ten line-of-battle ships into the town. I'll be damned if the French don't quit that very day."

"Commodore," said Pepperrell. "It will not be as easy as you make it out to be. The fog and lack of moon can work against us as well as for us. My men won't be able to see where they are going."

338

"Nonsense. I'll give you longboats and the finest helmsmen anywhere in the world. My men will get you there, but it will be up to you after we land you."

Pepperrell was boxed in. He had to go along. But he did not have to trust a man he detested. "Very well, Commodore," said Pepperrell finally. "We will attack the island tomorrow night. I would prefer Colonel Vaughan to lead the attack, however."

Warren looked shocked. "That is clearly your decision, sir," he said. "But if you will excuse my intrusion, it seems unfair to Pierce here. It is his plan, and I like the way he had the gumption to stand up and suggest it." Several of the army officers murmured agreement with the commodore.

Major Pomeroy interrupted. "I've been working with Vaughan's rangers these past few weeks. If any group of men can get the job done, it's these New Hampshire men."

"My Massachusetts volunteers can do the job better than any New Hampshire men," returned Pierce. It was a master stroke; by turning the debate into a Massachusetts versus New Hampshire one, he guaranteed himself victory. Soon all of the Massachusetts officers, even those who are suspicious of Daniel Pierce's motives, began to clamor for a Massachusetts officer to lead them—and by a Massachusetts officer they meant Daniel Pierce.

Pepperrell capitulated.

"It's settled then," said Warren, somewhat incredulous at this decision-making by majority opinion. "Pierce, I wish you luck." The commodore turned and left the wardroom.

Vaughan motioned Stephen to follow him as he walked over to Pepperrell's side. "Willy," said the general, "I don't like the way things are going, and I don't trust Pierce. More than that . . ." He was about to say more but hesitated.

"Neither do I, sir," said Vaughan.

"It's a waste—a diversion. Our objective should be the town itself."

"Is there no avoiding it, General?" asked Vaughan.

"No," said Pepperrell. Suddenly he seemed to come back to life again. "Willy, I want as many of your rangers as possible in that attack. Maybe I can't keep Pierce out of this thing, but I can guarantee that he will be surrounded by capable men."

"I'll volunteer, sir," said Stephen. "Captain Pierce and I don't exactly get along and I'm not sure I would like taking orders from him, but I think I could bring a fairly large force of rangers over to the island with me."

"Thank you, Mr. Nowell," said the General. "I'll remember that offer. Well, let's hope that tomorrow night goes well. I don't feel good about it but my premonitions are usually worthless. William, try to speed up the preparation of your guns."

Great waves of gray fog crept onto Isle Royale shortly after the sun set behind the Grand Battery. Under cover of the fog, the longboats, which had been rowed to the lighthouse the night before, were brought down to the waterline.

Stephen led his contingent of thirty-five rangers, including Israel and Socono, to the beach. Most of them had been released by Seth Pomeroy from the Grand Battery. Vaughan would need all of his men to mount his cannon on the new batteries at the lighthouse.

Stephen had not seen Socono for days, but he had shown up at the point in the morning. He seemed to sense danger and Stephen's involvement in it. When Stephen needed him, Socono was there. As for Kip, with only one good arm, it seemed foolish of the sergeant to volunteer. But he was determined to come and Stephen felt he could use his experience.

Pierce's men arrived with the fog. Most of them had been pulled off the docks of Boston—unemployed sailors or men released from the city and county jails in return for service in the colonial army. To lighten the burden of marching around the harbor from the main camp, Pierce had ordered a ration of rum for each man. They were noisy and laughing when they descended the path to the beach.

Pierce led the line down the slope and was the first to arrive on the beach. When he got close enough to see Stephen and Socono, he stopped. Stephen had expected Pierce to protest his presence, but instead Pierce took out his anger on Socono. "Who the hell's idea was it to take a heathen Indian along with us?" he said harshly, waving his hand in disgust. "Oh, well, what does it matter. You goddamn rangers are no better than heathens yourselves." He turned and walked farther down the beach.

"What do we do about that?" Stephen asked Kip, who stood beside him.

"We could shoot him. Or we could shoot the Indian. Or we could just ignore him. I suggest that we pay him no mind. Let's load the men into the boats and get the hell over to the island."

"Done," said Stephen. In Abenacki he told Socono to get into the first boat. The rangers were aboard within seconds and were manning their oars, which had been wrapped in cloth to cut down on noise. Many of the rangers had no experience as oarsmen, and their erratic rowing made the helmsman's task impossible.

"You goddamn arseholes are going to have to pull together," he said. "At my count, pull . . . , again, pull. . . . Hey, you, Indian, grab ahold of the oar."

Socono ignored him and continued to sit upright in the boat without touching the oar in front of him.

The helmsman cursed again. Stephen turned around and whispered to him, "He doesn't understand you. We'll make it to the island without his help."

"What a crew," the helmsman muttered and turned the boat toward the island.

The fog completely enveloped them. They had only gone a few feet from the shore, and already the beach was hidden. The black water of the harbor reflected nothing. The fog suppressed all light. Stephen shivered as he pulled on his oar. Hard work could not drive out the chilling effect of the fog, nor could it drive the misgivings from his mind.

With brief instructions from the helm, the rangers made steady progress back into the channel and across toward the landing beach. The only sounds were the soft lapping of the waves against the sides of the boat and the steady swish of the covered oars in the water. Kip, rowing with his one good arm, sat next to Stephen. Suddenly Kip lost his grip and the oar slipped from the oarlock. It was forced backward by the motion of the boat into the oar immediately behind. So silent was the night that the bump of oar against oar seemed to Stephen like the crack of a musket shot. He cursed silently to himself and pushed forward with all his strength to steady the oar and lift it back into place.

"Christ, you bastards are clumsy," whispered the helmsman. "You'll awake up every Frenchie this side of Paris."

The oar steadied and fell into place. Stephen breathed easier. The steady rowing continued. Soon Stephen could hear the sound of surf breaking against sand and rocks. With uncanny accuracy the helmsman had brought them to the narrow landing beach of the Island Battery. Two more strokes and the boat's bottom scraped softly against the sand of the beach.

Stephen and his crew leapt over the sides into waist-deep water. Some of the rangers slipped and fell in the surf, but soon all were on their feet and wading into shore. The battery was about one hundred yards directly ahead of them. No high vegetation had been allowed to stand in the way of the line of fire across the channel. There were no places to hide except behind the boulders that were strewn across the island. Stephen realized that, but for the combination of darkness and fog, they would be totally exposed to fire from the battery. He ordered his men to fan out and keep low. Nothing could be done until the rest of the boats landed their crews.

The next two boats were also filled with rangers. They made it safely and quietly to shore and joined Stephen's crew, lying flat on their bellies behind rocks or in the natural depressions in the landscape. They inched their way forward toward the island fortress. Stephen touched the shoulders of several rangers and signaled them to move off to his left. Several others were sent to the right, fanning out to confront the entire face of the battery. They were only fifty yards from the battery embrasures. Stephen longed to call out and check the position of the men, but he dared not. Any loud noise would give their presence away. He knew that Kip was immediately behind him. "Kip," he whispered. A hand touched his foot in response. "Crawl back to the beach and wait for Pierce's men. When they land, bring them up forward to me. Once we have all our men in place at this distance from the battery, we can make a rush for it. We can enter through the embrasures."

"That's running into the direct fire of some mighty heavy metal," responded Kip.

"It's the only way, I would not trust any suggestion from Pierce."

Kip slipped away.

Stephen lay quietly, afraid almost to move a muscle. He could hear Socono's heavy breathing next to him.

"This is a stupid way to fight a war, little brother," said the Indian. "I do not believe that the French are asleep. The toothless one worked for the man you call Pierce, and the toothless one was on his way here to warn the French of our coming when I caught up with him. I am sure this man Pierce also works for the French."

More and more men were creeping into the front line, volunteers as well as rangers. A breeze stirred the beach grass all around them and the fog began to move off. Suddenly Socono grabbed Stephen's arm. "We had best leave here, little brother." He shoved his hand in front of Stephen's face and pointed toward the far corner of the battery ahead. There was a faint light inside the embrasure on the far left. Then Stephen noticed a second light at the next embrasure.

"Good God," he said. "There's a light in each embrasure—a slow match for each gun." He started to crawl backward, whispering to Socono, "I've got to get the word out. It's a trap. The French are waiting for us."

He crawled to the man to his left. "Don't make any noise," he said. "Start back to the beach. Spread the word. Retreat." Then he crawled off to his right, spreading the same message.

The dark forms of men started to creep backward toward the beach. The man to Stephen's right cursed when his neighbor stepped on his hand. The men froze and listened for any reaction from the battery. There was none. Again the men moved backward. Stephen and Socono arrived at a depression, but they got no farther. From the beach twenty-five yards to his rear Stephen heard the unmistakable voice of his uncle. "We've made it, boys," Pierce shouted, "we've made it. Three cheers for Massachusetts."

There were some yells and shouts, but they were quickly drowned out by the roar of twenty heavy cannons loaded with grape and chain shot. There was nothing Stephen could do but lie face-down in the dirt, praying that the depression was shelter enough. The roar of the cannon was terrifying. When it subsided during reloading periods, small arms fire took up the slack.

Again the cannons roared. The blast seemed to sear the very air surrounding Stephen. He wondered why he was out of breath and then he realized he had been shouting, shouting for the guns to stop. He started to stand; he had to fight back. Socono threw him down again before his head rose above the top of the protective ridge.

"Lie still," he shouted. "The guns fire over our heads. They will not touch us. They kill the men on the beach."

Stephen collapsed. The guns roared again, but this time not together. They kept up a staggered and almost continuous fire for the next thirty minutes. Finally they stopped. Only musket fire continued, all of it from the battery. As far as Stephen was able to determine, no shots had been fired at the battery. If their failure to return any fire kept the cannons silent, Stephen was content to leave it that way.

They remained hidden behind the ridge until morning. When the sun rose, French soldiers left the battery and, with muskets at the ready, began to search the rocks and the landing beach. They found Stephen and Socono where they had lain the whole night, along with fifty other soldiers, ten of them dead. They all surrendered without a fight. Daniel Pierce and the longboats were long gone and there was no sense in resisting.

The commander of the Island Battery was Lieutenant Bertier. He did not recognize Stephen among the men who were rounded up for him to address in his very broken English. The last time Bertier had seen Stephen, he had had a beard; Stephen's very short hair and burned face aided his disguise. When asked his name Stephen gave a false one without any indication of rank. He did not wish to be identified as an officer and then be segregated from the other prisoners.

Just as Bertier completed his address and a large pot of gruel was brought to feed the prisoners, a dirty and bloodied Israel Kip was led into the battery. He joined the rest of the prisoners in the food line. Stephen walked over to him. "God, I'm glad you survived that," he said.

"So am I, my boy, so am I," said Israel. "I almost got away. If I had had two good arms, I would have. How I survived the cannon blasts I don't know. Just wasn't my time, I guess. Pierce and the others never left the boats, you know. Gave their God damn cheer in the boats offshore. Turned right around and rowed away. This dumb wound of mine opened again and I was bleeding some. If I could have swum, I would have made it to the boats. I got into some kelp beds and thought I would hide there until tonight. But as you can see, they found me."

"Pierce betrayed us," said Stephen. "The French had been warned in advance and they were waiting for us when we got ashore. He and the scout Wiggins were in on this from the beginning. Wiggins was in the fur trade and so is Pierce. Vaughan suspected them both."

Kip whistled. "The French must have promised them plenty to get them to take a chance on hanging for treason."

Stephen agreed. "They must also be fairly desperate," said Stephen. "I think Pierce sees Warren as the key to the siege. Pierce hopes that our failure last night will discourage Warren."

"You may be right, boy, but there is very little you're going to be able to do about it for a while."

"I'm determined to escape as soon as we set foot in

Louisbourg," said Stephen. "I've some old problems to set right and then we'll see what we can do about Daniel Pierce."

A French soldier, walking down the food line, told Stephen to shut up or he would fix it so that he could not talk. Stephen took the bowl of gruel over to the corner, where Socono sat on the floor. Kip dropped to the ground next to Stephen. "Christ, this paste tastes like garbage," he said.

"Big Bastard, no eat garbage then," said Socono in his own English style. Kip started to laugh. Every time he heard Socono speak English he laughed. Again the sentry told them to be quiet. As soon as he turned to walk away, Kip gestured obscenely behind his back.

Stephen began to speak quietly in Abenacki with Socono. "As soon as we land in the town, Socono, be ready for the signal. We should be fairly heavily guarded, but they will let down their guard somewhere, and when they do we will break for it."

"I will follow where you lead," said the Indian.

"We will take Kip with us."

The Indian smiled. "That will be good. I like Big Bastard." He said the last two words in English.

Once their skimpy meal was finished, they were herded down to the landing beach, now cleared of last night's dead and wounded, where three boats flying the white flag of truce were ready. Bertier placed two armed guards in each boat and told the prisoners to row themselves to Louisbourg. "If *les Bastonois* shoot at these *bateaux*, it is not a fault of mine," he said in his peculiar English. "Notice has been given and you fly the white flag."

The prisoners climbed into the boats and took up the oars. A French helmsman steered each, and the guard watched every move the prisoners made. The channel surf was calm and soon the boats were in the middle, pulling slowly around the island into the harbor. Behind him Stephen could see the lighthouse, where Vaughan and his friends would now be working harder than ever to offset the disaster of the night attack. Across the harbor stood the Grand Battery, her guns now silent. The helmsman steered them toward the harbor walls of the town. After almost thirty minutes of rowing against an ebbing tide, they approached the town. Stephen could see the Circular Battery—or what was left of it. It was almost completely in ruins. Stephen remembered when, as a boy, he had thought the walls were impregnable. The boat bumped against the wharf and they were ordered to get out. A small band of soldiers stood on the wharf to act as their guards as they were marched through the town to their jail cells.

They passed through the harbor gate into the town. Stephen saw no civilians and he was appalled by the damage.

"The guns haven't left much standing, have they?" whispered Kip, marching behind him.

"To the left—this way," ordered the corporal of the guard, and they were led toward the market building where Stephen had once picked up old Savard's bread for the nuns and priests. He turned around and started to walk backward, staring at the Jesuit house, which stood almost untouched down the street from him.

The corporal started to yell at Stephen to turn around, but before he could finish his sentence, his words were drowned out by the roar of guns and the crash of cannonballs off to the west. The corporal looked nervously toward the Grand Battery and told his prisoners to hurry along. Since among them only Stephen and Socono spoke French, it did very little good.

Again came the roar of cannon—but this time the balls came from the Grand Battery and struck into the market square. Pandemonium reigned. People came streaming out of their houses and ran for the shelter of the market house, which had a deep storage cellar. Several of the guards dropped to the ground as a ball struck the house to the left of the market and sent masonry flying in all directions. Everyone was screaming. The corporal attempted to force one of the fallen men to his feet by hitting him in the buttocks with the butt end of his musket, but to no avail.

Stephen moved quickly. He grabbed the corporal by the neck and swung him around. Socono was waiting for him and brought his knee swiftly into the corporal's groin. His scream was cut off by the crash of cannon shot falling in the streets. Several prisoners, seeing what Stephen and Socono had accomplished, began to run off in different directions. Stephen grabbed the fallen corporal's musket and raced back in the direction from which they had come, toward the house of the Society of Jesus. Socono signaled to Kip to follow and they soon caught up. Stephen stopped when he came to the kitchen door. He pushed. It swung open and the three fugitives stepped inside.

The smell of cooking greeted them. For Stephen it was like stepping back in time. Huddled before the stove was the form

346

of a much older Brother Richard. Stephen called to him in French.

"Who is that?" said the old man. "Speak up. I can't see too well any more."

"It's me, Etienne."

The old man dropped the spoon he had been stirring with into the soup pot and turned around. He walked over to Stephen and looked into his face. "You've changed, boy," he said finally. "But it's you. There's the scar." He walked over to Socono. "But you've not changed. Do you still say the prayers Father LaGarde taught you?" He did not wait for an answer but went right on to Kip. "And you—who are you?"

"A friend," said Stephen. "Tell me, Brother, what happened to Karl Stiegler? Where is he?"

The brother was silent for several moments. Stephen thought that perhaps he had not heard the question and was about to ask again when the old man finally spoke. "I don't think I'm allowed to tell you that."

"Did he go with LaGarde when he was recalled?" asked Stephen.

Again silence. The old man started to speak, struggled with himself and fell silent.

"Please, Richard," said Stephen. "I must find Karl and help him. Please tell me."

"You know, Etienne, all my life I have lived by the rules and by my vows. You know I have a vow of obedience and you know that I would die rather than break it."

"I know that, Brother."

"You know also," he continued, "that I have lived all my life with the consolation that my religious superior spoke with the voice of God."

Stephen was in despair. Perhaps he should begin a search of the house. But then Brother Richard surprised him. "God could not command what is going on in this house," he said. "Lalonde is not the voice of God. The evil he does is not God's work. The boy, Karl, was never a good boy like you, Etienne, but he does not deserve to suffer so. Father LaGarde took care of Karl; he nursed him back to health. But before he was fully recovered LaGarde had to go, and Lalonde took over this house. He put Karl into the basement, chained him to the wall. He goes down there often. I can't stand it any more."

"Karl is here? In the basement?"

347

The old man nodded.

Stephen started to rush to the basement door. "It's locked," said the brother.

"Where's the key?" Stephen yelled. Brother Richard reached into his habit pocket and drew out a large iron key.

Stephen grabbed it and raced out of the kitchen, with Socono and Kip following. Stephen fumbled at the latch but finally the key slipped into the hole and the lock snapped open. The cellar was dark, with only a ray of light streaming in from the tiny window to his right. It took a few moments for Stephen's eyes to adjust to the darkness, but even before they did, a low moan to his left drew him to what he was looking for.

Karl was hanging by chains from the wall. He was naked and his entire body was burned and bruised. His once-muscular frame had been worn and starved away. The ground at his feet was covered with dried excrement. The stench in the room was awful.

"Sweet Jesus," said Kip. "I don't believe that one man could do this to another."

Socono said nothing. He walked up to Karl and placed his ear against his chest. "He lives," he said to Stephen.

Stephen stood frozen in place, stunned. "Can we cut him down?" he asked.

Kip reached up and felt the hooks to which the chains were attached. "These hooks are nailed into the beams. I can pry them out but I'm afraid of hurting your friend."

"I don't think we could hurt him any more than he has already been hurt," said Stephen. "Wait, I'll pull out the other one."

Both men twisted and pushed the hooks, then slowly pulled them from the giant wooden beam above their heads. Kip's came out first. As Karl started to fall foward, Socono caught him. When Stephen's hook came free, the Indian carried Karl in his arms over to the stairway and laid him gently on a cleaner section of the floor.

"Let's try to get him upstairs into the kitchen," said Stephen.

"Is the old cook reliable?" asked Kip.

Stephen didn't know for sure, but he nodded.

"Doesn't say much, does he?"

"You're lucky we didn't come during Great Silence. We would have had to wait till tomorrow to find out about this," Stephen said with some bitterness.

They carried Karl up into the kitchen and laid him down on the table. Stephen turned to Brother Richard. "Where's Lalonde?" he asked.

"At your service," said a familiar voice from the doorway leading to the refectory. Lalonde stood just inside the doorway, holding a pistol in either hand. Beside him was the enormous hulk of a man whom Stephen recognized as François, the chief jailer in the citadel. "Drop your musket, Etienne. I really don't want to kill you, not when you can provide me with far greater entertainment than this dull lout." He pointed with one of the pistols to Karl's unconcious form. "Thank you for calling me into your kitchen, Brother Richard."

The old man looked at Stephen. "I couldn't help it," he said. "Holy obedience—I can't disobey. My vows." He started to weep.

"You're insane, Lalonde," said Stephen.

"I'm the martyr," Lalonde shouted at Stephen. "Do you know what those red devils did to me because of you, you filthy swine? I've prayed for the opportunity to get even with you. I had you in my trap and that fool, LaGarde, let you escape. All I had to play with was this dumb lummox. I thought I would have to remain content with hurting you only through your friend. Now I see that God has answered my prayers. My patience has not been in vain. I will make you suffer."

Neither Lalonde nor François saw Socono's hand move ever so slowly toward the pot of soup that sat on the stove. In one swift action he grasped the ladle and hurled its hot contents in Lalonde's face. The Jesuit screamed in pain. One of his pistols fired harmlessly into the ceiling; the other fell from his hand. Socono leaped at François, knocking his musket from his hand. The huge Frenchmen grabbed the Indian by the throat and, lifting him off the ground, raised him high over his head as if to hurl him aside like some rag doll. Kip reached for the pistol on the floor with his good hand. He raised it, aimed and fired. François stood dumbfounded, staring at the hole in his chest. Like some great bull in the slaughterhouse he crumbled, first at the knees and then the waist. He fell forward, letting go of his grip on Socono. Stephen picked up François' musket and pointed it at the temporarily blinded priest.

"Pull the damn trigger," Lalonde screamed at him from behind his hands, which covered his scalded face. "Kill me."

Stephen wanted to. He looked over at Socono, who nodded to him to pull the trigger. But he lowered the gun. "You can live with what you've done. That will be my revenge on you, Lalonde," he said softly.

The priest turned to flee, but Socono grabbed him, tearing his habit sleeve in the process. Kip took the musket from Stephen. Stephen picked Karl up in his arms and with Lalonde, under guard, in the lead, they walked into the Jesuit refectory, to the amazement of the fathers and brothers, who sat awaiting Richard's stew. Stephen carried Karl into what had been his own room in the brother's section of the house and placed Karl in his bed.

The soldier's eyes opened when Stephen placed his head on the pillow. "Stefan, is that you?" he whispered through his cracked lips. "I'm sorry I told them where to find you. I couldn't take the pain."

"It's me, Karl," said Stephen. "You're safe now. I've come back." Karl turned his head away and fell asleep.

Stephen left Socono to keep guard on the terrified Jesuits, while he led Lalonde, covered by Kip's musket, into the porter's lodge in the front of the house. Stephen forced him to sit in the porter's chair.

"Now what do we do?" Kip asked Stephen.

"Now we wait," said Stephen. "We wait for Pepperrell's guns and Willy Vaughan's guns to turn this place into a pile of rubble and set us all free."

Socono locked all of the Jesuits in the refectory for the night and then he, Kip and Stephen took turns standing watch in the porter's lodge. The guns pounded away at the fort and the town throughout the night. Twice the house was hit on the upper floor by cannonballs. Had they not been locked in the downstairs section, some of the priests would surely have been injured.

The firing continued throughout the morning also. Stephen ordered Brother Richard to prepare a meal for all the house. The brother obeyed him as if he were the new superior. Richard also placed some salve on Lalonde's face. Captors and captives alike sat down together to eat breakfast.

Kip, who had been standing guard in the porter's lodge, came running into the refectory. "Stephen, come with me," he shouted. Stephen rose from the table quickly and ran after Kip, toward the front door. "There's a force of French soldiers coming down the street, headed this way. They're stopping at every house for a few moments. It must be a search."

Stephen stared hard at the officer who led the marching soldiers. He recognized him instantly. It was Captain Duvivier. "They're from the citadel. Looks like the governor's guard," he said.

"They'll be here in a minute. Do we fight them?" asked Kip.

"What for?" said Stephen. "I've done everything I came here for. I don't think they will hurt Karl any more. He may be listed as a deserter, but it is clear he was held against his will in this house. Duvivier is a fair man. I don't want anyone else killed. If we surrender to the French, it will only be a matter of time before they turn themselves over to us."

The guard was now immediately in front of the door. Duvivier pulled on the bell. Stephen opened the door wide. The captain's eyes opened wide with surprise when he saw him. "Welcome, Captain," said Stephen.

Lalonde came rushing out of the refectory with Socono in hot pursuit. "Captain, these are English spies. Shoot them; arrest them," shouted the Jesuit.

"I don't think I am in a position to do that," responded Duvivier. "I have just come to inform all the residents of the town that the Island Battery was evacuated last night under heavy fire from the lighthouse. Governor Duchambon has just asked the English general for terms. This fortress is to be surrendered today."

Lalonde grabbed for one of the soldier's muskets, but Duvivier was too quick for him. He knocked the musket to the ground with his sword. "There are enough dead already, Reverend Father," he said with a sneer. "Let us have no more."

Lalonde stared at the group of men about him and then he turned and ran down the street away from the Jesuit house, his black cape trailing behind him.

Socono made a move to follow the priest, but Stephen checked him. "Let him go," he said to the Indian. "He is to be pitied rather than punished."

The firing from the lighthouse and the Grand Battery had ceased and all was suddenly very quiet. "It's over," said Duvivier to Stephen. "Soon it will be over for all of New France. Your next conquest will be Quebec. Then it will be Montreal and the west." His grief over the loss of France's New World empire was obvious.

"It was always part of the plan to push on," said Stephen.

"If you do," said the captain, "then the empire of North

America belongs to England, and France is forever banished from these shores."

"It will be ours by right of conquest, Captain."

Duvivier smiled. "New France may be dead today, monsieur, but the French people of this country will live on. We are its blood, its sinew and muscle. It is the people—not the flags—who will endure."

Stephen lay stretched out on the bed in his room at the Cromwell's Head. On a cot across the room Karl was snoring. Since their return from Isle Royale, Karl had done nothing but eat and sleep. His recuperation was remarkable. When he stared inquiring about the girls of Boston, Stephen knew his recovery was complete.

There was a soft knock on the door. Stephen rose from his bed to answer it. It was Hannah, bearing a basket of some of her bread and preserves. "There's a black man waiting for you outside," she whispered, not wishing to awaken Karl.

"That will be General Pepperrell's man," said Stephen. He reached for his coat, which lay draped across the couch. "After my meeting this evening," said Stephen, "I'll be coming to visit you and George in Charlestown. Karl tells me that you've invited him for dinner. Am I invited too?" he asked.

Hannah blushed. "Of course, Mr. Stephen. You know you're always welcome in our home."

The black man was not Pepperrell's servant at all but a rather nervous Josiah. "Mr. Nowell, sir," he said to Stephen as he entered the inn's taproom. "It's Mr. William Vaughan. He wants to see you before you go to the governor's reception."

"I thought I was supposed to meet him there," said Stephen.

"No, sir, he said that I was to bring you to his ship, the *Betsy*. He told me to hurry. I hired a carriage. I'll drive you."

Stephen nodded assent. He could tell by Josiah's agitation that something was very wrong. The man drove Stephen through the streets of Boston, which were thronged with celebrants. The governor had declared the day a holiday in honor of the victory, and rich and poor alike had taken to the taverns and the streets.

The slow ride took Stephen through Boston, retracing in reverse the steps he had taken that day when he had first entered the city. They traveled over the hill, past the graveyard and old Cotton Mather, down past the old North Church and across the creek to the south end. The celebration was even more raucous about "Funnel Hall." They turned at the market and passed the red brick State House, where Governor Shirley would be holding court later in the evening. They arrived finally at the *Betsy*'s mooring.

William Vaughan was waiting for Stephen on deck at the top of the gangway. Stephen was shocked by Vaughan's appearance. His clothes were disheveled and he had not shaved. He had always been meticulously neat in the past. Vaughan placed his arm on Stephen's shoulder. Stephen realized instantly that he had been drinking.

"Come with me, Stephen, to my cabin. I've some news for you."

Stephen followed him down the steps that led to the small cabin of the ship, ducking to avoid the timbers above him as he went. Once in the cabin, Vaughan threw himself on the bed and placed his arm over his eyes.

"I've been drinking, my lad," he said finally, "just in case your senses have failed you completely."

Stephen remained silent.

"I suppose you find that shocking, given my past."

Again Stephen said nothing.

Vaughan pulled his arm away and glared at Stephen. "Christ, can't you say something? Your mother would have read me out in purple by now."

"William, I don't feel it's my place to find fault with the one person who has tried to help me with no selfish motives."

Vaughan leaned back again onto the bed. "I'm not being fair to you. I should be much harder on myself. I've failed, Stephen. I've failed you, I've failed myself and I've failed her even more. They don't believe me about Pierce. I've gone to everyone with our story—to Pepperrell, to Warren, to Shirley. They say I have no proof. The locket, the attack on the island, the connection with Wiggins—all of it is . . . how did Shirley put it . . . supposition, unfounded supposition. No one will move against him."

"Do you mean to tell me that my uncle will not be charged?"

"Not be charged? Christ, they plan to reward him. They're giving him a seat on the governor's council. God help us, a French agent on the governor's council—a reward from good King George for a man who works for good King Louis." Vaughan started to chuckle but it was a sour laugh.

"You can't let them do it."

"I can't stop them. What do you think I have been doing all week? No doubt Pierce got wind of what I was doing and worked to offset me. Now that the charge has been made, even if unsuccessfully, he will be wary. At least his career as a French agent is over, but he will never be punished for it—not on this earth."

"We'll see about that," said Stephen as he turned toward the door of the cabin.

"Where are you going, boy?" asked Vaughan.

"I'm going to the governor's reception and I am going to expose that bastard so that all of New England knows what he really is."

"Don't run off yet," said Vaughan, his voice greatly softened. "You won't succeed, but if you must go, then you must go. But first I have something for you. Come over here." He opened his shirt at the neck and removed the gold locket he had worn ever since the day they first met. "This is for you," he said. "It was your mother's and I want you to have something of hers. This is all I have of her."

Stephen hesitated to take it. He knew how deeply Vaughan had loved his mother. Vaughan placed the locket in his hand and closed his fingers over it "Stephen," he said drunkenly, "I loved Sarah Nowell. She is irreplaceable in my life. Since she left me I've tried to fill the void with ambition but it has not worked. I really don't care that we have taken Louisbourg. I don't care if I'm rewarded or if I'm not. I miss her too much and too often. The one consolation I've had has been trying to help you for her sake, and I've grown to love you like my own son." He reached over to the desk and picked up a letter sealed with red wax. "This is my will. It declares that you are my heir. I don't have much—this ship, some fur trade shares and I suspect some land from the crown as a result of our recent venture. I want you to have it when I'm gone. Sarah got all of it for me anyway. I can repay her through you."

Stephen looked at him suspiciously, but Vaughan laughed. "Don't look so glum boy. I'm not planning to croak for some time yet."

Stephen relaxed and smiled at him. "Thank you, sir," he said. "I appreciate knowing that you care about me. I wish more than ever now that I had known my mother, or even could remember her. I admire you, sir, very much. And if she could stir so much love in you then she must have been a remarkable human being."

"That she was, Stephen," said Vaughan. He sat up on the

bed. "Now be off with you. Tell that son of a bitch Shirley what a traitor Pierce is."

"I'll do that with pleasure," said Stephen.

Vaughan lay back down on the bed. Stephen stared at him for some moments. "Will you be all right, sir?" he asked finally.

"I'll be just fine," said Vaughan.

Vaughan waited until he heard Stephen leave the ship. He sat up again on the bed and held his head in his hands. The boy worried him. He had been used so often and he was so gullible. He had none of his mother's quick wit. How would he ever survive in this harsh world? Well, he had done the best he could for him. He went to his sea chest and took another bottle of rum from it. He pulled out the cork with his teeth, spit it out and, throwing back his head, took a long gulp. He staggered toward the door of the cabin and practically fell through it. He yelled at his mate to take the *Betsy* to sea, setting a course for Cape Ann.

William Vaughan spent the night on deck sobering up. The sea was running strong and the spray from the bow of the ship covered the decks with water. On the quarterdeck, very little of the spray reached him, but the breeze and the cool sea air brought an alertness back to his mind that the rum had dulled. He had not had the heart to tell Stephen the final bad news: that everything they had fought for at Louisbourg had also been lost. Someone else—someone far more clever than he was—would have to explain that to all of the Stephens who had fought there. Now his only thoughts were of Sarah. He thought of the night aboard this very ship when they had first made love, and he thought of that other night when she had disappeared from this very deck.

His lookout sighted the white water of the reefs of Cape Ann. Night had taken possession of the sea about him, but the moon illuminated the reef off the port bow. Vaughan recognized it immediately. "There it is," he mumbled. "Where it all should have ended years ago." He still had the bottle of rum in his hand. He raised it toward the night sky. "Sarah, my girl," he toasted, "here's to you."

Seth Pomeroy greeted Stephen as he entered the front door of the State House. He shook Stephen's hand vigorously. They had not seen each other since their return from Louisbourg. "Everyone is here today, Stephen, except Willy Vaughan. Shirley's got them all under one roof—Pepperrell,

Warren, Waldo. Considering how they feel about each other, that may be a greater feat than the capture of Louisbourg."

"Well, Vaughan's not coming," Stephen said with some vehemence.

Before Stephen could explain the reason for Vaughan's absence, a footman greeted them and showed them into the governor's reception hall, which was filled with the officers of the recent expedition. Shirley stood in the center of the room with a glass of wine in his hand. He saw Pomeroy and Stephen enter. "Gentleman, your attention, please," the governor said loudly. "Now that our gunsmith has arrived, late as usual"—Pomeroy bowed to the governor—"I believe we can begin the festivities. I have some splendid news for you all. I have just received word from His Grace, the Duke of Newcastle, that the colony of Massachusetts will be reimbursed in pound sterling for our expenditures in the expedition against Louisbourg."

The merchant-officers in the crowd began to clap.

"And of course," continued the governor, "there are some splendid individual awards." He turned to Commodore Warren. "For you, Peter, their lordships in the Admiralty inform me of your promotion to the rank of Rear Admiral of the Blue."

A cheer went up from the officers. Warren, grinning, stood up from his chair to acknowledge their applause.

"It is also my understanding that His Majesty, in appreciation of your splendid efforts, has decided to award you with a munificent track of land along the Mohawk River in New York."

Again the officers cheered.

Then Shirley turned to the merchant-general, William Pepperrell. "For you, William, from His Grace also, word of a grant from the crown. You are now Sir William Pepperrell, Baronet."

The general was dumbfounded. The officers swarmed about him to offer congratulations. They were genuinely proud and pleased by the honor paid their leader.

The door to the next room swung open to reveal an enormous table, covered with a variety of specially prepared dishes. The governor pointed to the next room. "Gentlemen, our feast is awaiting us."

But Stephen was determined not to let it go like this. He rushed over to Shirley and grabbed his arm. "Your Excellency," he said. "What about the matter you discussed with William Vaughan?"

Shirley halted and turned toward Stephen. "That matter, sir, I have decided to drop."

"But why?"

"It is founded in supposition, circumstance and much that is contradictory. In short, I don't believe your story and unless you have more evidence, the matter is closed."

Stephen's face turned red. "You're going to let that son of a bitch off, aren't you?"

"The son of a bitch you refer to, sir, is one of the richest and most important men in this city and colony, someone I have mentioned to His Majesty as a worthy candidate for the governor's council, should the assembly see fit to elect him."

"He's rich because he stole his money from me," shouted Stephen.

"It would suit your purposes to see the man fall, wouldn't it, Nowell, to say nothing about your pocketbook?"

Stephen held his temper in check with difficulty. "But, Governor, Pierce almost prevented us from capturing the fort. If he had succeeded we would not be going on to Quebec and Montreal."

"Ensign Nowell, your arguments fall flat. We are not pursuing the matter; we are not going to attack Quebec and Montreal. This one victory is quite sufficient. I need no more. My obligation to His Majesty as Commander in Chief requires that I consolidate our gains."

"What? You won't be going on to Quebec and Montreal? But, sir, that will mean that the French will retain their hold on North America and be able to threaten us all in the years ahead."

"Ensign, you must learn to think from a broader perspective. The war has not gone well in Europe. The French threaten the balance of power on the continent. King George will have to make a peace, and part of that peace will include the return of Louisbourg to France. I see no reason, under those kinds of circumstances, to expend more lives and money taking Quebec and Montreal, only to see them revert to France in the end as well."

"You God damn Englishman," was all Stephen could say.

Shirley looked at him in amazement. "Pray tell me, sir, aren't we all Englishmen?"

"I know I'm not one," yelled Stephen. "I don't know what I am. But I'm sure that all of us settlers, Canadians or New Englanders, will never be free to run our own destinies as long as you English or French continue to dominate our lives. I believe that what happened on this side of the ocean is more important than what happens in England, France or Germany. You bastards let us work, sweat, suffer and die for something vital to us, which you are going to return to our sworn enemies to offset a loss in Germany."

"His Majesty's government—"

"To hell with His Majesty's bloody government!" Stephen shouted.

The whole room fell deadly silent.

Shirley turned from Stephen and walked through the doors to the banquet room. Stephen was about to follow him when he felt a hand on his shoulder. He turned to look into the face of his uncle, Daniel Pierce.

"You should guard your tongue, boy," said Pierce. "They'll have you up for treason. But I shall not wait for that day. The sheriff of this county has already, at the request of my solicitor, whom I believe you have met, issued a warrent for your arrest today—for fraud and blackmail."

"*You* are the traitor," Stephen said, "in league with the French."

"You're absurd, boy," laughed Pierce. "And even if your slanders were true, they are impossible to prove. Make sure you're out of town before the sheriff comes calling." He laughed loudly now and walked into the dining room.

Stephen was in a blind rage. He did not know if he should follow after Pierce or storm out of the building. Again he felt his arm grabbed, this time by Admiral Warren. "Where are you going, Nowell?"

"Anywhere," said Stephen. "Out of here."

"Look," said Warren, "Shirley told me all about your suspicions of Pierce, and as I told him and Vaughan and I am repeating to you now, I have no reason to defend the man, but you have no proof. Your proof died with Isaac Wiggins."

"That's ironic indeed," said Stephen. "In life Wiggins deprived me of my birthright and he does it again by dying."

Warren shrugged. "Don't pursue it," he said.

"Well, then I had better get out of town," said Stephen bitterly.

"I can arrange that," said the admiral. "Pepperrell thinks highly of you and so do I. I wish you and Vaughan had silenced that damn battery sooner. I would have loved to fire a few broadsides at the Frenchies. No matter," he shrugged, "a victory is a victory and this was a great one."

358

"For as long as it lasts," said Stephen sarcastically. "I understand that Louisbourg may be given back to the French. Vaughan will be furious when he hears."

"Vaughan? But he knows already. I have handsome holdings in New York in addition to what I have received today from the King. I've already sold some to Vaughan. He told me you would be handling his affairs for him. A wise choice."

Stephen looked at the Admiral in surprise.

"That is what I wanted to speak to you about. I'm sending my nephew William Johnson out to manage my estates. I want you to join him in New York City. He is all but ready to leave for Mohawk country. Do you wish to go with him?"

"I will have to speak with William Vaughan," said Stephen. "But I suspect that the answer will be yes."

"Good," said the admiral. "I'll arrange passage for you on one of my packet boats. How many of there are you in your party?"

Stephen was so taken aback that he had no ready answer. "Socono and Kip are off to Maine already," he said. "That leaves four of us, George and Hannah, Karl and myself—and of course William Vaughan if he is interested."

"Consider it done," said Warren.

Stephen could barely respond. To Mohawk country. He would be going back. He turned and walked from the reception room toward the front door. He stopped and looked back. He did not want to forget this sight. He knew that several persons had overheard his argument with Shirley. The charges against Pierce would not be forgotten by the men in this room, and even more, he knew that the Shirley statement about the possible return of Louisbourg to France was also passing from corner to corner of the State House. England would rue the day she had betrayed these men.

In the far corner of the banquet room, visible through the open door, Stephen could see his mother's murderer laughing as he conversed with the royal governor. Stephen felt sick. He had to get out of this room, out of this city where the vicious prospered and good men like William Vaughan were brought to their knees. It would be better among the Mohawks. He could find among them the courage and the honesty of a Molly Brant. He knew now that he was not Bastonois; he was not French. He had never been either. But maybe none of that really mattered. He would try again. He would retreat to the wilderness and begin anew.

ABOUT THE AUTHOR

A Canadian citizen since 1976, ROBERT E.WALL draws on his love for Canada and his native United States in creating the saga of *THE CANADIANS*. He perceives the histories of the two nations as deeply entwined and, influenced by the writings of Kenneth Roberts, seeks to teach these histories through the historical novel. *BLACKROBE*, the first in the series, is also Wall's first novel.

Robert Wall is married, has five children (one is an adopted Cree Indian, the most authentic Canadian in the family), and divides his time between New Jersey, where he is provost at Fairleigh Dickinson University, and Montreal, where his family lives.

A Special Preview of
the stirring opening pages of

BLOODBROTHERS
Volume II of *The Canadians*

by
Robert E. Wall

BLOODBROTHERS continues the sweeping saga
of Stephen Nowell and the conquest of a continent

The old man pulled the wolfskin closer to his body. Pain from the effort of closing his hands spread from his swollen knuckles up his forearm. He grimaced. The cold of winter was taking longer to leave his body every spring. Last winter had been the worst he could remember, and traveling here to Onondaga before the snows had left the valley had not been easy for a man who had already seen more than seventy winters.

The morning was a busy time in the longhouse but in deference to his position and age, no one approached the platform that had been assigned to the great sachem. His Onondaga Turtle clan cousins had done everything within their power to make the great sachem comfortable, even to the extent of hushing the naked little ones who would normally be scurrying about the house chasing dogs and playing warrior.

He was Tooniahigarawe, great sachem of the upper castle at Canojohari, known to the whites these many years as King Hendrick—high warrior of the most feared tribe in America, the Mohawk. Their very name had once struck terror in the hearts of everyone from Quebec up the great river to Montreal. Even Louis of France had cursed their name.

The English had taken Hendrick as a young man to visit their own Queen Anne across the seas. It had increased his respect for the English that they acknowledged the importance of the clan mother. The French did not understand such things. Now that he was much older, though, and had had forty more years to watch the English, he realized that his earlier respect for them had been misplaced as well. Every day the English moved more and more into the Mohawk lands. And who now feared the Mohawk? Once, the five other tribes of the confederation had acknowledged them as guardians of the eastern door of the Great Longhouse stretching along the river that bore their name all the way to the lakes of the far west. Now the English lived within the doorway.

Many of the Mohawk had fallen prey to the blandishments of the blackrobes and had gone off to found a new castle within eyesight of the hated Ville Marie—Montreal. If the Six Nations should go to war, he would lead no more than one hundred fifty warriors into battle. How the Seneca would mock him. But it did not matter.

The Great Council would begin with the setting sun and then he would have to put his plan into effect. Never before had the unity of the Longhouse been so seriously threatened. Geneseo and the Drunkard of the Seneca had become the lackeys of the French. The Keepers of the Western Door, and there were so many of them, had grown fat and rich carrying their furs to Niagara, ignoring the ancient way—the way it had been done even before Hendrick could remember. Going back to the time of the Dutch and after, it had been the honored custom to take the furs to Albany, near the land of the Mohawk. But no longer. Now the Seneca thought only of themselves.

Soyeghtowa, the Cayuga, the man of the golden tongue, would speak eloquently for them. The Cayuga had become lackeys to the lackeys. Together the Seneca and the Cayuga would call upon all Six Nations of the Iroquois to make war upon the English. War was sure to be the destruction of Hendrick's people and the Seneca knew this. They no longer cared about the good of the whole nation. They were beneath his contempt.

The old man pulled his legs from under him and stretched them out. Both of his knees ached. He reached with his right hand under his robe to scratch his armpit. With spring he would have to search his body and rid himself of unwanted visitors.

The key to everything was the Onondaga. And the key to them was their vanity. The Onondaga had also grown lazy over the years. They lived in the middle of the Longhouse and had been protected by the fierceness of the Mohawk and the numbers of the Seneca. They had gained their prestige not as warriors but as the peacemakers of the confederacy. Their castle was the capital of the nation —where the sacred council fire was kept forever lighted. The Onondaga would not cross him and they would understand his meaning. They would dissect his words to discover what it was that he truly meant. But his own people must not suspect.

He would have to trick even the white man Johnson, who had come to live among them years earlier. Now he was like one of them and sure to be adopted as one of them. Old Brant, sachem of the lower castle of his people, was deceived by Johnson, but Hendrick was not. Johnson might speak their language and dress like them, but he was not a Mohawk. He was an Englishman protecting English interests. His uncle was a commander of great ships like the one that had taken Hendrick to England forty years earlier. This Johnson had won over all the warriors of both castles. They screamed for the blood of the French as loudly as the Seneca called for that of the English. Hendrick could not openly resist them, but resist he must without seeming to resist.

The skin curtain of the doorway to the longhouse where Hendrick rested was pulled back. A large man, naked except for loincloth and moccasins despite the chilliness, stepped through the entryway and then straightened himself; his broad shoulders just barely allowed him entry without turning. His hair was jet black, as were his eyes. He waited for them to focus in the semidarkness of the longhouse. Then he discovered where Hendrick was seated and approached him.

"How is my cousin? Are you ready to address the council?" asked the newcomer.

Hendrick viewed him with his eyes narrowed to slits. It helped him to see inside the smoky lodge. "Dagaheari, how are you, my friend? I have spoken in council many times. It is you who should be preparing. Are you prepared to speak for the first time as a sachem of the Oneida?"

"I am not the orator that Skenandon was," said the younger man.

"Yes, we will miss him. He was a wise man who spoke well."

Dagaheari looked uncomfortable as Hendrick praised a man whom he had regarded as a fool and better dead. "Skenandon will be missed," he lied. "And the Oneida have had no revenge."

"Does that mean that the Oneida will speak for war with the French?" asked the old man.

"It was a French blackrobe who killed our sachem."

"But he fled to the English, Dagaheari. You yourself know that. You tracked him and his Abenacki friend."

"It doesn't matter. He was French and we will have our revenge on the French."

The old man was exasperated, but he did not let on. "Did not burning the other blackrobe provide revenge enough?"

"We did not taste his blood," said the Oneida, growing more angry. "Mohawk interfered and ransomed the priest."

Hendrick grunted in disgust. "It is clear that the blackrobe priest had nothing to do with the murder of Skenandon. That was done by the young blackrobe who speaks our language. He is the one you should have been seeking."

"It was no use," said Dagaheari evasively. "He fled and we could not reach him."

A woman brought the two sachems bowls of boiled meat. They sat eating for some minutes without talking. Finally Hendrick broke the silence. "I can help you and the Oneida, my cousins, in this matter."

The younger man looked at the Mohawk quizzically. "Do you know where he is?"

"No, but I know the whereabouts of someone equally important to you. I know where his son is. And I will put the boy in your power if you promise me two things." The Oneida said nothing and Hendrick took his silence as agreement. "First, you must promise me not to harm the boy. He is being raised Mohawk by old Brant, and he is his first great-grandson."

Dagaheari spoke coldly. "Do you mean to say that our Turtle cousin took the snake into her bed?"

"That is the way it is usually done," said the old man, smiling.

Dagaheari flopped down beside Hendrick on the platform. His initial anger had turned inward. "What else would you require of me?" he asked calmly.

"I would require that you and the Oneida and the Tuscarora, for whom the Oneida speak, vote to maintain the peace in the council tonight."

Dagaheari looked at Hendrick in amazement. His mask of indifference had disappeared totally. "But you have come to speak for war. The Mohawk wish war with the French. The Oneida and Tuscarora wish war with the French. If we can sway the Onondaga . . ."

"You have no hope of swaying our senior cousins. They will vote for neutrality. The Mohawk will call for war with the French. The Seneca will call for war with the English. The Cayuga will agree."

Dagaheari smiled a caustic smile. "The Cayuga have not thought on their own in many councils."

Hendrick nodded. "If the Oneida and the Tuscarora vote with the Onondaga, then a majority of the tribes will have called for neutrality and neither the Seneca nor the Mohawk will dare take up war hatchets in defiance of the council. But if only one tribe calls for neutrality, then the unity of our confederation might be broken."

"Old Brant will want your scalp, Hendrick, if he finds out what you have told me and what you have planned."

"But you will not tell him, Dagaheari. If you do, then you will never get your hands on his great-grandson. And no one else but you can tell my fellow sachem any of my plans. Are we agreed that you will speak for peace?"

The old man's face remained passive, but he knew that he had triumphed. The Oneida would do as he wished them to do. He pulled his creaking legs back up underneath him and grimaced again. "Besides," he said, "it is not old Brant I fear. What will Johnson do when he learns of what I am about to arrange? It is the white devil in our midst that I fear."

At that very moment in the next longhouse William Johnson stretched out his long frame. His toes touched the end of the platform, while his dark curls caught in the bark of the wood at the other end. The house was noisy and smoky. The women had kindled the fires and were pulling down dried vegetables and meats from the longhouse rafters, throwing them somewhat carelessly into the great iron pots hanging above the flames.

The girl next to him stirred but continued to sleep. Her mother hesitated to come and claim her from Johnson's platform, just in case he wished to make love to her again. He was a good catch, this Warraghiyagey—"he who does great things."

Once the fires had been started, Johnson had tossed off the furs that had covered his body during the cold night. The stiffness in his groin clearly indicated that his body would very much like another session with the Onondaga beside him, but even Warraghiyagey found it difficult to have sex in open view of all the families who shared the house. It was bad enough at night when only the sounds of lovemaking betrayed the activity on the sleeping platforms.

Johnson started to pull himself up onto his elbows to look about him, but his hair caught in the bark and pulled. He yelped. The girl awoke and smiled as she saw this giant of a man rubbing his head like a little boy.

"Is my brave lover afraid of pain?" she asked in her strange Onondaga dialect.

Johnson turned his gray eyes on her and smiled. He pulled back the furs that covered half of her lithe body so that he might look upon the whole of her. Most Iroquois girls would have protested the nakedness but not this one. Clearly both she and her mother were willing to put up with almost anything from him if it helped to get him into her longhouse.

The man feasted his eyes on her and his body reacted. The girl reached for him, but he pulled away. "Not this morning, my beauty," he said in an English laced with the sweet lilt of the Irish— a language the girl did not know. But she understood the motion of her lover's body as he pulled away. She pouted as he turned his back, threw his legs over the side of the platform and waited for his naked body to be ready for his loincloth.

He had much to do this day. Old Brant would begin the ceremony this morning. The sachem had agreed to help Johnson enter tonight's council, and the only way for him to do it was to be adopted into the tribe. The white man stood up, pulled on his buckskin leggings and slipped the loincloth between his legs. He did not look back at the girl but walked into the middle of the longhouse.

He saw old Brant on the far side, sitting on his assigned platform. The Mohawk delegation to the council at Onondaga had all been assigned to this one longhouse, except for King Hendrick. The segregation of the old sachem bothered Johnson. Had it been at Hendrick's own request or were the cagey Onondaga attempting to work on the old man's resolve to ask for war?

Brant's English-speaking granddaughter, Molly, sat by his side and served him his cornmeal breakfast. Her baby lay in the old man's arms, and he rocked the child back and forth. It was clearly a child of mixed blood, and Johnson had been amused to hear that the father was a Jesuit. He was a lapsed Catholic himself and had become an Anglican. How else did an Irishman make good in the Englishman's world? Since coming to the Mohawk country, however, he had prayed more often to the great Manitou than to King George's god.

Molly Brant smiled at him as Johnson approached their platform. It was a warm smile that turned her plain and slightly pockmarked face into a friendly, almost beautiful one. He smiled back at her.

Johnson looked at old Brant. "Will she be one of the maidens of the ceremony?" he asked in Mohawk.

"No," said the old chief. "My granddaughter is now one of the mothers of the Turtle clan. The maidens of the ceremony must be Mohawk virgins."

Johnson started to laugh. "There aren't any left."

Old Brant slapped his knee and howled. "Not since you came to live among us."

Johnson laughed again. "I am only finishing the work that you began, old friend," he said.

Again Brant cackled. The baby in his arms stirred and opened his eyes. Johnson was startled to see that the baby's eyes were blue. The child saw his great-grandfather's face and smiled. The old man smiled in return. "And this little one, my friend, he will continue the work after you and I are both gone."

Molly took the baby away from her grandfather, slipped open the front of her doeskin dress and held him to her breast. The child sucked hungrily.

"That's it," said Brant, "feed him good Mohawk milk. He will be a great warrior despite his French blackrobe father."

"His father was an Englishman, old fool," she said affectionately. "And his father was a man of great courage, much respected by the clan mother."

Johnson had heard the story of LaGarde, the blackrobe who had lived among the Oneida as a French missionary and who had killed the sachem Skenandon and then fled to the English towns, but he had never spoken to Molly about him. He had never heard her speak of him before either.

Molly looked very desirable as she sat there nursing her child. Her breasts were large with milk, and Johnson could not take his eyes from them. She looked up at him and spoke in English. "This is my son, Kanonraron Brant. His uncle, my little brother Joseph, will bring him to you someday, Johnson. He will be a great warrior. Joseph tells me that you will become the Great Father of all the Iroquois. I want you to know and honor my son."

Johnson bowed to her. There was something about her carriage, the way she sat nursing her child, that was both maternal and noble. He found these women so damned attractive—at one moment so blatantly sexual and the next so honorable and noble. They threw him off guard every time. All that he had learned about the Mohawks by living with them these past several years taught him to treat her now with the greatest respect. She was a Mohawk princess, a future clan mother, the mother of a future warrior of the tribe. Her father, Nickus Brant, grew more and more important as Hendrick and Old Brant grew more feeble. She was a formidable girl-woman, more suited for the marriage bed than for the pleasant evening on the sleeping platform.

Old Brant rose unsteadily from his platform and smiled at Johnson. "It is time, my young friend. We must get you into tonight's council, and if you are to speak to the council of all the tribes you must be one of us. The ceremony must begin." Brant signaled to the other Mohawk in the longhouse and soon all were crowded about him.

"It is time to end the differences that exist between Warraghiyagey and ourselves, my brothers and sisters," he announced in a loud voice. "Prepare him for the ceremony."

Young braves tore at Johnson's leggings, leaving him naked except for his breechcloth. A gnarled and wizened old man, a shaman of the Mohawk, approached him. He was followed by two assistants whose faces were completely covered by grotesquely carved wooden masks. Each assistant carried paint pots in his hands. The shaman mumbled a chant that Johnson, who knew the Mohawk language well, could not translate. The priest painted the outline of a turtle on Johnson's chest, over his heart. Lightninglike streaks were painted on each cheek. Old

Brant draped a belt of wampum over his shoulders and about his neck.

All of the Onondaga in the longhouse gathered eagerly around their Mohawk cousins. They had seen the ceremony of adoption before, but never had they seen a white man so honored. They had heard of such things among the Seneca and the Mohawk, but never had it happened here in Onondaga, the capital of the entire confederation, where the great mysteries of their people were preserved.

Brant spoke in a loud voice. His Mohawk dialect sounded funny to the untrained ears of the Onondaga children, but their parents hushed them, for Brant was a renowned orator. All listened to his words carefully.

"Warraghiyagey—'He Who Does Great Things' —is worthy to become a guardian of the eastern doorway of the Great Longhouse," said the old man. "He has lived among us for many winters. He has made his castle next to mine. He has fought by my side against our enemies, the French. He has obtained better prices for our furs by interceding for us with the merchants in Albany. And he has kept the white settlers away from our castles and made them pay us for the lands they take. He is a worthy brother."

All the Mohawk present grunted assent. A path was cleared and three young girls holding hands entered the semicircle.

"These three Mohawk maidens will now take Warraghiyagey to the waters to wash his skin and take from it all its whiteness."

Johnson smiled at Brant as he spoke of the maidens, but the old man pretended not to notice the white man's impertinence. Johnson allowed himself to be led out of the longhouse and down to the shores of the lake. The young girls giggled when Johnson modestly turned his back on them as he removed his only remaining garment. But when he turned around toward them, it was their turn to feign modesty and look away.

They grabbed handfuls of sand and dirt from the beach where the great canoes were landed; then they took him by both hands and both arms and led him into the numbing waters of the lake. The women splashed water all over him and, beginning with his hair, they scrubbed him from head to toe with the sand, rubbing his skin raw. Only the coldness of the water prevented the sensitive areas of his body from bleeding.

When they had scrubbed him to the point that Johnson had begun to wonder if they were planning to take old Brant's command seriously and scrub away any trace of white skin, they finally led him from the waters of Lake Onondaga, back to the longhouse. On the platform where he had slept the night before, there was laid out a whole new suit of buckskins covered with intricate and delicate decorations of porcupine quills. The maidens helped him to dress in his new clothes and then led him to face the sachem. The shaman and his assistants continued their chanting; their grotesque masks seemed to have become even more lewd. Brant gave him a smoking pipe and a tomahawk and placed his arm about Johnson's neck. "Now you are one of us, a brother, a true Mohawk. Let the other five nations call you cousin."

Johnson let out a war whoop that startled even

himself. He was now a Mohawk, an Iroquois. It was the first step on his path—a path that would lead eventually to war, war against the French and the final destruction of French Canada.

Read the complete book available August 1981 wherever paperbacks are sold.